"I am stuck because my appearance is not such that I can show myself," said Molly.

Was it his imagination or had she sounded on the brink of laughter?

"There is little moonlight here, as you have seen for yourself," he said. "I doubt that I could see whatever you'd liefer not show me."

"There is gey little to show, my lord."

He could not mistake it this time, definitely a near gurgle of laughter. His patience fled. More sharply, he said, "I can see nowt in this situation for humor."

"Nor do I, sir, I promise you. 'Tis not humor but hysteria, I fear."

"Whatever it is, I have had a surfeit of it for one night. Come out at once."

"I am nearly naked," she said flatly.

He pressed his lips together, suppressing the sudden strong urge he felt to see her. Something in the way she'd said those four words challenged him to *make* her come out.

"Charming...I eagerly await the next in the series."
—SingleTitles.com

"A fast-paced, action-packed story...Filled with passion, danger, Scottish allure, treason, and love. The romance and passion sizzle off the page...Ms. Scott has yet again created a dazzling story with a bigger-than-life hero and a feisty heroine. A must-read."
—MyBookAddictionReviews.com

THE LAIRD'S CHOICE

"Wonderfully romantic...[a] richly detailed Scottish historical from the author frequently credited with creating the subgenre."
—*Library Journal*

"Splendid scenery...Atmosphere abounds in this colorful romance."
—HistoricalNovelSociety.org

"A fine piece of historical romance fiction."
—TheBookBinge.com

HIGHLAND LOVER

"4½ stars! Excellent melding of historical events and people into the sensuous love story greatly enhances an excellent read."
—*RT Book Reviews*

"With multiple dangers, intrigues to unravel, daring rescues, and a growing attraction between Jake and Alyson, *Highland Lover* offers hours of enjoyment."
—RomRevtoday.com

HIGHLAND MASTER

"Scott, known and respected for her Scottish tales, has once again written a gripping romance that seamlessly interweaves history, a complex plot, and strong characters with deep emotions and a high degree of sensuality."

—*RT Reviews*

"Ms. Scott is a master of the Scottish romance. Her heroes are strong men with an admirable honor code. Her heroines are strong-willed...This was an entertaining romance with enjoyable characters. Recommended."

—FreshFiction.com

"Deliciously sexy...a rare treat of a read...*Highland Master* is an entertaining adventure for lovers of historical romance."

—RomanceJunkies.com

"Hot...There's plenty of action and adventure...Amanda Scott has an excellent command of the history of medieval Scotland—she knows her clan battles and border wars, and she's not afraid to use detail to add realism to her story."

—All About Romance

TEMPTED BY A WARRIOR

"4½ stars! Top Pick! Scott demonstrates her incredible skills by crafting an exciting story replete with adventure and realistic, passionate characters who reach out and grab you...Historical romance doesn't get much better than this!"

—*RT Book Reviews*

"Captivates the reader from the first page . . . Another brilliant story filled with romance and intrigue that will leave readers thrilled until the very end."

—SingleTitles.com

SEDUCED BY A ROGUE

"4½ stars! Top Pick! Tautly written . . . passionate . . . Scott's wonderful book is steeped in Scottish Border history and populated by characters who jump off the pages and grab your attention . . . Captivating!"

—*RT Book Reviews*

"Readers fascinated with history . . . will love Ms. Scott's newest tale . . . leaves readers clamoring for the story of Mairi's sister in *Tempted by a Warrior.*"

—FreshFiction.com

TAMED BY A LAIRD

"4½ stars! Top Pick! Scott has crafted another phenomenal story. The characters jump off the page and the politics and treachery inherent in the plot suck you into life on the Borders from page one."

—*RT Book Reviews*

"Scott creates a lovely, complex cast."

—*Publishers Weekly*

Moonlight Raider

Other Books by Amanda Scott

AMANDA SCOTT

Moonlight Raider

FOREVER

NEW YORK   BOSTON

Forever
Hachette Book Group
237 Park Avenue
New York, NY 10017

www.HachetteBookGroup.com

Printed in the United States of America

First Edition: September 2014
10 9 8 7 6 5 4 3 2 1

Forever is an imprint of Grand Central Publishing.
The Forever name and logo are trademarks of Hachette Book Group, Inc.

The publisher is not responsible for websites (or their content) that are not owned by the publisher.

To Debi Allen
for her consistent, unmatched, and
delightfully creative support.
Thank You!

Late, late in the gloaming, when all was still,
When the fringe was red on the westlin hill,
The wood was sere, the moon i' the wane,
The reek o' the cot hung over the plain
Like a little wee cloud in the world its lane . . .

James Hogg, the Ettrick Shepherd

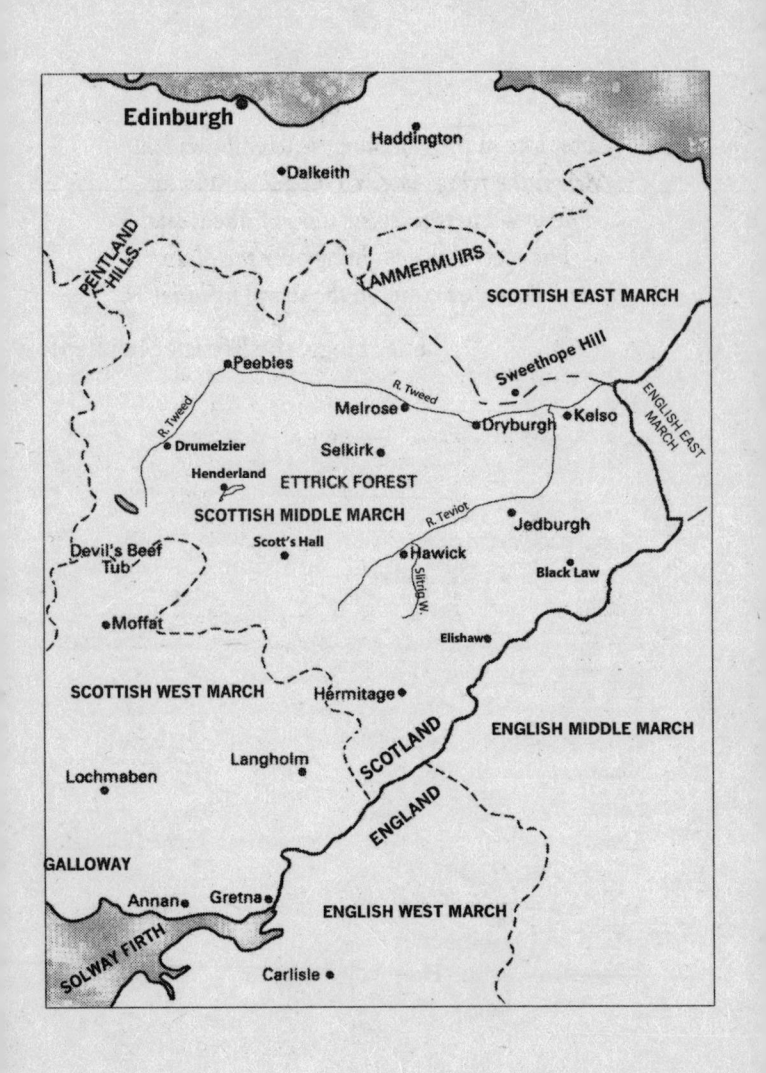

Author's Note

For readers' convenience, the author offers the following guide:

The Borders – refers to the English and Scottish areas near the borderline

Borderers –people who live in the Borders

Buccleuch – Buck LOO

Cockburn – COE burn

Father Abbot – proper form of address for an abbot

Haugh – HAW(k) = low-lying meadow beside a river

Hawick – HOYK

Herself – refers herein only to Lady Meg Scott

Himself – refers to the laird or lord of the manor

Keekers – eyes

Lassock – young girl

The Douglas – refers only to the current Earl of Douglas

Tuedy – TWEE die

Vespers – the clerical hour preceding supper, about 4:30 p.m. in November

Wheesht – as in "Hold your wheesht" – "Be quiet."

Moonlight Raider

Chapter 1  ————————

What was she thinking? God help her, why had she run? When they caught her...But that dreadful likelihood didn't bear thought. They must *not* catch her.

Even so, she could not go any faster, or much farther. It felt as if she had been running forever, and she had no idea of exactly where she was.

Glancing up through the forest canopy, she could see the waxing half-moon high above her, its pale light still occluded by the mist she had blessed when leaving Henderland. Although the moon had been rising then, she had prayed that the mist would conceal her until she reached the crest of the hills southeast of her father's tower. After she reached the southern slope in apparent safety, she had followed a little-used track that she hoped her pursuers—for they would certainly pursue her—would never imagine she had taken.

Experience had warned her even then that the mist might augur rain ahead, but the mist had been a blessing nevertheless. In any event, with luck, she would find shelter before the rain found her, or the light of day, come to that.

Long before then she had to decide what to do. But how? What *could* she do? Who would dare to help her? Certainly, no one living anywhere near St. Mary's Loch would. Her father was too powerful, her brothers too brutal and too greedy, and Tuedy—

She could not bear even to think about Ringan Tuedy.

A low, canine woof abruptly curtailed her stream of thought, and she froze until a deep male voice somewhere in the darkness beyond the trees ahead of her said quietly, "Wheesht, Ramper, wheesht."

Terrified, knowing that she was too tired to outrun anyone and dared not risk time to think, let alone try to explain herself to some stranger, eighteen-year-old Molly Cockburn dove desperately into the shrubbery and wriggled her way in as far, as quietly, and as deeply as she could, heedless of the brambles and branches that scratched and tore at her face and bare skin as she did. Lying still, she feared that her heart might be pounding loudly enough to betray her.

A susurrous sound came then of some beast—nay, a dog—sniffing. Then she heard scrabbling and a rattle of nearby dry shrubbery. Was the dog coming for her?

Hearing the man call it to heel, then a sharper, slightly more distant bark, and realizing that he and his dogs were closer than she had thought, she curled quietly to make herself as small as possible, then went utterly still, scarcely daring to breathe.

She was trembling, though, and whether it was from the cold or sheer terror didn't matter. She was shaking so hard that she would likely make herself heard if the nosy dog did not drag her from the shrubbery or alert its master to do so.

Above the sounds of the animal that had sensed her presence came others then, even more ominous. Recognizing the distant yet much too near baying of hounds, Molly stifled a groan of despair. They were doubtless Will's sleuthhounds, trained to track people, even—or especially—rebellious sisters.

~

Twenty-four-year-old Walter Scott, Laird of Kirkurd since childhood and the sixth Lord of Rankilburn and Murthockston for a scant twenty-four hours, had just taken a long, deep, appreciative breath of the energizing, albeit chilly, damp-earth-and-foliage scented forest air—filling his lungs and trying not to think of the myriad responsibilities that had so suddenly descended on him—when his younger dog gave its low, curious woof.

"Wheesht now, Ramper," he muttered. When the shaggy pup ignored him, its attention fixed on whatever nocturnal creature it had sensed in the always-so-intriguing shrubbery, Wat added firmly, "Come to heel now, laddie, and mind your manners as Arch does. I'd liefer you disturb no badgers or other wildlife tonight."

Hearing its name, the older dog perked its ears, and Ramper turned obediently, if reluctantly, toward Wat. Then, pausing, Ramper lifted his head, nose atwitch.

Arch emitted a sharp warning bark at the same time, and Wat heard the distant baying that had disturbed them himself.

"Easy, lads," he said as he strode toward the sound, his senses alert for possible trouble.

Both dogs ranged protectively ahead of him, but seeing torchlight in the near distance and now hearing hoofbeats over the hounds' baying, he halted a few yards past the area where young Ramper had sought whatever wildlife had gone to earth there. Calling both of his dogs to heel, Wat looked swiftly around lest there be other intruders nearby.

The misty moon's position indicated that the time was near midnight, so whoever was riding his way with hounds had not come to offer condolences to the new Lord of Rankilburn and hereditary Ranger of Ettrick Forest. That they might be raiders occurred to him next, but he dismissed that thought as unlikely, too.

A third thought and a companion fourth one that brought a near smile to his face led him to shout, "Tam, Sym, to me!"

Doffing his voluminous, fur-lined cloak, he draped it over nearby shrubbery, listened for sounds behind him, and watched the torches draw nearer as he waited.

Except for the ever-closer riders and dogs, silence ensued.

It was possible, he supposed, that neither Tam nor Sym, or perhaps only one of them, had followed him from Scott's Hall, but both tended to be overprotective of him, and had been since his childhood. At such a time, it was more likely that both men were within shouting distance than that neither one was.

As the riders drew nearer, Wat drew his sword and eased his dirk forward, hoping that he would need neither weapon.

His dogs were quiet now and kept close, awaiting commands. Hearing a slight rustle behind him, Wat said, "Are you alone, Tam, or is Sym with you?"

"'Tis both of us, laird," Jock's Wee Tammy said quietly. "We should be enough, too. It be just four or five riders, I'm thinking."

Even more quietly, Sym Elliot muttered, "Herself did send us out, laird."

At Rankilburn, "Herself" referred to only one person, his grandmother.

Wat said gently, "Are you suggesting that, had Lady Meg not sent you, you would not have followed me?"

Sym cleared his throat.

"Aye, well, I'm glad you did, both of you," Wat said, looking at the two shadowy figures as he did.

Jock's Wee Tammy, despite his name, had nearly sixty years behind him and was thus the older as well as much the larger of the two. A time-proven warrior and still fierce with a sword, he was captain of the guard at Scott's Hall. He and Sym had both served Wat's father and grandfather long before Wat was born, and he knew both men well and trusted them completely. "I was woolgathering as I walked," he told them frankly. "But Arch and Ramper warned me of our visitors."

Lanky Sym said, "Herself sent me to tell ye that her ladyship were a-frettin' earlier and restless. She said to remind ye that if she wakens—her ladyship, I mean—she'd be gey worried to hear ye was out roaming in the forest, so . . ."

"My mother and grandmother are both strong women," Wat said when Sym paused. "I do know that Mam is grieving, Sym. We all are."

"It were too sudden," Tam said.

"It was, aye," Wat agreed, stifling the new wave of grief that struck him. "We will miss my lord father sorely, but death does come to us all in the end."

"Not from this lot we be a-seein' now, though," Sym said confidently, drawing his sword. Tam's was out, too, Wat noted.

"Don't start anything," he warned them. "Take your cues from me."

"Aye, sir, we know," Tam said.

He knew that they did, but the riders were close. Their baying dogs were closer yet, and he hoped they were well trained. Arch and Ramper would fight to the death to protect him, but he didn't want to lose either one. He kept them close.

Seconds later, a pack of four hounds dashed toward them through the trees.

"Halt and away now!" Wat bellowed, shouting what the Scotts had long shouted to keep their own dogs from tearing into their prey.

Either his roar or his words were sufficient, because the four stopped in their tracks. Two of them dropped submissively to the ground. The other two hesitated, poised and growling, teeth bared.

Wat stayed where he was and watched the riders approach, four men in pairs, the two on the right bearing flaming torches. In the fiery glow, he recognized the two leaders and a man-at-arms who served them. He did not immediately recognize the fourth man although he looked familiar.

When the four saw him and wrenched their horses to plunging halts, Wat said grimly to their leader, "Will Cockburn, what urgency brings you and these others to Rankilburn at this time of night?"

Cockburn was a neighbor who lived at Henderland Tower on St. Mary's Loch. He was a wiry man several years older than Wat and known for leading brutal raids across the border and on the Scottish side, too. Such a reputation was common in the area, which was rife with reivers. Wat shared a somewhat similar repute.

However, the two of them had never been particularly friendly, and if Will had hoped that Rankilburn might be ripe for his raiding...

Will glowered at him. Then, exchanging a look with his brother Ned, beside him, he looked back at Wat speculatively, as if he hoped that Wat might say more.

Instead, Wat waited, expressionless, for the answer to his question.

At last, Will said, "One of our maidservants seems to have lost her way home. The hounds picked up her scent near St. Mary's Loch and led us here."

Molly nearly gasped. So she was a maidservant, was she? Not that it was far off the mark. But did they truly think that Walter Scott of Kirkurd would care about a missing maidservant? And, surely, the man must be Scott of Kirkurd if Will called him "Wat" and if they were on Rankilburn land near Scott's Hall.

"You fear that a maidservant wandered all the way here from Henderland?" Kirkurd said, his tone heavily skeptical. "Sakes, Will, 'tis eight miles or more."

"I ken fine how far we've come," Will snapped.

"Rather careless of you to lose such a lass," Kirkurd replied evenly, doubtless wondering at Will's curtness. "Do your maidservants often go missing?"

"Dinna be daft," Will retorted. "It be dangerous for a lass in these woods."

Molly could imagine the sour look on Will's face as he spoke and prayed that heaven would keep him from getting his hands on her after chasing her such a distance. He'd get his own back first. Then he'd turn her over to Ringan Tuedy, and Tuedy had told her what *he'd* do to her. A shiver shot through her at the memory.

"You won't find your serving lass here," Kirkurd said, his deep voice reassuringly calm. "My dogs would alert me to any stranger within a mile of here, just as they did when they sensed your approach."

A snarling voice that Molly identified with renewed dread as Tuedy's interjected, "So ye say! But since ye've no said what ye're doing out and about at such a late hour, how do we ken that ye didna come out tae meet some lass yourself? Ye kept them dogs o' yours quiet, for I didna hear nowt from them."

A heavy silence fell.

Molly had never met Walter Scott of Kirkurd, but her father had mentioned once that he was just six years older than she was. Tuedy, on the other hand, was older by nearly ten years. He was of powerful build, an experienced warrior, and a man ever-determined to have his own way. Would Kirkurd defer to him?

Shivering again, she hoped not.

Recalling then that Kirkurd's authoritative tone had stopped Will's dogs before they could surround her and reveal her presence to Will, she told herself she should be thankful for that one blessing and not be praying for more.

At last, in a tone that revealed only mild curiosity, Kirkurd said, "Tuedy, is that you? I thought you looked familiar, but it must be five or six years since last we met.

Do you often help others search for lost maidservants at midnight?"

Molly's lips twitched wryly, but her fear increased as she awaited the reply.

To her surprise, Tuedy said only, "I was visiting Piers Cockburn." He made it sound as if it had been an ordinary visit and not one that had turned her life upside down. "But ye've no answered me question, Wat. What be ye doing out here?"

"It is unnecessary for any Scott to produce his reason for a moonlight stroll on Scott land," Kirkurd said. "However, you may not yet have heard that my lord father died last night. We buried him today, so it has been a grievous time for us here. I came out into the forest to seek fresh air and peaceful solitude."

Robert Scott of Rankilburn was dead? Sadness surged through Molly at the news. She had met him only a handful of times, but unlike her brothers and her father, Rankilburn had treated her with the respect due a lady. He had been younger than her father, and she had thought him kinder, too. She wished she could see the men as they talked, but she was facing away from them and dared not move.

Tuedy said mockingly, "Ye come seeking peace, ye say. Yet ye come fully armed and wi' Jock's Tam and Lady Meg's Sym behind ye, also full-armed."

"Most Borderers carry weapons wherever they go," Kirkurd said.

Nay, but she must stop thinking of him as Scott of Kirkurd, Molly realized. Walter Scott was now Lord of Rankilburn and Chief of Clan Scott.

He added, "I certainly won't ask why you four are

armed or *why* you seek a missing maidservant instead of sending minions in search of her. But *you*, Tuedy, do seem over-familiar with my people."

"Sakes, everyone kens that Sym Elliot is your grandame, Lady Meg's, man. We also ken Jock's Wee Tammy and that he be captain o' Rankilburn's guard."

"Enough argle-bargle," Will declared curtly. "Ye willna object if we have a look through the forest hereabouts for our lass, will ye, Wat?"

Molly held her breath again.

"I do object to such an unnecessary intrusion," Scott replied, "especially whilst we here are grieving our loss." His tone remained even but had an edge to it, as if he disliked Will but tried not to show it. "Tammy and Sym were nearby," he added. "A few of my men always are. If I whistle, two score more will come."

Molly relaxed, although the thought of more men coming was daunting.

Another silence fell before Scott added amiably, "Methinks you should train your sleuthhounds better, Will, because they must have followed a false trail here. Moreover, you ken fine that you had no business hunting man or beast in Ettrick Forest without Scott permission. You would all be wise to turn around now and ride peacefully back to Henderland."

"What if we don't?" Tuedy demanded provocatively.

"You are on my land, Ring Tuedy, and you must know that I now wield the power of pit and gallows. Do you doubt I'd use that power against troublemakers whilst my lady mother, my sisters, and my grandame endure deep mourning?"

When yet another silence greeted his words, Molly bit

her lip in trepidation, fearing that Will and Ned might react violently to such a threat. Then, to her deep relief, she heard Will mutter something to the others, followed by the shuffling sounds of horses turning. Calling the dogs to heel, Will shouted, "Ye'd best not be lying to me, Wat. If ye've given shelter t' the maid, ye'll answer to me."

"I am not in the habit of sheltering misplaced maidservants, Will. If such a lass shows herself here, I'll get word to Henderland straightaway."

Although Molly was sure that Will had heard him, he did not deign to reply.

She listened intently until she could no longer hear any sound of horses, dogs, or men. When utter silence reigned throughout the nearby forest, she decided that Will and the others had indeed departed. Moreover, she had begun to feel the icy chill again. Tension stirred, nevertheless. Had everyone truly gone away?

Gathering her courage, she decided to risk moving and carefully wiggled the toes of one bare, chilly foot, grateful to find that her toes had not gone numb.

"They've gone," Walter Scott said quietly. "You can come out now."

Every cell in Molly's body froze where it was.

~

Ramper whined again but stayed obediently at Wat's side. The shrubbery did not move, but he was sure she was there. Will Cockburn's sleuthhounds, although as obedient as Ramper was, had quivered so much that if Will had been paying more heed to them and less to getting his own way, he would have noticed.

"Come on out, lass," Wat said again. "No one here will

harm you. I sent my lads back, so I'm the only one here." When there was no response, he added, "I have small interest in runaway maidservants, but I do lack infinite patience."

"I can't come out," she said, her voice no more than a hoarse squeak.

"Are you stuck in the shrubbery?"

"If you put it that way, I expect I am."

Her gentle, even educated, manner of speaking stunned him briefly to silence. She spoke as the women in his family did, so she was no ordinary maidservant. That thought gave him pause to wonder what mischief the Fates might have wrought by casting her into his path as they had.

"You will have to explain your situation more clearly," he said with a slight frown. "I do not know why it should matter how I put that question to you."

"I am stuck because my appearance is not such that I can show myself."

Was it his imagination or had she sounded on the brink of laughter?

"There is little moonlight here, as you have seen for yourself," he said. "I doubt that I could see whatever you'd liefer not show me."

"There is gey little to show, my lord."

He could not mistake it this time, definitely a near gurgle of laughter. His patience fled. More sharply, he said, "I can see nowt in this situation for humor."

"Nor do I, sir, I promise you. 'Tis not humor but hysteria, I fear."

"Whatever it is, I have had a surfeit of it for one night. Come out at once."

"I am nearly naked," she said flatly.

He pressed his lips together, suppressing the sudden strong urge he felt to see her. Something in the way she'd said those four words challenged him to *make* her come out. Ruthlessly reminding himself that he was a gentleman and that it was likely that the spirit of his father, a gentleman in every sense of the word, was still watching him, Wat said, "I have my cloak, lass. If I hold it up between us and give my word as a Borderer not to peek, will you trust me and come out?"

Silence.

"'Tis a gey warm, fur-lined cloak," he murmured, shaking off some dry leaves that it had picked up from the shrubbery. "It even boasts a hood."

"I'll trust you, sir. I have heard that your word is good. 'Tis just that I feel so...so..." The words floated softly, even wistfully, to him. Although she did not finish the sentence, he heard rustling in the shrubbery and knew that she was trying, awkwardly or otherwise, to wriggle her way out.

"Can you manage by yourself?" he asked as he held his cloak up high enough to block his view of the relevant shrubs. "Or should I try to help?"

"I'll manage alone if it kills me," she muttered grimly.

His lips curved, and he realized he was smiling. Until the Cockburns' arrival, he had felt miserable, grief-stricken, even forlorn. He'd worried about whether he was ready to step into his father's and grandfather's shoes and assume all the burdens of their immediate family, Rankilburn, all of Clan Scott, Ettrick Forest, and numerous other Scott holdings. Sakes, his father had even been an assistant march warden, with duties of which Wat had only slight understanding.

Nevertheless, the lass's grim fortitude had somehow banished his despair. Whoever and whatever she was, she was damnably intriguing.

A low cry from the shrubbery almost made him shift the cloak to see what had gone amiss.

"What is it?" he demanded.

"Just another scratch," she replied. "I'm nearly there."

He steeled himself to be patient, expecting her to remind him of his promise not to look. His younger brother and sisters often plagued him with reminders after he'd promised them something.

But she did not.

Silence at last from the shrubbery told him that she had extricated herself, and he sensed it when she stood.

"I'm here, sir," she said quietly as he felt her move against the cloak. "My shoulders are a bit lower down than that, though," she added.

Gently, he draped the cloak over her shoulders, noting that she was more than a head shorter than he was. When she pulled the cloak close around her, he saw that she was slenderly curvaceous. He could also see that her long, dark hair was tangled and full of leaves. When she turned, he gasped at the scratches he saw, even by the pale moonlight, on what was otherwise a pretty but exceedingly dirty face. A thin scar of about two inches ran from the end of her right eyebrow into her hairline.

"Are you going to tell me your name?" he asked, resisting an impulse to use his thumb and wipe away a bubble of blood from the deepest scratch on her cheek.

"I'm Molly, sir."

"Molly what?"

"Molly is sufficient for now, I think," she said. "It

is kind of you to let me borrow your cloak," she added quickly before he could reply. "Mayhap you know of a tenant or one of your servants who might lend me a cot or pallet for the night."

"We won't trouble anyone else," he said. "I suspect that you are not the maidservant that Will Cockburn and those others were seeking."

"What I am is cold and hungry, my lord. Those men and dogs frightened me, but I am as naught to them."

"Nevertheless, you are running from something, lass. No self-respecting female would be flinging herself into rough shrubbery, half naked, without good cause. And prithee, do not spin me a wheen of blethers about your being other than self-respecting. I shan't believe you."

"The truth is that I am not feeling at all self-sufficient," she said. "I simply acted when the opportunity arose, without thought. Consequently, the greatest and most fearful likelihood is that my so-impulsive act will prove futile."

"Sakes, then why did you run away?"

Giving him a direct, even challenging look, she said with resolute calm, "I have asked myself that question more than once tonight, my lord. The answer is that my reasons are ones that you are likely to deem insufficient, even senseless."

"Tell me anyway."

"Very well, I ran because it is or, more precisely, *was* my wedding night."

Molly didn't dare look at him, so certain was she that he would demand to know more. To her surprise, though, he put a gentle hand on her right shoulder and urged her forward as he said, "We'll go this way. You will be warmer walking than standing here."

"But you cannot mean to take me to Scott's Hall," she protested, as she huddled gratefully into the warmth of his cloak and tied its strings at her throat.

"Aye, sure, I will take you there. I cannot leave you out here wandering in the woods. For one thing, I'll want my cloak back. 'Tis nearly new."

"Well, if you want it—" She put a hand back to the bow she had tied.

"Don't be daft," he said more curtly. "You will wear it, and we will go to the Hall. You will be safe there, I promise. My mother and grandmother will see to that, not to mention my sisters and any number of maidservants."

"In troth, sir, I do not fear you, and your offer of warmth is sorely tempting," she said. "But much as I'd welcome your hospitality, I must not endanger you or your family. If you take me to the Hall, dire trouble may follow."

"I won't let any harm befall you," he said. "As for trouble, we've met with such before and will doubtless do so again. The Hall is fortified and well guarded, so you should feel safe inside our wall."

Although she kept silent to see if he would say more, he did not, and since she suspected that he would refuse to let her stay where she was, even had she been daft enough to want to, she walked with him in near companionable silence until she realized, to her dismay, that his lack of curiosity nettled her.

Not that she wanted to explain anything to him. She did not want to talk about herself at all and ought simply to accept that he was offering a refuge.

At that thought, she felt suddenly weak-kneed. It was as if the knowledge that she was safe, if for only a short time, drained what energy she had had left.

When she swayed, a firm hand cupped her right elbow, steadying her.

"You have come a long way, I think, and you are bare-foot," he said. "We have some distance to go yet, so I'll carry you if you like. You're small enough that I could do so easily."

Energy surged back, and she straightened, saying with forced calm that she hoped would seem to equal his own, "Thank you, sir, but I am accustomed to going without shoes in all weather. If I am tired, it is because of the late hour and the fact that I had nearly given up hope of finding shelter."

"As you like," he said amiably, adding in the same way, "Ramper, keep to the trail." But he did not move his hand away from her elbow, and she was grateful for its presence there. She seemed to draw strength from him, and she could not recall the last time she had felt such a thing with any man.

The silence between them continued as they walked. When she realized that he would make no further attempt to question her, she relaxed and began to pay closer heed to their surroundings.

Moonlight glinted on mist-damp leaves, providing enough light for her to discern the path they followed. The older dog kept to it. The younger one wandered off now and again but returned at a quiet word from its master.

"Why do you call him Ramper?" she asked him. "He's not an eel."

"No, but he squirms like one and can get out of any place I put him."

She glanced up at him, noting his firm, dark profile against the moonlight. He seemed completely at his ease, clearly trusting his dogs to warn of any danger.

Before long, torchlight ahead told her they were approaching Scott's Hall. A few minutes thereafter, they crossed a wide clearing and the gate in the high wall swung wide at their approach.

Her companion bade the man on the gate a good evening but said no more.

"Should you not have warned them that those men might return?" she asked, keeping her voice low so that only he would hear her.

"Nay, for my lads have received their orders from Tam and will keep a close watch, as always. Moreover, those men will not return tonight."

She was not as sure of that as he seemed to be, but she had seen enough to know that, try as they might, neither Will nor Tuedy would enter Scott's Hall that night. Its high wall and iron-barred gates would keep them out.

Inside, torches in the cobblestone yard revealed that the Hall boasted three towers. Her escort guided her to the central one. It was doubtless the keep, because its door opened onto an entryway where an alert porter rose from his stool.

A stairway beyond him took them up a few steps to the great hall. Just inside, his lordship paused and turned to face her. Frowning a little, and without warning, he put a hand to her chin and tilted her face up.

Involuntarily, Molly flinched, but he held her chin firmly and seemed to examine her doubtless filthy face. He had looked at her earlier, but not like this.

He looked as if he would comment but released her

instead when a young maidservant in a leaf-green kirtle, a white apron, and a white half-veil over curly reddish-blonde hair hurried toward them.

Molly fought to steady her senses.

"Good evening, Emma," his lordship said. "This is Mistress Molly, who will be staying with us for a time. Prithee, show her to a guest chamber and order hot water for a bath. She has been walking in the forest and is well nigh freezing, so the first thing is to warm her. She is also likely hungry and will need clothes to wear in the morning. She seems to be about the same size as the lady Janet, so..."

"I'll look after her, m'lord, aye," the lass said, giving Molly a warm smile. "Meantime, sir, Herself wants a word wi' ye. She said to bid ye come to her sitting room straightaway when ye came in."

Molly stiffened, wondering if Herself was his mother or even his wife to have summoned him in such a way. But she managed to retain the little composure she had left, telling herself that it was foolish to think he might abandon her.

As if he could hear her thoughts, he said reassuringly, "Go with Emma, mistress. I'll see you in the morning when you come down to break your fast. Emma will bring you down to the high table when you're ready."

Molly doubted that she would ever be "ready" for further conversation with the new Lord of Rankilburn. As she thanked him politely and bade him goodnight, she saw that his thoughtful frown had returned.

Chapter 2

Wat stood still, watching "Mistress Molly" walk away with young Emma Elliot. On Molly, his new cloak dusted the floor, and he realized that it had doubtless dragged along the forest floor, as well, and would need a good brushing. But his man, Emma's brother Jed, would take care of that for him.

Nevertheless, and despite Molly's bedraggled appearance, she carried herself with regal grace and revealed no outward sign of her difficult evening.

Her lack of proper clothing under the cloak would doubtless shock Emma, though. So would the bruise that was beginning to discolor her left cheek, and if Emma noticed the pale thin scar from their guest's right eyebrow to just above her right ear, those details might shock her, too.

Recalling Molly's wince, and her earlier dizziness, he knew she was still frightened. That increased his admiration for her fortitude and surface calm.

A smile touched his lips when it occurred to him that if he lingered much longer to watch her, he risked annoying his grandmother. Also, nearly a dozen men slept on pallets in the great hall. Most were warriors and thus light sleepers.

None would spread gossip abroad, but given cause to suspect that he'd taken an unusual interest in his new young charge, they might talk amongst themselves.

Therefore, collecting his wits, he strode back to the main stairway and up two levels to his grandmother's sitting room. He was well aware that, having summoned him, she would not retire without seeing him.

Opening the door after a perfunctory rap, he found her alone in the room, sitting comfortably, albeit soberly, in a cushioned chair before a small fire in the hooded fireplace. She stared into the flames, the stitchery in her lap forgotten.

The lady Margaret Scott turned her head as he entered. Smiling the warm smile that was his alone, she said, "So you are back at last. I am told that intruders dared to disturb your solitude."

Her voice was low and musical, her face and nose long and thin. Her mouth was so large and wide that before she married his grandfather, insolent wags had called her Muckle-Mouth Meg. However, her smiles, of every sort, were beautiful, and her figure was still graceful and slim. Her pale skin remained soft-looking with fewer lines than most women who boasted her nearly sixty years of age.

Her dark brown hair was graying, but she still wore it in the long, thick plait that she favored, draped now over her right shoulder. Her dark-lashed eyes were stone-gray, their irises black-rimmed, and their whites as clear as ever. Her head remained bare of veil or coif, and she had changed from the somber clothing she had worn to her son's burial into her favorite soft, pale-green robe.

Gesturing toward a nearby back-stool as Wat pushed the door shut behind him, she said, "Sit now and tell me about your visitors."

"Since Sym doubtless told you exactly what happened, Gram," he replied, bending to kiss her cheek, "I hope you don't expect me to describe it all again."

"Do pull up that stool or a cushion and make yourself comfortable, love," she said. "Sym did tell me such details as he saw and heard for himself, but..."

When she paused, Wat said, "If that is all he said, he must be failing sadly. Do you honestly expect me to believe he did not offer his own opinion of my visitors—aye, *and* of mine own actions and speech?"

"I would be wasting my breath if I said any such thing," she replied. "Sym speaks as frankly now as he did when he was a bairn, and I still find his opinions educational and often as highly amusing as they were then. He has changed in other ways since then, to be sure, especially since his Nelly died."

Wat knew Sym's history, as did nearly every other inhabitant of Scott's Hall. "I interrupted you, Gram," he said, drawing the back-stool closer to her and turning it so he could straddle it. "You were saying..."

"...that although Sym described the men and their actions and said that you had named two of them—Will Cockburn of Henderland and Ringan Tuedy of Drumelzier—neither one is a man I'd expect to come here unannounced at such an hour. Not peacefully, at all events. Sym said that Will professed to be hunting a missing maidservant. He also said that, in his opinion, it was a wheen o' blethers."

"I agree with Sym. Did he linger long enough to note aught else of interest?"

She shook her head. "He said only that Will had brought sleuthhounds with him and how sternly you ordered the men and their dogs back to Henderland. He said you also told him and Tammy to return here whilst you stayed out in the forest." Her eyes twinkled as she added, "Sym did say that, at another time, he might have stuck close, because he thought you were up to something. But now that you're the laird, he said, he thought he'd been wiser to obey you."

"Much wiser," Wat said, meeting her gaze.

"So what were you up to, love?"

"In short, madam, I found a young woman in the shrubbery."

"Mercy, who is she?"

"She says her name is Molly," he said, folding his arms over the top of the back-stool. "She did not provide a surname."

"Would not or could not?"

"She said only that she thought Molly would suffice for now."

Lady Meg frowned. "She sounds rather too sure of herself, then, to be Will Cockburn's missing maidservant, if such a creature exists."

"I am sure that she is no one's servant, Gram, although someone struck her recently. She has a bruise rising on her right cheek."

After a thoughtful pause, Lady Meg said, "Describe this Molly to me."

"When I turned her over to Emma, she looked like someone dragged backward through a bush, mayhap several bushes," he replied frankly. "When I persuaded her to show herself, she wore only a ragged shift. Her hair was tangled, and she had scratches all over her from burrowing into and out of the shrubbery."

"Hiding from whom? Might that still be Will Cockburn or Ringan Tuedy?"

"I suspect that it may be one or the other, even both. But I'm nearly certain she is wellborn, Gram. She speaks like a gently-bred lady."

"Did she tell you anything about herself?"

"Only that she had fled her wedding night," Wat replied.

~⌒~

While Molly waited for her bathwater in the pleasant bed-chamber to which Emma had shown her, the younger girl bustled about preparing for her to bathe. Dragging a large tin tub from the corner where it apparently lived, Emma next fetched towels and soap from a nearby kist and set them on a stool beside the tub.

"There always be hot water on the hob, mistress," she said with one of her cheery smiles as she shook out and refolded the larger of the two towels. Then, smoothing her apron over her green kirtle and pushing an errant red-dish blonde curl back under her veil, she added, "Our lads willna tak' long to fetch your water up here. I told one o' them to bring ye food, too. I hope bread and cheese will be enough. The kitchen ha' been closed yet a while."

"Bread and cheese sounds delicious," Molly said sincerely. "You seem gey cheerful and efficient, Emma, for someone I must be keeping up long past her usual hour for retiring. I am grateful to you, though."

"Good sakes, this be nowt," Emma said. "Me da serves Lady Meg and has done since ever she came to Rankil-burn. It be her rule that visitors should aye be well served and want for nowt that we can provide."

"That is kind and generous of her ladyship, but I expect you must be wondering how I came to be wearing his lordship's cloak," Molly said, certain that the maid would know it was his and not her own.

The comfort the cloak gave her had not lessened. Nor had the strong, albeit wholly unfamiliar, sense of security that the thick, fur-lined garment offered. It was huge on her but oh-so-warm and soft wherever it touched her skin. She could detect the rather spicy scent of Walter Scott when she inhaled. Nevertheless, she dreaded the fact that she would soon have to reveal how little she wore under it.

"'Tis nae business o' mine, mistress," Emma said lightly. "I did think your cloak looked much *like* his lordship's and wondered if it were a new fashion to wear one's cloaks so long. However, ye needna explain your doings t' the likes o' me."

Turning away to fetch a screen that stood against the nearby wall, she moved it nearer the tub. As she did, footsteps sounded on the stairs beyond the door, followed by a double rap, heralding the arrival of Molly's bathwater.

Two young men carried it in, in large buckets. They seemed to be as lacking in curiosity as Emma, and Molly decided that Scott's Hall was far better managed than Henderland was. Since Walter Scott had been its lord for only a day or so, she imagined that the deft hand behind such management must have been his father's . . . until she recalled Emma's casual mention of Lady Meg's rules.

"Is there not a Lady Scott, as well?" Molly asked Emma quietly while the men filled the tub. "Or is his late lordship's wife called Lady Rankilburn?"

Emma shook her head. "She be Lady Scott, aye, but the poor soul suffers from ill health. See you, though,

Lady Meg began running things here when she married his young lordship's granddad. I reckon she'll keep on running them till she dies unless his lordship marries someone wi' a stronger will than hers."

Emma's grin revealed doubt that such a person existed.

Recalling how swiftly his lordship had excused himself after receiving his grandmother's summons, Molly wondered if anyone dared to cross Lady Meg's will. The woman sounded fierce.

"You say that your father serves Lady Meg?"

"Aye, because the auld laird, *Sir* Walter, set him to Lady Meg's service the day they wed and said he was t' serve her till she didna want him nae more. He was nobbut eleven then, so he did it and he still does. And happy he is about that, too."

"Your mother must also live here, then, aye?"

Emma's expression clouded. "Me mam died when I were ten. We still miss her summat fierce."

"How old are you now?"

"Just on fifteen."

"That must have been very hard," Molly said sympathetically. "My mother died when I was a bairn, so I barely remember her, and my favorite grandame died when I was eight. She lived with us, and I do miss her. The other one lived longer, but in troth, the only thing I remember about *her* is that she always wore black gowns, had yellow teeth, and sat like a queen, as if she expected everyone to bow or curtsy to her. She certainly expected me to curtsy whenever I saw her."

Emma smiled. "Me grannies was both tartars sometimes, too, but I loved them both. Granny Gledstanes died last year, but Granny Elliot lives on. Everyone likes her, although they take good care to step out o' her path when she's on a rant."

The men, having finished filling the tub, left quietly and shut the door.

Molly stood where she was, yearning to get into the water and let it warm her but shy with the cheerful Emma, since she had never had a maid to aid her bathing.

His lordship's fur-lined cloak still felt like a refuge, but her shift was damp beneath it and beginning to cloy.

Emma adjusted the screen to conceal the tub and its occupant from the doorway. Then, giving Molly a direct look, she said, "I'm t' help ye as little or as much as ye like, mistress. I've put a wash-clout with them towels and some o' Lady Meg's own soap withal."

"I'll wash myself then," Molly said. With a small sigh, she added, "I cannot use his lordship's cloak as a robe, though, Emma. In fact, I ken fine that he'd like to have it back, and I've naught on underneath save a ragged shift."

"Then I'll fetch ye a warm robe and a pair o' the lady Janet's mules," Emma said without a blink. "And dinna be thinking she'll mind, for she won't. She has the warmest heart o' them all. Be there aught else that ye'll need straightaway?"

"A comb and brush," Molly said. "I'll just twist my hair up in a knot to bathe, but I do want to brush the leaves and such out of it afterward."

"I'll see to it all straightaway," Emma promised.

Blessing the girl's amiable, incurious nature, Molly waited only to hear the door open and shut before testing the water with the toes of one foot. It was hotter than she had expected, but she knew it would cool fast. So, draping the cloak over the screen, she peeled off the ruined shift and lowered herself gratefully into the tub.

Her scrapes and scratches made the process a penance, but she knew that her injuries would heal faster when they were clean. Lady Meg's soap smelled of spring flowers and she used it liberally, rediscovering the painful bruise on her cheek, where Tuedy had struck her, as she washed her face.

Soaking drowsily then, she let her thoughts drift again to her rescuer.

One new thing that she had noticed about him by the torchlight in the yard and in the great hall was that the new Lord of Rankilburn was handsomer than any man had a right to be. A head taller than she was, with chiseled features and hazel eyes, he possessed the strong, muscular shoulders and thighs of a swordsman and the otherwise lean and lanky body of one who spent many days on horseback.

She wondered if he always greeted unexpected events so calmly and how he was faring now with his fierce grandame.

~

Rarely was Wat able to stun his grandmother, so the astonished look on her face when he told her that Molly had fled her wedding night nearly brought a smile to his lips. Restraining himself, he waited politely for her response.

Her clear gray eyes narrowed suspiciously. "If I did not know you better, sir, I would suspect you of having a game with me. Are you actually telling me that the girl you found in the woods is a married woman?"

"Marriage is the only way I know to come by a wedding night," Wat said. "Having not witnessed the ceremony for myself, though—"

"Mind your tongue, sir," Lady Meg said.

He shook his head at her. "We must find out where she lives, Gram, and see that she gets safely home. My guess is that her new husband was rough with her and gave her a fright. But she belongs with him, nevertheless."

"You must not send her anywhere until we learn more about her, sir. Where is she? I want to see her for myself."

"At present, Emma is aiding her with a bath and providing food and clothing for her to wear. So, unless you mean to cross-question her in her tub—"

"You say she wore only a ragged shift?"

"Aye, or so she said. I did not peek when I gave her my cloak to wear."

"Then she fled because of fear rather than anger. I'll let her sleep tonight and see her in the morning. But we must give her sanctuary until we learn the truth."

"Must we?" Wat asked. He kept his tone mild but held her gaze.

Her composure withstood his challenge, but he discerned a twinkle in her eyes when she said, "So you would remind me of my place, would you, my lord? Aye, well, you are right to do so. The burden of decision here in all things is now yours to bear. But I would ask you to think carefully about this matter. If young Molly is who I suspect she may be, I have some right to speak for her. Only some, though, because I made no attempt to speak up during these many years past."

"I would attend closely to your counsel in any event, Gram," he said. "But why do you think you have a particular *right* to speak for her?"

"Because someone must. You are wise beyond your years, sir, but you have yet to think this matter through. Consider only what we know to be true. First, men from Henderland were seeking her. Don't bother to repeat that tale about a missing maidservant, because I refuse to believe that Will Cockburn would waste his time with such. He would wait for her return and then take a switch to her."

"I have said that I don't believe she is anyone's servant," Wat reminded her. "But I've never seen her before, so who do you think she may be?"

"Piers Cockburn of Henderland does have a daughter, you know," Lady Meg said. "I am sure you will recall that fact, because if I am not mistaken, your father once suggested her to you as an acceptable wife. Her name is Margaret. Her grandmother, Marjory Cockburn, was a dear friend of mine in the days before our sons took different courses politically. If your Molly is Margaret Cockburn, then I am her godmother and she is my namesake."

That would, Wat mused, explain why his father had *suggested* Lady Margaret Cockburn as a suitable wife.

"I do recall such a conversation, and Father did suggest such a marriage, but he did not press me to agree to it," he said. "Nor did he mention that you were Lady Margaret's godmother, Gram. You know as well as he did then that I was too busy training to win a knighthood to think seriously of marrying anyone."

"I know that you thought you were," she agreed with a smile. "I also know that you told him you would not marry anyone unless he commanded you to do so." Her smile faded. "Have you not also considered, love, who her husband must be?"

He had not, but he did now. The most logical answer was plain.

"If she is who you think she is, he cannot be one of her three brothers, or Will's man-at-arms," he said grimly. "So her husband is most likely Ring Tuedy."

"Sufficient cause for any lass to flee, I should think," Lady Meg said tartly. "Whilst she stays here, I suggest that you let her go on being just Molly. It will be more comfortable for her so, and word of her presence here is less likely to spread."

~

"God ha' mercy, mistress, what dreadful mischief befell ye?"

Startled at the sound of Emma's voice so nearby, Molly realized that she had sunk herself so deeply in thought that she had failed to hear the latch click open.

"I didna mean to give ye a fright," Emma said. "And I ken fine that it be nae business of mine. But when I saw all them scratches..."

Pausing, she added more gently, "I saw earlier that ye'd bruised and scratched your face, so I did bring the balm that Lady Meg keeps in the pantry. It may at least keep ye from getting another scar. I dinna ken what all might be in it, but when I cut myself wi' a knife, helping out in the kitchen, it healed gey quick."

"I'd be grateful if you would hand me the towel now and then rub some of your balm on my scratches after I'm dry."

"Aye, sure," Emma said. "I've brung ye a kirtle and shift, as well as a warm robe and slippers from Lady Janet's kists. I ken fine she'll say I ought to ha' brung ye her new kirtle, but I thought ye might be happier wi' one o' her older ones."

"You were right," Molly said with relief. "I'm most grateful to you for your thoughtfulness, Emma. I haven't had a new kirtle for an eon, so a well-worn one will suit me better, and that soft pink color is one of my favorites."

"I just thought how I'd feel, if it was me," Emma said. "I told one o' the lads t' bring up a hot brick for ye wi' your bread and cheese, too. He left them by the door, so I'll just fetch them in and slip the brick into the bed whilst ye dry yourself."

Handing Molly the towel, she disappeared around the screen again.

Molly dried herself quickly, listening as Emma moved back and forth in the bedchamber. The screen was too tall to see over, so she wrapped the towel around her for warmth and stepped around it.

Emma turned with a smile. "If ye'll sit on yon stool, I can rub the salve over the scrapes on your back, and ye can tuck into the bread and cheese whilst I do. Then ye can put on that robe, and I'll brush out your hair."

Ten minutes later, Molly lay snugly in bed, and the maidservant had gone, leaving her to her whirling thoughts. Savoring the warmth that the hot, flannel-wrapped brick provided, she reminded herself that for the night, at least, she was as safe as she could be.

If another thought followed that one, she was unaware of it and slept peacefully and dreamlessly until Emma opened the curtains and shutters the next morning to reveal a sky of drifting dark clouds, threatening more rain to come.

"Herself did say she'd talk wi' ye after ye've broken your fast," Emma said.

Molly's stomach clenched, making her hope she would

be able to eat before she had to face his lordship's grand-mother. However, when she followed Emma down to the great hall, she saw that his lordship awaited her on the dais, alone.

Wat stared at the young woman approaching the dais with Emma, skirting the two trestles of men still breaking their fast, and could scarcely believe that she was the lost waif he had found the night before. The soft pink kirtle she wore made her skin look like alabaster, and she car-ried a familiar-looking pink and gray wool shawl that he recognized as Janet's.

Her hair looked much lighter now than when it was damp. Then sunlight from a high window touched it, revealing streaks of gold. She had plaited it and twisted it at her nape, giving him a clear view of her well-scrubbed oval face. How had he failed to note that her lovely eyes were golden, the color of pine chips?

Her natural unplucked eyebrows and lashes were darker than her hair. The brows lay smoothly and nearly met above the bridge of her nose, a trait that he considered intriguing, even alluring. She would be a beauty when that bruise faded.

She eyed him with wary intensity, and he tried to imag-ine how it would feel to have run away from one's sacred obligations and accepted shelter in a strange household.

Despite her wariness, her pace did not falter and she carried herself with the dignity he had noted the night before. Nevertheless, and although the thought irked him, he was as dutybound to see her returned to her husband as she was to return.

He understood his grandmother's position. He could also sympathize with any woman married to Ring Tuedy. But none of that altered the fact that Molly was as much Tuedy's possession now as any other chattels the man might own.

Having run from him, she'd likely face punishment on her return. But no woman could hope to humiliate her husband on their wedding night with impunity.

Lady Meg was a wise woman with more experience of such matters than he had. She was also competent, courageous, and as practical as he was. But he disliked pretense of any sort, and in this instance, he thought that his position was the more realistic one and more likely to avoid unnecessary risk.

To draw the ire of a temperamental man like Piers Cockburn and his even more pugnacious sons must always qualify as risky. If Molly was Piers's daughter and Will's and Ned's sister as Lady Meg suspected, the Cockburns would take offense at any interference from Wat. So would Ring Tuedy, who belonged to one of the most ruthless families in the Borders. Moreover, Wat knew that such interference between a man and his wife was illegal and could land *him* in the suds with the Kirk, the King, and the Earl of Douglas, his own liege lord.

A wistfulness in Molly's expression as she glanced around the hall banished all thought of those powerful entities, leaving Wat with a stronger reluctance than ever to force her return, whether the situation was her own fault or not.

As she stepped onto the dais, he stood to greet her.

When she paused to make him a polite curtsy, he moved toward her.

"Rise, mistress," he said. "My grandmother will be down shortly, and she wants to talk with you. But you and I must talk more before then, I think."

"As you wish, my lord," she said softly. "I am grateful for your hospitality."

"Never mind that," he said, urging her to a seat beside his own. "Sit down and let them serve you. Emma said that you ate only bread and cheese last night."

"I shan't starve," she said, taking the seat he indicated. "*Should* I sit beside you, though? If your grandame is going to join us, or your lady mother—"

"If you eat quickly, we can be away before Gram descends," he interjected with a slight smile, "and my mother won't come down for hours. I'd like us to walk in the yard for a time, because I want to ask some more questions, if I may."

"Certes, you may, sir," she said. Turning toward young, fair-haired Edwin, who approached then to ask what she liked to eat, she said, "Prithee, I would like a lightly boiled egg, two slices of any cold sliced meat you have at hand, and toast."

"At once, mistress," Edwin said, turning away as Wat took his own seat again and took a manchet loaf from a basketful on the table.

"I've eaten," he told Molly. "But these are fresh-baked. Do you want one?"

"Nay, thank you," she said. "My egg and toast will take only a few minutes to prepare. What did you want to ask me?"

He hesitated, aware that men in the lower hall were watching them. Then, politely, he said, "Did you sleep well?"

She raised her eyebrows, doubtless aware that that was not one of the chief questions in his mind. But she said, "Better than I've slept in weeks, aye. My bed was much more comfortable than what I'd expected to endure, and quiet, withal."

"Is your own bedchamber so noisy, then?"

"It often is so when I go to bed," she replied. Casting a glance around the lower hall, she added, "Our men think of naught save their own entertainment."

"Your men?"

She gave him a quizzical look but turned away again when Edwin reappeared with a tray. "So quickly?" she said, revealing delight as well as surprise. "What excellent service you enjoy here, my lord."

Edwin chuckled. "This be gey quick even for Scott's Hall, mistress," he said, setting a bowl with her egg and a spoon before her. "See you, the chef had an egg on the boil for the housekeeper. When I tellt them both that I'd heard his lordship say he were eager to get outside, Mistress Ferguson said ye should ha' this one. All I had t' do was set bread to toast at the fire and slice your beef."

Thanking him, she fell to at once, and Wat did not question her further. Her enjoyment of her simple fare was clear. She broke her egg into the bowl, stirred it about, and used her toast to dip up egg before taking a bite. Then, rolling a slice of her beef into a tube, she daintily bit off an end and chewed.

"Will you take ale, mistress?" Edwin asked her, reaching for the pitcher.

Still chewing, she shook her head. Then, swallowing, she said, "I usually drink water when I break my fast. We have our own spring, you see. It bubbles right out of the rocks near the—" Breaking off, she looked down at the remaining toast beside the wee bowl and spooned the rest of her egg onto it.

Realizing that she would say no more, Wat said, "Prithee, Edwin, bring our guest some water."

Molly looked up and smiled at Edwin but looked quickly away again and went on eating in silence.

Wat glanced toward the archway leading to the private stair, half expecting to see Lady Meg step through it. But the archway remained reassuringly empty.

"Did you not want to ask me more questions?" Molly asked him.

"I do, but I'd prefer to talk in the greater privacy of the yard," he said, glancing again at the stairway.

Chapter 3 _____

Despite his lordship's apparent tranquility, Molly sensed his impatience to get outside. She dreaded the forthcoming interview with his grandame more than any questions he might ask, so she was perfectly willing to oblige him.

"I've finished eating, sir, if you want to leave."

"I do," he said, standing and extending his right hand to her. "The others will be down soon, and I want to know more before I present you to my grandmother."

"Like what?" Molly asked, automatically putting her hand in his warmer one. As she stood, though, she gave a sad little sigh, fearing that its warmth would chill when he learned her identity and realized who her kinsmen were.

She had nearly told him that the fresh spring water she usually drank with her meals sprang from rocks right near the kitchen door at Henderland. Few households in the Borders could boast of such a natural convenience.

He said no more but placed her hand formally on his left forearm and escorted her from the dais.

"You make too much of me thus," she muttered, uncomfortably aware that most of the men breaking their fast in the lower hall were staring openly now.

"Do I?" he replied *sotto voce*. "I think not."

Pressing her lips together but knowing better than to snatch her hand away, Molly resigned herself to behaving like a lady. Holding her head high, she let him escort her down the center of the lower hall toward its main entrance.

As they neared the archway to the stairs, she expected any minute to hear Lady Meg hail them from behind. Surely, the old woman would demand to know why they had left the hall before bidding her a civil good morrow.

Glancing up at his lordship to catch him looking back again toward what must be the privy stairs, she suspected that his thoughts matched her own. The notion relieved her worries until they reached the courtyard.

Her sense of comfort vanished after they had descended the long flight of wooden steps to the yard's still mist-damp cobblestones. They had taken only two steps on the stones when he said bluntly, "Is Piers Cockburn your father?"

Her hand twitched on his arm, and although a good night's sleep and long practice in hiding her feelings helped her avoid clutching that arm, she knew that he had likely detected her alarm. She also knew she dared not lie to him.

"Aye, sir, he is," she said. Anticipating his next question, she added bitterly, "And, may heaven save me, that villain Ringan Tuedy is my husband."

～

Wat gave Molly a long look. Her evident composure astonished him. So did the distance of her flight, the injuries she had endured, and the fact that she had dared to abandon her connubial duties. That she had escaped from such known brutes as Tuedy and her own kinsmen to do so was even more amazing.

Her bruise was darker, more prominent than it had been the night before.

She drew her shawl more closely around her and gazed fixedly ahead.

Either she was unwilling to see his reaction or unaware that her admissions might have shocked him. In either event, he hoped that he had concealed his feelings. Experience with his sisters suggested that she would tell him more if he could hear her out calmly without revealing his emotions.

She was apparently disinclined to volunteer much without coaxing, however.

Deciding to ask the most obvious question first, he said, "Why did you agree to marry Tuedy if you believe he is a villain?"

She looked at him then. "You did not seem friendly to him, yourself, sir. Do you think that any woman, knowing that man, would *willingly* marry him?"

"All you had to do was refuse," he said. "Scottish law is clear on that point. No one can legally make a Scotswoman marry without her consent."

The look she gave him then was scornful, the twist of her lips even more so. "So I thought, myself, my lord. I told them all, repeatedly, that I would *not* marry Tuedy. I even threatened to enter a nunnery if they tried to make me."

"Then how—"

"Mercy, sir, do you think that all Scotswomen are allowed to preach laws to their fathers and brothers? Surely, you must know what my father thinks of the King's laws. Your own father knew him. 'Tis why he and my father cooled their once close friendship. Recall that not long ago, Father ratified your lord father's charter when his lordship signed over his lands of Glenkerry to the monks of Melrose Abbey in exchange for your Scott gathering place."

"Father acquired Bellendean eight years ago," Wat said, surprised that she would know about that transaction. "They fell out only about *two* years ago."

"Aye, not long after King James expressed his determination to institute his own rule of law throughout Scotland. Father says that his grace is bent on undermining his nobles' heritable powers on their own lands."

That was not news to Wat, so he said, "Many men do believe that. But others believe that it will be good to have our laws apply to everyone equally and for everyone to understand what the laws are wherever they may be in Scotland."

"Aye, perhaps, but my father has spoken angrily about ratifying that charter ever since then. What he thought of Lord Rankilburn for failing to understand that his support of the King went right against the interests of all Scottish landowners to act as they please on their own lands does not bear my repeating."

"Then, prithee, do not repeat it," Wat said lightly. "I know Piers Cockburn disapproves of having one set of laws, determined by our Parliament, for all Scots to obey. But, on that point, I agree with my father and his grace, the King. Travelers should not have to worry about whether they are breaking any nobleman's private rules when they have to cross his land."

She opened her mouth to speak again, but he interjected firmly, "That is a discussion for another time, my lady. At present, I would prefer to know why your father thought he could ignore nationwide laws of both the King and the Kirk."

"Because he often does so and knows that he can," she said. "I believed, as you do, that I could refuse to marry Tuedy. So, I told Father and my brothers that I wanted no part of him. But it was useless. Tuedy and Will are friends, because they both love raiding," she added, giving him a look. "I doubt that you will hold their beliefs on that subject against them. I ken fine that you have led raids, too."

"I know that Will is a fierce raider," Wat agreed, ignoring the rest. "I did not know that all three of your brothers engaged in such doings, though."

"Thomas doesn't," she said with a slight smile. "He likes to build things and hopes to earn his own way when he is older. He kens fine that he'll get little from Father, because Will inherits all save my marriage portion and a house in Selkirk that will go to Ned. I like Thomas, because he is kind and wise, and loathes violence. Will and Ned *are* violent, and love raiding just as most Borderers do."

"I won't hold raiding against any man unless he chooses to raid *my* cattle or takes pleasure in killing innocent men, women, and bairns," Wat said frankly. "As for Will and Ned, they have often joined me to follow Douglas or to chase English raiders back to England. But I still don't see how your kinsmen forced you to marry Tuedy. Surely, *he* would refuse to marry a woman who didn't want him."

"You don't know him, then," she said, looking away, apparently studying the gates. "He sought a stronger bond with my kinsmen, because he has land abutting ours northwest of St. Mary's Loch. My father deemed him a good match for me, because Father had long feared a feud with the Tuedys of Drumelzier. You must know that, sooner or later, they feud with everyone they meet."

"So I have heard," he said. "Did Tuedy approach your father first, then?"

"Aye," she said. "And despite my refusals, Father told me yesternoon that it was my wedding day and that he would hear no protest from me. He had our own priest perform the ceremony, and Father and Will both stood close beside me."

"Are you so afraid of them?" Wat asked. "Was there no one to whom you could turn for help? Surely, the priest—"

"No one," she said. "Our Thomas was in Peebles, so there was no time to send for him. But even had he been home, he would not have opposed the others. I barely had time to prepare myself. I wore one of my old gowns and my mother's heavy wedding veil, which covered me to my waist. They bound my hands and stuffed a rag in my mouth. Will bound that in place, too. Then he gripped my hair under the veil. When the priest asked if I'd take Tuedy for my husband, Will jerked my head back and forth as if I were nodding."

"Surely, the priest could see that!"

"Aye, sure, he could, and he could hear me protesting over the gag as loudly as I could. But Father Jonathan owes his living to my father and is terrified of Will and Ned. He babbled the whole ceremony as if his life depended on finishing it in half the usual time. When it ended, he presented us—Tuedy and me—to my brothers, my father, and our household servants as man and wife. Then he blessed us and fled before blessing our bed, as Father had told him he should do at once."

Fighting his shock that any Borderer would treat his daughter or sister so, Wat refused to compound their brutality by asking her about the bedding.

"How did you escape them?" he asked instead, guiding her away from a group of lads setting up mats on the cobbles to practice wrestling.

"Pure providence," she said with a grimace. "Father had ordered a wedding feast, and they were about to serve it. Tuedy said it would not do for the servants to see me bound, so he'd take me upstairs to remove my veil and my bindings. I was terrified of him, but Father and the others just laughed and told him to take his time. He... he made me show him where my bedchamber was." Color suffused her face. "I...I don't want to tell you all he did then, but—"

"I will not ask you, lass," Wat said gently. "Tell me how you got away."

"I made him angry," she said, touching the bruise on her cheek. "God protect me, I called him a beast."

She drew a breath, adding, "He hit me and took away my clothes, all save my shift. Then he shouted for one of his men and told him to stand at the door and make sure I stayed inside until his return. Right there, with his man watching, Tuedy said he would school me then to respect my husband—with his whip, if need be—and teach me what he would expect from his wife."

Her voice had lost all emotion, Wat noted. She repeated the threat that must have curdled her liver as if she were reciting a list of foods to replenish a pantry.

She was staring straight ahead again with a set expression, as if she were remembering. Giving herself a visible shake, she met his gaze.

Since he could think of nothing sensible to say, he kept quiet, hoping she would continue.

The silence lengthened until he began to think he

would have to prod her to describe her escape. Just as he was about to do so, she gave him a rueful smile and said, "I did nothing heroic to escape, sir. Or even particularly dangerous. I confess, though, that I was more frightened, leaving, than I had ever been in my life."

"I believe you," he said more firmly than he had intended.

"I believed I had no choice, though," she said. "You see, I'd realized when Tuedy put his man at my door that he hadn't noticed the service stairway, because a tall screen stands before its door to prevent drafts. So, as soon as they left, I fled down those stairs to the kitchen. Nearly everyone was in the hall, serving the meal. I grabbed a roll and some cheese and slipped out through the scullery door."

"I do recall that Henderland has no wall around it."

"Naught save a stockade round the stables and sheep-fold. The tower itself is impregnable and boasts a wide view of the surrounding countryside. I waited until the men in the yard went in to eat and then made haste to the hills southeast of the tower. I knew that Tuedy would take his time eating and drinking. He had declared that having a guard at my door would be a lesson for me in humility."

Conscious of a strong urge to teach Tuedy a few lessons, Wat forced calm into his voice and said, "You were amazingly brave, I think."

"Do you? I assure you, sir, I did not *feel* brave. The worst part—before I heard Will's sleuthhounds, that is—was climbing our hill south of the loch. I knew I'd be in view of the tower then. But the mist had lowered, and light was dim."

"What made you choose to come to Scott's Hall?"

"Mercy, I didn't *choose* to come here," she said, offering him another rueful smile. "I got fearfully lost in the forest. It gets dark so early now, and with the mist trying to hide the moon, I had barely enough light to avoid walking right into trees, and I was terrified that I'd move in circles and find myself back where I started. I tried to keep the moon in sight and made my way as well as I could until I heard your dog. Then I heard your voice and Will's hounds."

"Which is when you dove into the shrubbery," he said. "I must tell you, lass, I know of no one who has ever gone to such lengths to avoid me before."

She gave him a look that ought to have withered him where he stood but made him fight back a smile instead.

Despite their circumstances, he had felt comfortable teasing her a little. Had anyone told him twenty-four hours before that he could feel so at ease with anyone, let alone a stranger, this soon after his father's death, he'd have denied it.

Molly felt herself relax, almost as if some unknown force had opened her up and let all the horror and fear she had been remembering drain out through her toes and fingertips. Magical as it felt, common sense told her that the feeling stemmed more from the solid, plainspoken man beside her than from any supernatural effect.

He seemed so sensible and strangely understanding for a man.

She wondered at herself for thinking so, because he had said nothing to indicate that he understood a single thing she had told him, although he *had* had the civility to glide right past the time when Tuedy had her at his mercy in her chamber.

He might just as easily have demanded to hear the details.

So his lordship was evidently a gentleman born as well as a nobleman.

His hazel eyes still glinted with his response to her glowering. She saw green flecks in them now but discerned no anger, certainly none to match what she'd have seen in Will's eyes or Ned's if she had glowered so at either of them.

In fact, had she been able to understand why Walter Scott might smile at the minatory look she had given him, she would describe that glinting as a twinkle.

He *had* spoken lightly about the lengths to which she had gone. Still, he must know that she dove into the shrubbery more to conceal herself from Will than from him. Any sensible man would know that, would he not?

"How did you guess who my father is?" she asked abruptly.

He shrugged. "I didn't. My grandmother deduced who you were. Even so, we could not be sure she was right without asking you."

"She deduced it! Mercy, how?"

"She was a close friend of your grandmother, Lady Marjory Cockburn. Moreover, Gram says that *she* is your godmother and you are her namesake."

"Lady Meg is my godmother? I didn't know. If anyone ever told me as much, I wasn't old enough or informed enough to know what it meant. Neither my father nor my brothers pay much heed to kirking, although I do remember going to kirk with my grandame Marjory.

When I grew older, I went because she said it was our duty to set a good example for our tenants and servants. In troth, though, I rarely understand what Father Jonathan preaches. He is not, I fear, a sensible man." She paused. "I don't think Lady Meg ever came to visit us after Grandame died."

"You must ask her about that," he said.

When she grimaced at the thought of quizzing Lady Meg about anything, he added gently, "I should tell you that she believes you should simply stay here. I disagree with her, though, because at some point you *will* have to sort this out with your family. The only sensible way to do that is to face them and have it out."

"Well, if that's what you think, I mean to cast my lot with Lady Meg," Molly said flatly, hoping for the first time that her ladyship was as fierce as she had feared. "Truly, sir, if you send me home, you might as well kill me yourself."

"Now you are exaggerating," he said mildly. "I expect that your father and brothers will be angry with you, lass. Tuedy, as well. But you did run away and doubtless caused them all considerable concern."

"Concern!" she exclaimed as a chill swept through her. "Do you think *any* of them cares a whit for me beyond my ability to run a household—a duty, I would submit to you, that my father and brothers were willing to sacrifice by forcing me to marry Tuedy. Prithee, my lord," she added with an unexpected catch in her voice, "do not send me back there. At least give them all time to let their tempers cool."

To her horror, she saw his face set and feared that he had made up his mind. She had already said more than she ought to have said, though, and had doubtless over-stepped what he would allow. Biting her tongue, she looked toward the keep and saw a small, dark-haired lassock standing in the entryway, watching them.

"I think that someone has come seeking you, sir," Molly said quietly.

Wat let his gaze follow hers and said, "That's my little sister Annabella." Meeting his gaze across the yard, Annabella waved imperiously. "If Gram did not send her out here to fetch me," he added, "I shall be much surprised."

"Before we go in, my lord, may I ask what you mean to do about me?"

"Aye, sure, you may ask," he said. "But you must know that I cannot hide you here indefinitely. Your family and your husband have a right to know where you are. You do make a good argument for letting some time pass before we tell them, though, and I agree that it would be unwise for you to face them alone."

"Most unwise," she said. "I know you think I've exaggerated—"

He shook his head. "I am not blind, lass. I can see your bruises, so you may stay until I decide what we should do. You will be safe here, and the women of my household should be sufficient to protect your honor."

"Thank you," she said fervently.

"We'll see if you thank me later," he said. "Such a delay may infuriate them all more. Also, if Will suspects that I had aught to do with your leaving—"

"Mercy, why should he?"

"I have never credited him with vast intelligence," Wat

said. "Moreover, you did come here, and he seems always to think the worst of people. He rarely, if ever, bothers to seek out the facts of a matter."

She bristled, saying, "Will can be hard, but he is not stupid."

"Come now, and meet Annabella," he said, determined to avoid that debate. Urging her back toward the keep, he added, "She is just eleven and will pelt you with questions, but you may snub her if you do not want to answer them. She knows she ought not to quiz our guests, but she cannot always contain her curiosity. Gram says that Bella is like her youngest sister, Rosalie, was at that age. She is named after their mother, our great-grandmother, who was Annabel Murray."

"I will never keep your family's names straight in my head," Molly said.

"It won't be so hard. You'll see." He was grateful to note that although she had taken offense at his description of her brother, she had recovered her calm.

Bella was bouncing on her toes with impatience, albeit looking as solemn as she had since their father's death. She had barely spoken since then.

As they drew nearer, he realized he had not yet decided whether to follow Lady Meg's advice and let Molly remain just Molly or to introduce her properly.

Apparently Annabella's notions of propriety failed to match his own, because, waiting no longer, she said in a voice that likely carried across the courtyard, "Gram says to stir yourself, Wat. She wants to talk with our guest."

Wat caught her gaze and said mildly, "Prithee, do not announce our grandame's wishes to the yard, Bella. Make your curtsy to her ladyship, instead." Then, to Molly, he said, "I pray you will forgive Annabella's enthusiasm, my lady, and allow me to present her to you."

"I would like that," Molly said, smiling at Bella, who promptly obeyed him by making an awkward curtsy without taking her eyes off Molly.

"No one told me you were noble, your ladyship," Bella said, rising as hastily as she had bobbed. "I thought—"

"Never mind what you thought, Bella," Wat interjected. "This is the lady Margaret Cockburn of Henderland, which lies some miles northwest of here."

"Did you come all by yourself, Lady Margaret?" Bella asked.

Seeing pitfalls at every new turn but grateful that his hitherto sorrowful little sister was taking interest in their guest, Wat said, "Unless you want Gram to hand us our heads in our laps, lassie, we should go in. You may ask your questions later."

Molly gave him a look then that startled him, because it was brimful of laughter, even mockery. To Bella, she said with a smile, "Prithee, call me Molly, Lady Bella. And, I beg that you will try to keep my visit here a private matter. My own family does not know where I am, and I hope to keep it that way for a time."

"Ooh, I love secrets, and even Wat will agree that I am good at keeping them," Bella said, returning Molly's smile with a winsome one of her own. "But Gram awaits us. And my lady mother and my sister, Janet, want to meet you, too."

"More names for me to remember," Molly said. "But why do you call your grandame 'Gram' instead of 'Grandame' or 'Nan' as many people hereabouts do?"

Wat said, "That is my fault. When I was small, everyone tried to get me to say 'Grandame,' but it came out 'Gram,' instead and stayed that way. I should tell you, though—and *you* are not to repeat this, Bella—Gram wanted me to introduce you to everyone as just Molly. Nevertheless, I'll present you properly to my mother and Janet. The servants will call you Mistress Molly, I expect, since Emma does."

"I understand, sir. I would not want to deceive any of them a-purpose."

"Then we are in agreement on that, at least," Wat said with a nod.

~

Molly followed Lady Annabella up the stairs with his lordship right behind them. *So far, so good,* she told herself. However, the easiness she had felt with him while walking in the courtyard faded again to uncertainty.

If Lady Meg was her godmother, why had the woman never taken interest in her? It had been a surprise to learn that she *had* a godmother, although not that her father had failed to mention such a woman's existence. Piers Cockburn held the institution of the Kirk in as low esteem as he held the current King of Scots.

Entering the hall with Wat and Bella, Molly faced the dais and three ladies seated there. The frail-looking creature nearest the center of the long high table she deduced to be Wat's mother, as the place next to him would rightfully be hers.

The older woman at Lady Scott's left sat stiffly upright. She was plain looking, quietly dignified, and the first of the three to note their entrance. However, although Molly knew that the woman must be Lady Meg, she did not look fierce. Shifting her glance from Molly, she looked speculatively at her grandson.

Next to her sat a dark-haired girl of perhaps sixteen, who, Molly decided, must be the lady Janet, his lordship's other sister.

"You were down gey early, sir," Lady Meg said evenly.

"Aye, Gram, I awoke sooner than expected and learned from Emma that her ladyship had risen and would soon come downstairs, so I hied myself down here. I have been showing her the courtyard by daylight. Good morrow to you, Mam, and you, Janet-lass," he added with a nod to each. "If you will permit me, Mam," he said to his mother, "I would present the lady Margaret Cockburn of Henderland."

Molly was still watching Lady Meg, whose lips tightened at hearing the introduction but relaxed seconds later. Deciding with relief that Lady Meg would not take his lordship to task, Molly hastily made her curtsy to Lady Scott.

"Welcome to Scott's Hall, Lady Margaret," her ladyship said in soft tones. "I knew your mother, but I have not set eyes on you since you were newborn. I fear you have come at a sad time for us, but doubtless Walter has told you as much."

"He has, my lady, and I, too, mourn your loss," Molly said as she rose. "But prithee, call me Molly. Our priest is the only one who has ever called me Margaret."

"Then we will call you Molly. This is my good-mother, whose name is also Margaret," Lady Scott added with a slight gesture. "But everyone here calls her Lady Meg. Sitting next to her is our Janet."

Janet got hastily to her feet and said with a warm smile, "It is a pleasure to meet you, my lady. I see that you've already met Bella."

Molly replied in kind and returned her attention to Lady Meg, who had kept silent since her opening remark. "Forgive me, madam," Molly said, "but his lordship has just told me that you are my godmother. I was unaware that I had one, but I am honored to learn of our connection."

"I am glad to meet you at last, too, my dear. I did meet you soon after your birth, but I fear I have been remiss in my duties to you since then. Your father... But we can talk later, for I do hope we'll have time now to get to know each other," she added with a pointed look at Wat.

He met the look easily, saying, "Her ladyship is welcome to stay as long as need be, Gram." With a glance including his sisters, he added, "Molly would keep her whereabouts private for a time. Prithee, be sure our people understand that."

Molly felt heat flood her cheeks and was wondering what they all must think of her when Lady Scott said in a fluttering way, "Then whatever did you mean by saying that she can stay 'as long as need be,' Walter?"

Chapter 4

Impressed by the easy grace with which Molly had greeted his mother and grandmother, Wat had continued to watch her. Having noted her nervousness when he'd mentioned Lady Meg's wishing to talk with her, he had expected to see that nervousness return when the two faced each other.

Instead, Molly behaved with the confidence he'd expect from Janet, rather than the awkwardness one might expect from a lass the Cockburn men had raised.

Lady Meg cleared her throat and glanced pointedly at Lady Scott.

Belatedly realizing that he had not answered his mother's question about how long Molly might stay, Wat said, "I meant that Molly will remain until I decide otherwise, Mam. I have business at Melrose Abbey, and I want to seek counsel with Father Abbot whilst I'm there. So, she will stay at least until my return."

His mother said, "You have much to do here, too, Walter. Mayhap your father somehow confided his every intention to you, and you will see to things as he would have desired. At present, though, one feels as if all here is in turmoil."

"I'll do my best to go on as he did, Mam, I promise. Moreover, if you need aught from me, you ken fine that you need only ask."

Aware that his grandmother was eyeing him quizzically, he returned his attention to her. "You and I might talk more about my visit to the abbey before I leave, Gram, if you like."

With an understanding nod, she said, "I, too, have faith in you, love. Prithee, extend my regards to John Fogo when you see him. He has been Abbot of Melrose for only three years, but he is a good man who gives sage advice. I believe he has knowledge of most laws that pertain hereabouts, as well."

"I mean to ask him about some of those laws," Wat said. Then, turning to Janet, he said, "I would ask you to be a friend to Molly whilst I'm away, Jannie."

Her warm smile dawned. "I will, Wat. I shall enjoy that."

"Prithee, do not forget that we expect your great-aunt Rosalie to arrive from Westruther within the week, sir," Lady Meg reminded him.

"She is bound to bring an entourage, Meg," Lady Scott said fretfully. "Ought we to be entertaining a host of visitors whilst we are in deepest mourning?"

"Lavinia, Rosalie is family," Lady Meg said firmly.

"But she has lived most of her life in England with those dreadful Percies, Meg. When they are not raiding our lands, they stir trouble elsewhere. We scarcely know Rosalie, after all. I have met her only once, years ago. Faith, but she is more Percy now than Murray, I should think, and we *are* in deep mourning."

Tears welled in her eyes, and seeing them, Wat felt

a pang of sympathy. He realized, too, though, that his mother often chose to forget that Lady Meg had connections to the Percies through her own mother, as did Meg's descendants, too, of course, including himself.

Molly looked as if she wished herself elsewhere. He nearly suggested that she take a seat and be more comfortable but decided he'd be wiser to keep silent.

Lady Meg said more patiently, "No matter how long Rosalie lived in England, Lavinia, she is still my sister. 'Tis true that she married our cousin, Richard Percy, but she is a widow now just as you and I are. Having stayed at Elishaw with my brother Simon for a month, she is now with my sister Amalie and Westruther. Moreover, we arranged her visit to us long ago. As for an entourage, unless Simon misled me, which I doubt, she will have an attire woman, a courier or some such thing, and an outrider or two."

"But all of them are English, are they not? With so many raids of late—"

"I believe Simon provided her outriders," Lady Meg interjected gently.

"Even so, the other two, her maid and this equerry or whatever he calls—"

"—will both behave themselves whilst they are here if they are wise," Meg interjected in a less gentle tone.

Wat had nearly smiled at the gentleness, amazed as he always was by his grandmother's capacity for patience with his mother.

The two women could hardly have been more different. His grandmother, twenty years the senior, was full of life and energy. His mother displayed little of either trait, although despite the indisputable local inclination for violence, she enjoyed a life of ease. He knew that she grieved because she had loved his father and depended on him for nearly every action she took and decision she made.

Knowing, too, that his own capacity for patience would never match his grandmother's, and sensing that Molly's tension had eased, Wat held his peace.

When silence fell at last, Janet said, "Molly, would you like to come to the kitchen with me? I promised to help pare apples for pies this morning. If you dislike such chores, of course—"

"I'd be grateful for anything that makes me feel useful," Molly said lightly.

Realizing that his lordship might think she sounded ungrateful, Molly turned hastily to him and added, "That is, unless you want to talk more, sir."

He smiled and she noted again how infectious his smile was.

"Nay, my lady," he said. "My grandame will have much advice to offer me before I depart for Melrose. I also have much on my mind, so I warrant you will enjoy Janet's company today more than you would mine."

Firmly stifling a sudden impulse to tell him that she strongly doubted that, she said, "Do you leave at once, then?"

"I should," he admitted. "I had planned to leave this morning to inform the abbot of my father's death and assure him that their agreements still hold. I want to avoid his ever wondering if I might try to alter any of them. Also, I must visit the Douglas in Hawick, if he is still there. He will already have heard of Father's death, for he has ears to the ground throughout the Borders. But he will expect to hear from me nevertheless. So, the sooner I get away, the sooner I can return."

"Then you might be away for a long while."

He shook his head. "I will return before you have had time to miss me. 'Tis but twenty miles to the abbey, and we ride fast. Also, as my lady mother reminded me, I have much to do here, and whilst your own situation remains unresolved, I must not tarry.

"Don't fret, lass," he added when she failed to suppress a gasp. "My men are skilled at protecting the Hall and our lands, so you will be safe. If you have concerns, you need only express them to Jock's Wee Tammy or to Gram."

"Or you might simply tell Emma," Lady Meg said, abandoning a murmured conversation with Lady Scott and thereby proving to Molly that age had not impaired the older woman's hearing. "Sithee," Meg added, "Emma is my Sym's daughter, and Sym is as skilled at keeping us safe as Tammy is. I think Walter will agree that Emma is also well suited to attend you whilst you stay with us."

"Thank you, my lady," Molly said, glancing at his lordship.

He nodded. "Emma is an excellent choice," he said. "She never gossips and has served us since she was old enough to insist that she wanted to work here."

"Come, Molly," Janet said, standing. "I have finished eating, so we can begin the apples straightaway. Then, perhaps, you and Bella would like to help with a few other light chores."

Bella grimaced, but Lady Meg said, "Aye, Molly, go along with Janet now, and I will talk with Walter. Then, perhaps, you will join me in my sitting room a half-hour or so before our midday meal, so that you and I can have a talk, too."

"Aye, madam, I would be pleased to do that," Molly said, there being no other acceptable reply.

She glanced at her host again as she turned away.

To her shock, he winked at her.

~

Wat saw Molly's astonishment and knew he had overstepped the line of acceptable behavior for a host toward a young lady guest. But his wink was pure impulse and occurred before he had known he would do it. Glancing at his grandmother, he noted gratefully that she was talking again with his mother.

Lady Meg nodded then and turned toward him. "I will see your mother settled in the solar, love," she said. "Then you and I can adjourn to my sitting room. I know you want to prepare for your journey, so I shan't let you linger with me."

"I'll be there anon, Gram," he said. "I want a word with Tam first."

"Surely, you won't take him with you!"

"Nay, Geordie will look after my men, and Sym's Jed will look after me, as usual," Wat said, speaking of the captain of his fighting tail and Sym's son.

He nearly revealed what he meant to tell Tam, but the hall was not the place for that. "I'll see you shortly."

She nodded and returned her attention to Lady Scott.

~

Finding Tam in the stable, talking with a pair of lads there, Wat waited only until he had dismissed them before saying, "I'd warrant you know that I want our guest's presence here kept as quiet as possible."

"Aye, laird," Tam said. "Ye'll no want trouble wi' the Cockburns."

"True," Wat agreed. "You have guessed"—he looked swiftly around to be sure the stable was otherwise empty—"that she is Piers Cockburn's daughter."

When Tam nodded, Wat went on. "I've agreed that we'll do all we can to protect her, so her family must not know where she is until I glean more facts about her situation and decide what is best to do."

"What o' Ring Tuedy?" Tam said mildly. "He seemed as set on finding her as Will Cockburn did. Ye'll no want trouble with that villain either, I'm thinking."

Wat sighed. "I'd like to say that what happens at Rankilburn is no concern of Tuedy's. But—and this is for no one's ears save yours and Geordie's, although Sym will likely hear it from Gram—the lady Molly is Tuedy's wife, albeit unwillingly so."

Big Tammy's thick, dark eyebrows shot upward. "Nay then," he muttered. "That villain has a foul reputation with the lassies, laird. He's been firm against marrying afore this, too. So what would ha' stirred him to marry her ladyship?"

"Cozying up to her father, I'd wager," Wat said. "They own adjoining lands, and her ladyship thinks Piers feared a feud with the Tuedys if he refused. Even so, that any self-respecting father could give his daughter to a man known the length and breadth of the Borders as a deceitful brute alarms me."

"Our lads will keep mum, and we've little to fear from the Cockburns," Tam declared. "Even so, the news will get out, sir. Such secrets always do."

"I know, but do what you can. Whatever happens, keep the lass safe."

After discussing other matters with Tam, Wat told Geordie, the captain of his fighting tail, that they would leave directly after the midday meal. "I will spend tonight at Melrose, Geordie, and tomorrow at Douglas's Black Tower in Hawick, if I must. But I want to return here as soon as I can."

"Aye, laird, I'll see to all, then," Geordie said.

Knowing that he had done what he could to protect Molly, and was leaving the Hall in good hands, Wat headed upstairs to his grandmother's sitting room.

Lady Meg would want to hear what orders he had given and would have last-minute advice for his trip to the abbey. But the morning was swiftly passing, and he could spare her only a few minutes.

⁓

"I am surprised that our fathers never presented us to each other, Molly," Janet said with a smile, as she deftly pared an apple. "I'm only a year younger than you are, so if they had, we might have been longtime friends by now."

"My father rarely mixes with other families," Molly said. "I used to think he avoided such gatherings because he missed my mother. Now I think he just prefers the company of men and dislikes anything more formal. I do agree, though, that your father would have encouraged our friendship. He was kind to me whenever he visited us, and I liked him. You must miss him sorely."

Tears welled in Janet's blue eyes, and Molly saw that Bella abruptly gave her full attention to the skinless apple she was slicing. The younger girl looked as if she were intent on making each slice equal to its predecessor.

Janet wiped her eyes on a sleeve. "Father would disapprove of us turning into watering pots," she said softly. "Whenever we succumbed to tears or what he called 'tragedy faces,' he'd remind us that emotions are for one's bedchamber."

"He did," Bella said. "But he was always gey quick with a hug when he said such things, Jannie. And his hugs—" Overcome, she stopped, swallowed hard, and fixed her attention again on her apples.

"I'm so sorry," Molly said sincerely. "I have wanted to express my own sorrow at his death, and my condolences, to you all. But one never knows what to say in such a case that will not upset the listener more than if one had kept silent."

"How true that is," Janet said. "I *never* know what to say. Gram always seems to know the exact thing, but even she has been quiet, so one knows that she is suffering as much as any one of us is. It was so...so sudden. He just put a hand to his chest and turned ashen pale. Within minutes, he was gone."

"Gram said he had been feeling sickly all day," Bella murmured. "He told her his arm and chest hurt. Then he said it was naught, that he had just been too busy and needed a good sleep. H-he couldn't have known."

"At least he was not sick or helpless for days or months," Molly said gently. "As for what to say to your grandame, mayhap you should ask *her* what you might do to make things easier for her now. I think she would tell you if you asked her."

Janet surprised her with a watery chuckle and quickly covered her mouth. "Oh, I ken fine that I ought not to laugh at such a time," she said through her slim fingers. "But the notion of Gram's *not* telling us what we might do, when she rarely misses an opportunity—faith, that just makes me want to laugh."

Bella said, "She told me once that offering advice so easily comes of having been the oldest of three girls. She said her mother expected her to look after the younger ones and to guide them, so it became habit later to manage things. Also, she is very good at managing. Mam never needs to lift a finger."

Janet met Molly's gaze and looked swiftly away.

Aware that she ought to change the subject, Molly said lightly, "It must be pleasant to have the company of other women. I have only men at home and the occasional maidservant whose parents will allow her inside during the day. None will let a daughter *sleep* inside our tower."

"Mercy, had you no personal maidservant, then?" Bella asked.

"Sometimes I did during the day," Molly told her. "But they never lasted long, especially as I grew older. Sithee, my brothers likewise grew older. Whenever a maidservant began to worry about drawing their attention, she would stop coming even by day. I didn't mind much, though, most of the time."

Both Janet and Bella eyed her sympathetically, and long enough so that she said firmly, "Truly, I did not mind. Sometimes, one *wants* to be alone."

"I don't mind that, sometimes," Janet said. "But I want to choose the times."

"I like having other females around," Bella said. "Without them... well, who can one talk to if one is all alone?"

"I had imaginary friends when I was small," Molly told her.

"I think Wat believes there are too *many* women here,"

Janet said with another little smile. "Since our brother Stephen began his knightly training..."

"He and Wat rarely had much to talk about before then," Bella said sagely when Janet paused. "Whenever Wat was home, Stephen would plague him to talk about all that he did when he was *not* at home."

"I think it is the nature of brothers to plague each other," Molly said. "I have three of them. I own, though, I've often wondered how it would be to have a sister."

"We can be your sisters for now, at least," Janet said.

"Aye, sure," Bella said, brightening.

The thought of having two such sisters warmed Molly all through. Then she recalled that she would soon have to go home and then let Tuedy drag her miles away to Drumelzier, his family's home on the river Tweed.

They were still talking and thoroughly enjoying each other's company when a stiffly upright, elderly woman entered the kitchen. She said, "Lady Molly, forgive my intrusion, but I am Lady Meg's woman, Brigid. She would have you bear her company now until they are ready to serve the midday meal."

"I must wash my hands, but then I will go to her," Molly said, taking off the apron that Janet had given her to wear while preparing the apples. Picking up the pink and gray shawl from the stool where she had draped it earlier, and assuring the others that she would help again as soon as she could, she hurried in Brigid's wake.

Her wariness of Lady Meg, having waned earlier, seemed now to have disappeared, vanquished by curiosity.

When Brigid opened the door for her to enter, Molly saw Lady Meg standing by a window directly opposite them. She turned with a smile.

"You came up quickly, my dear. I am grateful."

"There is no need for gratitude, my lady," Molly said, making her curtsy.

"Come to the window and take that stool," Lady Meg said. "We can enjoy the sun now that it has come out. 'Tis as if this early-November weather cannot decide whether to begin winter now or linger resolutely in autumn."

Taking the indicated seat, Molly said with a smile, "'Tis often the case at this time of year, though, is it not?"

"It is," Meg admitted. "In troth, I sought something to say other than to tell you again how dreadful I feel to have abandoned you as I did. See you—"

"You need not apologize," Molly interjected daringly. "I know my father, and since he never told me I *had* a godmother..." She spread her hands.

"Yes, but mayhap you should not blame him alone," Lady Meg said. "Marjory may not have told him. Only she, your mother, the priest, and I were present at your christening. As I recall, Piers had said..." She rolled her eyes musingly. "If I recall aright, he told Marjory that he had named three sons and thought a daughter's naming did not warrant disturbing a priest, let alone God."

"That sounds like him, aye," Molly said, stifling a grimace. "But I do think that Grandame ought to have told me about you before she died."

"I have heard that your father is a brutal man," Lady Meg said mildly in what seemed to be a non sequitur. "Has he ever raised a hand to you?"

"He used to skelp me with a switch, aye, whenever I misbehaved or made him angry. Do not most fathers do that?"

"They do, but yours has a reputation for being more

temperamental and violent than most Borderers are. Your brothers share that repute, so Marjory may have feared that telling you she had provided you with a godmother might prove dangerous for you. You must have been only seven or so when she died, aye?"

"I had just turned eight," Molly admitted.

"And your birthday is sometime this month, as I recall."

"The seventeenth," Molly said, impressed that Lady Meg had remembered. Piers Cockburn was not a man for remembering or celebrating birthdays.

When Lady Meg remained silent, Molly said, "It was kind of his lordship to rescue me. He was likely thinking then only of his so-recent bereavement."

"It was *good* for our Walter to rescue you, child. His father's death hit us all hard, but I think that Walter tends now to worry about the burdens he has inherited. His father also inherited the title much earlier than he had expected, you see, because my beloved husband died at the Battle of Homildon Hill."

Her lips twisted at the memory, and Molly could not blame her. The Scots had suffered dreadful losses in that battle, because they had endured exceedingly bad leadership from men who ought never to have been leading them. At least, that was what her father had often said.

"It must have been a terrible battle," she said.

"It was, but that is not why I mentioned it. Robert was eager to assume his new duties and was duly respectful of them. But he had no other ambition and few other calls on him to do otherwise. Walter, however, seeks to emulate his grandfather and become the second *Sir* Walter Scott in this family."

"He means to win a knighthood, then."

"Aye, for he thrives on battle and raiding just as my husband did. But Wat knows that all such activities must take second place to his duties here and on his numerous other estates. Robert recently acquired several new pieces of land and hoped to acquire the other half of one of them and rid himself of Murthockston, which is gey distant from here. I know he'd want Wat to do that if he can."

"Doubtless, his lordship is aware of his father's hopes," Molly said with a feeling that she should not be discussing her host so familiarly. To change the subject, she said, "It is fortunate that he was home when Lord Rankilburn died."

"I sent for him," Lady Meg said. Looking bleakly out the window, she added, "I kept having this odd sense of loving Robert too much. It came frequently and at odd times. I cannot describe it, other than to say that I'd experienced such feelings before, during a short period before my husband rode off to war that last time. I knew that our Walter would come home if I sent for him. So I did."

"How providential," Molly said, thinking it also sounded eerie. Then, noting that Lady Meg had turned from the window and was eyeing her rather speculatively, she wondered if the comment had seemed improper to her.

If it had, Lady Meg showed no sign of it. She said with a sigh, "The unfortunate thing is that Robert and Wat often saw things differently. Wat no sooner arrived than Robert asked him if he had turned his thoughts yet to marriage, which is a subject that Wat still avoids discussing."

"If he is reluctant," Molly said feelingly, "no one should force him."

"No one did. However, the fact is that he is more than old enough to take a wife and sire children, and now that he has inherited the title, he has a duty to provide himself with an heir. Perhaps I should begin thinking about who might suit him. I don't suppose you know any eligible young females."

"I...I have female cousins, madam, but I scarcely know them. In troth, I know only those females who have served us at Henderland."

"Certes, none of them would do, but I shall think of something." Lady Meg drew a breath. "Now, tell me how you came to marry that dreadful Tuedy. Do not think you will shock me, for I do not shock easily, and I want to hear *all* about it."

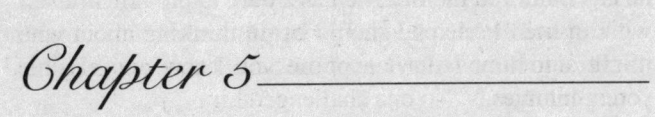

Chapter 5

After the midday meal, Wat left for Melrose with his manservant, Jed Elliot, his equerry, and a tail of six armed riders. That was half as many men as the King of Scots's orders and first Parliament allowed the Lord of Rankilburn.

Had he been crossing land controlled by an unfriendly clan, he'd have taken his full allotment. However, the Earl of Douglas controlled the land between Rankilburn and Melrose, and much of Teviotdale was Scott land.

Wat wore his fur-lined cloak over breeks, boots, and a leather jack, and he carried both sword and dirk. When his man, Jed, had draped the cloak over Wat's shoulders, an image of Molly wearing it the night before leaped into his mind.

She had looked small in it, not to mention sad, wary, bruised, and bedraggled. As he rode, he thought about her several times, wondering what to do with her.

Every time, the image of Ring Tuedy rose in his mind, making him wince.

He and his men crossed the river Tweed at the abbot's ford that afternoon and reached the abbey shortly before dark. Despite ever-threatening skies, they kept dry. Riding alongside the gray river, Wat heard baaing in nearby dusk-shadowed pastures and saw flocks of sheep, winter-heavy with the famous Melrose wool.

Beyond the next bend, a group of men-at-arms camped. Several took obvious note of the Scott banner with its gold crescent moons. No one challenged him.

Dismounting in the gravel yard, he handed his reins to his equerry and told Geordie to make camp downriver from the abbey buildings. "Tell them to keep clear of the lot west of here," he added. "They're likely friendly, but I saw no banner."

Taking only Jed with him, he crossed the yard through the darkening twilight to find a lay brother. He did not expect to see the abbot before morning.

"Methinks there be unusual activity here, laird," the lanky, redheaded Jed said as they walked toward the low-walled precinct and the newly whitewashed guesthouse east of it. Diverted from his imagined forthcoming talk with the abbot, Wat noted that the grounds near the abbey did seem to be busier than usual.

Alert now, recalling the camp to the west, he looked more closely. The precinct and newly restored cloister inside its low wall looked as peaceful as ever, but a few weaponless but still martial-looking men strolled through the abbey's winter-bare orchards. Others stood near its guesthouse or walked the river path.

A crunch of gravel drew his attention to a man in the plain brown habit and black scapular of a lay brother hurrying toward them from the guesthouse.

Wat recognized him from previous visits as Brother Kieran.

"Welcome, m'lord," he said as he approached, answering

the question hovering on Wat's tongue. News of his father's death had beaten him to Melrose.

"Good evening, Brother Kieran," Wat said. "You have learned of our so-unexpected and tragic bereavement then."

"We heard late yesterday, aye," Brother Kieran replied solemnly. "We have been praying for his lordship's soul since then."

"Thank you," Wat said sincerely.

"I'll show you to your room if that will suit you, sir. Father Abbot expects you to stay the night. He did say to warn you that his grace be resting in the main part of the guesthouse and that his reverence is to take supper with him there."

"The King is here?" That explained the unusual activity.

Nodding, Brother Kieran, said, "If you will agree, though, Father Abbot will meet with you as soon as you have had time to settle into your room. We put a pallet for your man in there, too. At present, we have no other rooms available."

"That is acceptable, thank you," Wat said. "If Father Abbot will forgive my riding clothes, I need only scrub off some of this dirt."

"Aye, sure, m'lord. We stand on little ceremony here, as you know."

Wat did know, but he also knew it behooved him to avoid offending the abbot. Therefore, it was always wiser to beg pardon *before* rather than after he did something of which he was uncertain.

Reaching his room and having no wish to delay the meeting, he attended quickly to his needs and told Jed to speak with Geordie and make sure the men were comfortable. "I want no difficulty between our lot and his grace's entourage."

"Geordie willna want trouble neither, laird," Jed assured him.

"No talk about the King being here, either," Wat added. "The lack of a royal standard flying must mean that his grace wants his visit kept quiet."

"Aye, then," Jed said.

Outside again and noting that Brother Kieran had vanished, Wat strode toward the chapter house. As he approached it, the Abbot of Melrose stepped onto the stone stoop outside its entrance, wearing the same unbleached, undyed woolen habit that all Cistercian monks wore. Only his heavy silver chain and cross distinguished him from the other monks. His tonsured hair and eyebrows were dark.

His demeanor as he watched Wat approach seemed unduly stern but his features relaxed sympathetically when he said in his mellifluous voice, "'Tis glad I am to see you, my son. I had hoped you would come to us. I know, though, that you have many more responsibilities now than you had three days ago."

"I do, Father Abbot. 'Tis regarding some of them that I seek your counsel."

"Then come into my parlor. We can talk privily there."

Located just off the entry hall of the chapter house, the abbot's candlelit conversation room was starkly furnished. Although the glow of candles and a small cheerfully crackling fire on the hearth suggested warmth, Wat kept his cloak on when he took his seat on a wooden stool facing the fire.

Taking a matching stool at a slight angle to his, so they could talk face-to-face, the abbot said, "Now, what counsel do you seek, my son."

"First, Father Abbot, I want to assure you that I will honor all of the agreements my father made with you regarding the properties he exchanged for Bellendean. The abbey will retain all of its hunting and fishing rights there."

"It never occurred to me that you might not honor those agreements," the abbot said. "Your father and grandfather were both generous to the abbey. Your grandfather honored his close friend, the second Earl of Douglas, who lies buried here. Your father did much, too, simply—he said—for the good of his soul.

"Both of them provided extra labor for our renovations," the abbot went on. "Thanks to them and others, and to Almighty God, we have rebuilt nearly all that the wicked English destroyed in 1385. We will forever be grateful for their aid."

"I mean to continue as they did," Wat said. "Next, then, I would extend my lady grandame's respects to you, Father Abbot. She respects your abilities and agreed that I would be wise to seek counsel from you."

"You may return my compliments and my deep condolence to Lady Meg," the abbot said. "She is a fine woman and has lost more in her lifetime than many would think such a woman deserves to lose. She must be deeply mourning—your lady mother, too. But, what matter is it that disturbs *you*, Walter."

"I want to learn about the laws of marriage, Father. You see..." He went on to explain, as briefly as he could, the situation that Molly faced.

Having done her best that morning to explain to Lady Meg how she had come to marry Tuedy, Molly had stopped at the point where her father's traitorous priest had declared her Tuedy's wife. Praying that her hostess would not demand more details than she was willing to share, she eyed her warily now.

Lady Meg just shook her head. "Sakes, child," she said. "I thought that *my* marriage was forced upon me. Your experience shows me just how lucky I was."

"I cannot imagine anyone forcing you," Molly said.

"You did not know me then." Meg grimaced. "Sithee, my father wanted to hang *my* Walter, but he gave him the choice of marrying me instead. Father didn't ask if I was willing. He believed, you see, that no other man would *want* to marry me."

"Mercy, my lady, how could he have thought such a thing?"

"I was sadly homely then," Meg said. "Not that I am any great beauty today. However, when one reaches a certain age, one's looks become less important to others than one's character. In any event, my marriage was happy but too short. It lasted long enough to give me children, but..."

She paused with a rueful look and added, "But you had to face your troubles alone. My mother was alive. In fact, I believe my marriage was her idea."

"It sounds horrid," Molly said frankly.

"Aye, but others would have suffered had I not agreed to marry Sir Walter. I had reasons of mine own, too. My mother would have insisted that I obey my father, but he would not have forced me had I refused. I made the decision myself, to avoid any hangings. You were not given *any* choice."

"True, so when the chance came…" Molly bit her lip.

"You fled, and were right to do so," Meg said matter-of-factly. "Heaven kens what the Kirk and the law will say to that, but I will do all that I can to protect you. Walter will, too."

Molly was not so certain of that.

They stopped talking then, because Brigid knocked to say that the midday meal was ready to serve.

Looking back on the conversation that evening as she prepared for supper, Molly could only hope that his Lady Meg was right about her grandson. She also hoped, too, that Lady Meg was satisfied with what little Molly had told her about her wedding day, and would seek no more details.

⁓

When Wat finished describing Molly's wedding to the abbot as she had described it to him, the abbot's heavy dark brows drew together thoughtfully.

Then he said, "'Tis true, my son, that a Scotswoman has the right to refuse marriage and that nae one can *legally* force her to wed against her will. However, God and Holy Kirk do also expect any unwed young woman to obey her father's commands, knowing that he has her best interest at heart."

Dryly, Wat said, "My opinion of her ladyship's father, if I may say so, your reverence, is that he rarely considers anyone's interest save his own. I will admit, though, that I do not know Cockburn personally. If I have met him, I have no memory of it. I do know his sons, though, and his reputation…"

"…is merely what other people think of him," the abbot said when Wat paused. "Hearsay, we call it. It can sometimes condemn a man without due cause."

"Aye, but I *know* Ringan Tuedy and would not let him near one of my sisters or female cousins. The man is a raider first, your reverence, a brutal one, at that."

"How did you learn of this wedding if you did not witness it, Walter?"

"I met her ladyship in Ettrick Forest yester-midnight, fleeing barefoot in only a ripped shift," Wat said. "She was spent, so I took her to the Hall and put her in my grandame's care. Molly's two elder brothers, Will and Ned, were after her with Tuedy and Will's sleuthhounds. When I asked what they were doing on Scott land, they told me they were seeking a lost maidservant."

"Such a lie bespeaks a guilty conscience, I think," the abbot said with a deeper frown. "Let me ponder this matter overnight and seek counsel from above. We can talk again tomorrow after we break our fast."

"Won't his grace still be here?"

"He will, aye, and for some days more, I believe. He treasures his solitude whilst he is here, though. So we should have time in the morning to talk."

It was a dismissal, and Wat had no objection. He wanted to think.

The fact was that if the Kirk expected Molly to obey her father and supported Piers Cockburn's right to her obedience, it would deem her marriage to Tuedy legal.

If that meant that she would have to return to Tuedy, he knew what Lady Meg would say. For that matter, the more he thought about it, himself…

~~~

Suppertime passed slowly for Molly. She sat between Janet and Bella, with Lady Meg next to Janet and Lady Scott beyond Meg. Since the ladies supped alone, privy screens were in place. The table seemed somehow smaller so, and quieter.

Molly had expected Janet or Bella to ask her about her conversation with Lady Meg or about life at Henderland. When neither one asked her any questions, she wondered if they simply lacked curiosity or feared that the older women would disapprove of such personal questions.

Just as she was recalling that Lady Meg had expressed her own curiosity but had not pressed her to describe the actual events that had led to her flight, Lady Meg's voice interrupted that reverie.

"Lavinia," she said, "I know you are sorely grieving. We all are. But I hope you will not keep to your chamber whilst Rosalie is here. She is looking forward to seeing you. Moreover, it will be good for us to have to show our best faces to her."

"I will try, Meg, truly," Lady Scott said in a voice so faint that Molly could barely hear her. "But Rosalie may prove less of an antidote than you expect, since she is so recently widowed herself."

"Richard Percy died over two years ago," Lady Meg replied. "In any event, if our Rosalie has turned into a watering pot, I shall be much surprised."

"Has it been two years?" Lady Scott asked. "It does not seem so long ago."

Janet said, "How long has it been since you have seen each other, Gram?"

"It must be ten years," Lady Meg said. "'Twas when my stepfather died. She met us at Elishaw, because Mother had decided to move back there and live with Simon and Sibylla. My brother and his wife," she added, reminding Molly.

Molly was content to let them talk of Lady Rosalie. But her contentment fled as they prepared to retire to the solar, when Meg said, "You and I will talk again tomorrow, my dear. I want to get to know you as well as I can whilst you're here."

～

Bright moonbeams pierced the forest canopy. They cast their silvery glow on the narrow pathway and made it sparkle as if someone had cast diamonds along its length.

She walked barefoot toward him in a long unbleached gown, like a monk's habit. Her long, lustrous hair was aglitter with golden highlights.

She smiled but did not speak, making him wonder if she was real or just a figment of his imagination. Her eyes looked more golden, and her dark lashes and eyebrows seemed more unusual than ever in such light.

She was near enough to touch, so he reached toward her.

As he did, the creamy cloth slipped from her as if magic fingers had pulled its top stitching free. Although he assumed that the fabric puddled at her feet or disappeared, he did not look down to see. His gaze fixed on her slender, shapely nudity.

The moonlight turned her smooth skin milky white. Her rosy nipples perked temptingly, inviting him to fondle her lovely breasts.

His hand had frozen in place when her garment fell

but extended now in response to that perky invitation. Before it touched aught save air, she vanished, saying in Jed Elliot's gruff, sardonic tone, "Wake up, laird. The abbot's man be here...

"...and likely gey sorry t' interrupt any dream that makes ye moan so."

Blearily, Wat found himself staring into Jed's twinkling blue eyes. The lad held a candle, but the rest of the room was dark. "What the devil?" Wat demanded.

"Father Abbot ha' been up for an hour or more, m'lord, or so his man did say. He also said to break your fast as quick as ye can. They dinna ken if his grace will keep to hisself or no t'day."

"As I recall, breaking one's fast here takes little time," Wat said with a sigh and a grimace. "'Tis nobbut bread and water or watery porridge."

"Aye, the porridge be nowt t' keep a normal man going long. The monks labor in their fields and orchards all day, though. They do eat well at midday, aye?"

"They do, and our supper last night was tolerable, too. Nevertheless, Jed, do you think you might find me some cheese to go with the bread?"

"I already did," Jed said, nodding. "I'm no me da's son for nowt, sir. I brung ye some fine ale, too."

"Did you now? And how do you know that it's fine."

"I wouldna give ye nowt that I'd no tasted first, would I?"

"I think you are getting above yourself, my lad," Wat said with mock sternness. "First interrupting my dreams—"

"It did sound like a good one," replied the unrepentant Jed. "Ye were moaning, like I said. But ye didna sound as if ye felt any pain."

"I'll thank you to leave my dreams to me."

"Aye, sure, sir. I just hope she were as pretty as the ones I dream up."

Chuckling, Wat got out of bed and dressed hastily. After eating his meager breakfast, he told Jed to check the men again, and took himself off to the chapter house, where Brother Kieran awaited him on the stoop.

Despite his simple habit, the lay brother looked as if he were unaware of the icy chill in the morning air. "Father Abbot awaits you in his parlor, m'lord," he said, opening the door for Wat. "I'll take you to him."

Following obediently, Wat was grateful to see the little fire again.

It was odd, he thought, that he could live off the land for days in any weather while leading a raid, going into battle, or chasing English raiders. But when he was indoors, he liked a roaring fire on a chilly day and plentiful food on the table.

The abbot stood before the fire with his feet apart, his hands behind him.

"Come in, Walter, and take your ease," he said. Gesturing toward the stool where Wat had sat the previous evening, he added, "I have thought hard on this matter."

"What did you decide?" Wat asked, tensing.

"I agree with you that if the Cockburn men forced the lady Margaret to marry Ringan Tuedy against her strongly expressed will, the marriage is illegal under the laws of Holy Kirk and Scotland, as well."

Wat relaxed only to tense again when the abbot added, "However, she can legally declare the marriage unlawful only if she is still a maiden, just as a bridegroom can declare his marriage null if his bride proves to be *un*chaste."

Wat's heart sank then. He was nearly sure that no woman, let alone one Molly's size and in her situation, could successfully deny a brute Tuedy's size his connubial rights on his wedding night.

Before he might have voiced those thoughts, the abbot continued, saying, "If they consummated their union, she must apply through the Kirk for an annulment."

"What does that mean?" Wat asked. Realizing his question was unclear, he added, "What is the procedure for such an application?"

"It requires a letter to the Pope and papal action. Since we do not have a papal legate in Scotland now, it will take months for such an application to reach him and for his reply to travel back to her. I must warn you, too, that His Holiness will likely refuse to grant the annulment, because he holds strongly that a woman is *always* better off with a bad husband than unwed."

"But if she declares that she is still virgin..."

"She would require examination," the abbot said, meeting Wat's gaze.

"I shall tell her what you have said, Father Abbot," Wat said quietly, feeling suddenly very protective of the lady Molly.

Then a new thought occurred to him. "When you say that she would require examination, whose word would the Kirk accept that she *is* still a maiden?"

"So you believe as I do that she is no longer intact," the abbot said gently. "Sithee, I am the person who would question the examiner, so I will tell you that the only person whose word I would accept without hesitation is Lady Meg's."

Wat would never doubt her either. At that moment,

though, he wished that his grandmother were not a woman known far and wide for her steadfast integrity.

"I should mention one other detail that you must consider carefully before advising the lady Margaret," the abbot said. He had put his hands behind him again and was staring at the floor.

Looking up, he met Wat's gaze and said solemnly, "Even if the lass can legally nullify her marriage, she should understand that word of it will have spread about quickly. She will need protection from the inevitable scandal, Walter, and likely from her infamously fractious kinsmen, too."

His protective instincts in full force now, Wat said without hesitation, "I promise you, your reverence, her ladyship will have my protection and that of my kindred for as long as she needs it."

"Consider carefully before you make *her* such a promise, my son. I mean to look further into her situation, but—"

A loud double rap on the door interrupted him. Sending Wat a rueful look that told him as clearly as words could that only one man would interrupt them in such a fashion, the abbot said calmly, "Enter."

A man in the royal Stewart livery walked in and held the door wide for the square-built, auburn-haired man behind him to enter the parlor.

Wat had never met the King of Scots, but he had no doubt that the second man was James Stewart, known to all and sundry when they spoke of him, as Jamie.

At thirty-two, he was eight years older than Wat, although his regular features and tousled hair gave him a deceptively boyish look. Of slightly less than the usual

Stewart height, he had dark, watchful eyes and a serious demeanor. He also possessed the broad, muscular shoulders of an experienced swordsman, was well proportioned, known to be extremely agile, and was a notable wrestler.

His gaze now became surprisingly direct, Wat thought as he met it. He felt as if the King were peering past his eyes, straight into his mind.

Except when swearing fealty, no Border lord knelt to the King of Scots, as the more feudal English did to their king. Wat simply returned the King's gaze.

"If you will permit me, your grace," the abbot said, "I would present Walter Scott, the new Lord of Rankilburn, Murthockston, and so forth."

Wat nodded politely then, murmuring, "Your grace."

"'Tis glad I am to find ye here, m'lord," James said. "Father Abbot told me of your father's untimely death, so I offer my condolences. I've also heard of your prowess on the battlefield and your relentless pursuit of English raiders who dare to invade our realm," he went on without pause. "Nae doubt, ye've inherited your father's lands and responsibilities along with his titles, but one prays that ye'll no refuse to aid your King. In troth, I had meant to visit your father and request your service for a particular task I have in mind."

"I am yours to command, sire," Wat said. He wondered if the task his grace had in mind might be one that could lead to his long yearned for knighthood.

The abbot placed his hand on the back of a two-elbow chair near the only window in the parlor. "Prithee, take this chair, your grace," he said, "unless you prefer to warm yourself here by the fire."

James frowned at the wee fire. "I'm warm enough,

Father Abbot, and 'tis a good thing, I'm thinking. This place is as cold as an icehouse. Even so, after all the freezing castles I lodged in during the nineteen years I was captive in England, I'll take the comforts *and* discomforts of Melrose or any other religious house over one o' my strongholds. At least, here, nae one locks me up, or could if he wanted to."

Wat had heard of the King's antipathy to his royal castles and knew that Jamie rarely spent a night in one.

"How may I serve your grace?" Wat asked him.

"D'ye ken aught o' one Gilbert or Gil Rutherford?"

"Aye, sure, a notorious and ruthless reiver," Wat said. "He raids throughout the Borders, not just in England but here, as well. He's never been caught."

"He also kills people," James said grimly. "Women, bairns, and other innocents. I told the Douglas to find and capture him, and he agreed. But he's done nowt. I do ken fine that the earl is your liege lord, but I'm sorely tempted to arrest him, either for defiance or sloth. Nae doubt, though, if I do, trouble may follow."

"Aye, it will," Wat agreed, wondering how he had managed to say the words calmly. "The Douglases would rise all together and in fury, I fear."

"'Tis likely, but your father was an assistant march warden. Since ye stand in his stead now, I'm asking ye to find this Rutherford chappie as fast as ye can. He plagues many powerful men on both sides of the line, and I want to avoid war breaking out over the antics of one iniquitous scalawag. Can ye do it?"

Delighted to meet his grace at last, and determined to prove his worth, Wat said, "I can, sire, and I will. I give you my word as a Borderer."

"That is good enough for me," James said with a nod.

"Moreover," Wat added, dropping to a knee and extending both hands, "I, Walter Scott, styling myself Lord of Buccleuch and Rankilburn to give proper honor to our first landholding, would hereby swear fealty on mine own behalf and that of my kindred to you and to yours for as long as we both shall live."

"Stand up, stand up, my lord," Jamie said as he clapped both of his own hands around Wat's. "I do accept your styling and most gratefully accept your oath. With God's grace and the help of men like you, we will bring law and order to these unruly Borders and to the rest of Scotland. But this demon Rutherford has too long wreaked havoc, and it must stop. Such behavior imperils all that I strive to do."

Dismissed soon afterward, Wat returned to his room, thinking that he had handled his business with the abbot and the King's surprising behest with ease.

He entered his room to find Jed packing the few items they had carried in.

Looking up at him, Jed said, "I suspected we'd be off again after the midday meal, laird. What wi' the King here and all, they'd no thank us for lingering. Do we return to the Hall or make for Hawick?"

Recalling that he'd meant to pay his respects to the Douglas and be sure the earl knew of his father's death, Wat saw an unexpected pitfall awaiting him now.

Not only did it make him reconsider his handling of events at Melrose, but in reviewing the culmination of his talk with the abbot and his brief discussion with the King, he realized that other, greater dangers also loomed ahead.

Jed, watching him, cocked his head. "Be aught amiss, master?"

With a grimace, Wat said, "Nobbut that I, who pride myself on my prudence, loyalty, and sense of honor, have just made promises to the abbot and to his grace that will almost certainly conflict with each other. I also recklessly promised to perform a task that my own liege lord has evidently ignored or refused to perform."

"Hoots, sir, ye're niver so daft," Jed said, eyeing him more narrowly. "Such doings would land ye in the suds soon or late, and nae mistake."

"Then it will likely be soon," Wat said with a sigh. "If we leave at once, we should make the Black Tower by midday. Fortunately, unless I anger Douglas at once, he will give us a much finer meal than the monks would, and will treat us to no prayers other than the grace before meat."

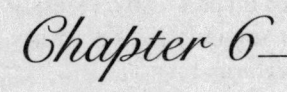

Chapter 6

Molly had feared that she might feel bereft and dangerously vulnerable after Walter left the Hall for Melrose. In truth, she barely noticed his absence.

Bella and Janet were delighted to have a new companion, and Molly liked them both. She only wished that her parents had blessed her with such sisters.

Being with the Scotts was more than pleasant but also made her realize how lonely she had been at Henderland. At home, her life was simply her life, one that she had had no choice but to endure. Now, living briefly with three generations of women who were kind to her, and equally kind men who treated them respectfully, she realized more than ever what a loss her grandmother Marjory had been to her.

That morning, as if the Scott women had not done enough by offering their friendship, Janet gave Molly a smooth leather girdle to go with the kirtles Janet had lent her. Depending from it were a sheathed eating knife, a tinderbox and flint, a needle case, and a pair of wee silver scissors.

"It is my old kirtle," Janet said with her warm smile. "But you should have your own eating knife and sewing things."

"This is much nicer than the one I have at home," Molly said, thanking her.

Lady Meg seemed especially determined to make friends with her.

Lady Scott, her actual hostess, was harder for Molly to read. Although she could tell that Wat's mother was truly grief-stricken by the loss of her husband, her lady-ship seemed unusually content to attend to her exquisite needlework and let her good-mother run *her* household and look after *her* daughters.

The women, except Lady Scott, spent the morning after Wat left preparing for the arrival of Lady Rosalie Percy, whose arrival they expected within the week.

"Did Aunt Rosalie take an entourage to Elishaw after Great-grandame Annabel died?" Bella asked as she and Molly helped Lady Meg count linens.

"She originally had an armed escort supplied by her husband's heir," Meg said. "But they returned to Dour Hill, England, after seeing her safely to Elishaw."

Turning next to Molly, Bella said, "Remember, Aunt Rosalie married into the powerful English Percy fam-ily. Men say that the Earl of Northumberland, Great-grandame Annabel's cousin, is the most powerful man in northern England."

Molly met Lady Meg's dancing eyes just as Meg said, "The Percies do say that he is, Bella, but other English nobles do disagree. In England, a man's power is mea-sured by how nearly connected he is to the English throne. The English king wields more power over his nobles than our King of Scots does wield over his."

"Aye, but the Percies *are* gey powerful," Bella said stoutly.

"They are, to be sure," Lady Meg agreed. "But in England, your grandaunt Rosalie is a 'mere female' and has few rights of her own. Moreover, since she and her husband had no daughters and only two sons, both of whom were fostered at the age of eight, she scarcely knows either one of them."

"What does 'fostered' mean?" Bella asked.

"Noblemen in England often send their sons and daughters to other families to raise. The children go when they are young and usually stay with their foster parents until they marry unless their birth fathers prefer to arrange their marriages."

"Mercy, why?"

"Nobles in Scotland do it, too," Meg told her. "Your father did not, nor did his. But others do. A Scotsman is more likely to send his sons to foster than his daughters, unless he hopes to marry his daughter into another noble family, mayhap one of greater stature. Then, he might arrange such a fostering. But fostering of any kind is more common in England than it is here."

"Well, I am glad that Father did not foster me or Janet," Bella said. "I like it here. As for marriage, I have never met a laddie I could bear to live with, except Wat, and he is not a laddie. Stephen is too bossy. So are most men, I think."

Lady Meg smiled. "Now, my dearling, you sound just like your aunt Rosalie did when she was your age. It was just a year or so later that she began scheming to marry an Englishman. She thought that living in England might be interesting."

"Was it?"

"You will have to ask her," Meg said. "For now, though, I am sure we have enough linen to provide for her and any number of others, so you may go and sit with your mother and attend to your stitching." When Bella's face fell, Meg added gently, "I want to talk privately, dearling, with Lady Molly."

Bella nodded then and turned with a smile to Molly. "I will see you at the table for our midday meal," she said. "I'm glad that you came to us."

"I am, too, Bella," Molly said sincerely. Watching the child dart away, she realized that she was looking forward to learning more from Lady Meg but hoped her ladyship would not press her to talk of things she'd rather keep to herself.

~

The sun had risen in a clear sky at last. But the day grew cloudy again and colder in the hours that it took Wat and his men to ride from Melrose, on the river Tweed, south to the town of Hawick on its high, narrow ridge of land in the sharp angle that the river Teviot formed with Slitrig Water at their confluence.

That angle between the two swiftly flowing streams, and the steep banks of both, made the town so easy to defend that it had served for years as a stronghold for Borderers, especially for the all-powerful Douglases.

They passed first through the haughs and woods of Branxholm, on the north bank of the river Teviot. Wat now owned half of that estate, thanks to his father's having traded half of their Murthockston estate for it.

The Branxholm ford was the nearest safe place to cross to the south side of the river, and since one had to approach Hawick from the southwest, where the town's sole entrance lay, Wat opted to cross the Teviot there.

As they neared the ford, stern images of his father and the older image of the gentleman that Wat had always visualized as his grandfather rose in his mind. It was as if they were reminding him to guard well what they had left him.

Gazing over the verdant, forested landscape and the river beyond, he reminded himself that his capable father had trained him well.

"I'll not let you down, either of you," he murmured.

"What's that, master?" Jed asked.

"Nowt," Wat said. "Water's flowing fast, lad. Keep to the center."

It was nearly midday when they topped the steep hill at Hawick's open stockade gate. As they rode into the town, Wat took a deep breath to steel his nerve.

He had known Archibald, fifth Earl of Douglas, for less than two years and could not say that he knew him well. Archie was more than twenty years Wat's elder, so Wat had simply done whatever Archie's captains had told him to do.

Even so, he had long since learned that the earl had no taste for battle.

Some years before, Archie, then Lord of Wigton, had followed his good-brother to France to support its king against encroaching English. After the costly victory of Beaugé, Wigton had come home and persuaded his father, the fourth Earl of Douglas, to join the French cause.

Meantime, Wigton, pleading ill health, had stayed home and thus missed the gruesome Battle of Verneuil. His father, good-brother, his brother James, and many other Scots had lost their lives. Wigton had become fifth Earl of Douglas.

Clearly, he also had little taste for tracking down ruffians, because Wat had heard naught of any hunt for Gilbert Rutherford.

Wat and his own men had tracked many English raiders

and a few Scots. But none had been men of Rutherford's ruthlessness. Even so, and despite the King's behest, he could not seek Rutherford without at least telling Douglas about his agreement to capture the vicious reiver.

What Douglas might reply was what concerned him now. The Douglases' Black Tower loomed ominously on the east side of the high street, shadowing nearby buildings. Dismounting in front of the tower entrance, Wat handed his reins to Jed and said to the captain of his tail, "Get food into all of you, Geordie, as soon as you stable the ponies. I doubt I'll stay long."

"We'll be returning to the Hall then, laird?" Jed asked, shooting an oblique glance at two Douglas guards flanking the tower entrance.

Aware that the two could hear their exchange as easily as his own men did, Wat said evenly, "That must be as the Douglas commands."

Nodding, Jed led his horse and Wat's toward the nearby yard. When the others began to follow him, Wat strode to the tower entrance. Acknowledging the nod of the guard on his right with a nod of his own, he passed through the doorway.

Inside, he took the steps two at a time to the tower's noisy great hall at the second landing.

Just inside, the earl's steward said with surprise, "M'lord, we didna expect ye. His lordship thought ye'd linger longer wi' yer family in yer time o' grief."

"I wanted to be sure the Douglas had learned of my father's death," Wat said. "If he is here, I would request a few words with him."

Nodding, the steward said, "He's here, sir. He be taking an hour's solitude, but if ye dinna mind waiting, that hour be nearly up."

"Certes, I'll be grateful for the warmth of your hall fire," Wat said. "It's devilish cold out today."

"I'll fetch ye m'self when Himself will see ye," the steward assured him. "We dine at noon, so I'll give orders to feed your men, too. I should just mention that his lordship ha' been a wee bit out of sorts. But he'll want to see ye, sir."

Wonderful, Wat thought sourly, turning toward the big crackling fire.

⁓

Molly followed Lady Meg to her sitting room but paused in the open doorway to collect herself before following her ladyship inside.

"Shut the door, my dear, and take a seat," Meg said. "I'd like you to be comfortable, although you must be *dis*comfited by this awkward situation of yours."

Obeying, Molly forced calm into her voice and said, "It would be more awkward, madam, were it not for the kindness that everyone here has shown me. I feel as if I have entered a new world."

Sitting on the cushioned bench in the window embrasure, Lady Meg said, "You make me wish more than ever that I had had the courage to confront your father and claim my rights as your godmother straightaway."

"I doubt he'd have heeded you," Molly said.

Meg sighed. "I was certain he'd refuse to *believe* me. I also feared that, with Marjory gone, your father's priest might refuse to support my claim."

Grimacing, Molly said bluntly, "Father Jonathan ignored the law and pronounced me married despite my struggles and my inability to speak. So you were right to mistrust him. Rankilburn was always kind to me, but he revealed no awareness of a relationship between our families other than his with my father."

"I did not tell Robert, either," Meg said. "My son had a knack for making friends and a determination to avoid conflict, so he'd have been even more reluctant to fight your father. You see, Robert's primary goal was to join his estates together and add to them, to increase the power of Clan Scott. He therefore exerted himself to be friendly with his neighbors, especially those with whom he disagreed politically. He also kept on good terms with the Douglas and, of course, with the King."

"That cannot have been easy," Molly said. "I know my father disagreed with him about the King's new laws and many other matters."

Meg nodded. "Maintaining friendships is also a risky business," she said. "Rather than risk his with Piers Cockburn, I think Robert would have strongly resisted any attempt I made to interfere between Piers and you. Had I thought you were in danger, I'd have acted differently, but I never heard that you were."

"I was not," Molly said honestly. "My father is not a loving man, my lady. Perhaps he was before my mother died—"

She broke off when Meg shook her head.

"I see," Molly said. "Even so, he has never been cruel, but he has seemed angrier since the King's return. As you must know, my father is strongly opposed to his grace's interference with his nobles' hereditary rights."

"I do know that," Meg said. "I don't take sides in such matters, myself, and I have not met the King. What one hears of him is mostly rumor, of course, but I've no objection to his desire for laws that everyone knows and must follow, noble and common alike. That seems only fair to me."

Molly smiled. "Me, too," she said.

Returning her smile, Meg said, "I do want you to be contented here, child. So, curious though I am to know all that has happened to you since Marjory's death, I shan't urge you to tell me aught that you are reluctant to discuss. And if you have questions for me…"

After that, their conversation proceeded amiably, although Molly could not quite bring herself to quiz Lady Meg about her past or even her present. Having little experience with polite discourse, she let her hostess guide their discussion and soon learned that Meg kept her word.

Although she asked a few questions about Piers Cockburn and Molly's brothers, she expressed stronger interest in Molly's activities at Henderland.

After describing some of them, Molly said, "I love to ride, my lady. I wonder, in fact, if I might be able to do so whilst I am here."

Meg began to frown, saying, "I have no doubt that you are as expert a rider as any other Border woman, my dear. I am concerned only about your safety, as I am sure that Tam will be."

"By my troth, my lady—" She stopped when Meg held up a hand.

"At best," Meg said, no longer frowning, "You must wait until Wat returns and ask him. I cannot take it on myself to put your safety at risk. Even if your father does not have men out looking for you, your brother Will surely does. Some may even dare to invade the forest again and come here."

"I suppose you are right," Molly said with a sigh. "I will ask his lordship, though. If he will escort me, or provide an escort—"

"He will escort you himself," Meg said firmly. "Now tell me more about your horses. For myself, I like a dependable Border pony. I was never as skilled a rider as my sister Amalie or my good-sister Sibylla. But, in my younger days, I did love riding out with my sisters."

Molly was glad to pursue that topic. By the time the bell rang for the midday meal, she had begun to feel as if she had known Lady Meg for years rather than two and a half short days.

She also realized that she was now yearning for Walter Scott to come home.

To Wat's surprise, the Douglas's steward came for him after a quarter-hour, just long enough to warm himself at the great-hall fire.

"His lordship will see ye now, sir. I'll take ye in."

They crossed the hall to the dais and across it to a door that a servant hurried to open for them. In the room beyond, known in most such establishments as the inner chamber, Douglas sat behind a wide table piled at one end with scrolled documents and a stack of four books at the other.

A smaller fire burned on the hearth there, but the room was comfortable.

Douglas was lanky and had a long face and dark hair that was graying, especially at his temples. He also had a dark tan, and his bushy eyebrows shaded eyes so dark that they looked black in the chamber's dim light.

'Twas no wonder, Wat thought, that people called him the Black Douglas.

His chamber boasted a beamed ceiling like the one in the great hall, and high windows. A walkway around its perimeter gave access to arrow slits on the west, facing the street, and on the side facing the stableyard. Openings on that upper level also led to corridors. The Black Tower, like its town, was easily defensible.

Douglas waved a hand, dismissing the steward as he said, "I'm glad ye came, Wat. I was sorry to learn of your father's death. He was a good man. Moreover, I ken fine that to inherit a powerful title from a powerful man is not just cake and ale. Still, I am sure ye'll bear the title well."

"Thank you, my lord," Wat said, still standing. "I mean to continue the work my father began. To that end, I must tell you that I visited Melrose before coming here, to assure the monks that nowt will change there."

"The Scotts have been generous to the abbey, I know," Douglas said.

"I should tell you that his grace was staying there," Wat said. "I met him."

"Did ye? Then I warrant he had cause to speak to ye."

"He did," Wat agreed. "A certain reiver has displeased him."

"Gilbert Rutherford, aye," Douglas said with a sigh. "Jamie wanted me to seize the man by the heels. I have too much to do to content my own clan, though. In troth, lad, the Rutherfords are more closely connected to the Scotts than they are to me."

"Then you will not object when I tell you that his grace asked me to see to the matter," Wat said. When the Douglas remained silent, he added, "I did agree."

"He didna command ye, then?"

"Not in so many words," Wat admitted. "But he wants Rutherford to stop killing innocents on both sides of the line. I know of no way to do that without capturing him and either locking him up or giving him to his grace."

"Jamie will hang him."

"I expect so," Wat agreed. "But so would any nobleman who caught Rutherford stealing his kine. That is, if any *could* catch him."

"I expect ye feel obliged to honor your agreement, then."

"I gave my word as a Borderer," Wat said.

"Then there be nae more to say," Douglas said with a shrug.

Wat felt an unexpected urge to shake the man. Having dealt primarily with Douglas's officers and spoken personally with the earl only twice that he could recall, he had spared little thought for the man himself.

His father had said that the fifth earl was a milder, less impetuous, less belligerent man than his predecessors. But Robert had counted that a good thing.

After all, the inexperienced, impetuous, determined-to-prove-himself fourth Earl of Douglas had gotten Sir Walter Scott of Buccleuch killed at Homildon Hill. The fourth earl's father, aptly named Archie the Grim, had been a much stronger leader by all accounts but had rarely endeared himself to others.

Wat could read the current earl well enough to be sure that Archie wanted nothing to do with confrontation or battle. He also knew that Jamie disliked this particular Douglas and that Archie tended to ignore the King. So, their relationship remained tense and unpredictable.

Aware that his best chance of knighthood would come from either Jamie or Douglas, Wat also knew he could create a political maelstrom if he acted unwisely.

That Douglas would likely avoid any fray suggested that a wise man should side with the King if the two disagreed.

However, Douglas was still the most powerful man in the Borders and could raise ten thousand men in a sennight, so Jamie needed him to keep the English at bay.

Since the earl apparently had no more that he wished to say, Wat said quietly, "Will that be all, my lord?"

"We'll eat anon, and ye'll sit wi' me," Douglas said. "I would hear more about your father's death. Also, I'd ask ye to extend my respects and condolences to Lady Scott and the dowager Lady Scott. Robert's loss must sorely grieve them."

"I'll tell them, sir," Wat said.

As he followed the Douglas from the inner chamber to the high table, he wondered how it was that, in the course of one short journey, he had unexpectedly trebled his responsibilities, and how his father had done all that he'd managed to do so deftly and without seeming ever to create new problems for himself.

His thoughts shifted abruptly then to his own most recent problem. Since he would be away chasing Rutherford, he would have to strengthen security at the Hall.

Therefore, the sooner he returned the better.

Molly's golden-eyed image stole back into his mind throughout the meal, so he counted it fortunate that the Douglas seemed not to notice his distraction.

Molly spent the afternoon with Janet and Bella, who took her on a tour of the Hall's three towers. As they left the third one, with the bell ringing for supper, Bella said with a sad sigh, "Whenever we come into the yard, I expect to see Father striding across it. I know he never will again, but..."

"You must miss him dreadfully," Molly said.

"I don't know how we'll go on without him," Bella said dismally.

"But you know that we will, Belle," Janet told her, patting her shoulder. "Wat will go on exactly as Father would have. Father did train him, after all."

"But Wat was away for a long time, training to become a knight," Bella protested. "He cannot know all that Father knew."

"He will have learned all about leading men, though," Molly said. "Is that not much of what a successful landholder must do?"

"I suppose," Bella said.

"Of course, it is," Janet said firmly. "Prithee, do not show that face to Mam, Bella. You know how sensitive she is to our emotions."

Bella nodded silently.

Entering the main tower, they hurried upstairs to tidy themselves. By the time they joined Lady Meg and Lady Scott on the dais, Bella had herself in hand.

Molly wondered what it was like to have loved a father so much. She wondered, too, when Walter would return.

Much as she liked his sisters, she was accustomed to more solitude and found that she missed it at times. That thought led her to recall Lady Meg's warning that Will's men were likely searching for her, that Will might even come to the Hall.

Could she trust Walter's people to protect her as carefully as he might?

That thought went to bed with her that night and continued to tease her mind until she lay sleepless, trying to find a comfortable position.

Giving up, she went to the window and opened the shutters to gaze out at the night. The moon shone brightly against a black sky until a cloud obscured it.

～

While he rode, Wat, too, was watching the moon play all-hide with the clouds. Its beams pierced the forest canopy and set pebbles on the forest path agleam.

The sight reminded him of the dream he'd had at Melrose. He wondered if Molly's eyes were ever as golden as they had looked in that dream.

"'Tis gey late, sir; mayhap we should stop soon," Jed said, rudely banishing that pleasant, most intriguing reverie. Sakes, did the man peer into his head that he could choose so easily to interrupt anything pleasurable there?

Giving him a look that made Jed's eyes widen, Wat said, "Not yet."

～

An hour later, still restless and abandoning sleep for at least a while, Molly tried to imagine any way to avoid returning to Henderland.

Instead, her head began to ache, and her thoughts became harder to control. Refusing to present a pleasant picture of living with her brothers and father, her imagination produced only her likely life with Ringan Tuedy.

Giving her head a fierce shake, Molly knew she needed to move, to go *some*where, if only to the bottom of the stairs and back again.

Recalling that if she took the service stairs, she would end in the kitchen, she decided to see if she could find something to eat. She had not been hungry for her supper, but her growling stomach made it clear that she was starving now.

Snatching up the robe that Janet had given her, she threw it on and took the service stairs, trying to recall what was in the storeroom that might assuage her hunger. Remembering apples and dried beef, she decided that an apple would do.

She made her way quietly. The last thing she wanted was to wake anyone.

Also, the stairway darkness was nearly complete. A window or other opening at the top admitted pale moonlight, but her own body blocked the light, keeping the area below her impenetrably black.

She felt a slight draft. Then she heard a sound as of light footsteps, doubtless a servant seeking his bed.

Or perhaps an invader who did not belong in the Hall!

With the rounding moon up as it was...a Borderer's aval moon...what if it was Will or Ned, leading others?

She stopped where she was and tried to peer through the blackness. Focused as she was on what she sought, when a man's solid form suddenly became clear, so certain was she that only someone with nefarious intent would behave so that, gasping, Molly whirled and fled.

When she reached the next landing, he was a step behind her. A strong hand caught her arm. Another clapped across her mouth before she could scream.

Chapter 7 —————————

Don't shriek, lass!" Wat muttered. "And, for the love of God, don't bite me. I ken fine that I scared the liver and lights out of you. I'm sorry for that."

She relaxed, and he saw that standing on the step above him as she was, she was nearly his height. Her back was against him, and his jack was open, so he could feel the warmth of her body through his shirt and the thin dressing gown she wore.

"You won't scream when I let go, will you?" he murmured into her ear.

She shook her head.

He could feel her trembling and felt guilty again for scaring her. Gently, he released her and turned her to face him. "Where were you going?"

"To the kitchen," she said. "I . . . I couldn't sleep, and I'm hungry. I thought I might find an apple."

"Come along then," he said quietly, turning. "I could do with a bite myself."

When she did not reply and he sensed no movement behind him, he wondered if she would follow or if she distrusted his motives. She would have to decide for herself, though. One could not command or persuade trust.

"I never thought you'd be back so soon," she said at last. Still, he felt an unexpected surge of relief when he heard her dressing gown rustle as she followed him. "When my brothers go away," she added, "they go for days, even weeks."

"My business at Melrose was brief," he said. "Then I went to Hawick to be sure the Douglas knew about my father's death."

"You did say you meant to see him," she said. "You also said you'd be back before I could miss you. You certainly did that."

She fell silent again, and although he knew she must be burning to hear all he'd learned from the abbot, she did not ask about that. Likely, she knew as well as he did that wisdom precluded speaking of such things in a stairwell.

When they reached the vaulted chamber housing the bake oven and buttery, he lit candles for each of them at embers in the fire. Then he opened the buttery door in the stone wall opposite the oven to find the apples.

"Do you want anything more?" he asked. "There's some good cheese here, too."

"Just an apple, thank you," she said, gathering the dressing gown closer around her. Her feet were bare.

"Art warm enough?" he asked, handing her an apple.

"Aye, sure, 'tis warm here," she replied, burnishing her apple on a dressing gown sleeve. Taking a dainty bite, she chewed and swallowed it before she said, "Do you mean to tell me what you learned from the abbot?"

Gesturing toward a nearby bench, he waited for her to sit on it. As she did, he noted again the exquisite grace with which she moved and decided that he'd be wiser to remain standing than to sit so close beside her.

With a hope of looking casual rather than concerned for her reputation, he set his left foot on the end of the bench. Leaning a forearm on the upraised thigh, he said, "First, I'll tell you what Father Abbot said about marriage laws."

⁓

The apple was good, but Molly scarcely tasted it after that first bite. The chamber was much smaller than the kitchen beyond it.

She had never been alone with any man who was not her brother, her father, a cousin, or Ringan Tuedy...until now. Nor had she ever experienced the feelings that had coursed through her since the moment he'd grabbed her on the stairway.

He was tall, a full head taller than she was and more, and muscular.

The muscles she had felt through her robe when he'd held her against him were rock hard. She had known it was he a scant minute after he'd caught her, though.

His very scent carried with it the same sense of shelter that his cloak had given her the first night. It relaxed her and made her feel protected again.

Something about the man just radiated safety.

"Art listening, lass?"

Startled, she realized he'd been talking and struggled to catch the echo of his words. Something about marriage laws and the abbot.

"What *did* the abbot say about them?" she asked, pleased that she had remembered. "Did you ask him about the laws, or did you just tell him about me?"

"I told him about that wedding of yours and asked if it fit within the law. He said he will look into it further."

Molly grimaced, having little faith in such a statement, even from an abbot.

"However," Wat added, "he also said that, in his opinion, your marriage to Tuedy is unlawful. You need merely declare the marriage so if you are still a maiden, he said. If not, you must apply to the Pope for an annulment."

"Mercy, sir, if I am married, how could I possibly still be a maiden?"

Since Wat had believed all along that Molly was unlikely still to be a virgin, the answer to that question was easy. "If you are not," he said, "we must talk more with the abbot and ask him how you should phrase your appeal. You should know, though, that he suspects such a plea will fail. The Pope—"

"But if an appeal will do me no good . . ."

"You cannot know that until you try," Wat said.

"But if I have to return to Tuedy, will it not look as if I *want* to be with him? After all," she added hastily when Wat frowned, "no one heeded aught save Will's forcing me to nod as if I'd accepted the horrid man as my husband."

"You will have my protection and that of my family for as long as you need it," Wat said. "You may stay here as long as necessary."

"Thank you, sir, but what if my father finds out that I am here and demands my return? Do the laws of Scotland not support his wishes over mine?"

"That is another question to ask the abbot," Wat said. When she looked right at him, guilt stirred again. He was nearly sure she was right about that point of law.

Visibly disappointed, she said, "I think I should go back upstairs. I doubt that your lady mother or Lady Meg would approve of us being here like this."

"Sakes, lass, I mean you no harm. They both know that."

"Appearance often means more to others than intent," she said, standing and blowing out her candle. "What should I do with this apple core?"

Shocked that she had challenged his assurance of the older women's trust but impressed with her quick intelligence, Wat was still seeking a sensible riposte to her challenge when she added the rider and held out the apple core.

"I'll take it," he said, surprised at the curtness in his voice as he did.

He wasn't angry with her, just irritated and feeling oddly helpless. If this day was going to set a pattern for the way he would handle Rankilburn's affairs and those of his other newly acquired estates, he thought, may heaven help his people!

Immediately recognizing the futility of such thinking, he took control of himself, tossed her apple core and his own into the smoldering embers but kept his candle alight.

Then, putting his free hand to Molly's shoulder as she turned away, he said quietly, "We'll take one step at a time, lass, but together we *will* find a way. Now, I'll see you safely to your chamber. Naught else must frighten you tonight."

Molly savored the warmth of his hand on her shoulder and had a sudden longing to lean into that warmth, to feel the length of his body against hers again.

Suppressing the yearning, she went quickly up the

stairs, trying to ignore the sense of him so close behind her. She dared not rely on such tantalizing feelings, or on his lordship. Men, in her experience, were never trust-worthy. And, sadly, Walter Scott was doubtless more like other men than not.

In truth, there were no saints in Borderer's clothing, and she knew that Wat led raids just as Will and Ned did. That meant that he was as much a man of violence as they were, and as Tuedy was.

A woman who trusted any man, she decided, was a fool.

Recalling again the odd sense of safety she felt with Wat made her wonder if she was being unfair to him. Whether she was or not, she reminded herself firmly, she must remain cautious and try to become more discerning.

She reached her landing, but his hand moved faster to the door-latch than hers did. When her fingers touched his, she snatched them back.

As the door swung open to reveal faint candle glow inside, she looked at Wat and found his face too close to hers. She could see his eyes searching hers and could sense intent of some sort in his posture.

Abruptly, he straightened and gave her a gentle push toward the doorway. "Get thee inside, lass, and go back to bed. We'll talk more tomorrow."

Her heart was pounding, and every inch of her skin seemed to have come alive in a new and astonishingly sen-sitive way. Even the unusually hoarse sound of his voice affected her, sending unfamiliar tremors through her body.

She opened her mouth to say goodnight, but no words would come. To cover her confusion, she whisked through the doorway, shut it behind her, and stood still, waiting for her reeling senses to return to normal.

How had she ever thought that the man was safe?

There could be *no* safety in the feelings he had kindled in her.

A vision of Ring Tuedy backed by her brothers and her father loomed in her mind's eye, looking larger and more dangerous than ever. Yet Ring had never stirred such feelings of danger as Wat had in those last few seconds at the door.

Tuedy inspired only fear bordering on terror and revulsion.

She shut her eyes, wincing, but Tuedy's image refused to fade.

⁓

Wat stood still on the other side of the door. He easily sensed that Molly had not moved farther into the room but wondered at himself for standing there.

Likely, she could sense him as easily as he sensed her.

To linger there would be as foolhardy as a bairn playing with fire.

Annoyed with himself for behaving so, he turned and went on up the stairs to his bedchamber. Only after he forced himself to focus on what he must do on the morrow did his mind cease tormenting him with images of Molly Cockburn.

However, as he prepared for bed, the torment began anew.

He had nearly kissed her. What kind of protector let himself even think of doing something so stupid? Such thoughts endangered not only the lass but also himself and his reputation.

He'd simply have to be more careful now that he recognized how perilously attracted to her he was. He would remain calm, serious, and practical.

In short, he would return to his normal self. He would approach one task at a time and concentrate on each until he had finished it. Also, he would more wisely leave Molly to his kinswomen to amuse. They would keep her safe, too.

His mistake was in believing that at Scott's Hall he could protect her from anyone. Tonight had warned him that it might prove hardest to protect her from himself.

With these thoughts, he took himself to bed, having dismissed Jed at the stables with the noble intent of making his own way silently up the service stairs from the kitchen to avoid waking anyone. Instead, only pure dumb luck had let him silence the lass before she could scream.

That thought brought memory of her warm lips against his palm and...

"Master Wat?"

Startled awake, Wat had no sense of the hour, only of an odd dream wherein he'd slain a fat dragon with Tuedy's face—a most agreeable memory.

"Be ye awake, sir?" Jed asked anxiously.

"I am now," Wat replied warily. "What's o'clock?"

"The sun just be a-peekin' over yon hills."

Wat groaned. He and his men had returned well after midnight, and he'd spent at least a half hour with Molly. He had slept less than five hours.

Resigned to duty, he shoved the covers off and sat up to let the icy air wake the rest of him. Then, sardonically, he said, "Is aught amiss, Jed? Or did you just decide it was time I got up?"

"Herself said that if ye'd come home, ye should bestir yourself, because the lady Rosalie Percy be arriving today," Jed said, obviously unimpressed by Wat's tone. "A rider brung us the news late yestereve."

"Then someone ought to have told me last night," Wat said, accepting the shirt Jed handed him and putting it on.

"Aye, but ye did creep in at the kitchen like a laird who'd been out tom-catting wi' his mates instead o' lying peaceful wi' his lady," Jed said. "Angus the steward did ha' the news, so if ye'd come in the front door as ye usual—"

"Enough," Wat said, silencing him.

He'd enjoyed coming in through the kitchen, as he had in his youth after sneaking out for adventure with lads that his father deemed his less suitable friends.

Last night's entry had lacked the exquisite sense of jeopardy that had accompanied such past doings when he'd feared he might find his father awaiting him. The more recent experience had certainly aroused other dangers, though.

His father had caught him only twice, with predictable results. Although Robert Scott had been a man of peace, he had reacted to such breaches of discipline much as any other father would. Certainly, Wat mused now, as he himself would if he were to catch any son of his daring to behave so recklessly.

Recalling his wits to the present, he said, "Did the rider say how soon Aunt Rosalie means to arrive?"

"Afore midday, me da did say," Jed said, making it clear to one of Wat's experience that Jed's orders had come from Lady Meg through Sym Elliot.

Nodding, Wat said, "I must organize a plan for tracking down and capturing Gilbert Rutherford. I need to talk with Tam and Geordie first, though, so they can begin getting the word out that I'll be looking for the man."

"Ye'll no want him to hear about it, though," Jed said thoughtfully.

"Right, so our lads must tread softly. I want to find his lair quickly, or at least his latest hunting ground. I don't want him running for cover in England."

"Shall I fetch Tam and Geordie in? Or will ye find 'em yourself?"

Wat's first inclination was to go and find the two men. However, he knew that if he did, he'd likely find other, more time-consuming tasks thrust upon him.

Preferring to avoid Lady Meg's displeasure if he failed to welcome his grandaunt's arrival, he sent Jed to tell Tam and Geordie that he'd see them in his privy chamber after he broke his fast.

Descending then to the great hall, he found his grandmother sitting in solitary splendor at the high table, eating a boiled egg and bread.

Ordering a larger repast for himself, Wat sat down beside her and said, "Where is everyone else?"

"Your mother is still asleep. Janet and Bella are waiting tactfully in the solar, hoping that your breakfast will render you docile enough to let them ride out and meet Rosalie. I've heard naught of our guest, so I presume she will break her fast later. Has she, by the bye, asked you yet about letting her ride into the forest?"

"As I only returned last night—"

"—and chanced to meet someone on the service stairs who sounded much like her ladyship," Meg interjected with a teasing smile.

Wat grimaced and was grateful when Edwin appeared with a jug of ale and a mug for him, as well as a warm manchet loaf in a basket. The butter pot being within reach, he extended the moment by reaching for it.

With his eating knife poised to cut butter, he looked at Meg and said, "Sym told you that?"

She nodded. "He was sleeping in the wee room above the bakery, because we got talking about the old days and talked longer than we'd intended. You ken fine that he sleeps like a cat with its ears wide open. He was like that as a boy, too."

"I know that little escapes him," Wat agreed, seeing Sym Elliot enter the hall and stride across the lower hall toward them. "It *was* Molly, Gram. I came in through the kitchen and scared her witless."

"Heaven bless the poor child! Why?"

"She was hungry, and we met on the stairs. So we went back down and pinched two apples from the bin. Then I escorted her upstairs to her door."

"Aye, so Sym said. I'm glad you look after her, love," Meg added. "I think she has led an uncomfortable life."

"With kinsmen like hers, I'm sure she has," Wat said.

"It must be hard for her to trust men, so it will do her good to spend time with one she *can* trust. Yes, Sym," Meg added, shifting her gaze as he stepped onto the dais. "Don't tell me that Rosalie has arrived already?"

Sym's boyish grin flashed as he said, "Nay, m'lady, her ladyship hasna changed as much as all that. I warrant we'll see her near midday, 'cause her lad said she'd take the Ale Water path. I were outside just to see if we'd have men enough to ride out wi' the young ladies and meet her if his lordship agrees that they may."

"Ahhh," Wat said, turning a gimlet eye on his grand-mother.

She met it with an innocent look of inquiry.

"I begin to see why you mentioned the girls' 'hope' to me, Gram," he said. "*And* why you wondered if Lady Molly had asked me yet about riding. Art suggesting that *I* escort the three of them to meet our aunt?"

"What an excellent notion, love," Meg said with her wid-est smile. "How clever of you to think of it! Your aunt Rosa-lie will be elated if you do her such honor. Sym, what did Tammy say about accommodating their ladyships' needs?"

Sym was eyeing Wat and, for once, did not immedi-ately answer her.

"Don't trouble Tam any further," Wat said to him. "I agree with Gram that the idea is a good one. If you can find your Emma, ask her if she can have the lady Molly ready to ride with us in an hour's time."

"Aye, sure, m'lord. I saw Em heading for the kitchen. I'll tell her."

When he turned toward the service stairs at the end of the dais, Wat said to his grandmother. "You might have just asked me, you know."

"I know, love, but you were right to remind me that you will make your own decisions. You make good ones, too, whether you know it yet or not. Even so, I know you are feeling your way, and I don't want to overstep or interfere."

"You are right about me feeling my way," he told her honestly. "I have much yet to learn, and I'm not sure..." He hesitated, because she was shaking her head.

"You are a natural leader, Walter-love. You will do well to follow your instincts. Your father, too, was young when he inherited, but he soon found his feet, and so will you. In troth, I think you'll have an easier time of it than he did. You seem to have inherited the best of both your father and your granddad."

Wat raised his eyebrows. "Sakes, madam, do you seek to flatter me?"

"Nowt of the sort," she retorted. "I speak only the truth. You have your granddad's skill with tactics, weapons, and horses. And you've inherited most of your father's good sense, as well as his ability to make friends and to parley with others."

"But I do lack many of my father's abilities," Wat said.

"Yes, but you are young yet. I have no doubt that your accomplishments will surpass his when you gain more experience."

Certain now that she had some goal in mind and was praising him before revealing her intent, Wat welcomed Edwin's hasty reappearance with the rest of his breakfast.

"Eat now, love," Meg said. "If you would talk more of such things, you need only say so." With that, she excused herself and left the dais, apparently forgetting that Sym was sending Emma to wake Molly, who would soon come down to break her fast.

Wat watched her leave the hall, still curious about her motives but beginning to wonder if perhaps she'd had none. She was usually frank with him.

Perhaps he was wrong to suspect more than her simply having arranged it so he'd feel obliged to escort his sisters and their intriguing guest to meet his grandaunt.

⁓

Molly entered the hall soon afterward, wearing another of Janet's kirtles, of primrose yellow. The narrow leather girdle sat low around her hips, its wee scissors, needle case, and tinderbox clinking lightly against each other as she moved.

She hesitated when she saw Wat at the high table alone, attacking a large breakfast. Guiltily aware that she had overslept and more aware of what some might view as her late-night tryst with him, she drew a breath to quiet her nerves.

Then, knowing that she had to eat, she continued toward the dais.

He stood as she approached and pulled out the back-stool beside him, saying, "Sit here, lass. Mam is asleep, my sisters have eaten, and Gram just went upstairs."

Waving Edwin over to attend her and behaving as if no tryst had occurred, he resumed his seat, saying, "I expect Emma told you that Jannie and Bella want to ride out to meet Aunt Rosalie's party."

"Aye, she did," Molly said. Turning at Edwin's approach, she asked him to bring her oatmeal porridge, sliced beef, and bread.

As he headed for the service stairs, she turned back to her host.

Smiling, he said, "Would you like to ride with them?"

Her tension vanished, and her spirits lifted. "I would, aye. Emma said that I might go with them, but will not Janet and Bella wear boots? I have none."

Frowning thoughtfully, he said, "In troth, I don't know. We shan't leave for a half hour yet, so you still have time to confer with them. It is cold out, though, so I think you *should* have boots, and you will also need a cloak."

"Then you have been outside already."

"Nay, but the shutters were open when I woke up, so I know it's icy cold."

"Is that why you were willing to wait for me? To let the day warm up?"

He shook his head, and she detected an odd glint in his eyes. "I was just talking with Gram. I must also talk to two of my men before we go, though."

She eyed him more closely. "Is aught amiss, sir?"

"Nay, but the King is at Melrose. I met him yesterday, and he asked me to track down a reiver who has been raising havoc with nobles on both sides of the line. I want my lads to see what they can learn about him."

The thought of riding again, instead of remaining as confined as she had felt for the past two days, was heady. But her elation vanished when the unwelcome image of an angry Tuedy loomed again in her mind.

With a sense of shock, she realized that, since waking to hear that she might go riding, not just with Janet and Bella but also—and most likely, Emma had said— with his lordship, she had utterly forgotten that she *had* a husband.

Swallowing hard, she said quietly, "Will it be safe if I go, sir? Might not my presence amongst you endanger everyone?"

The note of dread in her voice made Wat forget the food remaining on his trencher and look directly at her.

She had lost all color in her cheeks.

"You need not worry, Molly," he said, forcing calm into his voice. "I'll have my fighting tail with me. Moreover, my grandaunt travels with her own men."

"Even so—"

"We'll be on Scott land much of the time," he interjected in the same calm way. "And if Westruther does not send some of his men with her, I'll be surprised."

She looked thoughtful. "He is your grandame's good-brother, aye."

"He is. He married her middle sister, Amalie, and is a Scott cousin, as well. I can never recall the difference between first and second cousins, let alone cousins removed, but Westruther is my granddad's first cousin."

"You have a large family, I think," she said with a wry smile.

"Aye, with cousins from hither to yon."

The words gave him pause, and he nearly added that having so many close kinsmen was not always a blessing. But he was head of their clan now, and responsible for its well-being. He might confess his concerns to his grandmother, but it would ill become him to bleat about them to anyone else.

Reminding himself that his father had believed in him, and Lady Meg did, as well, he excused himself, and went to talk with Tam and Geordie.

A short time later, he met his sisters and Molly in the courtyard, and soon after that they were on their way.

He took six of his men with him and expected a peaceful trip.

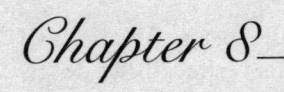

Chapter 8

The path to the Hawick road followed the Clearburn, which flowed from a loch northeast of the Hall to its confluence with the Rankilburn just west of it.

Despite the overcast sky, Molly reveled in the fresh air and lively conversation that she enjoyed with the ladies Janet and Bella. They seemed ever lighthearted and amiable, even when they disagreed. And they never talked only to each other, as the men in her family often did, as if she were invisible.

She had learned never to complain about such treatment, and to hide her feelings, as well. Neither Janet nor Bella had given her cause for complaint or concealment. With them, she was able simply to relax and enjoy the outing.

About a mile from the Hall, Janet pointed out a deep ravine through which the Clearburn flowed but that they were skirting.

"That is the Buck Cleuch," Janet said, enunciating both words carefully. "Seanachies say that an ancestor of ours killed a stag there. Then he carried it out of that steep cleuch on his back and laid it at the King's feet. As reward, the King named him Ranger of Ettrick Forest and

gave him land including the cleuch. That is how the name
Buccleuch came to be. Sithee, Granddad used it before he
inherited Rankilburn, because he and Gram lived in the
cleuch for a time at Raven's Law Tower. Wat means to
style himself as Buccleuch, too."

Wat was riding ahead of them with Geordie—the captain of his tail—and another man, while the rest of the
men followed the women. The two dogs Molly had met
the first night chased each other back and forth as they
traveled.

When the road narrowed and the three girls could no
longer ride easily side by side, Wat reined in and waited
for them to catch up with him.

"Bella," he said then, "would you like to ride ahead
of everyone with me to help Geordie and Ferg keep their
eyes out for trouble?"

Accepting his invitation with a grin, Bella barely
remembered to say farewell to her sister and Molly before
urging her mount to a lope beside his.

Watching them, Janet exchanged a smile with Molly,
who said, "Your brother is thoughtful, is he not?"

Janet's smile widened. "He is when it occurs to him
to be, doubtless because he was raised to know he would
inherit great responsibilities. Our brother Stephen has
only himself to consider and is not nearly as thoughtful."

"It must be more than that, though," Molly protested.
"My brother Will knows he will inherit our father's
estates, but Will does not care about anyone save himself.
My brother Thomas sometimes does. In troth, though,
the only other man I can recall meeting who gave true
thought to others, Lady Janet, was your lord father."

"Prithee, *do* call me Janet, Molly," Janet said with a

direct look. "Surely, by now, we can behave as sisters or at least close friends."

"You talk as if we have known each other for weeks instead of days," Molly said with a grin. "But I will try to remember."

"Good. As for men thinking mostly of themselves, I believe that is true at times of the best of them. But I'd wager that even your Will, villain though you paint him and villain though he must be, will have to consider the good of your clan when he does inherit those responsibilities."

"Perhaps," Molly said doubtfully. "At present, though, he resents any hindrance to getting his own way. My father is much the same, and as for—"

Realizing that she was about to mention Tuedy, Molly snapped her mouth shut, drawing a quizzical look from Janet. Hoping to cover the near-blunder, Molly said ruefully, "I should not speak of my kinsmen so."

Janet glanced ahead at Wat and Bella and the two men-at-arms behind them, with Ramper and Arch running now alongside them.

Then, looking over her shoulder at the other men riding some distance behind them, she said quietly, "You have said naught about *why* you came to the Hall, you know. I ken fine that I have no right to demand explanations, so I shan't. But if you would like to tell me, I'd like to know. I'm no gabster, I promise you."

Molly felt an unexpected prickle of tears in response to Janet's kindness.

Welcoming the opportunity to confide in her but uncertain of how much she should say, she said briefly, "I'm afraid I ran away from home, got lost, and hid in the shrubbery when I heard his lordship and his dogs coming toward me."

"Faith, were you afraid of Wat?"

"I'd have feared anyone then. Two of my brothers and a friend of theirs were searching for me, and I heard Will's dogs baying. His lordship sent the men and dogs away and took me to the Hall. He has said I may stay as long as I must."

"So you are afraid to go home," Janet murmured. "That makes me sad, Molly. Home should be the one place a person can always go—and be safe."

A tear spilled down Molly's cheek. Annoyed, she dashed it away, belatedly and painfully remembering her bruise. She avoided looking at Janet.

Janet laid a gloved hand on Molly's forearm and gave it a gentle squeeze. "This is not the best time to talk of this," she said. "But if you do want to talk without Bella's hearing, you need only ask me to aid you with something. Come to that, since you get on well with Wat, you might confide him, instead. He is utterly trustworthy when it comes to keeping one's confidence."

"I did tell him what happened, because he asked me," Molly said.

"There, then, you see. He has not said a word to Bella or me. He may have told Gram what he knows, but that is like talking to oneself. She will not repeat it."

"By my troth, Janet, I would like to confide in you, too. But I do think I ought to talk to him first. Not about you . . . about your trustworthiness, I mean—"

"I understand," Janet interjected with a grin. "You fear that Wat might think your tale unsuitable for me to hear. But I doubt that he will. He would not have brought you to us had he thought you were an unsuitable person for us to know."

Molly recalled then that Janet was just a year younger than she was. Moreover, Janet belonged to a family more willing to discuss certain subjects than the Cockburn men were. Accordingly, Molly decided to risk asking the question that had tickled her mind since learning what the abbot had said about her marriage.

"Janet," she said, lowering her voice even more, "having neither a mother nor a grandame to ask, I ken little of womanly things. Do you ken aught about maidenhood? I mean, do you know precisely how one stops *being* a maiden?"

"Why, one marries, of course."

"That's what I thought, too," Molly said with a sigh of disappointment.

Wat was listening with only half an ear to Bella's questions about the lady Rosalie and answering them as well as he could. At last he said, "Wheesht now, lassie. The truth is that I know almost as little about Aunt Rosalie as you do."

"Blethers," she retorted saucily. "You ken much more."

"If I do, 'tis only because I'm older and have quizzed Gram more often about her family than you have. When we meet Aunt Rosalie, we'll both learn more."

He had glanced back several times and noted with satisfaction that Molly and Janet seemed to be getting on well. He could not have said why it mattered to him that they did. However, it occurred to him now that if Molly had to return to Ring Tuedy, he would want to keep an eye on her for her own protection. That would be easier to do if she and his sisters became friends.

They rounded a turn a short time later and saw a dozen or more riders coming toward them. Wat recognized the Westruther banner leading them and noted the two women in the party, one more stylishly dressed than the other.

"There they are," he said. He raised a hand, greeting the oncoming riders and, at the same time, warning those behind him to rein in.

"Gram said Aunt Rosalie would have only her attire woman, a courier, and perhaps a pair of outriders," Bella said. "I see many more people than that."

"Cousin Garth must have sent some of his own. In fact," he added, belatedly recognizing the gentleman beside the stylish woman, "he has escorted her himself."

Sir Garth Napier, Lord Westruther, spurred his dappled horse to meet them.

His companion, in a fur-trimmed, blue-gray cloak, with her abundant still-dark hair confined in netting under a white veil, continued sedately on her gray palfrey.

As the two men met and shook hands, Westruther—a man with graying dark hair and beard, nearly sixty years behind him, and still a respected warrior with a warrior's physique—said, "We learned of your father's death yesterday, lad. I ken fine how it is to inherit sooner than one expects, for, as you know, that happened to me, too. So I've come to offer condolences and do what I can to aid you."

"I'm delighted to see you, sir, and with Quarter Day approaching, I do have a few questions for you. But first," he added as Molly and Janet rode nearer to join them, "may I present the lady Molly Cockburn, who is staying with us at the Hall."

Turning then to Molly with a smile, he added, "This is my cousin and granduncle, Lord Westruther."

Smiling back at him, Molly politely greeted Garth.

"And here is our Rosalie, impatient to meet you, too, my lady," Garth said, turning to introduce her. Wat-lad," he murmured with a boyish grin while the two women exchanged courtesies, "I must tell you that your *aunt* does not like to acknowledge that she is a grandmother, let alone a grandaunt."

"Art telling tales again, Garth?" Lady Rosalie demanded, her dark hazel eyes sparkling. "I'll not have you sullying Wat's ears with your nonsense. At least, I assume this is Wat. Are you not, my lord?" she added with an arch, even flirtatious toss of her head—more worthy of Bella, Wat thought, than a lady nearing fifty.

"I am Walter Scott, aye, my lady," he said, noting that another man some ten years younger than her ladyship, with light auburn hair and blue eyes, had eased his mount up beside hers.

"Let us talk as we ride, my lords," Rosalie said. "I want to see Meg."

"You might present your companion to them first," Westruther said dryly.

"Oh, aye, this is my steward, Len Gray," she said. "He has looked after me since my husband's death two years ago in Wales. Richard—my husband," she added with a glance at Molly—"sent him to me just before he died. Len is Scottish by birth, from Fife. But somehow he ended up in Northumberland with the Percies."

⌒

Recalling Lady Scott's worry that Rosalie might carry spies in her train, Molly looked carefully at Len Gray and decided that he did not match her notion of a spy. He was mannerly, good looking, and had eyes only for the lady Rosalie.

Her ladyship seemed to take his presence for granted but dismissed him, saying, "Look after Potter now, Len, if you please. She will be unhappy riding by herself, and I want to talk privily with my nephew and nieces, and their guest."

As he turned away, she added with a droll look, "Potter is my attire woman. I own, though, had she not been wondrous good about turning me out in style, I'd have dismissed her long ago. Sithee, Richard presented her to me soon after we married, and I'm sure he expected her to spy on me for him. He was ever suspicious of my behavior when I was out of his sight, although I vow I was a saintly wife to him. I missed him dreadfully when he died, too."

She chattered on cheerfully as they turned their mounts back toward the Hall, and her lighthearted manner fascinated Molly. It also shocked her, especially Lady Rosalie's airy admission that her husband had not trusted her. Surely, such a lack of trust must have been painful to endure.

By then, Wat was riding ahead of them with Westruther, but Molly knew that both men must be able to hear Lady Rosalie as she chatted on.

Wat glanced back a short time later, his eyes twinkling. He winked.

Molly felt heat flood her cheeks and ruthlessly suppressed a smile, lest her ladyship notice. But Rosalie was talking over her shoulder just then to Janet.

When they reached the Hall, the men dismounted swiftly. But when Wat turned to aid Rosalie, Molly saw that Len Gray was already helping her dismount.

Turning then to aid Molly, Wat said, "I hope you enjoyed our ride. I ken fine that it may not have been as long as you had hoped."

"I am grateful just to have got into the fresh air and beyond the wall, sir. Thank you for letting me go with you."

Then, noticing beyond him the straight-backed, slender figure appearing in the central tower's open doorway, she added, "I think your grandame must be as eager to see Lady Rosalie as Rosalie is to see her."

Her smile lingered as she watched the older women greet each other with fierce hugs and laughter. Next, Lady Meg hugged Westruther just as fiercely.

Glancing at Janet and Bella, and meeting Janet's twinkling eyes, Molly thought again of how wonderful it must be to have such a family.

The next day, Thursday, she saw Westruther and the ladies Meg and Rosalie only at meals. The women claimed that they had much catching up to do, and Westruther slept in and spent his afternoon with Wat in the latter's privy chamber.

Len Gray was like a wraith, Molly thought. He rarely spoke except to his mistress or her woman, or to relay requests to servants on their behalf.

She spent most of Friday with Janet and Bella. However, to her surprise—and clearly, to theirs as well—Wat offered to ride out with them early Saturday morning, saying that Westruther was sleeping late again.

They rode again Sunday morning before the family, their guests, and a number of their servants walked to Rankilburn Kirk. The walk was pleasant, but after the service, the rain that had threatened off and on for a sennight finally poured in a deluge that sent them hurrying back to the Hall.

Running across the courtyard with Wat, soaked to the skin but invigorated by her dash through the downpour, Molly looked up with a grin at the equally sodden Wat when he shoved the central tower's heavy door open to let her precede him inside.

To her delight, he grinned back as he pushed strands of wet hair off his face and followed her in. "I think you enjoyed that," he said.

"I did," she agreed. "But I must change my clothes before we sit down to eat." She glanced back at the others, walking fast but keeping their dignity.

"What is it, lass?" he asked.

"Until today, I did not know that you had your own priest," she said. "I ken fine that you may do as you please, but I do wonder why you rode all the way to Melrose to ask the abbot about marriage laws instead of asking your priest."

"Father Eamon is nearly my own age, as you must have seen," he said. "I doubt he can know much more about such things than I do. Even if he does, I have faith that the abbot will keep what I tell him to himself, but Father Eamon always kens the local gossip, which makes me suspect that he may contribute to it."

She nodded. "I ken fine that Father Jonathan, my father's priest, exchanges gossip with other priests. That is one way that Father gets his news. He also lets mendicant friars stay at Henderland, of course."

"We do, too, although we haven't seen one in some time," he said.

"Did you neglect to present me to Father Eamon

because you feared that he might speak of my presence here?"

"That is one reason," he admitted. "I think he knows better than to speak of anything that concerns me or my guests, though. And I did not mean to imply a lack of trust in the man. He is a good priest, just a young one and, as yet, untested."

"I saw Lady Meg talking to him," Molly said. "I thought he looked at me."

"He admires Gram. If she told him to keep a still tongue, I believe he will."

Molly had little faith in the young priest's sense of honor, especially if he was a friend of Father Jonathan, but Westruther joined them then, ending their private conversation.

~

Wat hoped he had laid Molly's fears to rest. He knew she was afraid that Father Eamon might reveal her whereabouts to her family, but in truth Wat himself had spared little thought for the Cockburns or the danger they might be to her.

His thoughts had been with the men out seeking word of Gilbert Rutherford. Several had reported, but none had found hint or clue of the reiver's whereabouts.

Monday was Martinmas and thus Quarter Day. By then he had spent two evenings with Westruther, discussing what Wat knew and did not know about his father's dealings with his tenants.

At the end of their discussion Sunday evening, Westruther had clapped him on the back and grinned. "I'm impressed, lad," he said. "You know much more about your estates and people than I knew when I inherited mine."

"Thank you, sir," Wat said sincerely. "I know that Father taught me well, but in troth, I surprised myself with how much I'd learned from him. I do feel more confident now about the meetings tomorrow, though."

"You'll do well," Westruther said firmly. "I'll be here, so if you meet with something that bewilders you, just order a brief halt, so we can confer privily."

Monday morning dawned with eerie stillness, gray and drizzly, but men came in pairs and groups to pay their rents. Wat spent the day in the Hall's inner chamber, meeting with one at a time, while Westruther sat silently in a corner.

Seeing him there, Wat recalled the many times *he* had sat there as a boy, watching and listening as his father met their people on Quarter Day. From then on, it was as if, instead of Westruther, Robert Scott was watching. Wat could even hear his father's voice in his head, offering advice, as he talked with people.

Besides seeing to affairs of business, and grievances, Wat asked each man he met what he knew about the reiver, Rutherford. Although most men recognized the name, none would admit knowing more about him than that he was ruthless.

Westruther knew no more than that about the reiver, either. "My estates, being far from the line," he explained, "lie well out of most raiders' territory."

⁓

Tuesday, midmorning, Wat gave orders to saddle horses, so he could ride out and see if any searchers had returned to their cottages. Geordie and Westruther had joined him in the yard when the tall gates opened to admit four horsemen.

The first two were men-at-arms. The third was a stranger in priestly garb.

The fourth rider was the Abbot of Melrose.

Handing his reins to Geordie, Wat said, "Look after my horse. Then take Kip and Aggie's Pete with you, and see what more you can learn from folks in the dale. If any searcher has gone missing, I want to know about it."

"Aye, laird, I'll see to that," Geordie assured him.

Westruther greeted the abbot, whom he clearly knew as well as if not better than Wat did. Then he said to Wat, "You won't need me whilst you talk with Father Abbot. If you don't mind, I'll go with Geordie and his lads. I'd like that fine."

"Aye, sure, sir," Wat said, smiling. "Prithee, convey my compliments or regrets wherever you believe they will do the most good."

Turning next to his visitors, he welcomed the abbot as that gentleman dismounted. The other priest was considerably more rotund than his reverence. Wat noted that the man remained mounted and eyed both of them warily.

"Come now, Jonathan," Father Abbot said briskly. "That horse won't bite you. Moreover, you will be much warmer and more comfortable in the Hall. I expect his lordship can even provide us with hot ale."

"Also food at midday if you are hungry," Wat said, eyeing the priest and wondering if it was the first time he had sat a horse.

A daft notion, Wat decided. Anyone living in the Borders, even those born elsewhere, soon learned to ride and ride well. But the fat little priest did not look like a horseman.

At last, with more grace than one might have expected,

the man dismounted and handed his reins to a waiting groom.

"My lord, this is Father Jonathan Graham," the abbot said lightly. "He serves mass in the wee chapel on St. Mary's Loch."

"Henderland's priest, then," Wat said, regarding the man more closely.

"I am, and I did nowt that I shouldna ha' done." The priest spoke brusquely but avoided Wat's gaze.

"That is no subject to discuss in a courtyard," Wat said. "We'll go inside where we can talk privily."

Leading the way to the inner chamber, he indicated cushioned back-stools near the wide table he had used to meet with his tenants the day before.

As he waited for the abbot and the priest to sit, Wat took his place behind the table. "What's this all about, Father Abbot?" he asked then.

"I brought Father Jonathan here so he could tell you what he told me. As you heard outside, he believes he acted properly. He insists he was merely following Piers Cockburn's orders with regard to his daughter."

"Does he?" Wat said with a look that ought to have withered the priest.

"He does," the abbot said. "I've reminded him that Lady Meg is her godmother and has therefore taken strong interest in Molly's...uh...disappearance."

Wat nearly raised his eyebrows but suppressed the urge. Clearly, the abbot implied that he had kept Molly's presence at Scott's Hall from the priest.

"I will talk wi' Lady Meg," Father Jonathan said curtly. "She must ken fine that even if she *thought* she enjoyed such a connection, she abandoned it long ago."

Molly and Janet were in the ladies' solar, mending linens, when Bella burst through the doorway. "Janet! You'll never guess who has come. It's the Abbot of Melrose. He has brought another priest, too, someone said. I saw Wat taking them inside from the yard, myself. So when Westruther rode off with Geordie, I hied me up here, because I knew you'd both want to know straightaway."

"The Abbot of Melrose?" Molly said, feeling such a shiver up her spine that she wrapped her arms around herself. "What does the other priest look like?"

Bella shrugged. "'A round little toad,' Geordie said. He *is* rather plump."

Molly shut her eyes, easily recognizing the description. The abbot had brought Father Jonathan to her refuge. She shot Janet a panicky look.

"Thank you, Bella," Janet said with a slight frown, "But Mam was looking for you earlier. You know you are not to go out to the yard or stables without first speaking to her. You must go to her, but tidy yourself first."

Making a face, Bella said, "I'll go. But do not think I am so dim as not to know you want to talk secrets with Molly."

"If I do, it is my business, dearling, not yours. Go along now."

When the younger girl had shut the door after herself, Janet said with visible concern, "What is it, Molly? Your face has turned nearly white."

"It must be Father Jonathan, the priest from Henderland—my father's priest. I fear that he has come to take me home."

"Wat won't *let* them take you. He promised you could stay."

"He may have no choice," Molly said. "How I wish we could hear what they are saying, but I don't suppose you have a laird's squint that we might use. My father has several at Henderland."

Janet's eyes danced. "If they are talking privily, Wat will have taken them to the inner chamber. Whilst there *is* a squint there, it overlooks the great hall and remains covered from the inside when not in use. One cannot see or hear aught in the inner chamber from the hall, only the other way round."

Grimacing, Molly said. "I doubt I could do it, anyway."

"I suppose we *could* creep down the service stair and mayhap hear some of what they say," Janet said. "However, if Wat has sent for food or hot ale, we'd likely run into a servant. I need not tell you that if anyone caught us, Wat would be furious. Still, if it is important for you to hear them, I'll go with you."

"I cannot ask that of you," Molly said, trying to conceal her dread of what Wat might do to his sister, or her, if they angered him so. "But, I *must* learn if they will join us for the midday meal. Father Jonathan would recognize me in a trice."

"He and the abbot have just arrived," Janet said. "It would be rude of Wat not to invite them to stay, so mayhap you should keep out of sight until they leave. I'll have Emma bring your food up here or to your chamber if you like."

"My chamber would be best," Molly said. "I'll go there now and stay until they have gone." So saying, she excused herself, picked up her skirts, and hurried down the main stairway to her chamber.

Entering, she paused to stare wistfully at the service-stair door in the far corner of the room.

⁓

After a glance at the abbot and a more intense look at the priest, Wat said, "Rather than allow you to affront my grandame, Father Jonathan, I will speak for her. I should warn you, though. We heard that the lady Molly steadfastly refused to marry Ringan Tuedy but that her father and brother forced the marriage. Is that so?"

"Cockburn did what he deemed best for his daughter," the priest said. "Bless me, but I did only what he told me to do. I ken fine that Scottish law and the Scottish Kirk say a woman may refuse to marry any man. But the Scottish Kirk and the Roman Kirk both hold that a lass must obey her father. Moreover, a priest who desires to retain his living canna afford to defy his patron."

"A priest worthy of the name should protect the weak above all," Wat said coldly. "I also heard that the lady's brother William tied her hands behind her and gagged her so she could not speak. Then he grabbed her hair to force her to nod at certain parts of the ceremony. Also true?"

"I expect so," the priest said, glancing at the abbot. "She didna speak."

Wat also looked at the abbot, who said, "I explained to Father Jonathan that he must not perform *any* marriage of an unwilling bride. However, he is also aware that her ladyship can declare her marriage illegal only if she can honestly claim that she remains a maiden. Did you manage to relay that information to her, my lord?"

"I did," Wat said shortly.

"Then that be that," Father Jonathan said on a note of

relief. "I ken Ringan Tuedy well, my lord. With a man of that stamp as her husband, that wee, slender lass could no ha' avoided consummation had she tried. You *must* agree with that."

"Then you admit that you assisted in her rape," Wat snapped, giving him an icy, silent stare. He feared to say more, lest he lose his temper.

"I did nae such thing," Father Jonathan declared indignantly. "Ye canna even persuade me that the lass was reluctant. How would *ye* know anyway? I tell ye, she went meekly wi' Tuedy after the ceremony. And *he* took her straight upstairs. She didna come doon to supper afterward, but that isna unusual, I think."

"Not if the lady has been brutalized," Wat retorted.

The abbot shot him a look that suggested he might be more tactful. Then he said mildly, "Did you ask Lady Molly if she *is* still a maiden, my son?"

Father Jonathan snorted derisively, then paused glowering at Wat. "D'ye ken where she is, then?" he demanded. "Mercy, if ye do and ye be keeping her from her rightful husband, ye're nowt save a wicked wife stealer!"

"The significant word would be 'rightful,'" Wat said, wanting to smack him.

To avoid making that desire clear to the man, he returned his gaze to the abbot. "I would not ask such a question of her ladyship under any circumstance," he said. "But I did tell my grandame all that you said to me."

"A good notion, that was," the abbot said, nodding.

"Aye, and if she finds opportunity to talk to Molly, she will ask her. Come to that, she may have done so already. She might not repeat what she knows to me."

Hearing noise beyond the service stair, he put a finger

to his lips. "Our ale is arriving, I think," he said. "We'll continue this discussion after the lad has gone."

The abbot engaged Father Jonathan in desultory conversation, but Edwin did not arrive for another minute or two. Wat wondered at the delay but doubted that either of the other two noticed. When the lad did enter, he bore a tray with a jug and three pewter mugs. Filling the mugs, he left the jug and vanished back downstairs.

"Now," Wat said to Father Jonathan, "you asked me, I believe, if I know where her ladyship is. I do not."

Chapter 9

Molly's whole body quaked, and she dared not move lest she make another sound. She had nearly let Edwin catch her listening to the men in the inner chamber.

She had been unable to resist the impulse to listen, so it was a relief that Edwin had gone downstairs again. He might as easily have come up, and she had dared not make noise by trying to get away.

Years earlier, her grandame Marjory had warned her that people who listened at corners heard only bad things about themselves. She ought to have added, Molly thought now, that one rarely learned all that one wanted to know.

She had rounded the turning above the chamber to hear a man ask if Wat had discovered whether she was still a maiden. Her breath caught in her throat then in an audible gasp. And when Father Jonathan asked if Wat knew where she was, she had grabbed wildly for the wall, fearing her knees would give way.

Hearing the fat priest declare that if Wat did know and kept her from her husband, he could be guilty of wife stealing had appalled her.

She'd heard Edwin coming upstairs then and had

whisked up and around the curve but dared go no farther lest he hear her and investigate.

Now she felt torn between wanting to know more and fear that Wat or someone else would catch her. Such an ill turn to serve a kind host, but—

A sound above her on the stairs decided the issue. Gathering her skirts and dignity, she continued upward, meeting Lady Meg's Brigid on the next landing.

"Faith, this be good fortune," Brigid said. "Her ladyship sent me t' find ye, m'lady. I looked first in the solar, but Lady Janet said ye'd gone t' your room."

"Does Lady Meg want to see me?" Molly asked quietly, wondering how far Brigid's rather shrill voice might carry.

"She does, m'lady, in her sitting room, if ye please. I'll take ye to her."

"I ken fine where it is, thank you," Molly said. Dismissing her, she hastened to Lady Meg's door.

Rapping and hearing the command to enter, she did so.

"I am glad to see you, my dear," Meg said as Molly shut the door. "Brigid said Father Abbot has come with another priest in tow. Do you ken aught of this?"

Licking suddenly dry lips, Molly said, "Aye, m'lady, Bella told Janet and me that two priests had come."

"Did you see them, or they you?"

"Nay, m'lady," Molly said and felt heat flood her cheeks, although the statement was true. She had not *seen* them.

Gently, Meg said, "Walter told me of your troubles, my dear. I suspect that the second priest may be your father's chaplain."

Molly nodded before she realized that, by doing so,

she might give herself away. Hastily, she said, "It is Father Jonathan. Bella said his lordship's Geordie called him a round little toad. The description is so apt that I am sure it must be he."

"I see." Lady Meg said with a thoughtful frown. Then, directing a narrower look at Molly, she said, "Wat's description of your escape lacked detail, I fear. Will you think me too intrusive if I ask you to tell me more about it?"

"I am too grateful to refuse you," Molly said. "I don't know how much his lordship already told you, though."

"He told me all I need to know about that dreadful ceremony," Meg said rather tartly. "Start with what followed it, and pretend that I ken naught of it."

Molly nodded, trying to gather her wits and decide what to say.

At last, drawing breath, she explained about the so-called wedding feast and Tuedy's concern about her bindings. "He put his face close to mine and said he'd make me regret it if I caused any trouble. I believed him. Then he ordered me to show him to my bedchamber, and one of his men followed us. When we reached my room, Tuedy told the man to wait on the landing, and then he…he…"

Shutting her eyes to the vision that appeared then, she fell silent.

"Prithee, sit down, Molly," Lady Meg said gently, gesturing toward a stool near her chair. "I know this is hard, but 'tis gey important. What happened next?"

"He…he shut the door and bolted it," Molly said, shuddering. "He is so big, and my chamber is small. He seemed to take up all the air in it. But when I backed away, just to breathe, he grabbed me and yanked off my veil."

"With his man still standing outside?" Lady Meg asked, visibly shocked.

"Aye," Molly said. "Then Tuedy grabbed my hair the same way Will had. He snatched out the pins and jerked off the netting. It hurt, so I tried to pull away, but he held me easily. He tore my bodice, trying to unlace it. When I protested, he told me to take off all my clothes and threatened to strip me himself if I refused."

"And then?" Meg said, her tone firm again, her expression insistent.

"I...I obeyed him. I took off all but my shift." Tears flooded Molly's eyes as she relived the terror and humiliation that Tuedy had made her feel.

Meg's expression softened, but she said, "Go on, dearling. I must know."

Molly murmured, "He took my clothes and my slippers and cast them aside. Then he...he..."

Tears streamed down her cheeks. Stifling a sob, avoiding Meg's eyes, she said, "He touched me, squeezed my breasts hard, and d-did other things. When I cried out at him to stop, he slapped me. I don't recall much else after that."

"Try," Meg said softly. "This is *most* important."

"I'm sorry." Molly met her gaze again. "'Tis as if my mind went elsewhere until he tried to rip off my shift. I-I must have wrapped my arms round myself and crumpled to the floor. I remember him grabbing an arm and forcing me to stand. Then he smacked my face again, harder, and threw me onto the bed."

Meg, visibly tensing, made only a slight gesture to indicate she needed more.

Molly sighed. The rest was humiliating but somehow easier to say.

"He walked toward me," she said. "Then he stopped and turned as if he'd heard something outside the door. I think he had forgotten his man was there."

"Then...?"

"Then he opened the door, saying I would need more usage before I'd be satisfactory and that my inexperience had put him out of temper. He was going downstairs to enjoy our wedding feast but would leave me to come to my senses. Also, he said he would bring his riding whip when he returned. Then, if I had *not* come to my senses, he said, he'd teach me to obey him. After that, he picked up my clothes and left, ordering his man to keep guard and see that I stayed put."

"But you escaped."

"Aye," Molly said. She told Meg about the service door behind its screen. "I'd never had a personal servant," Molly explained. "So I set the screen there years ago to block the draft from the stairway."

"And that's all?"

"Aye, for as soon as Tuedy left, I fled downstairs to the kitchen and out into the forest. Then, I just kept going... gey heedlessly, I fear."

"I think you were prodigiously brave, my dearling," Meg said.

"I'll have to go back to Tuedy now and face them all, won't I?"

"Perhaps, but you will not be alone if you do," Meg said firmly.

"His lordship said that the only way I could declare my marriage illegal is if I am still a maiden. But if I am married, I can no longer *be* a maiden, can I?"

Lady Meg was silent for a moment or two, and Molly

discerned a fleeting look of anger before she controlled it and said quietly, "I'm going to think about that, my dear. I ought to have realized how difficult this would be for you. But have faith in Walter, if you can. I can promise that you will have all the help we can give you. Meantime, I want you to stay right here for now. I am going down to take my midday meal with our guests. I will have Emma bring you yours here."

Molly said, "Janet already told her to serve it in my chamber, I think."

"Then I shall tell her otherwise," Meg said. "*No* one will disturb you here."

Molly believed her. She felt a little as if Meg were abandoning her, even so.

As Meg stood to leave, she said, "I may be some time, my dear, so I shall ask Emma to stay with you. That way, if sitting here grows tiresome, she can fetch Janet to you after we eat, and send Bella to bear her mother company."

"Prithee, madam, how long do you expect to hide me here?"

Meg smiled reassuringly. "Just until Father Abbot and Father Jonathan leave the Hall. Meantime, I mean to learn much more about all this."

When the door had shut behind her and Molly was alone, she began to wonder if she was truly safer or just learning that safety was ever-illusory.

~

After declaring to Father Jonathan that he did not know where Molly was, Wat turned their discussion to other, less contentious topics while they sipped the Hall's hearty ale. Father Abbot proved adroit at deflecting Father Jonathan from further defense of his actions. Even so, Wat more than welcomed the rap on the door informing him that the midday dinner was ready to serve.

Adjourning with his guests to the dais, he wished he had some magical way to make Father Jonathan support what was right for Molly.

Forced marriage, in Wat's opinion, should be illegal under any circumstance. As for the Kirk's notion that a woman was better off with a man like Ring Tuedy than unwed, that was utter lunacy.

That a father, any father, could treat his daughter as Cockburn had treated Molly shocked him. That a priest could collude in such a travesty infuriated him. It was all he could do to be civil to Father Jonathan.

Nevertheless, the man was a guest in his house and at his board. He would exert himself to be polite.

The fat little priest pulled out his back-stool and began to sit, with the abbot standing beside him at Wat's right. Recalled to duty but twitching with impatience, the priest folded his hands at his waist and looked piously down.

Wat doubted that the man was offering a prayer to the Almighty unless it was to get him out of Scott's Hall as soon as possible and away from Rankilburn.

Deciding he'd be wise to ignore him, Wat waited for the ladies of his household to appear. Men and women in the lower hall had found their places at the trestle tables there and stood quietly. Westruther and Geordie had not returned.

Janet and Bella came in, and Janet took her usual place, but Bella walked to Wat and said, "Our lady mother will eat in her chamber, sir. She said to tell you that if Father Abbot will pray for her and perhaps come to visit her another day, she would like to see him. She does not feel able to welcome a priest unknown to her at this sad time, though, and does not want to appear rude by receiving only one of them."

"Thank you, Bella," Wat said, glancing at the abbot and receiving a silent nod in reply. "After we eat, you may go and tell her that Father Abbot will do as she asks." Leaning nearer, he said quietly, "Since she is not coming to table, you and Janet should sit next to Gram."

"But what about Aunt Rosalie and—" Bella broke off when Wat frowned and turned away without mentioning Molly, letting him hope the priest would pay her no heed.

His grandmother entered and spoke briefly to Janet and Bella when she met them. When the three had taken their places, Wat said, "Where is Aunt Rosalie?"

"Visiting the Gledstanes at Coklaw," Lady Meg replied shortly.

"Then, Father Abbot, if you would be so kind as to say the grace…"

His reverence complied and was blessedly brief.

The meal likewise passed swiftly, because although it was the largest meal of the day, it was rare in Border establishments for such a meal to take long. People had chores to do, and the master of the house and his family customarily lingered longer over their supper than their midday meal.

While others at the high table waited for Father Jonathan to finish his food, Lady Meg leaned near her grandson and murmured, "If you mean to continue your discussion in the inner chamber, Walter, I would like to join you. If not, then I want a word with Father Abbot afterward.

Also, sir, if I look as if I might speak to that other worm, you must stifle me. I doubt I can be civil to him."

"Say what you like to him, Gram. I've stifled myself many times already."

She shook her head at him. "It is at just such times that you must try to emulate your father, love, *not* your granddad."

"And you, madam?" His lips twitched. "I doubt that you could be uncivil if you tried."

"Ahhh, but you do not know all," she said. "I'll have you know that I once tossed a full goblet's ale in your grandfather's face, right in front of his men."

Wat raised his eyebrows. "Pray, what did he do then?"

"That, my love, is no business of yours," she said, her dignity unimpaired.

Stifling a chuckle, Wat began to look forward to further conversation with the two clerics. Earlier, he had felt well out of his element, his antipathy toward Father Jonathan warring with his training to be respectful of all priests.

As it was, he barely waited for the man to wipe his eating knife before he stood and said evenly, "Father Abbot, my lady grandame will join our discussion in the inner chamber. As it may be long, I'd welcome you to spend the night with us."

"Nay, my lord, but thank you," the abbot said. "I have already told Father Jonathan that I must return to the abbey. Nor need you offer your hospitality to him. He told me earlier that Cockburn expects his return by suppertime."

"You give me more reason to press you to stay, Father," Wat murmured.

The abbot smiled but shook his head and turned to

Lady Meg. "I am glad to see you looking as well as ever, my lady," he said.

Meg said with her gentle smile, "You must reserve your compliments and consolation for my good-daughter, Father Abbot. Lavinia is beset with grief at present and will welcome your prayers and, in time, your sage advice."

"But you do not?"

"I did not say that." Quietly, she added, "I'm a Borderer born, your reverence. If we succumbed to our grief at every such loss, we'd have time for little else. Life goes on. My husband would not thank me for wallowing, nor would my father, mother, good-father, or my beloved son. I miss them all dreadfully but cannot bring them back, and life is a gift that one should not waste in sadness."

"So you mean to discuss your goddaughter with us, do you?"

When she raised her eyebrows, he said, "Aye, I asked Jonathan about that, and he does admit that he witnessed the event. He says you abandoned her."

"So he can be honest then," she said.

"He has been, aye."

"Then, I have the answer to your question for you and a declaration," Meg said. "But we should go into the inner chamber first, I think."

"Aye, we should," he agreed. Turning to Wat, he added, "Should anyone else be there, as well, my lord?"

Without missing a beat, and certain that the abbot meant Molly, Wat glanced at Lady Meg. Her headshake was so subtle that he doubted anyone else noticed it.

"We need no one else, Father," he said. "We'll go right in."

One of the younger menservants hurried to the inner chamber door and held it open for them.

Offering his arm to Lady Meg, Wat gestured for the two priests to precede him inside and to the table. Then he murmured to Meg, "Did you ask her, then?"

She did not answer but, head high, followed the priests to the table.

"Ale or wine, my lord?" the young manservant asked from the doorway.

"Not now," Wat said.

Recalling the noise on the service stair earlier and Edwin's delay with their ale, he dismissed the lad, moved to the other door, and secured it, as well.

~

"Me lady, ye've eaten gey little," Emma said, frowning at the food-laden tray she had set before Molly some time before.

Pushing it aside, Molly said, "I'm not hungry. I have things on my mind."

"Likely ye'll no tell me about them, and I'll no be asking ye," Emma said. "Me da would ha' the skin off me, did he hear I'd been prying into your business."

Feeling an urge to smile despite her concern about whatever was going on downstairs, Molly said, "Has he had the skin off you often, Emma?"

"Niver, but he's threatened it, and I'd no like t' test him. Our Jed says it doesna do t' vex 'im too far, and Jed would know. See you, he sassed Lady Meg once when we was small and smarted a sennight for that."

"They call your da 'Lady Meg's Sym,' do they not?" Molly said.

"Aye, so it doesna do t' vex Lady Meg even a wee bit, even if ye dinna sass her. Not if me da's around."

"And, I expect, he usually is."

"Aye, mostly, but she sent 'im out wi' the lady Rosalie soon after them priests came here," Emma said. "I dinna ken where Lady Rosalie were a-going, but I'd wager that steward o' hers went wi' them."

"Is that unusual?" Molly asked.

"I canna said what be usual wi' the lady Rosalie," Emma said. "Me da says nowt about her or Lady Meg's other kinfolk, and he doesna encourage questions. But I saw for m'self how that Len Gray watches her and keeps near."

"Your da does much the same with Lady Meg, though, does he not?"

"Aye, sure," Emma admitted. "But I havena heard nae-one ever say that me da fair dotes on Lady Meg."

"Faith, do they say that Len Gray dotes on the lady Rosalie?"

Emma shrugged. "Jed did say he's heard it said more than once in the stables. He said we shouldna tell our da, but I'm thinking we should. Da should ken such things if he's keeping his eye on her, aye?"

Molly had no answer for that question, but she found herself wondering afterward if ladies, even widows approaching fifty, enjoyed amorous adventures with their stewards. It sounded like a dangerous pastime, to say the least.

Moreover, the lady Rosalie was Lady Meg's sister, and Molly had a feeling that Meg might disapprove of such a pastime, herself. When her fertile imagination presented an image of Rosalie vexing Meg and Lady Meg's Sym taking the skin off Rosalie, Molly turned abruptly away from Emma to hide a grin.

Nevertheless, as Emma's da would say, it was no business of hers any more than it was Emma's.

⁓

"Shall we be seated," Wat said, pulling a back-stool out for Lady Meg.

Father Jonathan bristled. "I dinna ken what more we ha' to discuss. If ye've aided the lady Margaret Tuedy to escape her husband, ye're guilty o' wife stealing. To be allowing your nan to aid and abet ye is no the mark of a civilized man."

Margaret Tuedy! Wat nearly growled.

Aware of the abbot stiffening beside him and of Lady Meg's tightening lips as she took her seat, Wat caught and held the priest's gaze. "If Cockburn ever comes to his senses and throws you out, do not come here seeking sanctuary," he said with grim disdain. "When you speak of my grandame, you will do so with respect and you will omit such ludicrous accusations. Do you understand me?"

"Och, aye, I understand well enough that I ha' nae more to say here. I'll be taking me leave o' ye, then."

"You will go when I say you may go," Wat said icily. "Having made your ludicrous accusations, you will *sit down* and hear them answered."

Father Abbot said softly, "I think you will agree, Jonathan, that Piers Cockburn is likely to heed my advice, especially where his chapel is concerned. Therefore so should you. You *have* made several accusations since we arrived here. You would do well to hear what his lordship and Lady Margaret Scott have to say."

With a sullen shrug, the round little priest plopped

down on a stool and made a glib gesture as if to say they might proceed.

Wat glanced at the abbot, who took the seat he had occupied before.

Taking his own chair beside Meg's, Wat turned to face her. "You said you had information for us, madam. Are you ready to share it?"

"I am," she said, looking at the abbot and ignoring Father Jonathan. "You said that if Molly is still virgin, she can declare her marriage illegal, aye?"

"I did say that. Are you telling me that she is still chaste, my lady?"

"I am," Meg said firmly. "*And* that she does declare that marriage illegal."

"Blethers!" declared Father Jonathan. "I can tell ye o' me own knowledge that that lass was alone in her bed-chamber with her husband. Moreover, they were there long enough to make any claim of her continued virginity preposterous."

Wat gritted his teeth.

Before he could speak, Meg put a hand on his arm and said calmly to Father Jonathan, "You are offensive, sir-rah. You can have no such knowledge, since you did not see what occurred in that bedchamber. Nor, I'd venture to suppose, did Ringan Tuedy boast about it. If he spoke honestly, you would *know* that she is still chaste. If he said otherwise, he's an even poorer excuse for a man than I'd thought."

Turning to face the abbot, she said more gently, "Molly is as chaste as when she was born, Father Abbot. I will swear to it with my hand on the Bible if I must."

"There can be nae need of that, my lady," the abbot

said. "Your word is aye good. I will gladly support her declaration of the marriage's unlawfulness."

"If her ladyship's even *seen* the lass," Father Jonathan snapped. "Have ye?" he demanded belligerently of Meg.

"I have," Meg said, meeting his gaze, her disdain equal to her grandson's.

Wat murmured dulcetly, "Do you accuse *her ladyship* of wife stealing?"

Giving him a sour look, Father Jonathan refused to rise to the bait. "Fact is," he said, "the lass's chastity or its lack matters not a whit. Nor would it even if she submitted to and—by a miracle of God—passed a physical examination."

"Why not?"

"Sakes, if we can be sure of anything, we can be sure that Tuedy, being the sort *he* is, will *claim* that he consummated his union. And people, being the way they are, will believe him, not her. That lass's reputation will be shattered unless she returns forthwith to her husband. *That* be plain fact, and we all know it."

Wat heard truth in the man's words and his heart sank. Catching the abbot's gaze, he fought to calm himself. Beside him, he sensed his grandmother's distress, although a glance reassured him that her demeanor remained tranquil.

Father Abbot said, "You give us cause to ponder, Jonathan. Yet I ken fine that you have obligations to see to at Henderland Chapel. If his lordship will excuse you, we need keep you here nae longer."

"Aye, sure, I'll excuse him," Wat said sincerely. "Have you men to travel with you, sirrah, or would you like some of mine to escort you?"

Father Jonathan hastily disclaimed any need for a bodyguard. His nervous manner suggested a suspicion that Wat's men might be a greater danger to him than armed bandits would be.

Wat did not reassure him. Barely waiting for the irritating priest to leave the room, he said to the others, "'Tis a bigger coil than we had imagined, is it not?"

To his surprise, Father Abbot got up, walked to the door, and opened it. Leaning out, he waved at someone. Moments later, Wat heard him muttering.

When the abbot shut the door and turned back into the chamber, he smiled at Lady Meg and said, "I knew you would worry about Father Jonathan's safety, m'lady. You will be grateful to know that I have asked one of my men to see him safely to St. Mary's Loch."

"How wise you are, your reverence," Meg said. "I own, I was more concerned that he might linger to stir trouble here."

"You should have told your man to confer with the captain of my guard, Father Abbot," Wat said.

"That would be Jock's Wee Tammy, aye?" the abbot said with a twinkle.

"It would," Wat agreed.

"Aye, well, I did just mention to my chappie that he might tell Tam what my orders were. If that was overstepping, my lord..."

"Not a bit," Wat said, grinning. Then he imagined what Molly would feel, first learning that the abbot would support her and then what little good it would do.

The grin vanished. He said, "Jonathan's point does remain valid, Father Abbot. Although Molly has declared her marriage unlawful and refuses to return to Tuedy, she will have to return to Henderland and face her family. I'd not wish that on any young female, let alone one whose family has betrayed her as Molly's has."

"She can stay with me as long as she likes," Meg declared.

"Gram, you know that holds true only until her father commands her return," Wat said. "We cannot legally prevent that."

"Then we'll do it *illegally*," Meg said. "We need not tell him she is here."

"Just how long do you expect her presence to remain secret?" he asked.

"Not long enough," the abbot said when Meg grimaced. Turning to Wat, he added, "But mayhap you have forgotten your promise to me, my son."

"What promise?" Wat asked him a split second before the echo of his own words at Melrose flooded his conscience and brought heat to his cheeks.

"Why, you assured me that her ladyship would have your protection and that of your clan for as long as she requires it," the abbot replied. "In my experience, my lord, the best way to provide such protection is to make the young lady your wife."

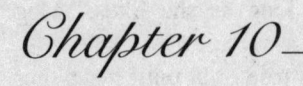

Wat fought to keep his countenance after the abbot reminded him of his promise, while every fiber in him wanted to shout, *That's not what I meant!*

He could scarcely tell the man that he had been offering protection for Molly only until it was safe for her to go home, not to protect her for the rest of her life.

Not only was he ill-equipped to accept another huge responsibility on top of those he had just inherited, but to do so could also mean war with the Cockburns. They were unlikely to agree that her marriage to Tuedy was unlawful.

The silence in the room grew heavy. Reminding himself that Father Abbot had done naught but echo his own words back to him, Wat stared at his hands. He dared not look at Lady Meg. He had neglected to tell her about that promise of his.

Feeling her gaze on him, he was as certain as he could be without looking that her gray eyes had widened and her expressive mouth was agape.

He was devoutly glad that Father Jonathan had left the Hall.

"Well, my lord?"

Wat met the abbot's steady gaze and swallowed, collecting his wits.

"I ken fine that you are a man of your word," the abbot said gently.

"I am, aye," Wat said. "I did not expect it to bring me to this pass, though."

"Most understandable," the abbot said, nodding. "We can never know what God's plan for us is. That is why a wise man takes care to think before giving his word. Thinking first can prevent one's feeling forced to gainsay himself later."

Fighting down irritation at what sounded like a rebuke, albeit one he deserved, Wat said, "I must give this matter more thought, Father Abbot. In troth, I remain uncertain that marriage, *any* marriage just now, is the sole way to protect her ladyship. Moreover, she may well refuse such a course."

He saw the abbot's gaze shift to Lady Meg and rest there.

Glancing at her, Wat saw no reaction to that steady gaze until, rather abruptly, she stood and extended a hand to the abbot.

"It was kind of you, your reverence, to look into Molly's situation as you did. The matter is now much clearer to me. I'm sure it is also clear to his lordship."

Getting to his feet, the abbot took her hand between his two and said, "You are gey wise, m'lady, and I am ever at your beck and bay, as you know. I'll have a word with Piers Cockburn if you like. I think he is poorly served by his priest."

"Forgive me, Father," Wat said, rising to stand beside Meg. "I agree that Jonathan Graham ill becomes his post, but I'd liefer you leave him be for now."

The abbot cocked his head. "But, my son—"

"Whatever I decide about the lady Molly's protection," Wat went on, "I must talk first with her and with her father, because we cannot continue to conceal her whereabouts from him. I will make my opinion of that forced marriage known to him, though, and will tell him she has declared it unlawful before witnesses. May I also tell him that the Kirk agrees that the marriage was illegally done?"

"Aye, sure, and name me as 'the Kirk' if you like. I assure you that any honest priest will agree with me. Jonathan will get nae sympathy from the bishop or any other kirksman in Scotland, though he is welcome to try."

"I'll walk out with you," Wat said. "Do you come with us, madam?"

"I should go to my sitting room," Meg said with a meaningful look. "I must attend to that other matter awaiting us, unless you wish to do so yourself."

Interpreting those words to mean that Molly was likely impatient to learn what had happened, Wat shook his head. He had no wish for that confrontation yet. "Nay, do as you please," he said. "I want to avoid trouble elsewhere first if I can."

"Then it shall be as you wish," Meg said. "Perhaps I will walk out with you and Father Abbot, after all. Rosalie will be returning soon. As I told you, Sym took her to visit the Gledstanes at Coklaw. They are Murray cousins, you see," she said to the abbot. "Rosalie has not seen any of them since her marriage."

"'Tis a long time then," the abbot replied. Scanning the yard, he added, "My men stand yonder, m'lady. Prithee, do not feel obliged to walk to the gate with us. All will fall into place now as God commands."

They bade him farewell. Then, as they watched him approach his men, Wat murmured with a wry smile, "What you meant, Gram, was that you sent Aunt Rosalie away so she'd be less likely to quiz you about Father Abbot's visit."

"True," Meg answered, unabashed. "And you should be thanking me instead of smirking, my lad. I doubt that Rosalie's curiosity has faded one whit over the years. But Father Abbot is waving. We must not be uncivil."

As she waved, she added, "Did you want me to tell Molly that the abbot agrees her marriage is unlawful, love? More important, do you mean to include me when you do discuss all of this with her?"

Wary now, Wat gave her a speculative look. "Don't tell me that you, too, think I must marry her."

"Your father did consider such a union, after all," she replied musingly. "I think he agreed then that you were not ready. But such a marriage would have pleased him. Moreover, he believed in keeping those opposed to his views close when he could. That was better, he said, than letting them become greater enemies."

"Well, whatever comes of all this, I do not want to keep the Cockburn men any closer than they are now," Wat said bluntly.

"Then again, I say, it shall be as you wish, love. I see no sign of Rosalie or Sym so I should go to Molly now. If you fear that I may say too much…"

"Tell her whatever you like, madam," Wat said. "Just do not commit me to anything yet. I want to ponder the matter for a time before I decide what to do."

And it won't be marriage of any sort, he added silently to himself. *I'm not ready to marry yet, and when I decide that I am, I'll choose my own wife.*

Molly sat silently, listening to Emma tell her about a small cousin who had a knack for flinging himself into the briars.

"Me uncle Dod says he's just like me da were as a bairn, but me da insists that *he* had gey more sense in his cockloft than what Wee Gibby has."

"Sym did have more sense than Gibby does," Lady Meg said from the doorway, startling both young women. "Sym was then and still is one of the most sensible men I know. Young Gibby rarely thinks before coming to grief."

"Did me da never come to grief then?" Emma asked.

Meg shut the door as quietly as she had opened it and without apparent effort. "I cannot say that," she said with a twinkle. "The day I met Sym, he came to grief. Sithee, he was not yet eleven but had followed your uncle Dod and my Sir Walter straight into the briars. *After* they had ordered him to stay home."

"Aye, he would," Emma said, nodding as if it made sense to her.

Molly, however, was watching Meg, whose gaze shifted next to her. "Have you had your dinner, Emma," Meg asked, still holding Molly's gaze.

"Aye, m'lady," Emma said, getting quickly to her feet. "But if ye mean to stay wi' Lady Molly, I ha' dunamany other things t' do."

"I do have some matters to discuss with her," Meg said.

Smiling at Molly, Emma whisked herself out of the room and shut the door carefully behind her.

"Have the priests gone, my lady?" Molly asked.

"They have," Meg said. "I must tell you straightaway, though, that you are not out of the briars yet."

Molly sighed. "I did not suppose that I could be. Must I go home, then?"

"Not yet. That much I can tell you with a clear conscience."

"What else can you tell me? What did they say?"

"Father Jonathan insisted that he had followed your father's orders. He said that he does not believe you were reluctant to marry Tuedy."

"A holy priest should not tell such lies!"

"Nay, but he seems to think that his loyalty should be to your father, rather than to the Almighty. He fears that Piers will punish him if he admits the marriage was unlawful. He stuck to its lawfulness even in face of the abbot's displeasure."

"Did the abbot say the marriage was unlawful, then?"

"He did, aye. He agreed to support your declaration that it was."

"Then someone must have told him that I'm still a maiden," Molly said, furrowing her brow.

"I did," Meg said.

Molly shook her head. "I don't understand how that can be."

"I said it because I believe it," Meg said. "Tell me, Molly-lass, just what do you ken about a wife's duties to her husband?"

Molly frowned again, gathering her thoughts. "She bears his children and looks after his household, of course. I'm not sure what other duties she has, except," she added with a sigh, "as Tuedy said, to obey his every command."

"The only uncertainty I had earlier was when you said you did not recall all that he did to you," Meg said quietly, drawing up a stool to sit facing Molly.

Remembering her encounter with Tuedy, Molly felt a distinct shiver. "He touched me in places where no one had touched me before. He terrified me. All I could think about after he left was how I might get away from him, from them all."

"Did he take off *his* clothes?"

Molly shook her head. The thought of him doing so made her throat close and her stomach churn, although she did not know why it should. She had seen naked men—her brothers, father, and occasionally one of the men-at-arms who slept on pallets in the great hall. But the thought of Tuedy naked . . . She winced.

"Never mind," Lady Meg said. "We can talk more about this another time, if you decide that you want to. I know this has been a difficult day for you. Sithee, before my wedding, I knew less than you do about a woman's duties in her marriage. My mother told me just to obey my husband, so I did."

"Ay-de-mi," Molly muttered.

"So I thought, myself, but my husband was of a different cut from Tuedy, and I came to love him with all my heart. I also had respect for my mother's wisdom then. I still do. Even so, if you ever do want to know exactly what happens on a normal wedding night, you need only ask me. I will tell you."

"Thank you, my lady," Molly said, hoping she need not. Somehow, despite her ladyship's kindness, the thought of talking about such intimate things with her increased her stress rather than easing it.

Meg smiled. "I think I know how you feel, but the truth is that you can talk to me about anything you like. You won't shock or upset me, and I won't repeat what you tell me to anyone. You have no reason to believe that or to trust me yet. I understand that, too. Moreover, I do think that when that time comes, you will know whom to ask and will feel comfortable enough to do so."

"Thank you, my lady," Molly said, relaxing. "Is there anything else that I should know?"

To her surprise, Meg made a wry face and rolled her eyes as if seeking help from heaven. Then, drawing breath, she said, "Look at me. I have just said that you can trust me, and then you ask me a question about something that the head of my family has as much as told me to keep to myself."

"As much as?"

"Aye, and that's the rub," Meg said. "Our Walter said that I should tell you we will discuss what to do next and he will decide. However, since you have suffered quite enough from people making decisions on your account…"

When she paused, Molly said, "Did he not intend for me to be one of those involved in that discussion?"

"Faith, I wasn't sure that he meant me to be involved," Meg said. "Then, he told me I might tell you what I pleased." Grimacing again, she added, "He said it in that tone a man uses when he means he *will* be displeased if you say too much."

"Do you fear his displeasure, madam?"

"I don't fear it," Meg said thoughtfully. "The truth is that I've never endured it. I have seen how it can be, though. My husband had a volatile, fiery temper. He would explode, sparks would fly, and whoever got in the way of it might suffer. But my Wat's anger, like most such fury, burned out quickly. Wat's anger is the opposite. His is ice cold and sometimes long-lasting."

A shiver shot up Molly's spine. "One would not want to anger such a man," she murmured.

Meg's expression softened. "He will not lose his temper with you, dearling. Once our Wat has taken someone under his wing, that person need never fear him. He will guard you as if you were one of his sisters."

Molly found no reassurance in that statement. She did not *want* to be Wat's sister. Nor did she want anything from him that would make her feel further obliged to him. As it was, she could never repay him for the kindness he had shown her.

"There is one other thing that I think you should know," Meg said. "I must warn you not to put much stock in it, because I doubt..."

Pausing, she drew another breath and eyed Molly with unusual wariness. "Sithee, my dear, Wat evidently promised the abbot that you'd have his protection as long as you needed it. Today Father Abbot reminded him of that promise and pointed out that in your situation as it is now, with people likely knowing of your marriage to Tuedy, and then learning that you have declared it illegal..."

"Tell me," Molly demanded when Meg paused.

Bluntly then, Meg said, "His reverence believes that the only sure way to protect you now, from scandal and such, is for Wat to marry you himself."

"Nay," Molly said sharply. "I won't do that. Nor would he!"

After Meg left him in the yard, Wat went to find Tammy. "Any word yet on Gilbert Rutherford?" he demanded.

Tam gave him a shrewd look but said mildly, "Not yet, laird. One o' the lads did say that he'd heard o' someone who kent someone else who kens Gil Rutherford. But I didna set much store by that. I sent a lad t' follow yon priest and see he went straight home t' Henderland," Tammy added. "Father Abbot's man said—"

"You did the right thing," Wat interjected. "Saddle a horse for me, Tam, and another for the lady Molly. I'm going to take her out for a while. It will be just the two of us, so have one of the lads saddle a mount for himself, too, or find Jed."

Tammy nodded, and Wat strode back to the great hall, where he saw Emma with one of the other maidservants. Catching Emma's eye, he summoned her with a gesture and said, "Prithee, go and tell the lady Molly that I will take her riding, if she'd like to go. Be sure that she has a warmer cloak than the one she wore the other day to meet Lady Rosalie. I thought she looked chilly then."

"Aye, sure, laird," Emma said and hurried away.

When she had gone, Wat wondered what had possessed him and what he would do if Molly refused to go. For all he knew, she was still with Lady Meg, and heaven knew how much Meg had told her. He'd have been wiser, he decided belatedly, if he had just talked with Molly himself. At least then he could have controlled what and how much she learned.

The abbot was right. He had not been thinking clearly for some time now. Doubtless, his father's death had affected him more than he'd known.

He was pacing the hall impatiently when movement from the main stairway caught his eye, and he saw Molly coming toward him. She wore the soft primrose-yellow kirtle that she had worn to meet Rosalie, and the same threadbare cloak.

"You won't be warm enough in that cloak," he said.

"Aye, sure, I will," she said. "I wore it the other day to meet Lady Rosalie and did not feel the cold at all."

His lips tightened, but he did not want to argue with her. Since they needed to talk, he would be unwise to anger her before they began. Nor could he let her stir his temper.

Accordingly, he smiled and said, "You know best, lass. I thought we might ride to a wee burn that I know, where some hardy flowers are still growing. Sithee, I think we must talk, and we can talk as well on horseback as we could inside."

"I'd certainly rather ride," she said. "I was accustomed at home to walking or riding out every day. I miss having such daily exercise here."

"Well, you must not go out on your own," he said flatly. "You'd likely bump bang into Tuedy or one of your brothers."

She raised her lovely, dark eyebrows. "I thought you said that your people always warn you of intruders on your land."

"They do, aye," he admitted, remembering that she had heard all he'd said to the men searching for her that first night. "But my lads watch for raiding parties and would pay little heed to noblemen who say they are coming to visit here or crossing my land to visit someone else," he said. "Now, come. I've ordered the horses saddled, and I don't want them standing about, getting chilled."

"Certes, sir, but I am not the one who has kept us standing here."

His lips twitched. He said, "Again, you are right, lass. I'm the one at fault."

⌁

Molly accepted Wat's arm and let him take her from the hall to the stairway. As he led the way down, she admired the way he moved and the way his shoulders filled out the tan shirt beneath his sleeveless leather jack. If anyone was going to get cold . . . However, she had noticed before that he seemed never to heed the weather.

Outside, he offered his forearm to her. As she rested a hand on it, a young groom emerged from the stable leading three horses.

Recognizing one of them with pleasure as the same well-mannered sorrel she had ridden to meet Lady Rosalie, she took her hand from Wat's arm and hurried to greet the horse. The groom made a stirrup with his hands for her, and she mounted easily. Then she watched Wat mount the well-muscled bay that he'd ridden before.

"We will want to talk privily, Oliver," Wat said to the groom as the lad mounted his own horse. "Be sure you keep us in sight, but stay far enough behind us so you don't find yourself overhearing our conversation."

"Aye, laird, I ken that fine."

The tall gates opened, and within minutes the forest had swallowed Scott's Hall behind them. Ramper and Arch ran alongside for a time but then darted into the shrubbery after imagined or scented prey until Wat whistled them back.

Molly watched him peripherally, trying to gauge his mood without staring. He seemed perturbed, and recalling his grandame's words to her, she decided that he must be as annoyed as she was about the abbot's solution to her predicament.

When he had been silent long enough to let the Hall vanish behind them, she said lightly, "If you are trying to think how to tell me that the Abbot of Melrose suggested we marry, sir, I should tell you that her ladyship has already informed me of that absurd scheme. And, as you have likely guessed, I want no part of it."

"You might have no choice," he said bluntly. "I might not, either."

"Blethers," she said, struggling to keep her tone light. "You don't want to marry me any more than I want to marry you, sir. You must choose your own bride, and I strongly doubt that she will be anything like me."

"I made a promise to the abbot."

"Aye, sure, to offer me protection as long as I need it. Her ladyship told me that, too. But surely, you did *not* mean to take me on as a burden for life."

"I'll admit that I didn't mean it the way he is choosing to take it," Wat said. "But I did say the words. I ought to have been clearer about my meaning."

"But you *don't* want to marry me," she said.

"I must think of mine honor, too, Molly. And you do need a husband."

"I don't need any such thing," she said more curtly than she had intended. "In troth, sir, I think your pride rather than your honor is at stake here. I'll wager that you dislike being told what you must do as much as I do."

His lips twitched, and she was relieved to see it. Speaking as sharply as she had had warned her that her temper was stirring. It would not do to lose it with him.

With a sigh, he looked at her. "There is much in what you say, lass. I do tend to resist, strongly, when someone tells me I must do something his way because it is 'the only way' to do it. If that is pride speaking, so be it."

"Then, what now?" she asked him. "You don't want to marry me."

"I have never said that. By my troth, I like you and would welcome you as a friend. I am simply not ready to marry anyone yet."

"Nor am I, as I think I have been at great pains to tell everyone."

"Your case is different," he said flatly. "You cannot go on living under my roof whilst I help you conceal your presence there from your family. Not only might it stir talk, but your father has a right to know where you are."

She wanted to scream at him, not in anger but panic. Fighting the impulse, she said, "But if you tell him, he will order my return and hand me over to Tuedy."

"The abbot has said that he will talk to your father if your daft priest does not, and will explain that that wicked marriage was illegal under every law. Your father will have to accept that, that he cannot force you—"

"If you believe that, you will believe anything," she said with asperity. "My father does as he pleases at Henderland. He has his own laws there, my lord, just as you have your own here. And he kens fine how to make anyone do what he wants them to. Faith, how could anyone stop what he does there, legal or otherwise?"

"He will know that people are watching," Wat said. "That I am."

"But you are as domineering in your way as he is in his!" she exclaimed. "You make decisions, issue orders, and

expect obedience without debate from all around you—
even the sun and the moon, I should think—just as he does.
If you think for a minute that I can withstand him—"

"I meant what I said, Molly," he interjected. "You *will*
have my protection."

"Ah, bah," she snapped. "You *are* like him in *every*
way, thinking your word is law when it is not!" With that,
unable to hear another word, she kicked her horse, leaned
forward, and urged the beast to a gallop through the forest, little heeding where it took her, as long as it took her
away from Wat Scott and Scott's Hall.

~

Muttering a curse, Wat glanced back at the wide-eyed
groom and shouted, "Keep us in sight, Oliver, but don't
interfere."

Without waiting for an answer, he gave his mount a
touch of his whip and followed her.

She could certainly ride, but what a vixen! To berate
him as she had when she was the one losing her temper
and spouting absurdities! When had he ever tried to command the sun or the moon? The woman was daft.

Doubtless he had offended her by admitting that he did
not want to marry. He had never been so rude as to say
that he did *not* want to marry *her*. He had taken care to
say only that he was not ready to marry anyone.

Sakes, he had even said that he liked her, and he did.
How could he not? How could any man not? She was
extremely attractive, even with scratches and that finally
fading bruise on her cheek.

She was also intelligent and delightfully witty when
she wanted to be (and sometimes when she didn't). But

she was *not* the woman he wanted to marry. She was too quick to speak her mind, for one thing.

Naturally, he did not want a simpleton, but neither did he want someone who would ride off in such a dangerous way. Nor did he want one who would rant at him as she had. Her father or brothers would have smacked her for such impertinence.

That thought dammed up the tumbling stream of such thoughts in its course. In its place, a vision leaped to his mind of how Piers Cockburn, not to mention his iniquitous sons, was likely to greet Molly if she did have to go home.

Despite his mental perplexity, Wat had not lost sight of her. Even if he had, Ramper's enthusiastic barking as he careened after her would have shown him the way. She seemed to be riding blindly, heedless of the terrain, but had had sense enough to give her mount its head. The animal was as savvy and surefooted as any other Border pony. But if it put its foot in a burrow or gopher hole...

The thought sent chills up Wat's spine, and he urged the bay to a faster pace.

"By heaven," he muttered, "if she *were* my wife..."

Then, suddenly, ahead of him, Molly's horse reared, and he saw her wrench its head to her right and bring it to a plunging halt. At the same time, he realized that she had nearly run headlong into a party of other riders, coming toward her.

Slowing his mount, Wat fought to rein in his temper.

Chapter 11 ————————————

Good sakes, Molly, do you always ride so recklessly?" Lady Rosalie demanded. "I vow, you frightened my poor palfrey nearly out of its skin. What reason could you possibly have to be riding so fast through this forest?"

The palfrey had already calmed, Molly noted. But that was small comfort.

"'Tis only by God's mercy that you weren't harmed, madam," Len Gray said tersely, urging his horse nearer Rosalie's. "As for this foolish young woman—"

"I beg your pardon, my lady," Molly interjected, still breathless. "I did not expect to meet anyone else in these woods."

"Now, see here—" Gray began.

It was neither Lady Rosalie nor Len Gray who drew Molly's attention then but the long-limbed man with graying red curls beside her ladyship. Sym Elliot's stern gaze disconcerted her more than Lady Rosalie's complaints or Gray's displeasure had, because the way Sym was looking at her stirred memory of Emma's saying that her dad had threatened to have the skin off her if she behaved badly enough to vex him.

Molly wondered if Sym was having similar thoughts now about *her*. She certainly wasn't going to ask him.

Then Wat's chilly voice right behind her banished all thought of anyone else.

He said in a tone that brooked no discussion, "Take Lady Rosalie and her party home, Sym. Take Oliver, too. I'll bring Lady Molly with me."

"Aye, laird," Sym said with a glance at Lady Rosalie as he lifted his reins and urged his mount forward.

"But surely, my lord, we must explain to her young ladyship how badly she frightened us," Len Gray said haughtily. "No female should ever ride so wildly, as I am sure you will agree."

"Will I?" Wat asked, his tone so icy now that Molly shivered.

Gray apparently recognized the folly of trying to pursue the conversation. When Lady Rosalie said with amusement, "Come along, Len," he nodded and followed her and Sym as they took the lead and vanished into the trees.

The nearby forest had fallen silent. Even the dogs were still.

Molly felt another shiver and a strong desire to look anywhere but at Wat.

"Get down," he said.

Swallowing hard, she managed to say, "What are you going to do?"

"*We* are going to talk," he said in that same chilling tone. "I just want to make sure that you won't do such a hare-brained thing as to ride off like that again whilst we do."

"I was angry," she said to the arch of her horse's neck.

"And you will likely be angry again," he said. "Can you get down by yourself, or shall I help you?"

Aware that any attempt to escape would be futile but

unsure that she could trust him only to talk, she hesitated long enough to hear a near growl from him.

Knowing she had to answer him, she said, "We're just going to talk?"

"Aye, lass," he said. A touch of weariness entered his voice as he added, "I ken fine that it may be hard for you to trust me, or anyone, come to that. But we must talk this out, and I can't have you endangering my horses."

She stiffened. "Your *horses*!"

He dismounted, dropped his reins, and moved toward her. "Get down, Molly, or I swear, I'll pull you off of that animal, myself."

In answer, she leaned over the horse's neck, swung her right leg over its rump, and slid to the ground in front of Wat. Still gripping her reins in her left hand, she avoided his gaze.

Silence hovered between them for several long moments before Wat put his hands on her shoulders and, although she expected him to shake her, said quietly, "Don't *ever* do that again. You frightened me witless."

"I didn't think," she admitted, staring at his broad chest. "I just wanted to get away. I don't like other people making decisions for me, especially people I scarcely know."

"Look at me."

She drew a breath, aware that he likely thought she was being childish. But she was too aware now of how close he was and of the warmth of his hands on her shoulders, to think properly. She could smell the spicy scent of his clothes. She could hear him breathe. And she could feel her own heart still pounding hard.

She did not want to see his anger. Hearing it in his voice was bad enough.

A bird chirped in the distance.

"Molly."

She raised her eyes to his chin and saw his lips pressed tightly together. A small dimple revealed itself a half-inch or so below and to the left of his mouth.

He put a warm hand under her chin and raised it, forcing her to meet his gaze or shut her eyes.

She licked her lips and drew a shuddering breath.

"Ah, lassie, you mustn't fear me," he said quietly. "I may not be keen on marrying just now, but my promise to you is good, as was my promise to the abbot. I know that I told you I never meant I'd take responsibility for the rest of your life. And 'tis true that the abbot took that very meaning and did so without considering your feelings or mine. But I gave him cause by not making myself plain. We cannot know the future, but you are welcome to stay at the Hall for as long as you like. Mam and Gram will provide all the protection your reputation requires, and I will protect you from your kinsmen, however I must."

"Thank you," she muttered, wondering why, instead of feeling reassured, she felt an unexpected wave of disappointment.

What did she want from the man? Certainly not marriage and what else could a woman hope for from a man unrelated to her *but* marriage?

He drew a finger along her cheek. "Don't look so sad," he said.

"You were so angry." The words were out before she could stop them, before she realized how much it meant to her that he had been angry and frightened for her safety. Also, that he had admitted *being* frightened.

"I was furious, lass, and I'll doubtless be angry again,

too," he said. "But I won't harm you. Nevertheless, you must not dash off by yourself as you did, on a horse or without one. This is the second time I know of that you have tried to run away. You must not make it a habit, or you will make me very angry indeed."

Those words stirred new feelings in her, unfamiliar but pleasant ones, and she began to wonder if she was losing her senses or just mixing them all up.

Without thinking, she put a hand to his arm, noting how hard his muscles were as she looked into his eyes and said with deep sincerity, "I'm sorry I frightened you. I don't think clearly when I'm angry. In troth, I fear that whenever my temper gets the better of me, I do try to get away, but only to try and calm myself. Losing my temper has often…"

She paused when his expression altered rather strangely.

"You should not look at a man like that unless you want him to kiss you," he said softly.

"But I do," she replied honestly and without hesitation. "No man has kissed me since my granddad died, and I think I would like you to, if you don't mind."

A voice deep within Wat shouted a warning of where such a kiss might lead, but he ignored it, cupping her chin again with one hand while he drew her closer with the other. Then, gently and ever so slowly, savoring the moment for himself, he lowered his mouth to hers and kissed her.

Her rosy lips were feather soft and warm against his own. Her slender body snuggled against his and seemed to fit there unusually well. When she moved her lips beneath his, kissing him back, he shifted the hand that had cupped her chin to cradle her head beneath her veil, marveling at the soft silkiness of her hair.

She moved her lips as if to taste different parts of his, and another part of his body stirred strongly in response.

The urge to take her then and there nearly overpowered him, and as much to distract himself from that dangerous urge as to answer the invitation her lips were offering, he pressed his tongue between them and began to explore the intriguing, moist interior of her mouth.

She gave a gasp, then seemed to stop breathing. But when he continued his exploration undaunted, she inhaled with a moan and touched her tongue to his.

Her breath was whisper soft and clean, and her breasts pressed against him, tantalizing him and making his fingers itch to stroke them. That thought provided stronger warning than the voice in his head that he was treading dangerous ground.

Remembering his vow to protect her but wise enough not to break their embrace too abruptly, he eased his tongue from her mouth. Then he kissed her more lightly on the lips and again on her forehead.

"We must go back, lass. I should not have done that, but I'm not sorry I did."

"*We* did it, sir," she said, looking solemnly into his eyes. "Faith, I invited it."

He shook his head at her. "Believe me, if my father were still alive, and I were to tell him exactly how it happened, he would have much to say to me, none of which I'd want to hear. But I'd deserve every word."

"Sadly, he is not here to scold you," she said.

"Aye, but Westruther will give me an earful if *he* hears

about it. You are an inexperienced maiden who was naturally curious, whilst I am…"

"…much experienced at such things?" she said for him when he paused.

"More experienced than you, I'd wager," he said with a sudden grin. "But we are not going to discuss my experience, now or ever, my lass."

"Well, I am not your lass, but I can understand that you would not want to talk about what you have done with other women," she said. "Is that why Father Jonathan said that if I stay here, Tuedy might accuse you of wife stealing?"

His grin vanished in a trice, and she knew she had made a grievous error.

The ice was back in his voice when he said, "Do you often listen at doors?"

Meeting his gaze, she said ruefully, "Not often. But, sometimes, it is the only way to learn what the men at home are thinking. It has often saved my hide. Even so, I knew I should not do it. I just couldn't stop myself."

He held her gaze for a long moment, silently. She had the feeling that he was looking deep inside her, that he could see things there that she had thought she had hidden away from everyone. She could not even blink but gazed seriously back.

"At least you are honest," he said at last. "I think I can see how you came to do such things, but that does not mean that I will tolerate them."

"Are you still angry with me?"

"Only if you mean to continue listening at doors, careering through this forest on horseback, or running away when circumstances are not to your liking."

"Then I will try to avoid doing those things," she said, still solemn.

He put an arm around her shoulders and gave her a gentle squeeze. "Then we are friends again. I suggest that we go home now before Gram comes looking for us or sends Westruther after us."

"Mercy, would she do either of those things?"

"What do you think?"

Her eyes widened, making him smile again.

~

Molly's senses were whirling, and she knew the sensation had nothing to do with Lady Meg or whether she might come in search of them or not.

It had everything to do with Wat Scott and that kiss.

She had never imagined putting her tongue in someone else's mouth. The thought of such a thing would doubtless have repulsed her before now. But who could possibly imagine that when Wat did it, it could stir so many never-before-experienced, certainly unimagined, feelings throughout her body.

After he released her, she stood where she was, staring at him and wondering what had just happened to her. Why had she so impulsively wanted to kiss him in the first place? And why had he been able to make her feel so?

The one thing that Tuedy had not done was kiss her. She knew that husbands and wives did usually kiss each other, though, whether they were noble or common.

Tuedy had wanted only to paw her and intimidate her, to make her obey him. To be sure, he might have thought of kissing her had she not made her antipathy to him as plain as she had. But antipathy was the feeling she had experienced with most men. Until Walter Scott had found her.

"Molly, why are you just standing here? We need to go."

He was gazing at her in bewilderment, so she gave herself a mental shake and decided that she was just reacting to the first kind man she had met in a long while. "I don't know why," she said straightening her shoulders and forcing a smile. "Will you help me mount my horse?"

"Aye, sure," he said. Cupping his hands to make a stirrup for her left foot, he held her steady while she caught the sorrel's mane and swung her right leg over its rump to ride astride as she had before.

Although he handed her reins to her, she waited while he mounted his horse and whistled for Ramper and Arch, who had vanished into the shrubbery after scents. Then, as he turned toward the Hall, she said quietly, "I wanted only to see what kissing was like, sir. It did not change the way I feel about marriage."

Such a lie that statement was that she felt the warmth in her cheeks spread through her body. It was as if blushes covered her skin from tip to toe, although she had never known blushes to do any such thing.

Fortunately, he was not looking at her but watching for the dogs. Nor did he look at her until he said, "I ken that fine, lass. 'Tis just as well, too. I've no time for a wife, because I've too much else to do. You will recall that the King wants me to lay a notorious reiver by the heels. Until I find that villainous creature, I'll have time for little else."

She nodded, remembering that his men were seeking such a man, and they spoke of ordinary things until they reached the Hall. Then, he escorted her inside only to find Sym Elliot awaiting them.

Sym smiled at Molly and said to Wat, "Herself wants to see ye, sir."

"I'll go to her straightaway," Wat said.

Summoning a lad, he sent him to find Emma and then said, "Go up to the solar, Molly. You'll find Janet and Bella there now, and Emma will find you."

He gestured for her to precede him. As she did, she told herself that, just as she had surmised, he was like any other man, giving orders without a thought for what she might have preferred to do.

Not that there *was* anything like that, but it would not have mattered to him if there had been. It was just as well that he did not want to marry her, nor she him.

~

Wat followed Molly only as far as the landing outside Lady Meg's sitting room. He paused there, though, long enough to watch as Molly silently rounded the next turn of the stair and wonder what she was thinking.

Reminding himself that she was entitled to her thoughts and had no reason to share them, he rapped once on the door and opened it.

"So you are back," Lady Meg said, setting down her needlework. "Did you enjoy a pleasant ride?"

Deducing from this greeting that neither Sym nor his aunt Rosalie had spoken to her yet of their meeting—the startling nature of it, at least—he said, "It was invigorating to ride in the forest again with no duty demanded of me."

"As to duty, love, have you learned aught more about that reiver?"

"I don't recall telling you about Gilbert Rutherford," Wat said with a knowing smile. "I must suppose that Sym did."

"Should he not have done so?" she asked, raising her eyebrows.

He chuckled. "What would you do if I said he should not?"

"You know very well that he tells me all he knows. And I doubt that short of hanging him, you could stop him, which I doubt you would do."

"It would never occur to me, Gram. I owe Sym too much. Although, if memory serves me, he did put me across his knee a few times when I was young."

"Aye, because your father and I both told him he should if the occasion arose. We trusted him then, and I trust him now."

"As do I. So why did you ask me about Rutherford?"

"I recalled the King's presence at Melrose whilst I was thinking about the abbot, and my thoughts flew next to Rutherford, that's all," she said. "His reverence put you in a bit of a corner today, though, did he not?"

"He tried to put both Molly and me in a corner, and I suspect that you tried to aid him by telling Molly what he had suggested," he said bluntly.

"I had no such intention," she replied. "I do believe that Molly deserved to know we were discussing her future. She has that right, Walter."

"Aye, but I was right in saying that she'd not take kindly to the idea."

"You were. So did she tell you to your face that she won't marry you?"

"She did, and I only made it worse when I tried to

explain my position. I shan't tell you the details, but she did something rather dangerous."

"Mercy me," Lady Meg said. But her eyes were twinkling.

"It was not funny then, I promise you," Wat said. "I told her that I agree with her about our marrying but will do all I can to protect her from her ill-willed family for as long as she requires protection. I still disagree that only marriage can save her reputation. She is clearly an innocent. Anyone of sense can see *that* at a glance."

"True, but you cannot go on keeping her whereabouts from her father."

"I agree, so I will ride to see him tomorrow," Wat said. "If you have any advice you can offer me about engaging with him, I'd welcome it."

"Just remember that Piers and your father were good friends before the King's return from his English captivity," Meg said. "Even after they realized how strongly they disagreed about Jamie's intention to curtail the powers of many of his nobles, your father managed to stay on good terms with Piers *and* with Jamie."

Wat grimaced. "I'll find it hard to forget the way Cockburn has treated Molly. Thanks to the way her menfolk behave, she finds it hard to trust any man."

"Then whoever her future husband may be, you will be doing him a great favor if you can teach her to trust you," Meg said gently. "To do that, you must first learn to trust yourself and your own instincts. It might also help to consider that you can do her *no* good by further alienating her father."

Wat remained silent, thinking about her words.

"I might tell you something more about your granddad,"

Meg said, instantly regaining his attention. "You have heard the tale of our marriage."

"That he was caught reiving and given the option of marrying you or hanging," Wat said with a smile. "I'm glad he made the choice he did."

"I, too," Meg said. "But I was dead set against it then. Not that I had any choice. My mother said the marriage would be good for our family, and that was that. Afterward, my father fairly shoved the two of us into my bedchamber together. Then he stood outside the door, listening. We could hear him there."

Wat choked off a laugh. "I warrant Granddad said a few words about that."

"Let us just say that he resolved things," she said. "My reason for mentioning it, though, is to help you understand Molly's frustration. Imagine if you can how you'd feel if the abbot had the same right to order you to marry Molly that my parents had to order me to marry your granddad."

"It is not the same, Gram."

"Why not? Simply because you are male and Molly and I are female?"

"Aye, sure. It is a father's duty to find husbands for his daughters. And when he does, it is their duty to obey him and marry them."

"Not according to the law as it has stood in Scotland for centuries past," Meg said. "Scottish women have rights, too, my laddie, and you know that."

"They do get rather mixed up with a father's rights, though, don't they?"

"A loving father has no difficulty finding a path through the maze, Walter. Nor will a loving brother when that time comes, I think."

"I suppose you are right," he said. "In any event, Molly understands that no one here means to force her to do anything she dislikes."

"Then we understand each other," Meg said.

Rather cryptically, Wat thought.

But he did not question her. His thoughts had already shifted back to Gilbert Rutherford. An idea had occurred to him that he wanted to discuss with Tam.

Excusing himself, he said, "When you see Sym, Gram, prithee tell him I'd like a word with him when he has a moment. I'll be with Tammy."

~

As Wat had said she would, Molly found Janet and Bella in the solar with their lady mother and their stitchery. Molly had seen little of her hostess, so she was pleased to see Lady Scott looking well rested, if rather solemn and quiet.

Janet was quiet, too, but Bella was restless enough to draw a rare look of censure from her older sister.

Making a saucy face at her, Bella welcomed Molly's entrance with, "I am glad to see you. It has been gey dull in here and I am tired of stitching hems."

"I'll work on yours for a time if you like," Molly said. "Good afternoon, your ladyship," she added, making her curtsy to Lady Scott.

"You need stand on no ceremony with me, Molly," her ladyship said. "You are our guest and therefore must make yourself comfortable here."

The words were gracious, but Molly had the distinct feeling that Lady Scott said them only for civility's sake. Nevertheless, she thanked her with sincere gratitude for the safety that Scott's Hall provided her.

"One doubts that you want to spend your time hemming sheets, though," Lady Scott added. "Bella should attend to her own chores."

"I don't mind, my lady. I enjoy such tasks, because I can let my thoughts wander whilst I do them. It is even more pleasant to do them here at the Hall, where I have other women to bear me company."

"Molly has no other females to talk to at home, Mam," Bella said.

"How unfortunate," Lady Scott said. "None at all?"

"We do have two women who come in to aid the cook and see to some of the heavier chores," Molly said. "But they come only by day. It is rare for any family to let their women stay in our tower overnight."

"But why not?" Bella demanded.

"That will do, Bella," her mother said. "One must not be inquisitive."

"But how can I learn things if I may not ask?"

"I don't mind, my lady," Molly said.

"It is not a suitable subject for tender ears," Lady Scott said.

Bella's eyebrows shot upward, making Molly certain that the younger girl would find opportunity to ask her again. As it was, Janet changed the subject to a safer one, and a few minutes later, Emma came in.

She said, "Herself would like ye to visit wi' her for a time, Lady Molly."

"I'll go when I finish this hem, Emma," Molly said. "I've only inches to go."

Emma waited patiently, and Molly soon tied off her thread and stood.

"Should I tidy my hair, Emma, or will I do?"

"Ye'll do. Herself isna used t' waiting long," Emma warned.

Molly smiled. "Then, let us hurry, aye?"

⌐⌐⌐⌐

Wat found Tammy leaning against a stall in the stable with his brawny arms folded across his chest and one ankle crossed over the other. He was watching one of the younger lads curry the horse that Molly had ridden.

"I have an idea, Tam," Wat said. "Come to the tack-room where we can talk."

"I've learned summat, too, laird," Tam said. "I were talking to Sym," he went on as he followed Wat to the far end of the stable and into the room where they kept most of the gear. "He tells me Rutherford were seen in Redesdale nobbut a sennight ago. Afore that, he were farther east. What I be thinking—"

"He's moving westward, aye," Wat said. "Did he raid in Scotland or in England before Redesdale?"

"Scotland," Tam said. "He'll avoid anyplace near Berwick if he's wise. Too many English soldiers there. Nor will he venture through any o' the larger towns."

"Likely you're right about that. Sithee, I've been thinking that, rather than looking for the man, we might draw him closer to us."

Tam frowned. "To raid us?"

"To suggest it, aye. We might let him think I'm moving horses or kine to Rankilburn, perhaps from Kirkurd, since I mean to visit there tomorrow. Or mayhap we could say I'm moving kine from here to Melrose."

"Methinks that would sound more likely," Tam said.

"Aye, it might. Rutherford must know that we Scotts

help support the abbey. The trick would be to get word out and about without being too obvious about it."

Tammy grinned. "We'll need Sym, then, won't we? The man kens every road, path, and deer's track in the Borders. On both sides o' the line, come to that."

Wat nodded. "He's studied them since he was a bairn when he took more than a few licks for his explorations, he said."

"True, but his knowledge has proved useful to us afore now and will likely be useful again. Moreover, he kens near everyone for miles and can drop a word here and there where such words will be useful."

"Exactly what I want," Wat agreed. "I don't mean to travel with kine, though, just to give Rutherford reason to head toward us, rather than away."

"Ye'll be wantin' a full tail when ye ride t' Henderland and Kirkurd, tomorrow, aye?"

Wat hesitated, but he knew Tam was right. To take only his usual six men would be foolish when he did not know what reception he would meet at Henderland.

Chapter 12 _____

Dismissing Emma at the sitting-room landing, Molly entered to find Lady Meg standing by the window at the far end of the room, looking out. As Molly shut the door, Meg turned and said, "Come right in, my dear. I understand that you had an interesting ride today."

Feeling a twinge of anxiety, Molly forced herself to meet Meg's steady gaze and said ruefully, "I suppose that the lady Rosalie must have told you what happened, madam. I am—"

"Nay, nay," Meg interjected, coming toward her. "Rosalie stopped in here long enough only to tell me that she had returned, ordered a bath, and intended to wash her hair. She was never a talebearer, even as a child. I should be amazed if she were to begin now."

"Then..." Absurdly distressed by the thought that Wat might have told her, Molly almost named him but thought better of it.

She was glad that she had when Lady Meg smiled warmly and said, "Walter did not tell me, either. My informant...Ah, but I see that you've guessed. You have a most expressive face, my dear."

Realizing with another tickle of trepidation that Meg

had a more discerning eye than Cockburn or her brothers did, Molly said, "I remembered that people have reason to call him 'Lady Meg's Sym.' I gave thanks at the time, too, that I was not his daughter," she added. "I am not the only one with an expressive face."

"Nay, Sym's has always revealed his feelings," Meg said with a twinkle. "I expect your wild ride did stir thoughts of retribution in his head. But you need never fear Sym, or Wat, although I'd wager he was angry, too."

Remembering that icy anger and then his kiss, Molly felt heat flood her cheeks again. "He *was* angry, aye," she said. "His voice froze the marrow in my bones. But he is kind, my lady. Despite his anger, I could still talk to him. He even let me offer an explanation with my apology, which is unusual for a man, I think."

"Aye, he is a good listener, is Wat, and one cannot say that of many men. My father rarely listened to what we said. He..." She paused, then said calmly, "But we are talking about Wat. I feared that if he scolded you, you might feel unwanted here, or as if you were imposing."

"I don't," Molly said. "Even Lady Scott said she wants me to be contented. And Janet and Bella make wonderful friends. I own, though, that I am a trifle concerned that Wat—Walter, that is—means to tell my father that I'm here."

"You do see why he must, though," Meg said, moving from the window to her usual seat and gesturing toward the stool opposite her.

"I trust him not to stir coals," Molly said, taking the seat. "But my father is not the only one who worries me. My brothers..." Fear swept through her, choking off her words. She spread her hands.

"I see. Cannot your father control them?"

"In troth, I no longer know the answer to that question. He controlled them easily when they were young. But now, Will and Ned are big men, too. And Will takes orders from no one.

"He rarely defies Father to his face," Molly went on. "He just takes his own road and makes his own friends. And Ned is like his shadow. Will was the one who decided I must marry Ringan Tuedy."

"I see," Meg said again. "I'm glad you've told me this, Molly. I want to learn as much about you as I can. I missed so much of your life, fearing that I'd draw Piers's ire down on both of us if I spoke up." Shaking her head, she added, "Rarely am I such a coward, but Marjory's own inability to tell him she had named me your godmother daunted me."

"I don't blame you, my lady. When my father is in a fury, he can terrify anyone. And Will…" Feeling another shiver up her spine at the thought of Will, Molly shook her head and fell silent.

"I see that the men in your life have been poor examples of the creatures," Meg said in a lighter tone. "I hope you will not judge all men you meet by them."

"How could I?" Molly asked. "I have met Lord Westruther, who is very kind, and his lordship. Come to that, the men who live and work here are all different from those at Henderland. Yours are respectful and kind. I have not met one who has behaved disrespectfully to me or to anyone else."

"Nor will you if our lads know what's good for them," Meg said tartly.

Molly smiled. "I did hear that you'd hand them their heads in their laps."

"So I would, if Wat did not do so before me," Meg said. "Now, tell me what you remember about your grandmother Marjory. Then I will share some of my memories of her, as well."

The time passed so comfortably after that that Molly was startled when Sym rapped on the door to ask if they were coming down to supper.

"I must change my dress," Molly said hastily as she stood.

"There is no need," Meg replied. "We do not stand on ceremony at supper."

Nevertheless, Molly felt that telltale heat in her cheeks again when she stepped onto the dais and her gaze collided with Wat's.

Turning swiftly away, only to find Lady Meg eyeing her speculatively, she collected her wits and said, "Do you expect Lady Scott this evening, madam?"

Learning that her ladyship had declined to come downstairs, Molly moved to her usual place. She noted gratefully then that Bella and Janet were entering the hall.

Later, when she was alone in her chamber, her thoughts flew back to the forest and lingered on Wat's kiss. She wondered if she might dream about him, then called herself a fool for thinking such a thing. One thing was certain, though. She had been wrong, very wrong, to believe that the man was not dangerous.

He was climbing a mountain taller than any he had seen before. Indeed, the mist-occluded peak seemed to grow taller the nearer he came to it. More oddly yet, the sunset had turned the gauzy mist and the peak within it an orange-gold color.

As he watched, the peak turned pure gold and re-formed itself into a chair or royal throne. A figure took shape on it then. It was not the square-built figure of his grace but someone more slender, more curvaceous, more graceful. Finally, obviously, it became a young female sitting there.

His lips burned with sudden memory. His body stirred below as if it remembered the young woman before he could make out her features.

He saw her hair first, in plaits, the way Bella wore hers. The sun's last strong rays outlined the young woman's plaits in gilt.

She beckoned to him.

Abruptly, without sensing movement, he stood before her.

The throne was no longer a throne but a two-elbow chair, just like his own at the high table, which still felt so alien, as if his lord father were not ready yet to relinquish it, despite being in his coffin and six feet underground.

Daringly—at least, it felt daring—he extended a hand to the lass. When she put her much smaller, much more fragile hand in his, he drew her to her feet.

Her eyes widened, their irises pure gold now, her pupils expanding until they narrowed the gold to just a rim for each enormous pupil. Her rosy lips parted.

He could bear it no longer. Sweeping her up into his arms, he strode forward. The chair vanished. Beyond it by a pace or two stood a curtained bed. Its curtains parted invitingly, and he was not a man to reject that welcome invitation.

Their clothing had apparently vanished with the chair or as they swiftly and magically made their way into the bed. He could feel her, warm in his arms and against his body, as hungry for him as he was for her. His lips found *hers, and he knew instantly that he would recognize the taste of her in pure black darkness, anywhere, anytime.*

She moaned softly, her tongue pressing against his lips, seeking entrance. As he willingly allowed it, his right hand stroked her silken body, moving lower and lower, to see if she would offer reciprocal submission below. Her skin grew hotter to his touch, and when he reached the soft curls at the juncture of her legs..."

...curtain rings rattling on their rod startled him awake in a dark room. The shadowy shape of his man loomed beside the bed, shoving the bed curtains aside.

"Jed! What the *devil* are you doing here at such an hour?" Wat demanded.

Stepping hastily back from the bed, Jed raised both hands. "I didna mean t' startle ye, sir. But ye did tell me last night that I should wake ye early, so ye could ride to Henderland today. Be Lord Westruther a-riding wi' ye?"

"Part of the way, along Ettrick Water," Wat muttered, rubbing sleep from his eyes. "I'll follow it to Tushielaw, then ride through Cross Cleuch to St. Mary's Loch. He'll follow Ettrick Water to the Tweed and Melrose, then home from there."

Glancing toward the shuttered window, Wat noted a slight lessening of the darkness through cracks in the shutters, suggesting the incipient gray light of dawn. In the silence that had fallen, he heard a soft hushing sound outside.

"Is it raining?"

"So far, aye," Jed said. "Me da says it will turn intae snow if it gets much colder. Ye'll be wanting oilskins, heavy gloves, and your good cloak."

"If it's cold enough to snow, I'll also want the red wool cap that the lady Janet knitted for me."

Nodding, Jed moved to pour hot water into the basin and to fetch a fresh towel. He remained silent, a sign that he was still wary of his master's mood.

But Wat was awake now, although remnants of his dream lingered. His skin tingled where he had felt the warmth of her body. His cock stood alert, too, until the chilly air struck it—when he shoved the covers back—and lowered it to half mast.

An hour later, having broken his fast and collected his tail of a dozen men-at-arms, and Westruther's, the two set out in the continuing rain. They parted company when Wat and his men forded Ettrick Water to continue northwest to Henderland, and Westruther continued along Ettrick Water with his own men.

While Wat's party stayed in the forest, the rain was just a nuisance dripping through the canopy. But when they emerged from Cross Cleuch into thinning trees above the narrow, southwest tip of St. Mary's Loch, they felt the rain's full force.

"Cockburn's tower be yonder," Geordie said, pointing across the loch.

"Still a mile or more to go then," Wat said, peering through the rain.

"Aye," Geordie said. "Tam did say that this loch be three miles long, southwest to northeast, but scarcely a half-mile across at its widest point."

They entered denser woodland again as they descended into the vale and skirted the loch's southern tip.

When they came to a narrow, bubbling, rain-dotted burn, Geordie said, "That will be Megget Water, Tam said. The tower lies ahead, up on the brae."

The tower became visible as they forded the burn, and

Wat saw that flatter ground lay below it near the confluence of the Megget Water with the loch. The tall keep was massive but offered little that he found of architectural interest. It was ominous looking, though, looming as it did through the icy rain.

As Wat peered at it, a snowflake drifted past his nose. He sighed. The last thing he wanted to do was to beg hospitality from Piers Cockburn.

"I didna think to ask Tam where they keep their stables," Geordie said.

"I ken where they be, now that I see the place," a man called Aggie's Pete, with shaggy corn-colored hair, said from behind them. "I came here twice wi' the auld laird," he added. "There be a low building and a stockade farther up the cleuch for their beasts. They should ha' room for ours, too, laird."

Thanking him, Wat led the way to the tower. Before they reached it, two riders came toward them from behind it.

"Geordie, you and I will ride ahead and meet them," Wat said, raising a hand to stop the others.

They met the two armed riders near the loch, and Wat told them who he was. "Is your laird at home to visitors?" he asked.

"Aye, m'lord, and pleased he'll be tae see ye," the spokesman said. "We were all shocked tae learn o' Rankilburn's death."

"He is a great loss to us all," Wat said.

Signaling his men to follow, Wat rode with Cockburn's men up past the tower to a graveled yard. There he dismounted and said quietly, "Geordie, I'll take Aggie's Pete and Kip in with me. You stay with the others, and keep your eyes and ears open. I don't trust the Cockburns at all."

"Nae one does," Geordie muttered. "Even the auld laird trod softly here, they say, man o' peace though he was. I'll learn what I can from them whilst I tend to the beasts."

Wat nodded, knowing that Geordie had a knack for picking up odd bits of information. And, since they were still hunting for Rutherford...

He had no more time for thought then, because one of the two men who had met them was waving him toward the tower. Aggie's Pete and a younger lad named Kip Graham followed Wat across the yard to the timber stairs leading to the main entry.

When their leader shoved the thick wooden door open to let them in, Wat noted the heavy iron yett against the torchlit wall, ready to swing into place and, if necessary, to bolt into the entry wall, further strengthening that thick door.

Glancing up, he half-expected to see a portcullis like the two at Hermitage Castle, ready to drop into place and trap an unwary visitor.

The ceiling revealed only bare stonework.

They went up six steps, through an archway, into the great hall. Even by torchlight, the lack of feminine influence was clear. Men's gear lay everywhere. The only sign of tidiness was the stack of about a dozen pallets by the huge fireplace.

Six men squatted by the fire, rolling dice. Others played board or table games.

"Laird, ye've a visitor!" their escort bellowed in tones worthy of the royal chamberlain.

"If he's friendly, dry him before the fire," a male voice shouted from behind the privacy screen on the dais. "If he's not, throw him back outside."

"It be the new Lord o' Rankilburn," the man-at-arms shouted back.

Piers Cockburn came around the screen. About fifty years old, he had a lined, leathery face, dark hair and eyebrows, and a rangy, loose-jointed frame. His midsection suggested more interest in eating than fighting. Peering down the length of the hall at his chief visitor, he displayed an air of dour inflexibility.

"If ye're dry under them skins," he growled, "I've whisky tae warm ye. Just leave your men by the fire and come up for a swig—or a guzzle, come tae that."

Wat nodded, handed his oilskin and cloak to Kip, and muttered, "Keep these with you, and stay alert. They seem friendly, but we'll take nowt for granted."

At least, he thought as Kip and Pete moved to join the dicing men at the fire, no one had tried to take their weapons. He had his small sword and his dirk.

Striding to the dais, he stepped onto it and moved around the screen. The welcome aroma of roasting meat wafted from the archway at the end of the dais, so he was surprised that neither Will nor Ned Cockburn sat at the table. Judging by his rumbling stomach, it was about time for the midday meal.

Piers Cockburn sat alone with a jug and two mugs before him.

As Wat approached him to draw out a stool, Cockburn poured amber liquid into a mug, shoved it toward him, and lifted his own mug to his lips.

"I were sorry tae hear about your da, lad," Cockburn

said almost affably, setting his mug down with a clunk. "He were a good man. Weak-minded about summat and nowt but kind and peaceful withal. I've heard ye be of a different cut."

"Thank you for receiving me, my lord," Wat said politely. "I'm gey grateful for the whisky, too. The rain is turning to sleet with a few snowflakes added."

"Ye're welcome tae stay the night," Cockburn said. "Me own lads be away the noo, but they'll likely return on the morrow."

"I thank you for the offer, sir, but I must return to the Hall," Wat said. "As you may imagine, I have much to do and much to learn before I will be confident about acceding to my lord father's place."

"Then ye must ha' had good reason for coming out in this weather."

Having hoped to ease into the subject of Molly, Wat was nonetheless willing to take a straightforward course. Thinking swiftly, he said, "I met Will and Ned in the forest the night after my father's death."

"I did hear that, aye."

"They were riding with Ring Tuedy," Wat continued, aware of his host's narrowing gaze. "Will said they sought a maidservant who had lost her way."

"Did he now?"

"Aye, sir, so imagine my shock to discover that your daughter, the lady Margaret, had fled Henderland."

"And how did ye come by such news?"

"You will be relieved to hear that she is safe at Scott's Hall with my mother and my grandame," Wat said. Sipping his whisky, he swallowed and added lightly, "My grandame, the lady Margaret Scott, was a close friend of your own mother, as you must know. Evidently, she is also Molly's godmother and was glad to take her under her wing. She has invited Molly to stay with us as long as she likes."

"I'm thinking that our Molly failed to tell ye a thing or two," Cockburn said. "She's married to Ring Tuedy, and he's displeased that she's run off. If ye're wise, lad, ye'll be bringing her back here straightaway. Ye'll no want to be making an enemy o' Tuedy. Nae sensible man wants that."

"Molly has officially declared her marriage illegal," Wat said mildly, as if such declarations were perfectly natural.

"Blethers! Me own priest performed that wedding."

"But Father Jonathan admitted that Will gagged Molly and forced her to nod her head. That makes the marriage illegal under Scottish law and the Kirk's laws, as well. Mayhap you were unaware that Will forced her."

Cockburn bristled and looked as if he would fervently deny any lack of such knowledge. Instead, he hesitated, frowned, and said, "I might look further into that if me lass comes home and tells me all this herself."

"Molly is afraid to come here. Her bruises and scars support that fear."

Cockburn shrugged. "As I ken the matter, if a man takes a wife and doesna declare her unchaste, that marriage is legal however it happened. Me own opinion is that she belongs to Tuedy now. 'Tis likely that he'll declare it perfectly legal."

Wat took another sip of whisky and said, "I won't stay to debate the matter, sir. I'd suggest instead that you talk with your priest. Perhaps you might also talk with the Abbot of Melrose before you make a song about this."

"Be davers, what does that auld devil ha' to do wi' this?"

"You will have to ask his reverence," Wat replied, setting down his mug. "I came here because I thought you would be worried about Molly. You were also my father's friend. So both honor and duty demanded that I tell you she is safe."

"I thank ye for that," Cockburn said grimly. "I'll tell ye another thing, too. Ye lack all o' your father's good sense if ye think ye can steal Tuedy's wife from him. And that's being kind, me lad. Fact is ye're nobbut a wife-stealing dafty."

"We'll see," Wat said quietly as he stood. "I will take my leave now, sir. I thank you again for the whisky and the warmth of your hall."

"Sure ye willna stay the night?" Cockburn said, wolfishly baring his teeth.

~

That gloomy day passed slowly for Molly, although Janet and Bella had made good company throughout the morning. Now, the lady Rosalie was helping to pass the time during their midday meal by telling them about England and her deceased husband's family.

Nevertheless, Molly's imagination had played merry havoc with her nerves all morning. Her thoughts kept flying to Henderland.

What if Will and Wat had got into a fight? What if her father ordered Wat's arrest and then wielded his power of the pit and gallows to do away with him? It would hardly be the first time that Cockburn hanged someone who had irked him.

And what on earth could Wat say to him that would *not* irk him?

To be sure, her father was usually of milder temperament than Will, and less likely to fly into the boughs over something another man said to him. Cockburn would more likely bide his time, although he might spend that time planning how to get even with that person later in some devious and unexpected way.

Will was more forthright and quicker with his fists or any other weapon that came to hand. And Ned, of course, would do whatever Will told him to do.

If Thomas was home, he would try to keep things calm. But Thomas was more often in Peebles now than at Henderland.

Knowing she would not rest until Wat was safely home again, she tried to persuade herself that she would fret over anyone confronting Cockburn in his lair. However, the truth was that the more she saw of Wat, the better she liked him.

As for the feelings he had stirred with his kiss…She paused, thinking. What if any man's kiss could make her feel so?

A stupid question, that was. Will's or Ned's kisses, had they ever offered any, would likely repel her. As for Tuedy's, the man himself repelled her.

When Tuedy touched her, she'd nearly lost whatever food she'd still had in her stomach and been grateful that she'd eaten nothing since breakfast. What he might have done had she vomited all over him did not bear imagining.

"Molly, are you going to answer me?" Bella demanded, breaking into her reverie. "Or are your thoughts so private that you do not want to tell us?"

"What?" Molly stared at the younger girl in guilty bewilderment. "I'm afraid I *was* lost in thought, Bella. Did you ask me a question?"

With a gurgling, merry laugh, Bella said, "Aye, sure, I asked what you were thinking about so hard that you did not even smile when Aunt Rosalie said how often she used to get scolded for asking too many questions."

More bewildered than ever, Molly looked to Janet for help.

Janet shook her head. "Never mind, Molly. Bella knows better than to ask others what they are thinking. Our thoughts, thank heaven, are private. I hope that this weather does not augur a long, cold winter, but Sym told Gram he thinks it will snow." Brushing an errant wisp of fair hair off her cheek, she added, "Did Wat tell you how long he expects to be away?"

Molly shook her head. "He told me only that he was riding to Henderland."

"Henderland?" Lady Rosalie raised her neatly plucked eyebrows. "Where is that, precisely? How far away?"

"About eight miles northwest of here," Molly said when no one else spoke.

Rosalie sighed. "After living so many years in England, I'm finding naught about Scotland that looks familiar, except Elishaw, of course. But Simon is too bossy to stay with for long. I've decided henceforth to make a circuit of my visits."

"A circuit?" Janet said, raising her eyebrows in much the way that Wat did.

"Yes, for during my lovely visit today with our Gledstanes cousins, I decided that I don't want to *live* with anyone," Rosalie said firmly. "Sithee, after two years of widowhood, I find I strongly dislike men who tell me what I must or must not do."

Lady Meg chuckled. "As I recall, you had a strong aversion to such men in your childhood. But then you could nearly always wrap men round your thumb, dearling. Have you lost your magic?"

Rosalie, disclaiming any such loss, laughed merrily, and their conversation continued without Molly.

Agreeing wholeheartedly with Rosalie in her aversion to men who ordered women around, Molly had returned to her reverie.

Perhaps, she mused, that was why she liked Wat Scott. Although she had told him he was as domineering in his own way as her father and her brothers were in theirs, Wat listened when she spoke to him—even when he was angry with her.

When he had not returned by dusk, she began to fear the worst.

Chapter 13 —————————————

Wat paid only a brief visit to Kirkurd. Having sent word of his father's death and his own new status to his steward there immediately after Rankilburn's death, he stayed long enough only to be sure that all was well with his people and to lend verisimilitude to any later suggestion that he might move kine south from Kirkurd.

His burly steward, who had served the Scotts for nearly thirty years, assured him that all was well, adding, "Ye'll do well, looking after all your new estates, m'lord. We ken fine that your da had every faith in ye, but we here at Kirkurd ken better than most that ye make a good master."

"Sakes, Jock, I've been away with the Douglas more than I've been here," Wat protested. "If all is well, it is due more to your skills than to mine."

"Aye, sure," the older man replied, nodding. "But many of us here ha' known ye since birth, laird, so we know we can trust ye. We'd no let ye down."

Wat swallowed hard, thanked the older man, and clapped him on the back.

Riding away with his men afterward, he felt strangely mixed emotions. His people's trust reassured him and boosted his confidence. But it humbled him, too.

He sent a brief prayer aloft that he would not let them down.

Kirkurd lay some miles northwest of Henderland, so darkness began closing in long before he and his men reached Scott's Hall. However, they had prepared for that likelihood and had already lit torches.

Wat was tired by then but grateful that, other than its miserable weather, the day had passed without further incident.

To be sure, Cockburn's menacing smile had given him pause, but the man was more of a nuisance than a menace and did not frighten him. Had Cockburn's sons been at his side, the meeting might have taken a more dangerous turn.

But his sons were not there, which meant that their men were away, too. Their absence had left their father and thus Henderland with a much reduced force.

Moreover, the Borders were relatively peaceful, the English not having attacked across the line for months. Reivers remained plentiful, to be sure. But they were not an army, and Borderers took what precautions they could against them.

He knew that his own reputation and that of Clan Scott had afforded him protection at Henderland, too. He had kept his temper with surprising ease, feeling confident that Cockburn would not dare try to keep him at Henderland. Nor had he.

Satisfied that he had honored his duty to Molly's father and had done so without rising to the man's baiting, Wat realized that the Cockburns would not let the matter rest. Now that they knew Molly was at Scott's Hall, he would have to double his guard there.

They had ridden silently for some time more when Geordie said, "I did learn summat at Henderland, laird. Leastwise, I been pondering, and I think I did."

Aware of how easily voices carried through the still night air, Wat said, "Let us ride a short distance ahead before you tell me."

"Ye can trust our lads, sir."

"I know that," Wat said. "But I'd liefer give them no cause to gossip, even amongst themselves. We barely know Lady Rosalie's people yet, after all. One of them might still be loyal to the Percies or even to the English king."

Geordie nodded, took a torch from Kip Graham, and motioned for the others to fall back a bit more.

When Wat was satisfied that no one else would hear them, he said, "Tell me now, Geordie. What did you glean?"

Instead of answering directly, Geordie said, "D'ye ken aught o' what this grievous Rutherford chappie looks like?"

"Nay, just that he's a ruffian who discards all civility when he raids."

"Aye, but we hear that about Will Cockburn and his lot, too," Geordie said with a straight look. "I were thinking this Rutherford chap must have size to 'im, and muscle. But whilst I were a-drying our horses and seein' they got feed and water, I heard two lads talking o' someone they called Wee Gilly."

"Such a name could refer to almost anyone, male or female," Wat said.

"Aye, sure, 'cept the one lad said this Wee Gilly wouldna like summat. Then t'other one said he wouldna want tae be nearby did Gilly fly into a tirrivee again, like

he did after the Redesdale raid. The first man told the second tae hold his wheesht, and I went on about me chores
like I didna hear nowt."

Wat considered the image that Geordie's description
suggested.

Geordie kept silent, evidently having said all he meant
to say.

At last, Wat said, "You've been pondering that since
we left Henderland, Geordie. Why did you not tell me at
once, or when we stopped at Kirkurd?"

"We was later than we'd meant t' be, sir," Geordie said.
"I could see ye was impatient t' be away again. Then, too,
I were none so sure o' me thinkin'. See you, I'd thought o'
this Rutherford as a great, fiery fiend on horseback. The
notion that he might be a puny one just didna set right wi'
me until I bethought me of our own Jock's Wee Tammy.
Could be, I thought, that the brute be a brute and the name
be nobbut one as ha' stuck wi' him since he were a bairn."

Wat nodded. "That could be, aye. Men at Henderland might call him so because they've known him since
then—or their masters have. Or those two you over-
heard might have been talking about some other chap
altogether."

Geordie did not reply, but Wat could tell that he was
thinking. His own gut told him that Rutherford was just the
sort of villain Will Cockburn might know and would follow. And Ned would go where Will went. As for Thomas...

Recalling Molly's assurance that Thomas loathed violence, Wat dismissed Thomas but continued to consider
Will and Ned as Rutherford's possible allies.

The rain had stopped an hour later when they reached
the Hall, although clouds still blackened the sky. Wat dis-

mounted, turned his horse and his oilskin over to Geordie, and went straight inside, looking forward to his bed.

Heading upstairs, he rounded the curve in the stairway below the cresset-lit landing outside Lady Meg's sitting room and came to an abrupt halt.

Molly, fast asleep, leaned sideways against the wall by the door with her knees bent up under her skirt. Her left cheek rested on her knees, and her arms were wrapped round her shins. Her rosy lips had slightly parted.

He stood looking down at her. A slight, if weary, smile curved his lips.

She resembled a child who had slipped downstairs after being sent to bed, to listen to or even peek at what the grownups were doing. He suspected that she had been listening for his return, wanting to know what had happened with her father.

The orange-gold cresset flame made her skin look softly gilded and lit golden highlights in her hair. Her eyelids had a bluish cast, as if they were too thin to do their job properly.

Gently, he touched her shoulder, hoping to avoid startling her into crying out and waking Lady Meg.

Her thick, dark lashes fluttered. Nothing else moved.

"Molly-lass, wake up," he murmured.

Her lashes fluttered again, and her rosy lips twitched, reminding him of how they had tasted, soft and a bit salty. Her body stiffened then, as if it had just become aware of his hand on her shoulder.

~⌒

Molly, waking from a dream of Wat's voice to the reality of hearing it, opened one eye. Meeting his slightly amused gaze, she sat bolt upright and looked around, trying to recall where she was and just how she came to be there.

"You're sitting in front of Gram's sitting-room door," he said quietly. "You *should* be in bed."

She wanted to tell him that she was perfectly capable of deciding when she should go to bed. But since she had no idea what time it was, she muttered instead, "I...I got worried. I thought you would return before sundown."

What, she wondered, would he think of that? Will would tell her that *his* business was none of hers and that a man returned when a man returned.

"I rode on to Kirkurd, to see to things there before turning back southward."

"I didn't know," she said, stretching her legs and arms out slowly to see if everything moved normally. When a cramp erupted in her right calf, she shifted both hands hastily to massage it.

"I'm sorry, I ought to have known you'd worry," Wat said then. Those simple words, spoken in that soft, rather sensuous murmur, seemed to float on the air.

She gathered her wits. "What happened? Was Will there? Was Tuedy?"

But he was watching her rub her leg. He said bluntly, "What's amiss, lass?"

"Just a wee cramp. I don't know how long I've been sitting here."

"Let me," he said, dropping to a knee.

Gently, he touched her hand and eased it out of his way. Then, cupping the still skirt-covered calf, he hooked his long fingers over her shin and pressed the heel of his hand into the calf muscle, kneading it.

Silently, she stared at that hand for a time before she relaxed and said, "Do you not want to tell me what happened, sir?"

"I saw only your father. He said Will and Ned were away. He also insists that your marriage was legal and that Tuedy has every right to have his wife back. I told him to talk to Father Jonathan about that and, if necessary, to Father Abbot."

"He must be furious with me," she said, wincing.

"Did I hurt you?" Wat asked sharply, releasing her calf.

"Nay, don't stop," she pleaded. "That feels good. I winced, just thinking of Father's anger and Will's, not to mention Tuedy's."

"Forget Tuedy, lass," he said, returning his attention to kneading her calf. "That marriage is as if it never happened. The abbot said he would speak for the Kirk. Recall, too, that his grace was at Melrose and likely still is."

"I doubt that the King knows who I am or cares a whit about my marriage."

"I don't know if Father Abbot told him why I'd come," Wat admitted. "But he cares about Scottish law. He has exerted himself to learn what laws are good and which are bad, so the abbot may have told him about you. If he did, Jamie might take an interest. Sakes, if I can lay this reiver he wants by the heels, I'll ask him."

"You have mentioned that reiver before," Molly said. "But you have not told me his name. Who is he?"

⌒

Realizing only then that he had omitted Rutherford's name on purpose, Wat hesitated to tell Molly more without thinking first about whether he dared trust her.

His men knew enough to ask their questions without noising it about that he sought to bring the reiver to justice. But Molly was still new to him. He did not know her well enough to be sure she would keep such news to herself.

Swiftly deciding that they would be wiser to talk elsewhere and after they'd slept, he said, "We'll talk in the morning. I'll tell you then what your dad and I said to each other but not on these stairs. Do you think you can stand on this leg now?"

"Aye, sure, the cramp was just reminding me of how foolish I was to sit for so long in one position."

"Come then, and I'll see you safely upstairs." Extending a hand, he helped her to her feet.

Her hair was tousled. She blinked sleepily. The impulse to offer her a hug was strong, but he resisted, reminding himself that she was his guest.

He had no right to behave so in any event, he told himself firmly. Moreover, the always alert Sym might be sleeping in the tower again and be wakeful.

When they reached her door, Wat opened it for her. However, when she turned toward him, standing much too close, he stepped back a pace.

"Good night, Molly," he murmured. "Sleep well. We'll talk in the morning."

She nodded, met his gaze one last time, and slipped inside the dark room, shutting the door quietly behind her.

Wat stood there, wondering at his own feelings and recalling his talk with his grandmother. He had never contemplated marriage before, not with serious intent. And heaven knew he had more than enough to do without thinking about it now.

Molly stared into the blackness around her. She had dismissed Emma hours before, meaning to go right to sleep. But her imagination had immediately begun sending a stream of pictures through her mind, suggesting horrid things that might have happened at Henderland if her father had lost his temper or if Will had.

When a fear struck her that Will had locked Wat in the tower dungeon and meant to leave him there to starve, she had scrambled out of bed again, put her kirtle back on, and crept downstairs.

She had meant to listen for his return and then, reassured of his safety, to steal swiftly back to her chamber. Instead, like a dafty, she had fallen asleep.

Having failed to light a candle before leaving her chamber, and too sleepy to find her tinderbox and light one now, she padded in darkness to her bed. Pulling off her kirtle, she laid it at the foot of the bed and climbed back in, in her shift.

She was asleep before she gave a thought to sleeping and awoke when a shaft of sunlight through a crack in the shutter touched her face, telling her she had slept longer than usual. That meant either that Emma had peeked in and decided to let her sleep, or that Wat had told the maidservant to leave her be.

Fearful, but nonetheless eager to hear what had transpired between Wat and her father, and to ask Wat what he thought Tuedy might do next, she washed her face with cold water and donned the pink kirtle. Reattaching her tinderbox to her leather girdle, she adjusted the girdle around her hips and buckled it in place.

Then, draping the pink and gray shawl across her shoulders, she flipped one end over the other in a loose knot at her breast, slid her feet into woolen slippers, and hurried down to the hall.

To her disappointment, only Bella and Lady Scott remained at the high table.

Edwin met her as she stepped onto the dais.

"I'll have my usual boiled egg and a slice of cold beef, please," she said.

"And toast, m'lady?"

"Aye, thank you, Edwin."

"You are gey late, Molly," Bella said. "Could you not sleep last night?"

"I must have been more tired than I knew," Molly replied with a smile.

Lady Scott said quietly, "When one is tired, one must sleep."

"Aye, madam," Molly said, turning her smile toward her ladyship. "In troth, I am used to having so many chores at home that I am often up late and again with the dawn. Having much less to do here, I fear I am becoming lazy, so if I can do aught to aid you, prithee tell me so."

Bella said cheerfully, "I have been learning to milk cows, Molly. You could help me with that."

"I'd like that," Molly said. "I'm a good milkmaid."

Bella giggled.

"Not today, however," Wat said from the far end of the great hall, his voice carrying easily over Bella's giggles. "If you have broken your fast, Lady Molly, I would speak with you."

"She has only just told Edwin what she wants to eat," Bella said.

"I'll wait, then," Wat replied, approaching the dais. "I had meant to ask you to walk in the courtyard," he said to Molly. "However, despite the sun, it is icy cold out there, and my men are practicing their skills, so 'tis noisy, too."

As he stepped onto the dais, Lady Scott said, "If you would have speech with our guest, Walter, you may do so in the solar. Bella is going to help milk the cows, and Janet is sitting with Rosalie and your grandame in Meg's sitting room. I mean to join them when I have finished here."

Edwin served Molly's breakfast then, and she gazed down at it, expecting someone to mention the impropriety of leaving her alone with his lordship. No one did, and she did not want to mention it herself, so she focused on her food.

While she ate, Wat chatted amiably with his mother and sister. But Molly had barely set down her spoon when he said, "Art finished, lass?"

Meeting his gaze and finding it more intense than usual, she wiped off her eating knife and slid it into its leather sheath on her girdle.

"Aye, sir," she said then, feeling suddenly shy.

⁓

Wat watched color flood into Molly's cheeks but made no comment.

His mother's suggestion that they talk in the solar had surprised him, but he knew it was his responsibility as master of Rankilburn never to discomfit a guest.

Moreover, the topic they had to discuss was more personal for Molly than it was for him. Believing that he understood her vulnerability, he reminded himself to choose his words carefully when he described his visit to Henderland.

"We'll take the privy stair," he said, gesturing toward it.

She preceded him, and when they reached the solar, she walked across it to the window embrasure and turned to face him.

"We can sit if you like," he said, thinking she might be nervous with him.

"Prithee, just tell me what happened, sir. I spent yesterday imagining all manner of horrors befalling you. You said, though, that Will and Ned were away."

"They were, and I saw no sign of Ringan Tuedy. Nor did your father mention his whereabouts. He said only that Tuedy believes the marriage was legal. Won't you sit down, lass?" he added when she frowned. "You will be more comfortable on that cushioned window seat. I promise I'll keep my distance."

A twinkle lit her eyes, surprising him. "Do you think I fear you, sir?"

"I think you are unaccustomed to being alone with a man you barely know," he said. Reaching for a back-stool, he turned it around so he might straddle it. "I would like to sit, too, but I must not unless you do."

"Aye, sure, then," she said, sitting obediently on the window seat.

Wat sat, too, and rested his forearms on the stool's back. "Now," he said, "I'll tell you what happened yesterday." He went on to describe his conversation with Cockburn but did not mention the menacing smile at the end of it.

"He disliked the fact of your being here," he added. "But he did not demand your return. Instead, he wanted to know why the abbot had involved himself."

"What did you tell him?"

"That he should ask his reverence, of course," Wat said with a smile. "I meant only to assure him that you are safe, but we may have learned something helpful, nevertheless. It has to do with that reiver I mentioned last night."

"Why have you not told me his name?"

"Because it was unnecessary at first, and we were on the stairway last night," he replied honestly. "Moreover, lass, I was so tired then that I could scarcely think. Sithee, I'd liefer the villain not learn that I'm searching for him, and he has many allies on this side of the line who would warn him."

"I am certainly not one of them," she said, cocking her head quizzically. "So, now that you *have* thought, do you mean to tell me who he is?"

"I decided this morning that I must," he admitted. "His name is Gilbert Rutherford. Have you ever heard your brothers speak of him?"

She shook her head. "I ken fine that Will and Ned do go a-reiving, but I know few of their friends. I don't know who goes with them on raids."

"Thomas never does?"

"Nay, I told you, Thomas is a man of peace. Moreover, he has been away for two months, helping a man near Peebles build a new house on his estate."

Wat said, "Geordie, the captain of my tail, heard something at Henderland that makes us suspect that your brothers might ride with Rutherford. Will's repute is so much like his that I'd be surprised if they don't at least *know* each other."

"Will and Ned can be violent," Molly said stiffly. "But they don't kill people. And if the King wants this Rutherford caught, I expect that he does kill."

"He and his men have murdered many, aye, and I doubt that your brothers tell you all that they do. Art sure you've never heard them speak of Rutherford?"

"I am certain," she said tersely. "I may not like Will or Ned much, my lord, but they are still my brothers. I know they're angry with me, and I expect I've given them cause to be. But I won't help you hunt them down. No one who is kin to me could be as brutal or as ruthless as you tell me this Rutherford person is."

"Have you heard of someone called Wee Gilly?" he asked.

"No, and I don't want to continue this conversation. Moreover, it is unfair of you to say that because they go a-reiving they must be so wicked. After all, you have also led raids into England. Doubtless, they call *you* a reiver. Is that not so?"

His temper stirring, Wat nearly denied it. After all, he had done only what was necessary to follow orders the Douglas had given him. The earl's commands were often simply, "Take care of it," or "Look into that. See it doesna happen again."

Knowing he would be wiser to be honest with her, he said, "I've led raids into England at my liege lord's command, aye. We were usually retaliating for English raids on our people here, to dissuade the English from doing it again."

"How does that differ from what this Rutherford does?"

Deciding it was unnecessary to carry honesty so far as to admit that in his youth he had ridden with Clan Scott reivers until his father put a stop to it, he said grimly, "Rutherford has burned innocent people, even children, in their homes, or cut them down with Jedburgh axes. We have done our share of burning, lass. But we empty the places of innocents first."

He knew that many Scots were as ruthless as the English and Rutherford were. Nevertheless, she had accused him personally, and his men had orders against such doings. They knew that he would hang any man who purposely killed a child, a woman, or any other innocent person, regardless of where the killing occurred.

"Try to understand," he said quietly. "To serve his grace, I must bring this villain to justice. And, if your brothers are in league with him..."

"But I tell you they are not," she said, standing again and fisting her hands. "I won't listen to more of this. If you deem me disrespectful for that, so be it."

"I don't want to fratch with you, Molly," Wat said, also standing and stepping away from the back-stool. "But you must see that men who treat you as your father and brothers have are more likely than not to ill-treat other women and bairns."

"I don't see that at all," she said more heatedly. "How would you like it if I accused Janet or Bella, or the lady Rosalie and her steward, of such things?"

"We will leave my family out of this discussion," he said, irked again.

"Aye, sure, because they are *your* family," she retorted. "Even *you* once suggested that your aunt's steward might be a spy for England. Yet you instantly defend them all. I am doing no more than that, my lord. Even so, I will not speak again of your family. In fact, I will speak no more to you today."

So saying, she moved toward the door, but he reached

out when she would have passed him and caught her by an arm.

"Wait," he said, striving for calm and finding it more elusive than expected.

She stiffened and glowered at his hand on her arm. "Release me, sir. If you do not, I shall know that you *are* just like my brothers and my father."

"You know that I am not."

"*Just* when I'd begun to think you might be different, too," she added, as if he had kept silent. "It pains me to admit that I had even begun to hope, to imagine, that if I am truly free of Tuedy, our friendship—which is to say yours and mine—might grow much stronger, even w-warmer."

~

Furious with herself for the slight stutter and hoping that Wat had not heard it, Molly scowled at him. His lips had parted slightly, but he had not said a word.

Nor did he release her.

She knew he was angry. So was she. "Did you not hear me, sir? Let me go."

"I heard you," he said with unnatural calm. He released her.

Angrier with herself for spouting her most intimate feelings at him than she was with him for expecting her to disown her family, Molly strode toward the door. Certain that he would stop her again before she reached it, she increased her pace, only to feel a surge of disappointment when he did not even try.

She hesitated, hoping he would at least say something to keep her there. When he did not, she opened the door, walked out, and slammed it behind her.

Having no other sensible place to go, since it was doubtless as cold out as he had said it was, she went to her chamber. Standing inside, by the door, she listened for his footsteps and, when she heard none, called herself a fool for doing so.

⁓

Muttering imprecations to himself, grateful that he had managed *not* to say such things to Molly, Wat strode to the solar's window embrasure to make sure its shutters were firmly fastened against the worsening weather.

Such loyalty to kinsmen who had betrayed her and opposed their rightful King, as well, seemed irrational to him. He had expected her to be grateful for his protection and his friendship. Instead, she had turned on him like a spitting wee cat.

His first impulse was to go after her and shake some sense into her. His next one was to appeal to his grandmother to support and advise him. Somehow, though, as he pictured himself telling Lady Meg that Molly ought to be grateful…

He was a fool. He didn't want her damn gratitude. He wanted to understand her. He wanted her to see that her kinsmen were dangerous to her and to others. He also wanted her to stay and fight with *him* when she believed she was right.

It was the second time she'd stormed away from him, and she had promis—

Stormed?

He strode back to open the shutters that he had just secured.

The sun hid behind a sullen dark cloud. Its cousins rushed to join it, and the air was icy enough to stiffen the hairs in his nostrils. Snow was coming. Moreover, the last time she'd fled, the fool lass had tried to lose herself again in the forest.

"God help me," he muttered, "if she has run outside again…" Picturing her across his knee stirred visceral satisfaction, then other, more sensuous thoughts.

When those images abruptly gave way to one of her frozen to an ice statue, a noise erupted from his throat that sounded suspiciously like a growl.

He crossed the room again and wrenched the door open before he took a breath. What the devil, he asked himself, had stirred such unusual panic in him?

Molly was no dafty. Why was he behaving as if she were?

Collecting his scattered wits, he went down to the great hall.

He found Sym there, alone with Lady Rosalie's steward, Len Gray.

"Has either of you seen the lady Molly?" Wat asked.

"Nay, laird," Sym said. "I thought she was with ye."

"We did have a talk," Wat said, striving to keep an even tone. "I have more that I'd like to say to her, but she seems to have vanished."

"She may be wi' Herself," Sym said, eyeing him more shrewdly. "The ladies Rosalie and Janet, and your mam, be in the sitting room wi' her now."

The thought of trying to extricate Molly from that group daunted him. Nor did he want to ask all four women in concert if they knew where she was if she was *not* with them. Thanking Sym for the suggestion, he decided to ask people in the kitchen and outside in the yard before he sought her elsewhere.

Both courses proving futile, he found himself at a standstill. No one else had seen her. The remaining likelihood, therefore, was that she was with Lady Meg.

But if she wasn't... Truly growling now, he decided the abbot was right. The lass *needed* a husband. No matter how many times he or anyone else called her marriage to Tuedy illegal, the only way Molly could permanently escape the brute was with a husband who had the power to protect her and to stifle Tuedy.

If *he* were ready to marry, he might easily choose worse than Molly for a wife. His father had considered her for him, and he did feel as if he'd known her all his life, not just for a fortnight. Surely, he could think of *someone* suitable for her.

He could talk to her, and she could talk to him—until her temper erupted. Aye, sure, they did sometimes disagree. But those conversations had all stimulated him to want more. The fact was they got on well together, except when they didn't.

Smiling at the turn his thoughts had taken, he decided that he would find her, wherever she was, and do what he could to straighten things out between them.

He would discover then if she remained firmly opposed to marrying or might consider doing so if he could find a man who would protect her *and* persuade Tuedy that his misbegotten marriage was beyond recovery.

Chapter 14

Molly awoke from her nap to hear the click of her door latch followed by the hushing sounds of someone entering her room. Realizing that she had fallen asleep at the foot of her bed with its curtains half drawn, she sat up to see who it was.

Her first thought was that Wat had come in, but she banished it as most unlikely even before she saw Emma cross the dusky room to the washstand.

Emma turned with the ewer in her hand and gasped, nearly dropping it. "M'lady, I had nae ken that ye was here," she said. "'Tis sorry I be if I woke ye."

"Don't apologize, Emma," Molly said, swinging her feet to the floor. "And, prithee, do not tell the ladies Janet or Bella, or Lady Scott, that you found me asleep again." When Emma shook her head, Molly added, "What is the hour?"

"It be nigh midday, m'lady. Be ye ailing, d'ye think? Mayhap ye should get under them covers. It be freezing cold out, and me da says if it doesna snow afore bedtime, he'll be fair astounded. He's always right about such, too, me da is."

"I think your father is wise about many things, Emma.

I've heard men say that he kens the Border roads and trails better than anyone else in Scotland."

"Aye, he's a canny mannie, is Da. Shall I brew ye a tisane, m'lady?"

"I'd liefer you pretend that I've just come up here to change this kirtle for the other one that Lady Janet lent me," Molly said. "I expect that you should tidy my hair, too, though, and put it in a net for me."

"I can do that, aye, but Lady Janet's sent ye a new gown, too," Emma said, gesturing toward a length of fabric draped over a stool. "She said she thought this bright green one that the lady Rosalie brought her would suit ye better than her."

"Oh, but I cannot wear something that Lady Rosalie meant for Lady Janet," Molly protested. "What would Lady Rosalie think?"

"Och, it willna trouble her," Emma said, grinning. "Lady Janet said the lady Rosalie saw for herself that such a bright green willna suit a lass wi' her light-blue eyes and straw-colored hair. Lady Rosalie even said it might be more suitable for you, because o' the green flecks she saw in your eyes when first she met ye. And, too, your hair being darker, she said, the color willna overpower ye."

Molly suspected that Janet had put those words in Lady Rosalie's mouth, if Rosalie *had* spoken them, or in Emma's if she hadn't. Even so, it would be churlish to refuse such generosity. "You leave me nothing to say, Emma. I'll try it on."

Minutes later, Emma stood back, nodding and smiling with satisfaction. "'Tis a pity we've nae looking-glass in here, me lady, for ye should see yourself. It becomes ye mighty well, I think."

Molly wondered if Wat would agree with Emma. Then she recalled that she had infuriated him to a point where he probably would not care what she wore.

Moreover, he was her host and the man who had protected her from her brothers' anger and her father's right to insist that he send her home.

In return, she had vented her anger on him and fled again. The last fact was the worst, since she had promised to try not to run away again.

Not that she had no right to defend her family, she reminded herself. She just ought to have been more civil to him.

Suddenly nervous about seeing him again, she prayed that he would not let others see his vexation when she went downstairs. To her relief, when she entered the hall, he stood on the dais, talking with the lady Rosalie and smiling.

When his gaze shifted to Molly, he stopped talking to watch her approach.

His face revealed none of his thoughts. And, although his gaze seemed to encompass her without meeting her eyes, she could not look away from him. Something about his demeanor—or perhaps it was no more than her own pride—stirred her to thrust back her shoulders and raise her chin.

"I knew it!" Lady Rosalie exclaimed, clapping her hands. "God might have created that color just for you, Molly. I am delighted that it suits you so splendidly. Sithee, I'd forgotten that our Janet is so delicately pale."

"Janet *said* the dress would suit you, Molly," Bella said. "She was right, too."

Rosalie's comment had diverted Molly's attention from

Wat to her ladyship. Now, she saw that the other ladies stood at their places near the table. As she turned to go join them, Wat stepped off the dais and blocked her path.

Perforce, she stopped. Looking up at him, hoping that the lower-hall noise of men and women finding their places there would keep her words from anyone else's ears, she said quietly, "I'm sorry I angered you."

"Nay, lass," he replied, matching her tone. "'Tis I who must apologize. I've no evidence to support my suspicion that Will knows Rutherford. I must remember, too, that no matter how your family treats you, they are still your family."

Molly glanced toward the other ladies. "I should take my place now, sir."

"Aye, you should." As she turned away, he added softly, "I like that dress."

"I, too," she said, touching the soft fabric with one hand. With the other, she raised her skirt high enough to be sure she'd step onto the dais without tripping.

He looked down. "You need shoes, Molly. It's too cold now to go unshod."

Giving him a look, she said, "I'm *usually* unshod, and my skirts are long enough to keep my feet warm. Are you ordering me to wear shoes, my lord?"

He met her gaze with a rueful smile. "I won't order you, but you do need shoes, and netherstocks, too. Talk to Janet, or I can talk to Gram. I'll want to talk more with you later, too, if you will consent to further discussion with me."

"Perhaps," she said airily. As she moved toward the ladies' end of the high table, she assured herself that she was *not* daring him to order her to talk with him.

The green fabric made her eyes look deep green instead
of green-flecked golden hazel, and the regal way she carried herself made Wat suspect that an age had passed
since she'd had a new gown.

A notion stirred to provide her with the clothing due to
her rank. Again, he pondered over who, among the men
he knew, might make her a suitable husband.

For one reason or another, he eliminated each name
that came to mind.

Despite her contrary attitude, he *would* speak to her
after the meal. For one thing, he probably ought to ask her
if she knew any man she might *like* to marry. But, then, he
recalled how fiercely she'd denied wanting to marry anyone.

Undaunted, he took his place at the table and signaled
for his carver to begin.

He wished he had thought to discuss Molly's predicament with Westruther. Garth was a sensible man, a
fine warrior, the head of his own family, and not a man
inclined to tease his grandnephew. But he had known
Molly only as their guest.

Accustomed as Wat had been to seeking advice from
his father, he felt the late lord's loss more acutely than
ever. He could think of no other man in whom he might so
easily confide his concerns and his feelings.

The fact was that he was beset by women, only one of
whom had earned his confidence as an advisor. Talking to
any woman about this, even one as sensible as Lady Meg,
would hardly aid him as much as talking to his father might.

Seeing Sym cross the hall from the main stairway and
pause to speak to Brigid, Lady Meg's woman, Wat got

impulsively to his feet, excused himself to his mother, and headed toward him.

"Sym," he said as he drew near, "have you eaten?"

"Aye, sure, laird," Sym said. "Be summat amiss?"

"I want advice, and I'm hoping that you might provide it."

Sym's curly, still red eyebrows arched upward. "Ye want advice from me?"

"I do," Wat said. "I think you ken much about Lady Molly's situation, aye?"

"As much as Herself does, I warrant," Sym said warily. "I ken fine that ye went to see auld Cockburn and did nae more than let the man and his gallous sons ken where her ladyship be staying."

Wat grimaced. "True, although his gallous sons were away at the time."

"Likely raiding," Sym said, nodding.

"Possibly," Wat said. "At present, the Cockburns don't concern me. You've been seeking word of Gilbert Rutherford's whereabouts, I believe."

"Ye ken fine that I've been a-putting out word that ye mean to move beasts to Melrose. So far, I've learned nowt, as ye must likewise ken fine. Chance be, I'll hear summat anon, but that canna be the advice ye seek now."

"Nay, although I do suspect that the Cockburns may be in league with Rutherford. The lady Molly says they are not, but..." He shrugged.

"Them thatchgallows? Aye, sure, they could be. I'm thinking Will Cockburn would join wi' the devil hisself to gain a farthing. And Ned will follow Will to hell or wherever he ends up. That Ned has nary a thought to call his own."

"What about Lady Molly, Sym? What think you of her?"

Sym's craggy features softened. "She's a rose amongst thistles, that 'un, and ye ken that much, yourself, Master Wat. 'Tis writ all over ye when ye look at her."

Wat frowned. "I think you give your imagination too much rein, Sym."

"Aye, perhaps," Sym said, his eyes atwinkle. "Or may-hap I put more faith in the auld laird's ability to choose well for ye, and yours to choose for yourself."

"She is just a friend, Sym, and I do not want to see her hurt. I'm thinking the abbot was right, though. The only way to be sure she need never return to Tuedy is to find her a husband powerful enough to protect her from him."

"Aye, that be what I'd advise, too. I ha' me doots there be anyone else wha' could do that better than yourself, though. Be there aught else I can do for ye?"

Wat glanced at the dais to see that the ladies, including Molly, were still at the table. "Nay, Sym. 'Tis clear that I must resolve this dilemma for myself."

⁓

Sitting between Janet and Bella, with Lady Rosalie at Janet's right and Lady Meg and Lady Scott beyond Rosalie, Molly was still eating. She was also fighting a strong temptation to watch Wat and Sym, when Bella said abruptly into the silence, "Who is Gil Rutherford, Molly? Do you know?"

"Gil?" Molly noted that Janet was deep in conversation with Lady Rosalie.

"Gil *Rutherford*," Bella repeated, evidently thinking that Molly had not heard his surname. "Our Bessie, who sees to Janet and me, said her father and her brother had been talking about such a man. But Bessie failed to hear much of interest, she said, because when they caught her listening, they got angry and sent her away."

Thinking that Bessie ought to have known better than to repeat such a thing to the child, Molly shook her head. "You should ask his lordship about that, Bella. Or perhaps you might ask Janet."

Bella grimaced. "I did ask Janet. She said that curiosity ill-becomes a bairn like me. But I want to know, Molly. Mayhap I *will* ask Wat."

Although Molly hoped, for Bessie's sake and perhaps Bella's as well, that Bella would think twice before asking her brother about Rutherford, she did not dwell on that hope. Her thoughts had stuck instead on the reiver's name as Bella had said it. Although Gib and Gibbie were the usual nicknames for a man named Gilbert, some people might easily call such a man "Gil" or "Gilly."

It was true, she reflected, that she had never heard of Gilbert Rutherford or anyone called Wee Gilly until Wat had asked if she knew those names. But she did recall a discussion between Will and Ned a fortnight or so before, about someone called Gil—or perhaps Will had been talking to Tuedy. She couldn't be sure.

She might not have recalled the incident at all, had Bella not mentioned that Bessie's father and brother were angry with her for overhearing them.

Will had slapped Molly when he'd seen her in the doorway that night, and scolded her. He had said that she had no business lurking in corners, listening to men talk. She hadn't been lurking, though. She had just been doing her chores.

That hadn't mattered to Will.

Her memory of the incident failed to supply a picture of which men or how many had been with him at the time. Her focus then was on Will, although she could not be sure whether he or someone else had mentioned the name Gil first.

Putting a hand to her cheek, she could almost feel Will's heavy hand there instead, although the most recent bruise he'd given her was nearly gone.

She wondered if the Gil mentioned then could have been Rutherford. Trying to remember more of the incident proved useless, so she decided that any attempt to explain it to Wat would only stir the coals of their recent argument.

He would be certain that that Gil *was* Rutherford when he might have been someone else. She could prove nothing and knew no more than the name.

It was a pity, though, that she could not somehow send for Thomas. She could tell him what she knew, and he could warn Will and Ned to stay away from the Gil that they knew lest he *was* the dangerous reiver.

The more she thought about that, the more worried she became that she might again be ill-serving her host. But if Wat leaped to the wrong conclusion, she would have distorted the entire situation for him. Telling him would also stir more trouble between the Scotts and the Cockburns. She had caused enough already.

She would bide her time, and likely Wat would capture the reiver.

It occurred to her that she might be unable to avoid telling him if he pressed her again to talk about her brothers. She would certainly lose her temper if he insisted that she believe the worst of them. And he might well do both. Therefore, she decided, she would be wise to avoid all discussion with him for the nonce.

Accordingly, noting that Wat had left the great hall with Sym or shortly afterward, she went with Janet and Bella to the bedchamber the two shared. The three of them talked long then about all manner of things, except Wat.

Molly's thoughts wandered back to him, though, when Bella said in her abrupt way, "Do you think Len Gray is in love with Auntie Rosalie?"

"Mercy me, Bella, what a thing to say!" Janet exclaimed. "Even if we suspected such a thing, and I do *not*, it is most unbecoming of us to talk about Aunt Rosalie behind her back."

"Well, I did think of asking her, but I thought you'd liefer I ask you instead."

Molly choked on a bubble of laughter and clapped a hand over her mouth when Janet shot her an admonitory look. "I'm sorry," Molly gurgled through her fingers, trying to stifle her mirth. "I can't help it." She paused, trying to regain her composure. "To...to imagine your lively aunt in love with that pompous stick..."

"I never said that Auntie loved *him*," Bella protested. "She couldn't!"

"That will do, the pair of you," Janet said in a stern voice, albeit with dancing eyes. "We must talk about something else."

Bella looked at Molly, cocked her head, and parted her lips as if to ask another question.

Certain that it would as awkward as the previous one, and one she would not want to answer, Molly said hastily, "Janet, do you have any dice?"

"We do," Janet said. "Bella likes to play for pebbles. Do you like to play?"

"I haven't diced for years," Molly confessed. "But I did enjoy it when I was Bella's age. My brothers were kinder then, at least when my grandame was near."

"Our brothers are both kind to us," Bella said. "But we won't ask Wat to dice with us, because he always wins."

"We'll just stay here then, where he is unlikely to disturb us," Molly said.

Janet gave her a speculative look. Then, getting gracefully to her feet, she said, "I'll fetch our dice and the pebbles. Oh, and, Molly, Gram reminded me that you need shoes. You should wear a pair to supper, I think."

~

Wat endured a veritable stream of second thoughts after leaving Sym. No matter how hard he tried to stem the flow, it persisted.

Sym's notion that he should marry Molly must, he knew, have originated with Lady Meg. Nevertheless, Meg had already given him food for thought. Sym's advice seemed only to underscore much of what he had thought, himself, except as to who should become Molly's husband.

He knew without false pride that, thanks to his father's many kinsmen and allies, the Scotts were one of the most powerful clans in the Borders. He also knew that he was not his father, but as clan chief, he did intend to build on his father's legacy, to acquire more land and, somehow, win a knighthood and provide as many well-trained men as possible to serve his liege lord and his grace the King.

Hitherto, Wat had thought primarily of achieving those goals. Nevertheless, the fact remained that he did someday have to provide himself a wife. He was already years past the age that his father had been when *he* married.

Perhaps marrying Molly was not a bad idea, he thought when he saw her at supper, still wearing the green dress... and shoes. She was beautiful, and she certainly attracted him. He could not see her without wanting to touch her, and his memory of the kiss they had shared was enough to stir his whole body to life.

Also, he had promised to protect her, not just to find her a protector. If he persuaded someone else to marry her, would he not be pushing that responsibility onto another chap—shirking it, in fact?

That stream of thoughts, for and against, continued throughout the evening but always came to the same end. He, a Borderer, had given his word.

"That's it, then," he muttered as he prepared for bed at last.

"What's that, sir?" Jed asked, turning from the kist he had just closed.

"Nowt," Wat said. "Just nattering."

But it wasn't "nowt."

He had deduced from Molly's demeanor at supper that she was still out of charity with him. He hoped, though, that she would be calm again by morning. He would seek then to learn if she might willingly accept a husband.

If so, he would offer to marry her.

❧

Molly awoke early and quickly donned her yellow kirtle. Sitting on a stool, she pulled on the knitted netherstocks that Janet had given her the previous evening and the raw-hide boots and gloves she had borrowed to meet Lady

Rosalie. Then, flinging Janet's old cloak over her shoulders, she went quietly down to the kitchen.

Avoiding comment or interference, she made her way through the bakehouse to the scullery door and out to the yard. The air was icy, the sky clear.

If Sym's snow had fallen overnight, no sign of it remained. The gray dawn light was turning golden.

The high wall made it impossible to see more than a few treetops beyond it, and Molly knew that the men on the gates would not open them for her, so she contented herself with a brisk walk around the cobbled yard. The stones were dry, and her boots and gloves kept her feet and hands warm.

Her breath produced clouds of steam. Only her nose was cold.

The crisp, fresh air smelled faintly of woodsmoke and baking bread. Men busied themselves with chores around the yard, and she saw Tammy in the stable doorway. He stood with his back to her, but seeing him warned her that her time outside might be curtailed if he turned around.

She did not want to go back inside yet. Although the high table would be ready for anyone wanting to break her fast, she was not as hungry for food as she was for fresh air and exercise. None of the other ladies of the Hall enjoyed the early-winter outdoors as much as she did.

The changing seasons had always fascinated her, and she did not know Ettrick Forest or the Teviotdale countryside as well as she knew the areas around St. Mary's Loch. She wanted to see all of it.

Perhaps after Wat captured his reiver, he would take her and his sisters on more frequent rides. He had not invited them since Westruther had gone home.

As quickly as she could go without drawing Tammy's notice, she headed back to the scullery, remembering with a smile the night she and Wat had stolen apples from the pantry near the bake oven.

The warm scent of baking bread stirred her taste buds to life.

"I've some hot rolls, m'lady," the baker said with a smile. "Would ye like one tae soothe yer hunger?"

Eagerly agreeing, Molly watched him slice one and slather butter on it before handing it to her. Deciding that she need not go upstairs yet, she went warily back outside and saw Tammy disappear into the stable. The yard thus being safe again, she crossed it swiftly to find the milkmaid.

Wat entered the great hall, certain that Molly would be there and might like to ride after breakfast. While they rode, he could learn if she was agreeable at least to the idea of marriage, if only as a way to protect herself.

So set was he on his plan that her absence from the dais came as a shock. Everyone else, including his mother, was at the high table, eating.

"Where is Molly?" he asked as he stepped onto the dais.

Bella shrugged.

Lady Meg said, "I expect she's still abed, love."

"She is usually up early, Gram," he protested. "Has no one seen her?"

Learning that none of them had, he sent a lad to find Emma. She hurried in before Edwin brought his food but disclaimed knowledge of Molly's whereabouts.

"She dressed without me, this morning, m'lord," Emma said. "I thought she must ha' gone riding with ye."

Alarm stirred. Surely, his men would not let her ride out alone. Forgetting breakfast, he hurried downstairs to the yard, only to meet Sym on his way in.

"One o' the lads just came in, m'lord," he said. "That Rutherford lout be heading west now, the lad said, mayhap toward Liddesdale."

"Good news, but I was looking for Molly," Wat said. "Have you seen her?"

"Nay," Sym said, giving him a shrewd look. "She'll no ha' gotten outside the wall, so she must be inside somewheres. She does like to wander about, ye ken."

Wat knew that that was true enough. Relaxing, he said, "Where is the lad with news of Rutherford?"

"Still a-talking to Tam and Geordie in the stable."

"Find Molly, Sym. I must talk with her before we leave."

"Aye, laird, I'll find her." Sym turned away.

"And, Sym?"

Sym turned back, eyebrows raised.

"Send someone for Father Eamon. Tell him to come straightaway and to bring his missal and whatever else he might need to perform a wedding."

Sym grinned. "Aye, laird, I'll see to that, and I'll wish ye good fortune. I'm thinking ye may be holding your head in your lap, though, afore this day be done."

Having finished her roll and a mug of warm milk in the company of the cheerful milkmaid, Molly bade her good day and returned to the tower through the main entrance. Stepping into the great hall, she saw Lady Meg and Janet at the high table. Sym was with them, too, bending to talk with his mistress.

As Molly approached the dais, he looked up and straightened.

"His lordship be a-looking for ye, m'lady," he said.

"Was he? Where is he?"

"In the stable, a-talking wi' Tam and Geordie. Likely he'll come in here when he's done, though, and he'll want to talk with ye then. If ye havena broken your fast, ye'd be wise to do it now."

"I've eaten, thank you," Molly said, but Sym had shifted his gaze to some point beyond her.

Turning, she saw that Wat had entered the hall and was striding toward her, looking grimly determined. The determination faded to wariness when his gaze collided with hers. Then his features hardened again.

"I want to talk to you," he said. "Privately."

Although she hoped that Lady Meg or Janet would object, neither one did.

"Aye, sir," Molly said with careful courtesy. Suddenly unable to look him in the eyes, she fixed her gaze on his chest instead. "Where do you suggest we go?"

"To my father's . . . that is, to *my* privy chamber upstairs."

Fearing that he might have learned that her brothers and perhaps even her father *were* in league with the reiver Rutherford, she could not swallow, let alone talk. Nor did she dare look up to try to read more in his expression. So, she stood frozen until he put a hand to her shoulder and urged her gently toward the stairway.

Climbing the stairs ahead of him, she felt his gaze—all the way up.

Chapter 15 ―――――――――

Wat followed Molly up the stairs, enjoying the sensuous way she moved. Some women trudged up stairs, putting one hand to the outer wall for support and using the other to lift their skirts. Some went briskly, clutching their skirts up before them in both hands. Molly held hers up with one hand and let the other move as it would, making her hips sway enticingly with each step.

He had seen the way she'd avoided his gaze and wondered at it. The only times she had done that before were when he'd let her see that she had vexed him.

He was not angry now. He felt only purposeful and determined to see her well protected before he left the Hall to capture Gilbert Rutherford.

Because if anything went amiss with that...

"It is that door on your right," he said as she approached the landing.

She hesitated in front of the door, so he moved up behind her and reached to open it. His chest brushed her shoulder as he did. He could smell the floral aroma of whatever it was that his sisters used to scent the clothes in their kists, as well as something else, rather enticing, that he thought might be Molly's own scent.

"Go in, lass," he said. "Sit on one of the back-stools if you like."

"I'd liefer stand, sir, than have you loom over me," she said. Turning toward him as he shut the door, she kept her eyes fixed again on his chest.

"Then look at me," he said more sharply than he'd intended. Gentling his tone, he added, "My face is up here. I don't want to talk to the top of your head."

To his consternation, her gaze dropped lower, to his feet or her own.

Putting three fingers under her chin, he forced her to look at him.

"Am I such an ogre that you cannot have civil discourse with me?"

He saw her swallow. Then, to his dismay, tears welled in her eyes.

With what seemed to be more effort than should have been necessary, she drew a breath at last and said, "You are not an ogre, nor are you like Will or Ned. I'm afraid it is a habit of mine to avoid looking at anyone who is angry with me."

"But why, lass?"

In response, she touched the faint scar on her right temple. Then, abruptly, she shoved a strand of hair back as if that were what she had really intended to do. Still, she said nothing.

"I would not have taken you for a sullen one," he said provocatively.

She grimaced. "I don't think I am sullen," she said. "Just wary of what I might say if I let myself speak or afraid of what might happen if I do."

"Is that why you run away and hide?"

"Usually, I *walk* away so that I may keep my temper."

Keeping his tone even, he said, "When I make a suggestion for someone's benefit, I expect that person to consider my advice as potentially beneficial and to be willing at least to discuss it. When you won't look me in the eye or talk to me, that irks *me*. It is as if you cannot be honest with me."

She met his gaze at last. "If I look at my father or Will, or try to speak whilst they are scolding me, they declare me insolent and slap me, or worse. Will calls it teaching me to be properly submissive to their authority."

Through clenched teeth, he said, "Is that how you got that scar?"

She blinked at his tone but did not look away. "It is, aye," she said.

As he fought to subdue his outrage, Wat wanted nothing more than to teach Will Cockburn to keep his hands off Molly. Instead, he drew a steadying breath and reminded himself that Will was beyond his touch ... for now.

For the present, he would focus on his immediate goal.

"I agree that your kinsmen are brutes," he said evenly. "But, if you hoped your explanation might persuade me to accept such intolerable behavior, you have missed your mark. I've never given you cause to avoid talking with me, Molly, and I'll always listen to you. Sakes, I know you have courage, and I've given you my protection. But as things stand, any protection I provide you must be temporary, regardless of what either of us might desire. You do see that, do you not?"

She licked her lips as if they had dried. But although she had clearly disliked suffering his rebuke and looked wary again, she did not look away.

Molly struggled to control her tumbling thoughts and answer Wat's question. Whatever his reason had been for this so-private discussion, she decided that he had not discovered a connection between her brothers and the villainous Rutherford.

So what was Wat up to? Although her unfortunate reaction to his demand for private speech had angered him, and she had shivered at the iciness of his tone, she had stood up to his anger before and had told him what she thought. She had fled only because her own temper had threatened to leap beyond her control. If he had frightened her it was because she had feared he could prove she was wrong and that Will and Ned *had* become villains like Rutherford. If that was not so...

"I do know that my stay here must be temporary, sir, since Father has the legal right to demand my return," she said quietly. "I wonder why he did not demand it at once."

"I don't know," Wat said. "The Cockburn I saw two days ago was much less confident than I'd imagined him. It might have been because your brothers and their men were away. But he said only that Tuedy would demand 'his wife' back."

"And now they will know where to find me," she said. "But since the abbot has agreed that my marriage to Tuedy was unlawful..." She paused when Wat began shaking his head. "Did he *not* say that?"

His slight, knowing smile aroused her annoyance, but she suppressed it easily.

"You are too innocent, lass," he said soberly. "Father Abbot did say that, and someday the laws of Scotland and the Kirk may apply to men and women equally. At present, though, despite the law and the abbot, the power of the sword is still strong. If a man claims that a woman is his wife and can produce witnesses to agree with him—her own kinsmen, say—neither the law nor the Kirk will gainsay him."

"But surely, if I refuse to leave here—"

"For how long?" he asked. "I ken fine that I said I would protect you for as long as you need protection. But are you willing to hide behind my walls for much of the rest of your life, riding out only when I can provide an armed escort?"

"What choice do I have?"

He did not reply. He just held her gaze. His expression seemed sympathetic at first, but his narrowing eyes told her he expected more of her.

"What?" she repeated, feeling her temper rise again.

"You *know* what," he murmured.

She wanted to look away but could not. Nor did she think that doing so would be wise after what he had said about his tolerance for such conduct.

He looked as if he peered into her thoughts, hoping to influence them. The only solution she'd heard anyone suggest that *might* offer her permanent safety—

She refused to think about that.

"*I'm* willing," he said softly. "I become more willing every day, Molly, even when your behavior disturbs me."

"*Disturbs?*" She clamped her teeth together to quiet her unruly tongue.

A double rap sounded on the door, followed by a youthful male voice, saying clearly, "Laird, be ye in there? Father Eamon said t' tell ye he's here. He wants t' ken who be a-getting married and where the wedding will be."

Molly's temper ignited.

~⁓

Seeing color surge into her cheeks, and her mouth and fists tighten, Wat put a warning finger to his lips and said loudly enough for the lad at the door to hear him, "Tell Father Eamon I'll be down directly."

To his relief, Molly kept silent until the lad's footsteps faded down the stairs. But the respite did naught to ease her anger.

"How dare you!" she exclaimed. "You had no right to summon your priest for another forced wedding, my lord. Nor will I take any part in it. *You* may be willing. *I* am *not*."

Tears spilled down her cheeks, but she dashed them aside and drew a long, shuddery breath. Her tears had not damped the fire in her eyes.

Wat said with strained calmness, "What makes you think I'd force you?"

"God-a-mercy, you sent for your priest, just as my father did."

"I am not your father, Molly. Nor would I want to be."

"You're twisting my words."

"I am not," he said, adding a touch of ice to his voice. "I was trying to discuss a delicate matter with you. I'll admit that I did send for the priest, but only because my men have learned where Rutherford is, and I must ride with them today to have any chance of finding him soon. By my troth, Molly, I want only to know that if I fail to return, my name and my people will protect you."

Molly stared at him, her anger gone. The thought that Wat might die in his attempt to capture the reiver was terrifying. She had not even thought about his leaving, but of course he had to go. And, although she had seen enough of Jock's not-so-wee Tammy to know he would do all he could to protect her, the thought of remaining immured at Scott's Hall for who knew how long without Wat...

"See here," he said in that same chilly voice, "you must know that as long as you remain a maiden..."

"Why do you say that?" she demanded. "How could you think that I am?"

"Because Gram gave the abbot her word. And Gram never lies."

"But how could *she* know?"

He frowned. "Did she not examine you?"

"What do you mean, examine?"

Wat's lips parted as if to reply, but did not. A long moment passed before he said, "Are you telling me that she did not check to see if you are still intact?"

Molly shook her head, confused. "I don't know what you mean. She asked me to describe what happened after the wedding, and I did. I think she could see that I did not like talking about what Tuedy did or all that he said to me, but—"

"Well, you're going to talk about it now," he interjected. "I want to know exactly what you said that persuaded her. You told *me* that Tuedy hit you and stripped your clothing off. What happened between then and when he left you nearly naked in your chamber, with his man outside your door? Did Tuedy take off any of his own clothes or hurt you in any other way whilst he was with you?"

Molly's eyes widened, her jaw dropped, and Wat saw what his grandmother had seen in her. "Lady Meg asked me that about Tuedy's clothes, too, but he did not take any off," she said. "Why would he when he had not yet had his supper?"

"Then he did not—" Breaking off, recalling his conversation with her after he'd told her what the abbot had said about illegal marriages, he realized at last just how innocent she was. To destroy such innocence now would be brutal.

Seeking a more tactful approach, he said, "When you and I talked after I'd visited Father Abbot, you expressed surprise that anyone might think a married lady could still be a maiden."

"Aye, sure," she said. "I asked Janet about it, too. She said that one ceases to be a maiden when one marries, so..." She spread her hands.

With a sigh that was as much relief as anything else, Wat said, "Molly, what do you ken of marital duties, specifically of coupling?"

She thought for a moment. "My father and Will said I need ken no more than to obey my husband. Since my mam and both of my grandames died when I was a bairn, I never had anyone else to ask until now. Lady Meg did offer to explain them to me," she added. "But I did not feel..." She paused, nibbling her lower lip.

"Your husband is the one who should explain such things to you," Wat said. "I have already said that I'm willing to *be* your husband, lass, but you must make that decision. Sithee, after a man and a woman are married, they do things together that only a husband and wife should do. You have horses and kine and such at Henderland. Surely you have seen how they mate."

Her widening eyes gave him the answer before she exclaimed, "But people don't do such things! Do they?"

He had not realized how tense their conversation had made him until he felt himself relax. Gently, he said, "They do, aye. I swear to you, though, it *can* be a most enjoyable and satisfying pastime."

"You swear it?" She gave him a narrow look. "But if those are things that only a husband and wife should do, then how is it that you—?"

"*Pax*, Molly," he pled, choking on a rueful laugh. "You can ask me anything you like after we marry. *If* we do," he added hastily when she frowned. "For now, I just want you to understand that you do need the protection of my name."

Her frown deepened. "I ken fine that Will and Ned, and Tuedy as well, talk and joke about women they say they have enjoyed. But I never imagined that they were behaving like animals do, with *women*!"

Wat moved closer to her. "Don't fret about their behavior, lass, or any previous conduct of mine, come to that. If you will agree to marry me, I give you my word as a Borderer that I will be faithful to you and to you alone."

He put a hand on her left shoulder. When she stiffened, he put the other one on her right shoulder, gently, to see if she would pull away from him.

She didn't, but her beautiful face grew pale.

⌒

Molly stared into Wat's face, wondering what he thought. She felt dizzy at the idea of marrying him but strove to make sense of her emotions and to think.

The strongest urge she felt was to melt into his arms and let him hold her. There was something so solid about the man, so reassuring. That primal urge nearly overpowered her. But if she cast herself into his arms, he would believe that she had cast all her doubts aside, and she had done no such thing.

Nevertheless, the safety he offered her was more than tempting, and she suspected that rejecting it would be foolhardy. When men spoke of powerful Borderers, they usually spoke first of Clan Douglas. But amongst the other powerful clans, she had heard most often of Clan Scott.

To be sure, they were nearer neighbors than most and her father's rank, although older, equaled the Lord of Rankilburn's. And, although Wat might still have to prove himself worthy of the position he had so recently inherited, Molly believed he would do so easily.

Even so, would he be more patient with a reluctant wife than her brothers and her father had been with a recalcitrant sister and daughter? Would any man?

Finally, searching Wat's eyes as she spoke, she said, "I hear the words you say, sir, and I want more than I can describe to believe them. Wait," she added, holding up a hand when he looked about to speak. "I believe that you mean them and that you are an honest man. I also know that I would be foolish to reject the offer you make me. Nevertheless, I remain uncertain."

"You could do much worse, I think, than to marry me."

"Sakes, I have already done much worse!"

When he bit his lip, clearly struggling not to laugh, she smiled. "By heaven," she said impulsively. "I'll do it."

"Good lass," he said. "Go and put on the gown that

Aunt Rosalie gave you, and meet me on the dais. I'll take care of everything else whilst you dress."

"Mercy, right now?"

"Now," he said firmly. "I must be away within the hour."

Swallowing hard, she drew a deep breath and let it out. Then, taking another breath and nodding, she turned on her heel, strode to the door, and opened it.

Turning back, she said, "Art sure, my lord?"

"Completely, my lady."

Fighting a sudden, unexpected urge to cry, she turned again, stepped through the doorway, and hurried upstairs to her chamber, wondering if she had gone mad.

⁓

Molly had left the door ajar, so Wat went to the landing and watched her to the next turning of the stairs. Then, he went down to the hall.

His grandmother and Janet still sat at the high table, talking. Father Eamon and Sym had joined them there.

"Sym," Wat said, "did you send someone to tell Jed I'll need my gear?"

"I did, laird, aye, and Geordie will ha' the horses ready." When Wat nodded, Sym added with a gesture, "Father Eamon be here, too, sir, as ye see. I didna tell him nowt save that there'd be a wedding, 'cause I didna ken what else to tell him."

"You can perform one straightaway, can you not, Father?"

"I can, m'lord, if that is what you desire me to do. But where—good sakes, who—are the bride and groom?"

"I am one. The lady Margaret Cockburn is the other."

"But I heard that the lady Margaret had married."

"She has declared that marriage forced, thereby illegal, and the Abbot of Melrose and her own priest agreed with her. Therefore, that so-called union need trouble us no longer. However, since her erstwhile husband may not be willing to accept her declaration, I have offered her the protection of my name."

"But—" Meeting Wat's gaze, the priest hastily broke off. "Aye, m'lord," he said with a nod. "I'll see to it all as ye wish if the lady be willing."

"She is." Wat glanced at his grandmother and saw her smile.

"Have you mentioned this intent of yours to your lady mother, love?"

"Not yet," Wat said. "I was rather hoping that you—"

"Don't be daft," Meg said. "You must tell her yourself and straightaway. Moreover, love, do not turn into an iceberg if she refuses to attend. I can tell you that her strongest argument will be that this is much too soon after your father's death even to be *thinking* of bridals."

He nodded. "Aye, you're right. I'll go to her now. Jannie, if Molly comes down before I return, stay with her. *Don't* let her get cold feet."

Janet's eyes were sparkling, but she said, "Art sure about this, Wat? I adore Molly, and so does Bella, but—"

"I'm sure," Wat said. And he knew as he said the words that he was.

⌁

"I did not expect to find you here, Emma," Molly said when she entered her bedchamber to find the maidservant already shaking out the bright green dress. "How did you know I would want that dress?"

"Me da told me, m'lady. He said Lady Meg suspected ye might want it."

"I do," she said. Strange but comfortable warmth filled her at the thought that Lady Meg and Sym evidently approved of Wat's decision. That thought brought another with it, though, of Lady Scott, and Molly's worries flooded back.

She had told Wat she would do it, and so she would, if only because once she was Lady Scott, Tuedy could do her no more harm.

"I'll brush your hair first, m'lady," Emma said, pointing to a nearby stool.

Sitting on it, Molly put everything else out of her mind but preparing for her wedding, and soon she was ready to go back downstairs.

Entering the hall, she saw that Bella had joined her sister and Lady Meg on the dais and that Sym and some other men had moved the high table back to make room for a makeshift altar. Father Eamon, in his clerical robes, stood aside from the others and appeared to be quietly praying.

Molly wondered what he must think of such a wedding. But she had little time to dwell on that thought before sounds behind her from the main stair archway announced the return of Wat with his lady mother.

Lady Scott looked shaken, and although she glanced at Molly, she looked quickly away toward the dais. The lady Rosalie stepped through the archway just then with her ever-present steward, Len Gray, a step behind her.

~

Wat escorted his mother to take her place on the dais with the other ladies. Receiving a nod from Lady Meg, he could be nearly certain that the lady Lavinia—as his mother would henceforth likely style herself, instead of as the dowager Lady Scott—would remain at least until the ceremony was over.

He had persuaded her to come easily enough, merely by letting her see that her refusal would displease him. He was nearly certain, though, that he could trust her to be kind to Molly while he was away.

His mother was by nature a kind woman, if a fragile one. He knew that the shock of his father's death had undone her. As Meg had predicted, she did insist that it was too soon for a wedding, let alone one that no one had expected to occur at all.

"I have promised Molly my protection, Mam," he had said in response. "You would not want me to break my word. Nor would you want to upset her by refusing to witness our marriage."

Lady Scott had agreed that whatever had happened was no fault of Molly's, and that had been that... for the nonce.

Noting that Molly stood alone, looking rather forlorn, he excused himself to his kinswomen and went to her.

"You look beautiful, lass," he said warmly. "I do like that dress, and I like your hair all loose and hanging down your back like that, too."

"Emma said that was how it ought to be," she said with a nervous smile. "Are you still sure about this, sir?"

"I am," he said, gesturing to Father Eamon to get on with it.

⁓

The ceremony was over so quickly, compared to the seemingly unending horror of her first experience, that Molly was unsure that she was married. She could see that its brevity stunned Wat, too.

Her previous ceremony, she realized with surprise, had likely been the same one. She recalled little of it beyond the pain of Will's fist in her hair and the abrupt declaration of Father Jonathan's that she and Tuedy were husband and wife.

She had been helpless then. Now she felt safe and increasingly confident.

After Father Eamon had declared them husband and wife, he added in stentorian tones to the rest of the hall, "My ladies, my friends and kinsmen, I present to you Walter Scott, Lord of Buccleuch and Rankilburn, and Lady Scott."

Feeling heat flood her cheeks, Molly stared blindly ahead of her until the assembled company began to cheer and to gabble among themselves. Seeing only smiles and nods then, she relaxed.

When Wat put a strong, possessive arm around her shoulders, she looked up at him with a grin.

"I brung ye some good claret, laird, and m'lady," Sym murmured, appearing beside them with two silver goblets. "I thought ye might like some afore ye…that is, afore his lordship has to leave."

Wat nodded but not, Molly noted, without first shooting her a speculative look. "'Twas a good notion, Sym," he said then. "Here, lass, drink some of this," he added, taking one of the goblets from Sym and handing it to her.

She sipped obediently but handed it back to him. "With respect, my lord, I'd liefer keep my head clear."

He leaned closer and murmured, "The wine will help you relax, Molly, so drink some more. Remember, we still have our connubial duty to see to."

Heat swept through her, but she said the first thing that came into her head. "Surely, not yet. Do we just leave everyone? I...I couldn't! Just the thought..."

When she paused, he said, "Sym, tell the lads I want to be away soon after we dine. Meantime, what did you do with that wine jug?"

"'Tis yonder on the high table," Sym said, pointing toward the end farthest from the makeshift alter.

Molly noted distractedly that servants were clearing the altar away to make way for the midday meal. But thoughts of what Wat had described as coupling made thinking of anything else difficult. Then he put a hand to her shoulder and urged her toward the stairs.

The warmth of that hand penetrated her skin and spread through her body, making it impossible to think at all.

Wat did not speak. He picked up the jug from the table in passing and guided her toward the privy stairs without a word to excuse them from the company.

She thought she should protest, but words failed her when he urged her ahead of him up the stairs. Conscious of his footsteps on the treads behind her, and his breathing, she realized she felt none of the fear she had felt with Tuedy.

Her emotions had stuck somewhere between chaos and keen anticipation.

Just before they reached his bedchamber landing, she wondered what he would do first. Might he expect her to do something to him? If so, what? Could she just ask him? Would he kiss her? He hadn't done so since that first time.

The thought nearly stopped her in her tracks, because with it came a wave of desire unlike anything she had ever known. She *wanted* him to kiss her again.

On the thought, she turned to face him and discovered

that she was not yet eye-to-eye with him when she did. He'd stopped a step below her but was still a few inches taller. His mouth was right before her eyes.

Looking up into his eyes, she saw a twinkle.

"There's no escape now, lass," he said with a half-smile tugging his lips.

"I don't want to escape," she said. "I want you to kiss me again."

He drew her into his arms then and touched his lips to hers. When she responded, he kissed her more thoroughly. He had just eased his tongue through the opening of her mouth when Sym's voice sounded from below.

"Laird, Geordie's just talked to a chap wha' says the gallous Rutherford be a-heading toward Edgerston and Jed Water. He left others to keep watch, but they be hours away from here, so the chap says ye'll want to hie yourself."

"I must see to my lady wife first," Wat said. "Have the horses ready and be sure we have oatcakes aplenty, and apples. I'm going to miss my wedding feast."

"Please, sir," Molly said. "Surely, *we* need not make such haste. I ken fine that you are not anything like Tuedy, but..."

He grimaced. "I don't blame you for your uncertainty, Molly-lass. By my troth, the last thing I want to do is frighten you. But we must consummate our marriage now. Otherwise, if something should happen to me..."

Unexpected tears sprang to her eyes. She squeezed them shut and turned swiftly away to hurry upstairs, hoping that Wat had not seen them.

*Chapter 16*_____

Noting Molly's tears, Wat glanced back to be sure that Sym could not see the two of them. Then, concerned lest she return to her own chamber, he followed quickly but saw that she had stopped on the landing outside his bedchamber.

She stood silently there, staring at the door.

"Don't cry," he murmured.

"I'm not, not really," she said just as quietly, without looking at him. "I just don't want anything to happen to you."

Relieved, he reached past her, unlatched the door, and pushed it open. The bed was ready, its coverlet and quilts turned down in welcome. His thoughts sped to the duty that lay before them, and his body stirred in eager anticipation.

Molly stepped inside and stopped, gazing either at his bed, against the wall opposite the door, or at nothing in particular. Wat could not tell which it might be.

Shutting the door, he slid the bolt home quietly and moved up behind her.

When he put his hands on her shoulders, he expected her to stiffen as she had before. Instead, she stood as she was ... silently.

"Look at me," he said softly.

She turned then, her gaze solemnly meeting his. Her eyes were clear, her tears gone. "I do trust you," she muttered. "I will do as you say."

Wat felt an absurd urge to shake her, but he realized that his frustration was with himself, not with her. He said, "I dislike this haste, too, Molly. Consummating a marriage is not an act that anyone should do hastily, certainly *not* with an inexperienced maiden. I want us—both of us—to enjoy coupling, and I fear that if we rush this, you will hate it and perhaps fear it even more than you do now."

Still looking into his eyes, she said, "I don't fear you, sir, truly. But, although I know you want only to protect me from Tuedy, such haste discomfits me."

He could think of no way to convince her quickly that she would enjoy coupling. Therefore, aware that each minute with her was a minute he lost in finding Rutherford, he exerted himself to seek a compromise that might address her feelings and his need to be away quickly.

"I can make it easier for you," he said at last. "First, though, do you recall when I asked if Lady Meg had examined you to see if you were still intact?"

"I remember the question. But since I do not know what you meant—"

"Maidens have a sort of barrier a short way inside them that breaks during their first coupling and thus ends their maidenhood. You may have heard tales of a man returning his bride to her father in disgrace because the man discovered on their wedding night that she was not intact."

She shook her head. "I never heard of such a thing. Do you mean that a man can marry a woman and then give her back?"

"Only if she is no longer intact. A new husband views such a breach as proof that the woman has lain with another man before him."

She looked thoughtful. "So, if you were to breach mine," she said slowly, "would Tuedy no longer want me?" Before he could think how to reply to that, she added, "Is there no way to breach me without behaving like animals?"

"I could do it with my fingers," he admitted. "But, should anyone ask me afterward if we had consummated our union, I could not honestly say that we had."

Frowning, she nibbled her lower lip. "Would you hurt me?"

"It will likely hurt some no matter how I do it," he said frankly. "Your body has to adjust to the intrusion. But if I'm careful and you are willing, it should hurt only the first time, and we can stop as soon as it's done."

She drew a deep breath, expanding her breasts enticingly.

Feeling his cock stir again, Wat fought to ignore it.

She exhaled. "What must I do?" she asked.

His cock replied energetically.

Swallowing, Wat said as calmly as possible, "We'll take off our clothes first. If we were taking our time, I'd undress you. But unless you need my help—"

"I don't," she said hastily, looking away. "I need only unlace my bodice, and the rest will come off easily."

Wat swiftly disrobed himself, watching her as he did and marveling at the creamy smoothness of her skin and her enticing curves. Feeling tightness in his throat, he swallowed again and said, "Now, lie down on the bed and close your eyes. I'm less likely to hurt you if you can relax.

Also, I can show you that some—perhaps even much—of this will be pleasant."

Without hesitation, she turned and moved to the bed.

Knowing that he watched her stirred new feelings in Molly's body. It was as if she could feel every nerve in it and could feel his gaze touching her bare skin.

The bed was waist high for her, but she hoisted herself onto it quickly and leaned back against the pillows piled at its head.

He had followed and now stood beside her. His gaze held hers as he pulled two of the pillows away, leaving one under her head. She dampened her lips.

"Scoot over a bit, lass," he said rather hoarsely. "I want to sit beside you."

Obeying, she kept her eyes on his face. His gaze was intense. His eyes seemed darker than ever, but she could not decipher his expression.

He said, "Shut your eyes now, and try not to think about what I might do."

A near giggle, more of a chirp, escaped her lips. "You must be jesting," she said. "How can I *not* think about that?"

He smiled. "Just close your eyes and be still. I do want you to *feel* what I'm doing and to think about nowt save those feelings. I'm going to touch you, to stroke you as I might stroke a kitten. It will be easier for you, I think, with your eyes shut."

The thought of him stroking her like a kitten sent a wave of heat through her body that she could feel right to her cheeks. Licking her dry lips, she tried to relax but continued to watch him. Having seen her brothers' cocks dangling softly when they stripped, she could not imagine how one could hurt her.

Hitching his left hip onto the bed, Wat put his left hand to her right shoulder and gently stroked down her arm as he watched her face. His broad, bare chest was well muscled with soft dark hair growing thicker in the center, then trailing lower until—Shocked at the rampant erection she saw then, she shifted her gaze swiftly back to his face.

His eyes twinkled. "I told you to close your eyes, but you needn't fear me." Sobering, he used two fingers of his right hand to stroke her left cheek. Then, so softly that she barely felt them, he touched one each to her eyelids.

Having little choice then, she shut them and realized with astonishment how sensuous his feather-light touch felt there.

The hand on her right arm had stilled, but it moved now to stroke her right eyebrow slowly from the end near her nose to the scar that touched its other end. Then he traced the scar into her hairline above her right ear.

The hand moved on, cupped her head briefly, and then stroked her hair. Enjoying the intense feelings that produced, she realized that his other hand was moving, first to stroke her left cheek and then to outline her left ear.

When he touched the ear's inside curve, Molly felt a tingling sensation that flamed to the core of her body. She moaned.

～

So far, so good, Wat told himself, wishing he could control his own reactions as easily as he could stimulate Molly's. His cock was clamoring to claim her.

Her lips parted invitingly, and he yearned to taste and savor them. Putting thought to action, he leaned slowly closer until his lips barely touched hers.

When her eyes flew open, he kissed her harder as he stretched out beside her, leaning on his left elbow, and purposely brushed his right forearm across her breasts as he did. Hearing her breath catch, he moved his hand lightly along the same course, teasing her nipples. Then, cupping her left breast, he tweaked its tip lightly between his thumb and forefinger as he eased his tongue gently between her lips.

She moaned again, and her body twitched as if it urged him to be less gentle.

"Doucely, lassie," he cautioned. "Try to relax."

Pushing his tongue away with her own, she muttered. "Would you relax if I did such things to you?"

He chuckled, but his body fairly leaped at that suggestion.

"Shhh," he said, raising his left hand to tease the nipple on that side while his right hand moved more purposfully over her ribs and waist. "It won't be long now."

Her moan changed to a gasp when he cupped her between her legs.

~

Molly could hardly breathe. Never had she suspected that a man's touch could stimulate such feelings in her body. That Wat could do so with little more than touching her eyelids, or the tip of a breast with his thumb, astonished her.

His hand between her legs was another matter.

Modesty stirred, only to vanish when that warm hand

stroked her left thigh down to the knee. When he shifted it to her right knee and upward, she gasped again. Unfamiliar feelings coursed through her body, stirring heat and unexpected anticipation. Her legs spread of their own will. Did she *want* him to touch her there?

She realized with shock that she did. She ached for his touch. She pressed her lips together to keep from demanding it. What would he think of her if she did?

~

Watching her lips thin, then part, Wat knew she was as ready as she could be for what must come next. Without haste, he stroked the soft honey-bronze hair at the juncture of her legs, then stroked down the inside of one thigh and up the other again before gently inserting his middle finger into her moist sheath.

She stiffened with a kittenlike squeak.

"You're ready," he said quietly. "I'm going to take you now, lass."

This time her moan revealed discomfort rather than passion.

His cock strained to accomplish its task, and heaven knew that he was as eager to conquer her as it was. But he had also made her a promise, and much as he'd like to tell the lads to wait, he could not. So, he eased the head of his cock into place, gritted his teeth, and focused as much on diverting her attention to her breasts and lips as he could, while he continued to press himself slowly, carefully in.

The urge to plunge in and take her with primal fierceness was strong.

When she cried out, he pushed all the way in to be

sure that he had taken her maidenhead and then carefully eased himself out. He realized he was panting just from the effort it had taken to control his urges.

"Is it done?" she asked, her eyes wide again.

"Aye, lass, it is," he said, grateful to hear his normal voice rather than the hoarse grating he'd expected. "You're no longer a maiden. There will be some blood, and that's natural, but you'll want a cloth to clean yourself."

So saying, he got up and went to the washstand to fetch her a damp cloth.

His body was strongly protesting his decision, and his cock fairly shouted at him to grant it release. Ignoring its demands, he handed her the cloth.

She took it and sat up, eyeing him searchingly, even cautiously.

Recognizing her uncertainty and doubtless modesty, too, he turned back to the washstand and dampened a cloth for himself. His cock protested more while he cleaned it and more yet when he donned his breeks.

Quickly, he put on the rest of his clothes. Then, deciding that she had had enough time to herself, he said briskly, "I'll take another kiss now, madam wife. Then I must be away, but see that you behave yourself whilst I'm gone. There must be no more dashing out into the woods."

"Yes, my lord," she said with a wary smile. "I do know that much."

He bent, put two fingers to her chin, and kissed her gently on the lips. Then, turning, he strode to the door and unbolted it.

As he opened it, she said, "Walter?"

He turned back. "Aye?"

"Come home to me, sir. I want to learn more, *much* more."

Grinning with delight, he said, "I'll teach you all I know, Molly-lass. Then we'll see what else we can discover to amuse us . . . together."

She smiled, and he knew he would carry that smile with him until he returned to her. He had, he decided, made rather a good bargain.

Minutes later, he was in the saddle, his cock still throbbing in complaint of its bereavement. His ride would be uncomfortable for a while, but Molly was safe.

With luck, he could take his irritation out on Rutherford when he caught him.

After tidying herself, Molly went downstairs, still marveling at the feelings Wat had stirred in her and wondering if he expected her to sleep in her own bed or in his now. She entered the hall to find everyone awaiting her.

"There you are, Molly!" Bella exclaimed loudly enough for everyone to hear. "Gram would not let them serve us without you!"

In the laughter that followed that outburst, Molly wished that Wat had waited long enough at least to escort her to the high table. Reminding herself that she was now the lady of his household, she squared her shoulders and approached the dais.

To her surprise, Lady Scott stepped forward before she reached it. With a sad little smile, she extended a hand to Molly and said, "You must take your proper place now, my dear. If it pleases you, I shall take mine at your left hand. You must also call me Lavinia now, I think. I have already told the servants to address me henceforth as Lady Lavinia, because you are Lady Scott now, after all."

Taking her ladyship's slender hand in both of her own," Molly said sincerely, "Madam, I hope you know that I had no thought of this marriage until Walter insisted. I certainly must not displace you. Mayhap when he returns—"

"Nay, nay, child," Lady Lavinia said, turning her hand to give Molly's a squeeze. "Walter would be wroth with us both if we awaited his return. He would be right to feel so, too. You do not displace me. I am pleased that he has taken a wife, and I ken fine that my beloved Robert approved of you. He told me more than once that he wished he had been able to arrange for Walter to meet you."

"Mercy, madam, was he so set against me?"

"How could he be when he did not know you?" Lady Lavinia smiled with true warmth. "The truth is that he resisted marriage itself and the responsibilities that accompany it, because he had set his heart on winning a knighthood like his grandfather did. It was only through the greatest good fortune that he was here when his father died. He had come to seek Robert's advice, I think. Had he not," she added with a sigh, "then everything would have been *much* worse."

Molly glanced at Lady Meg, remembering what she had said about sending for Wat. She met only Meg's steady gaze.

Without hesitation, Molly said sincerely, "His coming home when he did was providential for all of us, madam."

Janet and Bella insisted then on greeting their new sister with hugs, and Rosalie hugged her, too. Lady Meg beamed her own satisfaction withal, and they took their places at the high table in complete amity. Noting that Father Eamon eyed her expectantly, Molly nodded for him to say the grace before meat.

After the meal, Lady Lavinia excused herself for her usual postprandial nap.

Lady Meg invited the other ladies to retire with her to her sitting room, and Molly accepted the invitation with relief and gratitude.

She had just realized that she had no idea what she should do next.

Gathering her courage, she waited only for the ladies Meg and Rosalie to take their seats before she said to Lady Meg, "Prithee, madam, advise me. I do not want to offend anyone, but I am at a loss to know what my duties are now."

Meg smiled warmly. "I know just how you feel, my dear. When my Wat brought me here, his parents were still alive, and neither had the least notion that he was bringing a wife home to them. His father was furious and his mother shocked to the bone. She was gey chilly to me. Your Wat inherits his temper from her."

"I see," Molly said. "Did she possess his kindness, too?"

"Bless her, she did," Meg said, smiling. "My Wat left me with her almost at once, so I did what I could to please her and soon learned how kind she was. Then my goodsister, Jenny, suggested I take up residence at Raven's Law, Wat's peel tower in the Buck Cleuch. Although he'd been living there, he'd decided that the place was unsuitable for me and I should stay with his parents. I moved to Raven's Law whilst he was gone, though, and began setting it in order. He was livid when he found me there," she added, twinkling.

"But Walter doesn't live at Raven's Law," Molly said.

Janet laughed, and Bella said, "Nay, just Sym's family and some of the other men live in that peel tower now. It is not nearly as comfortable as the Hall is. You will be happier here, Molly, I promise you."

"In any event," Lady Meg said, "this is your home and Wat's now, Molly, so I suggest that you let things go on as they have for a time. Get to know Agnes Ferguson, our housekeeper, and ask her to guide you. My good-mother was kind enough to show me how to go on, but Lavinia has little energy for such things."

"Moreover," Janet said with a twinkle, "Agnes dotes on Wat and will be delighted to tell you what he likes and how she manages the household."

"Yes," Meg agreed. "Soon, you will feel at home here, Molly, and will want to make changes of your own. Wat will certainly expect the pair of you to move into his father's rooms."

Molly could not imagine herself ousting Lady Lavinia from the bedchamber her ladyship had shared with her husband, or giving orders to Wat's people. But she did know something about managing a household of men, so she thanked Lady Meg and moved to the window embrasure with Janet, who had brought her mending.

Taking a ripped pillow cover from Janet's pile, Molly began unstitching the damaged end while Rosalie and Meg talked quietly nearby over their embroidery.

Bella sat near them, hemming a cambric handkerchief.

Molly heard Len Gray's name just before Lady Meg said with a chuckle, "You must know that the poor man is in love with you, Rosalie."

Molly and Janet exchanged a surprised look. Glancing

again at Bella, Molly wondered if her own eyes were as big as the child's were.

"Don't be a dafty, Meg," Rosalie said sharply. "Len Gray is my steward, that's all. He is an excellent steward, to be sure. But that is *all* he is to me."

"It may be all he is to you, but I have seen how *he* looks at you, my love. You must take care. If he is important to you, you don't want to offend him, but you must make your position clear to him. What do you know of his past, after all?"

"Isn't he an Englishman?" Bella asked, only to receive quelling looks from both ladies *and* from her older sister. She quickly began tying off her thread.

"He is a Scot," Rosalie snapped. Turning back to Meg, she said, "I have nearly forty-eight years behind me, Meg. I daresay I can look after myself."

"I meant no offense," Meg said mildly. "But if you have failed to see—"

"There is naught to see, and I ken as much of Len Gray's past as I need to. I would liefer discuss this no further."

"As you wish," Meg said. "Bella, if you have finished your hem, you may sort these threads for me. I have let them get into a tangle."

As Bella moved to sit beside Meg's sewing basket and draw the threads into her lap, Rosalie said quietly, "I did not mean to be discourteous, Meg. Do you think Walter will succeed in capturing Gil Rutherford? The man is a dreaded menace, but he has hitherto eluded every effort on both sides of the line to capture him."

"It will likely take longer than Wat expects, but he will do his best to keep his promise to the King. Don't look so worried, Molly," she added. "Wat took forty of his lads with him, and they are good, reliable men."

"Yes, my lady," Molly said, looking down at her work to conceal her worry, albeit not for Wat's safety. Rosalie's having mentioned Gil Rutherford reminded her that she had failed to tell Wat that she suspected her brothers might know the man even if they had not abetted his reiving.

If Lady Meg's Sir Walter had been angry merely because she had moved into Raven's Law without his permission, how would his grandson feel if he found Will, Ned, and perhaps even Tuedy with the reiver when they captured him?

He would be angry that she had not told him of her suspicion and would not care a whit that she had heard just the name Gil, never Gilbert, Gib, or Rutherford. She knew him well enough to be sure he'd say she ought to have told him all the same. Even so, and little though she liked Will or Ned, they *were* her brothers.

But even Lady Rosalie had referred to the reiver as *Gil* Rutherford.

Moreover, Wat was her husband now. He had a right to expect her to be more loyal to him than to her brothers or any of their so-called friends. So, Molly wondered, was there any way she could remain faithful to Wat *and* to her family?

Would he believe that in the chaos of their marriage talk, their wedding, and their connubial duties, she had simply forgotten about Will and Ned? Perhaps, or perhaps not, but how likely was it that he'd capture Rutherford straightaway or that Ned and Will would be with the reiver if he did? Not likely at all . . . she hoped.

Rutherford had eluded capture so far, and with apparent ease. How could Wat and his men succeed quickly when so many others had failed?

The reiver could be anywhere by now. So Wat would be home again before any capture took place. She would tell him then what she suspected.

~

Wat and his men rode fast through the forest until they reached Borthwick Water and followed it into Teviotdale. When it turned east toward Hawick, Wat told Geordie to take Kip Graham and half of the other men and head southeast.

"I expect your chap can find the lads he left behind to follow Rutherford, can he not?" Wat added.

"Aye, sure, sir. They'll use our usual markings," Geordie said.

"Then get word to me when you can. I mean to keep the others north of the Teviot and head east toward Ormiston and Kelso. I'm thinking Rutherford will keep clear of Hawick and Liddesdale. If he stays south of the Teviot, he may head for Jedburgh."

"Ye're a-hoping to catch 'im betwixt us then, eh, laird?"

"Hoping, aye. His estates lie between Roxburgh and Melrose, so he knows all of Teviotdale well."

Telling his men to spread out as they rode, and to keep one another in sight, Wat kept Jed Elliot with him on the highroad north of Hawick that led to Melrose.

He called a halt at dusk in a shallow vale southeast of Ashkirk, while there was still enough light to make camp. Sundown came earlier each day, and he knew the moon would rise late that night.

Ordering his men to tend their horses and eat sparingly from the provisions each carried, he made a circuit of their encampment's environs to be sure the area hid no surprises and that the secret markings he and his men used were in place.

As he prepared to sleep, Aggie's Pete strode through the increasing darkness toward him, his corn-colored hair subdued in the dimness. Pete was wiry with long arms and legs for his height, and was a savage brawler with a Jedburgh axe.

"I've set lads to watch both sides o' the vale, laird," Pete said. "Others will relieve 'em in two hours. But I doubt the moon will rise afore midnight."

Wat agreed. "Rest will do us all good," he said. "We'll ride again when the moon's glow appears behind the Cheviots. I hope to glean more news of Rutherford and his men before noon tomorrow."

"Sym said the man rides wi' just a score o' lads on his raids," Pete said as if he were reminding himself rather than Wat. "Still, I'm thinking we'd ha' been wise to add some o' Douglas's men at Hawick to ours, if the Douglas still be there."

"He's at the Black Tower," Wat said. "But I'd liefer avoid obligation to him in a task that his grace has entrusted to me. Archie Douglas disapproves of raiding unless he orders it. And, much as he ought to *want* to see Rutherford hanged, he likes his own life to be peaceful. His grace told me to see to Rutherford, so I will."

"Aye, sure, laird," Pete said. "I'll just put me head down for a bit then."

Bidding him goodnight, Wat lay on his back with his hands cradling his head and gazed at the sprinkling of stars beginning to appear in the dusky northern sky. He wanted to think through his plan and visualize various routes connecting areas where men had recently reported seeing Rutherford.

Before long, his thoughts drifted to Molly. Theirs was not a love match or one based, as many were, on alliance of powers. But it *was* a marriage.

His discovery that his lightest touch could stir her senses and that she could stir his as easily was an unlooked-for boon. It had been a strange wedding day for them both, but it had certainly been a better start than they might have had.

Lying there, thinking about her, he felt his cock stir and realized that if he let his thoughts dwell on their activities that afternoon, he would soon be aching again.

Jed's quiet return reminded him that he needed sleep, so he cleared his mind, took a last look at the stars, and shut his eyes. Long practice as a soldier who slept wherever and whenever he could did the rest. He slept until a rustle of nearby movement brought him instantly awake to soft moonglow outlining the Cheviots.

Rising swiftly, he picked up his cloak, scattered his temporary bed of grass and leaves, and noted that Jed had already returned his own bed to its natural state and was likely saddling their horses. Wat could see Pete's rangy figure moving to men who were slower to waken, urging them to make haste.

They were off again within minutes, and Wat munched an apple as he rode. Others had oatcakes. Some had cheese or hard biscuits, and a few had brought sliced meat or chunks of it that would keep well enough in the November chill.

The night was still dark, but the half-moon's cap showed between two dark Cheviot peaks, lighting the way well enough for men accustomed to riding by moonlight. Before dawn, they reached Ancrum, some three miles northwest of Jedburgh and four miles south of Rutherford's family estates on the river Tweed. There, they learned from a priest that Rutherford had not yet shown himself in the area. The news reinforced Wat's belief that the reiver would stay east of Jed Water.

Continuing eastward along the Teviot toward Eckford, Wat sent men to scout the rolling landscape to the north whilst the rest kept their eyes on land south of the Teviot, to be sure they did not miss Rutherford by passing him. Aware that the reiver would also be sending out watchers, Wat spaced his own men well apart, in pairs here, single riders there, and one foursome.

Anyone riding toward them would see only scattered riders on any nearby road or path, which was typical traffic near the borderline by day or night.

⁓

Molly descended to the great hall Saturday morning with Emma at her heels to find a smiling Janet at the high table, chatting with Lady Rosalie.

"I'm glad you are up early," Janet said. "But it must seem gey strange to be married less than a day and have no husband at your side."

"Nearly everything that has happened to me this fortnight and longer has been strange," Molly admitted. "Are you two the only other ones up?" she added as she took her place at the table. Emma was already ordering boiled eggs and toast for her from a hovering Edwin.

"Oh, no," Rosalie said with a laugh. "Meg broke her fast an hour ago and is downstairs with your cook, arranging an appropriate celebration of your marriage to take place when Wat and the others return. Lavinia is still abed, of course, but *I'm* yearning for exercise. I was just persuading Janet to ride with me. You should come, too, Molly. The day promises to be a fine one, and mayhap a ride will keep you from thinking about Wat, or worrying about him."

"I think he expected us all to stay inside the wall," Molly said.

"Perhaps, he did," Rosalie agreed. "But I care naught for that, because whatever may be said of the forest, Rankilburn Glen should be safe enough."

"We could ride along the Clearburn if you like," Janet said.

"I have seen everything that way," Rosalie said. "My lady mother and I stayed with Meg when Robert was born, and we rode to the Buck Cleuch then."

"But that was *long* ago, and Molly has never seen it," Janet said. "It is a narrow trail, though. We won't be able to ride fast."

"I'd prefer a path where we can let the horses out," Rosalie said. "Len suggested riding south along the Rankilburn toward your kirk. In troth, though, I'll accept anything that gets us beyond these walls."

Janet said, "An ancient motte that we might visit lies not far from the kirk. Men say the motte is centuries old, but only fairies and other wee folk live there now," she added with a grin.

"I do doubt that his lordship would approve of our leaving," Molly said.

"He must know that we are safe in the glen," Rosalie protested. "His people keep good watch here and would report any stranger at once."

"That is true," Janet said. "Moreover, Wat left no orders for us to stay inside the wall. At least, if he did, no one has told me."

Molly nearly declared that Wat *had* told her that she was not to dash out into the forest while he was away. But, in the silence while Edwin set her boiled eggs and toast before her, she decided that Wat had meant the sort of "dashing" she did alone to avoid losing her temper. He had not forbidden their morning rides, and Rosalie was right. No one would interfere with them so near the Hall.

Accordingly, and meeting no objection from Lady Meg, their little party departed a half-hour later, including Emma. The maidservant, to Molly's surprise, had followed her downstairs and out through the main entrance, taking up a brown wool cloak that lay on the porter's bench in the entry on her way.

"Do you want to ride with us, then?" Molly asked her.

Color crept into Emma's cheeks, but she said steadily, "Aye, m'lady. I'm meant to keep near ye."

"Mercy, did his lordship order you to follow me about?"

"Nay, m'lady, 'twas me da said I should keep close. He said there be enemies about as might mean harm to ye. And, upstairs, Herself did give me a wee nod when ye said ye were riding out. So, I'm thinking she might ha' thought the notion up herself. Or mayhap she and me da conjured it up betwixt 'em."

"So, it would be useless for me to send you back, aye?"

Molly said with a smile. When Emma flushed, she added, "Don't fret, I welcome your company."

Evidently, though, Tammy took a dim view of Emma as Molly's protector, because he sent along two extra grooms, as well. So, with Janet and her groom, plus Rosalie and Len Gray, they became a party of four women and four armed men.

Chapter 17 —————

The day was as glorious as Rosalie had promised. A light breeze rippled dry leaves that lingered on the birches, oaks, and ash trees in the forest.

The Hall stood east of the Rankilburn, near its confluence with the smaller Clearburn, flowing into it from the northeast. Molly and her companions followed the path south along the Rankilburn's east bank, uphill toward its source, as they had on Sunday.

Birds chirped, squirrels chattered. No one was in a hurry.

"The motte sits on yon hill across the burn," Janet said after a time, pointing.

By then, they were riding single file. A steep, densely foliaged hill rose on their left, and the burn chuckled cheerfully downhill on their right. A short time later, Molly saw that the burn bent westward ahead. A sike, or rill, tumbled downhill there, and she recalled that the bridge lay near where the rill flowed into the burn.

"Look yonder," Rosalie said. "Is that not Father Eamon striding toward us?"

"It is," Janet replied as Molly followed Rosalie's gaze. "Moreover, by the look of those white robes his two companions wear, they are Cistercian monks."

"Likely, they come from Melrose, then," Len Gray said.

"They have seen us," Janet added when Father Eamon waved.

"We shall have to be civil, I expect," Rosalie said.

Molly looked at her. "Would you just ride on to the motte if you could?"

Grinning, Rosalie said, "I have wanted to ride since I awoke this morning, so aye, I would go on. That is, I would if I were alone and could be sure that Father Eamon would not betray me to Wat or to Meg. However, one must not offend Wat's priest, or yours, Molly, let alone two of the good men from Melrose Abbey."

"'Tis odd that they wear their cowls over their heads," Len Gray said.

"Oh, don't be so suspicious all the time," Rosalie said tartly. "Must you see bogymen even in priests, Len?"

"It is my duty to protect you, madam."

"Pish tush," Rosalie said. "Doubtless, their heads and ears get cold in this weather. My hood is up, and *you* are wearing a wool cap to cover *your* ears."

Gray lapsed into dour silence, and Molly watched the clergymen.

The three men stopped on the far side of the bridge.

Over the gurgling sounds of the water, Father Eamon shouted, "If we may beg leave to delay you, your ladyship, we bring news."

Fear shot through Molly. Urging her mount onto the plank bridge, she said, "Has something happened to his lordship?"

"Nay, nay," the priest assured her hastily. "I should have said we bring *good* news. Brothers Joseph and Harold here are messengers from Father Abbot. See you, my lady, his reverence has persuaded your father to meet with you and is bringing him to Rankilburn Kirk now to do so."

"To meet me? Why?" Molly demanded. The last thing she wanted was to see her father, certainly not without Wat beside her.

The priest turned to the monks. "Brother Joseph?"

The taller, thinner monk said in a gravelly voice, "Father Abbot would mend the rift between you and your father, m'lady. Cockburn fears dire consequences will result from your so-hasty flight. He believes that renouncing your marriage and taking shelter at Scott's Hall was unwise, mayhap even dangerous. Father Abbot persuaded him to see for himself that you are safe at the Hall."

"Then why did he not bring Lord Cockburn to the Hall?" Janet asked.

Giving her a look of irritation, the monk said to Molly, "Cockburn would not agree to that, and he knew that you would not agree to meet at Henderland. Father Abbot suggested Rankilburn Kirk as a compromise, and the laird agreed."

"Then where are they?" Molly asked, forcing herself to remain calm.

Father Eamon said, "They will be at the kirk when we return, my lady. His messengers came ahead to inform me, and the three of us hied ourselves to fetch you. That we found you so quickly is quite providential."

"Providential," Molly repeated, glancing at her companions.

"I do hope you will meet with him," Father Eamon said earnestly. "We should aye seek to amend dissension. Your friends are welcome, too, of course, although you may prefer to meet privately with your father and the abbot."

Molly glanced at Rosalie, who shrugged. "I expect you have a duty to see him, my dear. If you want us there, we will come. I do fear that we might make an intrusively large audience for your father, and rather a large distraction for everyone else, if we have to wait for you outside in this chilly air."

"I don't want to meet him," Molly said frankly. She was unwilling to ask the impatient Rosalie to go with her and had *no* wish for Len Gray to be there. "Still, I expect I must see him if Father Abbot has gone to such trouble to arrange it."

"His reverence rarely goes to such extremes, m'lady," the hitherto silent monk said. "He does feel summat responsible for his own part in it, withal."

Molly knew she owed more to the abbot than a brief meeting in his presence with her father, especially since neither of them seemed to know yet that she had married Wat. "I'll see him," she said. "You others should ride on to the motte. If we finish talking before you return, someone will see me safely to rejoin you here."

"I will do that myself," Father Eamon assured them. "Such a meeting should take less than an hour, so you may look to see her ladyship in good time."

"I'm a-coming wi' ye, m'lady," Emma said flatly.

Molly nodded, grateful for her company.

The two monks exchanged a glance but did not object. Nevertheless, that glance led Molly to suspect that the two of them might try to dissuade Emma from staying with her while she met with Cockburn.

She decided to keep Emma at her side, whatever happened.

Len Gray said to the two grooms Tammy had sent,

"You lads stay with her ladyship, too. The other ladies will be safe with me and Lady Janet's groom."

Recalling things she had heard rumored about Len Gray, Molly hesitated.

Lady Rosalie waved her on. "Stay as long as you like, my dear," she said. "If we return before you do, we'll wait here until you come."

Molly and Emma watched them turn away and then followed the priest and the two monks back the way the three of them had come. Looking over her shoulder minutes later, Molly saw that the others had vanished into the trees.

The journey to the kirk took longer than she had expected, although the three men strode rapidly ahead of the riders. At last, she saw the small building on its rise above the burn. Water meadows spread round the base of its hillside.

"I see four more horses now," Father Eamon said cheerfully, casting a smile at Molly. "Just as I promised, m'lady, his reverence and your father are here."

No one stepped out to meet them, so the Scott's Hall grooms dismounted quickly and moved to help Molly and Emma.

"You lads walk them horses," the shorter monk said. "It willna do t' keep 'em standing in this chill, and we willna be long enough t' stable them."

The tall monk opened the kirk door, gestured, and said in his gravelly voice, "That way, m'lady. Through yon door t' yer left."

The nave of the small kirk was dusky, lit only by clerestory windows high in the wall above the door through which she entered and above the altar and rood screen straight ahead. She could barely make out a door to the left of the screen.

Sensing Emma right behind her, Molly glanced at her.

"I dinna hear nowt," Emma whispered. "Would we no hear voices if—"

A strange, gurgling cry behind them, followed by a hushing sound and a thump, made both young women whirl around to see Father Eamon slumped on the floor, his eyes and mouth open, blood pouring from a gash in his neck.

The shorter of the two monks stood over him with a bloody dagger in hand.

Emma opened her mouth, but before either she or Molly could scream, the tall monk grabbed Emma by an arm, swung her hard away from Molly, and let go of her to grab Molly. Seeing Emma crash to the floor, striking her head hard on a prayer stool, Molly screamed as loudly as she could.

"Hush that row," the man holding her snarled as he slapped her, hard.

The one with the dagger cast off his robes, revealing breeks, a leather jack, and a mail shirt underneath. "Dinna stand like a stone, man," he said curtly to the other. "Stuff summat in her gob and bring her along."

"I'm going nowhere!" Molly snapped. "Someone had to hear me scream."

From behind her, someone else said, "Aye, woman, *I* heard ye. But if ye meant them lads ye brung wi' ye, they be dead by now."

Molly's breath stopped in her throat. The very sound of that voice made her sick. She had heard nothing behind her until he spoke. But she knew who it was before she turned and saw him standing in the open doorway near the rood screen.

Of medium height, broad-shouldered and barrel-chested, Ringan Tuedy boasted a beard of tight red curls with more bristling from under his leather bonnet. He stood with his hands on his hips, grinning at her in fiendish triumph.

Emma, sprawled as she was between them with what looked ominously like a large pool of blood beneath her head, had not stirred.

Molly looked from one to the other, ignoring the huge lump in her throat to say gruffly, "You must be mad, Ring Tuedy."

~

Wat and his men covered the territory between Ancrum and Eckford by midday without meeting a soul who admitted seeing or hearing aught of Rutherford. Suspecting that the reiver and his men had moved faster and more stealthily than expected or, and more likely, had not yet crossed the Teviot, Wat forded the river at Eckford and headed southwest along the river until it met Jed Water.

A mile or so later, following the Jed toward Jedburgh, he spotted a lone rider coming toward them at speed. Recognizing Kip Graham's black pony before it was close enough to identify its rider, Wat whistled for the others to close in.

Kip would not be riding so hard unless he had news of Rutherford.

"Where is he?" Wat demanded as Kip wrenched his pony to a rearing halt.

"He cut west on a path that'll bring him northward

'twixt Jedburgh and Denholm, laird. Geordie thinks he'll seek one o' his hidey-holes hereabouts. But methinks the reiver has more mettle than sense to show hisself in Tevi-otdale wi' his grace at Melrose, Douglas at Hawick, and your lordship at the Hall not twelve miles from the Black Tower. Mayhap Rutherford doesna ken aboot the Doug-las, though."

"He's too canny not to know," Wat said. "To have evaded capture all this time, he must have superb sources of information. How fast was he moving?"

"If he keeps the pace he were setting, he'll likely make camp near Denholm. In one o' the cleuchs 'neath Black Law, Geordie thinks. With all these clouds, it'll be a gey dark night, so likely he'll rest till the moon rises. *If* it shows itself."

"He has no beasts with him, then."

"Just their own mounts and spare ponies. I heard that when his men go a-raiding, they keep only what they need t' feed theirselves. They hide what booty they take in caches, hither and yon. See you, three nights ago they razed two estates in Redesdale, so Northumberland wants 'em now as bad as his grace does."

"Take a fresh horse and ride back to Geordie, Kip. Tell him to be careful, especially if he is close to Rutherford. We don't want to stir any dust that the man might sense. I want him to think that he and his lads are as safe as lambs in a fold."

Watching Kip ride away, Wat drew his men in closer and told them what Kip had learned, adding, "Don't grow too confident, though, lads. Rutherford can change direc-tion at any time. And he will have watchers out, too, so we'll ride scattered as we did before. Keep your eyes open, and if any of you kens a place other than Black Law where you think they might make camp, speak up."

As a variety of shouted suggestions flew at Wat, Jed said quietly, "D'ye think the man comes this way, thinking to lift your beasts, sir? Seems daft, that."

"He'd be greedy enough," Wat replied. "But he might be heading northwest for some reason other than those rumors of ours meant to draw him this way."

"The Rutherford estates lie nobbut five or six miles east o' Melrose," Jed said musingly. "The man may be heading for his own country."

"If he is, he's a fool, because Jamie's men will be watching those estates closely," Wat said. "But we have seen no sign that Rutherford is a fool. He has sympathizers in Tweeddale besides his kinsmen, though, men who are just as lawless and ruthless as he is."

"Aye, them wicked Tuedys t' name one lot," Jed muttered.

Wat glanced at him, wondering how much information Jed had gleaned about Molly and Tuedy, but he did not ask. Whatever Jed knew, he was Sym's son and would keep his knowledge to himself or within his immediate, equally trustworthy family. Still, Tuedy *was* friendly with the Cockburns, so if, as Wat suspected, Will and Ned were in league with the reiver, then Tuedy likely was, too.

Watching his men spread out along the darkening grassy hillsides, Wat kept Jed with him, aware that the lad knew the area near Black Law even better than he did himself. Jed was Sym's son, after all, and was nearly as skilled a tracker.

Molly had no idea where she was.

Tuedy terrified her, and she was sure that Emma was as dead as Father Eamon and the grooms were. Both lads had died outside the kirk in the same manner as the poor, unsuspecting priest had died inside.

Tuedy's men had left Emma where she lay, not bothering even to cover her body. The pool of blood under her head and lack of any sign that she breathed had told them all they wanted to know about her.

When Molly had tried to go to her, Tuedy jerked her back and snarled, "Ye'll come with me, woman. 'Tis time ye learned to obey your husband."

"You are *not* my husband," she retorted. "I am lawfully married to Walter Scott of Buccleuch and Rankilburn now. He will kill you for this."

"Ye terrify me," Tuedy said, rolling his eyes. "I'm no afeard o' Wat Scott, and his fool priest be dead. Certes, a woman canna be married to two men, so ye be my wife, will ye, nil ye. Now, dinna speak again unless ye want to feel my hand."

With that, he'd dragged her from the kirk to the waiting horses, whereupon she saw that, besides the two false monks, he had four more ruffians with him.

Taking a rope from one of them, Tuedy tied one end of it to her left wrist. Then, he helped her mount her horse, looped the rope under the horse's neck, and tied the other end to her right wrist. When she pointed out that she could not sit up straight without choking the horse, she earned herself a hard slap across the face that might have knocked her to the ground had Tuedy not retained his iron grip on her wrist.

"I told ye what I'd do if ye didna hold your tongue," he growled when she glowered at him. "Ye've rope enough t' hold on to the pony's mane, so dinna fall off. If ye do aught to slow us down, I'll bare yer arse and take leather to ye."

With that, he mounted his horse and, leading hers, set a fast pace southward and away from the kirk. After they crested the first hill, he increased the pace.

The circuitous route they took upset Molly's sense of direction. The hilly, often wooded country further disoriented her, and gathering dark clouds soon hid the sun. Worse, she saw no one who might heed her cries had she dared make any.

It occurred to her that even if she weren't afraid of Tuedy, screaming would avail her naught. He would just tell anyone who tried to interfere that he was disciplining a wayward wife, and that would be that.

Claiming to be Wat's wife would do her no good, either. Tuedy would likely claim that she was daft.

They reached their destination in the late afternoon, but it revealed nothing useful. She saw only a long, thatched, stone cottage in a deep cleuch with a rivulet running through it. Two decrepit outbuildings and a wooden stockade stood nearby.

The larger outbuilding appeared to be a stable or barn, the other a shed of some kind. The thatch on all three buildings was long overdue for replacement.

When the seven men dismounted, Tuedy untied Molly's hands and stood back to let her slide down off her horse. "Ye can talk now, if ye must," he said. "But dinna sauce me, or ye'll feel me hand again."

Determined not to let him see how frightened she was, she said with what she believed must, under the circumstances, be admirable calm, "Is this where you live? What do you mean to do with me here?"

"I live at Drumelzier wi' me da and four brothers, as well ye ken," he said. "As to yourself, ye'll bide here whilst I tend to important business. I'll leave ye food and water, and quilts, but ye'll ha' nobbut your own thoughts for company whilst I'm awa'."

A surge of grateful relief swept through her at the welcome thought of his impending absence. Surely, she could find a way to escape while he was gone.

She was exerting herself to conceal her relief when he added, "Lest ye think I've forgot that ye did me out o' me wedding night, I did nae such thing. We'll attend to that as soon as I ha' me supper."

A chill shot up Molly's spine, and she swayed where she stood.

Collecting herself, she said, "I hope you won't expect me to prepare your meals, for I don't know how to cook." That was not perfectly true, but her father had expected her only to oversee the preparation of their meals.

Tuedy said, "Me and me lads ha' long seen to our own needs, lass. We willna starve. But come along now, and I'll show ye where ye'll stay." '

"Do you trust your people here not to harm me before your return?" she asked, searching his eyes in hope of reading truth or falsehood in his reply.

"People?" He grinned. "I ha' nae people here, but I'll be gone just for the night and mayhap a bit o' the morrow. Ye'll ha' time to think on your sins and decide to behave. I've told me da and me brothers that we're wed, so they'll expect to see ye soon. But I canna take ye to Drumelzier until ye learn to mind me."

"Why do you want me?" she asked bluntly.

"Sakes, ye be the only woman I've met that I *do* want. There's aye the land your da promised as your marriage portion, too. A man wi' four brothers..." He shrugged.

"But your marriage to me was unlawful, and mine to Walter Scott is legal. He has already...that is, we are *truly* man and wife. You and I are not."

He shook his head again. "If ye mean to say that ye've lain with him, I'll no hold that against ye, though I'll enjoy making ye a wee bit sorry for it when I claim ye for m'self. Ye'll no be thinking o' him after I'm done wi' ye. I promise ye that."

"He *will* kill you," she muttered.

Tuedy laughed and said, "I'll welcome him an he tries. Now, come and I'll show ye where I mean to keep ye whilst I'm awa'." His bruising grip on her arm reminded her that she would be wise to obey him until she escaped.

Then, I vow, Ring Tuedy, if no one else kills you, I'll do it myself.

~

Wat and his men met Geordie and his lads soon after dark at the northwestern side of a vast, cleuch-ridden circuit of hills southeast of Denholm, cresting in the thousand-foot peak known as Black Law. Shortly afterward, two more of Geordie's lads rejoined them, reporting that Rutherford was making camp on the south bank of a steepsided, burn-fed cleuch descending eastward from the summit.

Wat quickly gave his orders: "We'll flank them, Geordie. We'll send men ahead now in pairs to locate their watchers. Then you'll take the north side of the cleuch, so keep your lads as quiet as mice in a mill as they near that encampment."

"Aye, laird, I ken what to do."

"I know you do. But wait until they've had their heads down for a time. Then come down into the cleuch on foot. The less noise we make the better, so await my signal before you ford that burn unless one of Rutherford's men raises the alarm."

"And if one does?"

"We'll descend on them like banshee warriors," Wat said with a grin. "But with luck, we'll have them surrounded and helpless before anyone wakes up."

With only scattered starlight to guide them, he left Geordie and his men to find their way over the nearby hills and took his own men to skirt the wooded hills south of the peak. One- and two-man scouting parties cleared the way for both groups. Men and horses all moved in well-practiced silence.

Topping the forested slope on the south side of the cleuch, Wat reined in well within the trees. Peering down into the deep valley below, he breathed a sigh of satisfaction. Even by cloudy starlight, his night vision was keen enough to make out shapes of men sleeping in a clearing on the south side of the burn, nearer the woods than the water, their horses grazing or dozing a short distance away.

To Jed, he murmured, "We've taken out their watchers, but I doubt this lot has had their heads down longer than an hour, so some may yet be wakeful. The wee burn's babble would aid us more had they slept closer to it, but Rutherford's too canny for that. We'll go afoot, though. I want to get close enough to surround them without waking them before we're ready."

Giving the dismount signal to the rest of the men, he tethered his horse to a nearby branch. Then he and his men made their way cautiously down the hill.

Jed murmured, "Their ponies be as used to keeping quiet as ours be, sir. I'm thinking I could slip down and move 'em right out o' their reach."

"Nay, we'll want those horses after we capture the men. We're nobbut ten or twelve miles from Melrose, so we'll take them straight to Jamie. If he's left the abbey, we'll deliver Rutherford to him wherever he's gone."

Jed nodded, and they continued in silence.

Wat noted that he could hear only an occasional soft rustle behind him. When he and Jed neared the clearing, he paused again, trying to discern movement beyond the burn. At first, he feared that Geordie's men were not yet in position. Then he detected a moving shape on the ground, creeping toward the burn.

To Jed, Wat whispered, "You have your horn, aye?"

"Aye, sure," Jed hissed back, his toothy grin barely visible.

"Good, then pass the word back that when I raise my hand, the lads must creep close enough to form a line around the reivers, with their weapons ready. Once they're in place, blow your horn."

Sword in hand now, Wat moved toward the reivers. He heard one softly snoring and counted sixteen men in a semicircle, its flat side facing the water.

Unable to discern any of the sleeping men's features in such darkness, Wat tried to imagine where their leader would most likely sleep. His own men having scoured the woods, he was sure that Rutherford must lie near his men.

Wat raised his arm then. Ghostly figures crept up

silently behind, beside, and beyond him, until his men and Geordie's encircled the reivers. With swords and dirks drawn, they would easily prevent any escape to the woods or the water.

Noting that Jed was back in place on his right, Wat nodded to him.

Jed put the horn to his lips.

Its clarion blast seemed almost to levitate the sleeping men, startling them all into scrambling for weapons.

Pricking the man before him with his sword point, Wat shouted, "We surround you, and we're twice your number. Leave your weapons on the ground!"

A deeper voice roared, "Dinna heed the man! At them, lads!"

But splashing and shouting from the burn drowned out his words to all save a few. Most of the reivers stayed where they were.

Those who did not quickly learned their error.

"That chap," Wat muttered to Jed. The one standing alone amidst those others still sitting. I'm nearly certain he is the one who shouted."

"Aye, laird, me, too," Jed said. "I'll just ha' a look."

With a smile, Wat watched Jed walk through a group of the raiders as Geordie's men secured them and say casually, "I think ye dropped this, Gil."

When the man turned, saying, "What did ye find?" Jed deftly secured him.

The difference between the two men in size was significant. As Wat watched them, he heard Geordie say with a chuckle, "I told ye he were a puny one, laird."

Their success in capturing the reiver was cheering, but Geordie's next words were not. "One o' me lads said he'd seen two riders coming down yon hill behind us, laird, afore we crossed the burn. When they saw us attack, he said they whipped round and vanished in the darkness. He and another lad chased 'em but didna find nowt."

Summoning Jed, Wat told him what Geordie's men had seen, "Find out where they saw those riders, and see if you can find tracks enough to follow them."

"Aye, laird. Where will ye be if chance be that we can?"

Wat said, "Right here, I expect. I don't want to try moving this lot before the moon rises... and, with these clouds, likely not until dawn breaks."

Chapter 18 _____

Molly had no sense of what time it was because her current quarters had no window and thus no light. She was sure, though, that she had been there for hours.

Too tired to think after Tuedy left her there, she had wrapped herself in her cloak and dozed but had no idea for how long. The only good thing about her situation was that Tuedy had not yet made good his threat to claim her for himself.

Either he had not finished his supper or he had forgotten her. She heard frequent shouts of male laughter.

At Henderland such laughter would mean that the men were drinking more than they were eating. If she was lucky, Tuedy would drink himself senseless.

If not, she would be in more danger than ever.

Although she wished she could make herself believe that he had forgotten her, she knew it was more likely that he just wanted to let her fear of him increase. Moreover, if she kept thinking about him, that was exactly what would happen.

Knowing no more than that he had locked her in a windowless, pantrylike storage area, she decided to focus her thoughts on learning all she could about the place and finding some sort of weapon.

Her sense of touch told her that the walls were stone, likely up to the thatch, which was out of her reach. The floor was hard-packed dirt. The shelves, built of rough-hewn boards, stood free and were wobbly enough to fall on her if she tried to climb them. The only possible weapon she found was a long-handled wooden spoon called a spurtle, customarily used to flip oatcakes or stir big pots of porridge.

She couldn't imagine Tuedy making porridge, but the thought made her wonder if a servant might come in by day when he stayed there. That tiny flame of hope died quickly though. If one did come, she could be sure that he, or even an unlikely she, would either be too fiercely loyal or too terrified of Tuedy to aid her.

Feeling her way blindly around the small room, Molly discovered two loose stones in its walls. Both formed part of what she believed must be the outer wall, but when she tried to wriggle the first one loose, she could not.

The door of the room had opened outward, and she had seen the slotted steel hasp and staple now holding it shut. After Tuedy locked her in, she had tried to move the door but could not budge it. She was also unlikely to dislodge whatever he'd inserted through the staple to keep the hasp in place. Nothing had even rattled.

The second loose stone she found moved more easily than the first. It was no bigger than her two hands together, but she hoped that if she could wiggle it free, others would come out more easily. Testing that hope would at least fill her time.

Tuedy had assured her that no rescue would come, and she believed him. But she had escaped him by herself before. With luck, she would do it again.

The spurtle's bowl was too large and its end too rounded to make it a useful tool for digging. But the tip of its handle fit into a crack between the loose stone and one next to it. Taking care not to break the handle, Molly scraped bits of rubble away, working by touch and smoothing the debris across the dirt floor.

When she tired of digging, she searched from shelf to shelf, trying to guess what things were by their feel. The only useful items she found were a basket of apples and two candles, tallow ones by their noxious odor.

It had not occurred to Tuedy to search her, other than to take her eating knife from its sheath on the leather girdle Janet had given her. So she still had her tinderbox and flint, her needle case, and her wee sewing scissors.

As she went back to work, her thoughts jumped to Wat. Was he safe? Had he caught Rutherford? Did he know yet what had happened to her?

Knowing that she was more likely on her own, she gave herself a mental shake and reminded herself that she was comfortable enough for the time being. Finding the candles had given her hope, although she could not imagine why it should.

The thatch might burn, but as damp as it had been of late, it was unlikely, even if she could reach it. Stone walls would *not* burn. And, even if she could burn the wooden shelves or the door, a fire would just fill the room with smoke.

However, if the darkness became too much to bear, or if she wanted to judge what progress she made with the stones, she could light a candle with her flint and the tinderbox. If the stirring of hope came only from that small fact, so be it.

Deciding at last that Tuedy and the others must have fallen asleep, she lay down, covered herself with her cloak, and dozed again only to wake abruptly and in dread at the noise of male voices excitedly—nay, angrily—raised.

She could not discern many words, and the ones she did hear told her nothing until she heard the name Rutherford. That voice was not Tuedy's, nor did Molly recognize it. Getting up, she put an ear to the door, hoping to hear more.

She heard Tuedy say, "Snirk, ye'll go to Scott's Hall, so saddle a pony. I'll tell ye what to say after ye've done that. They'll do nowt to harm ye or keep ye, so take young Jack if ye want him. Make haste, though. We've nae time to spare."

If the man, Snirk, responded, Molly did not hear him.

"You lot," Tuedy went on, "pack up what's left from our supper to take with us. I'll settle the lass in a twink, and then we'll ride."

Hastily stepping away from the door and feeling her way back to her cloak, Molly lay down and shut her eyes, hoping Tuedy would not hear her fast-thumping heart. What had he meant by 'settle the lass in a twink'?

She heard metal scrape against metal as he released the hasp.

The door swung open.

Blinking, and trying to do so as one normally did when rudely awakened, Molly sat up and pushed her hair out of her eyes.

Tuedy filled the doorway, the golden light of candles or cressets behind him making him look like a giant black shadow looming there. He held a large bundle under one arm and a jug in his free hand.

"I've brung ye some oatcakes, a jug o' water, and a pallet for the night, lass," he said, dropping the bundle to the floor. "I'm leaving now, for I've business I must see to. Just use yon pail in the corner when ye need to relieve yourself."

"I heard the name Rutherford," she said impulsively. "Do you know him?"

"Aye, sure, everyone kens Gil Rutherford."

"But do you know him yourself?" she persisted. "I heard he's the most successful raider in Scotland. Do you ride with him?"

"Everyone goes a-raiding," Tuedy said, reaching to set the jug on a shelf and extracting three oatcakes from inside his jack to set beside it.

"Mercy, do my brothers ride, too?"

"Ye must ken fine that they do. Gil Rutherford be the king o' raiders, but your brother Will has a long reputation, too."

"I meant does he ride with Rutherford? Does Ned?"

"Now ye're asking too many questions. If ye want t' ken what your brothers get up to, ask them."

"What about the Elliots?" she asked quietly. "Do any Elliots ride with him?"

His lips tightened. "I told ye t' shut your gob," he said. "All ken fine that Elliots will go a-raiding with anyone. Why would ye ask such a daft question?"

"Because that lassie you killed in the kirk today was Sym Elliot's daughter, Emma," she said, fighting back tears to eye him closely. "Since he is Lady Meg's Sym, a thousand or more wrathful Elliots and Scotts may be hunting you by now."

To her shock and dismay, he just shrugged.

"Do you *want* them after you?" Molly demanded.

"Sakes, lass, by capturing ye, I've already invited the wrath o' the Scotts. A host o' Elliots willna trouble me."

"Why not?"

"Because Wat Scott has more to lose. I ken fine that he only married ye to spite me, but he thinks ye're his now, and he's a man as would keep what he owns. He'll soon be thinking o' nowt save how to get ye back."

"He'll succeed, too," she said more curtly than she had intended.

"Nay then, he won't," Tuedy said. "I'm no going t' let ye go. Ye canna get out, and nae one will come to aid ye. I'll be back afore sundown tomorrow, and if I find that ye've tried to escape, ye'll no ha' your sorrows to seek, I promise ye."

"What if you *never* come back? What if Wat kills you?"

"Ye'd best hope he does nowt o' the sort," he retorted. "Me lads willna come here without me. And by the time me brothers come, ye'll ha' starved to death."

⁓

Wat awoke to a light touch on his shoulder. The sky was as dark as it had been when he'd shut his eyes. Only the hushing babble of the burn and someone's uneven snoring disturbed the cleuch's silence. Jed—his shadowy shape as identifiable to his master in darkness as by daylight—dropped to a knee beside him.

"Did you learn where those men who ran away are headed?" Wat asked him.

"Nay, laird," he murmured grimly. "'Twas gey rocky, and torchlight didna help much. We ha' visitors, though. Me da followed our signs."

Wat sat up quickly. "What's amiss?"

Jed was silent long enough to make the hairs on Wat's neck stand up. "Has aught happened to Mam or Gram, what?"

Bluntly then, Jed said, "'Tis Lady Molly, laird. Some-one's taken her."

Wat started to speak, only to have the words stick hard in his throat. Pausing to swallow, fighting against clearing his throat lest he waken their captives, he said, "You say Sym brought the news?"

"Aye, but he says ye'll want to talk wi' Len Gray. He's brung him, too."

"Len Gray?"

"Aye, laird. They be waiting amidst the trees up yonder."

"Show me." Wat got up, grabbed his sword, and flung his cloak over his shoulders. The air was icy, and the chill that had struck him earlier lingered, making him feel even colder. *Which of the men that Molly knew had taken her, and how?*

He and Jed moved swiftly but silently up to the tree line. From behind a large oak, Sym's murmur drifted to Wat's ears. "Here, laird."

Finding him, Wat said as quietly, "Who did it, and how, Sym?"

"We ken fine who it was," Sym said. "But it be best that Lady Rosalie's Len tell ye what happened," he added, ges-turing toward the lean, dark shape beside him.

Keeping his voice low, Len Gray said, "We rode out this morning, my lord, to visit Rankilburn Kirk and the motte nearby. The ladies Rosalie, Janet, and Molly went, as well as Sym's Emma. We also took Lady Janet's groom and two others."

"They were armed, aye?" Wat said, certain that Tam would have seen to it.

"We all were," Gray said. "Not that it mattered. We met your priest, Father Eamon, and two Cistercian monks near the wee bridge across the burn. The priest told us the Abbot of Melrose had persuaded Lady Molly's father to let him arrange a meeting with her at Rankilburn Kirk. Father Abbot would be there to—"

"Father Abbot would have conferred with me first," Wat interjected with a frown, glancing at Sym. "Also, I doubt he'd send monks to fetch my lady to him."

Sym remained silent.

Gray said, "We realized that afterward, sir. Meantime, Lady Rosalie did offer to ride with them to the kirk, but we all realized that an audience would make Lady Molly's meeting with Cockburn more difficult. Sakes, sir, we were certain that she would be safe with the abbot, Father Eamon, two monks, and her own father."

"My Emma did go with her ladyship, laird," Sym said quietly.

Something in his tone alerted Wat to a heavier meaning in his words. "Did those villains capture Emma, too, Sym?"

"Nay, laird, but one o' them so-called monks—may God send him straight to hell!—knocked her down so she cracked her skull on a prayer stool. Then them perfidious bangsters left her a-lying in a pool o' her own blood."

"Sym," Wat said, grief surging through him as he reached to grip Sym's shoulder, "I'm so sorry! I swear to you, we'll see them hanged for her murder."

"They do be guilty o' murder, laird, but it isna Emma's," Sym said. "They killed Father Eamon. But God be thankit," he added before Wat could express his dismay, "our Emma has me own hard head and me keen wits, too. She lay like one dead, so they must *think* they killed her, whilst she were a-holding her breath as best she could and listening hard. She said her ladyship talked right back to them monks. Then a new voice spoke up, and Emma heard her ladyship call him Ringan Tuedy."

"So Tuedy has her," Wat muttered. Suddenly, the relief he had felt at learning of Emma's survival made his fear for Molly nearly overpowering.

It occurred to him that if Tuedy *had* Molly and claimed that the two of them had consummated their union at once, proving otherwise would be impossible even if a magistrate let Lady Meg testify to Molly's intact virtue after the forced wedding.

Struggling to clear his mind so he could think, Wat asked the most important question first. "Where might Tuedy have taken her?"

Without hesitation, Sym said, "I dinna ken that yet, but he must ha' known ye'd left Rankilburn, sir. He'd never ha' tried such a daft plan had ye been home. See you, he sent word to us hisself o' what he had done."

"What? Taunting me?"

Sym hesitated but said, "Perhaps, a bit. But the important thing be that when he did send word, he must already ha' known that ye'd captured Rutherford."

"Be damned to the man!" Wat muttered. "How could he have known that?"

"The two men Geordie saw who hied themselves off, laird," Jed said quietly.

"Ay-di-mi," Wat said, putting a hand to his brow. Gathering his wits, he looked again at Sym. "What exactly did Tuedy's messenger say."

"'Twas a pair o' lads," Sym said. "They said they didna ken nowt but that Tuedy had sent them to tell us he has our lady Molly and will give her back to ye only in exchange for Gil Rutherford. Ye ha' till tomorrow's dawn to save her."

"By God, that's no time at all," Wat muttered, "I'll—" He broke off, unable to think beyond his overwhelming desire to see Tuedy's head on a pike.

"Tuedy said ye're to meet him at Peat Law wi' Rutherford, laird," Sym said softly. "If ye're no there on time, he said, he's a-going to keep her hisself and make her sorry for ever letting ye touch her, if he doesna kill her."

                            ⁓

The second stone came out of the wall more easily than the first had but only if one discounted the time it had taken to scrape away the mortar that had bound it to stones above and at its sides. The process was slow, and the room stayed dark.

Nevertheless, Molly could put a hand through the hole she had made and be nearly sure that she felt outside air. She thought she could feel a slight breeze.

By putting her head right to the floor, she could see through the hole, but that brought no satisfaction. Reminding herself that the sky was likely overcast again or the surrounding hills hid any stars, she went doggedly back to work.

Again, she lost track of time. Lighting one of the candles and sticking it in its own tallow on the lowest shelf, she saw that it merely reassured her that no mice or large spiders were inclined to disturb her labors.

However, if Tuedy returned, he would surely notice the candlelit hole.

Also, she might have greater need for the candles later, so reluctantly, she pinched it out. Then, feeling her way, she began working on the next stone, and a new problem arose. The air outside was considerably colder now than the air in the storeroom. Moreover, it occurred to her that if she could not make her hole large enough to crawl through before Tuedy returned, the hole would admit enough daylight to reveal itself to him when he came into the room. What he would do then...

She refused to think about that.

～

Wat found it hard to breathe after learning of Tuedy's threat, but he knew he could not dwell on what might be happening to Molly. If he was going to find her, he had to concentrate on that and that alone. One of his strengths, according to those who spoke of such things, was his ability to focus on one task at a time without losing sight of others that remained to do. He would have to prove that skill now.

Sym and Jed remained silent, and Wat ignored Len Gray until Gray said, "We did learn from young Emma that tracks of at least a half dozen or more horses led away from the kirk, my lord. Despite her injury, the lassie managed to follow them until their trail led up out of the glen. We found her senseless soon after that."

"How was she when you left the Hall?" Wat asked Sym.

"She'll do, laird. Like I told ye, she inherited her da's hard head. Tammy did send men to follow their trail, but it led them hither and yon until they lost it. One o' our lads said it looked to him as if they was keeping close to Teviotdale, though."

"Not heading north toward Drumelzier?"

"Nay, for all the twists and turns they did take, the lad said, they kept aiming more eastward than north." Sym paused, glancing at his son.

Then, he said. "Jed told me about them two chaps that got away when ye captured Rutherford, laird. We may be able to track them when it gets light. Tam sent trackers after the two wha' came to the Hall. He sent others out to raise the dale and said they should all gather at Bellendean. One way or t'other . . ." He paused.

"We'll find her ladyship, laird," Jed said. "We must."

"Aye, we will, but we must not linger here any longer," Wat said. Gesturing toward the sleeping men below, he added, "Get these men up and ready to travel. Put sacks over their heads and have our men lead their horses. Tell Geordie I want Rutherford near me with at least four of our lads flanking him."

"I don't know this area, my lord," Len Gray said. "Where is Peat Law?"

"It rises amidst a maze of hills just northwest of Selkirk, not far from where Yarrow Water flows into the Tweed. It is distinctive, taller than Black Law."

"Them wha' tracked Lady Molly did see Ettrick Water *and* the Yarrow in their wandering," Sym said. "Tuedy did say ye must come alone wi' Rutherford. Ye willna do that, but we canna take all these ruffians wi' us."

"We'll be heading toward Melrose, nevertheless," Wat pointed out. "Geordie can take Rutherford's men on to Jamie at the abbey. He can also promise his grace for me that Rutherford will soon follow. Jamie has enough men-at-arms with him to see that all of these louts get to Stirling for hanging."

"He'll no be a-hanging them at the abbey, more's the pity," Sym said.

"He'll want to," Wat said. "But likely Father Abbot will disagree."

"Hawick's closer than Melrose," Gray pointed out. "We could take them there and leave them with Douglas for the nonce."

"Aye, but I'd spend more time getting Douglas out of bed and persuading him to lock this lot up than taking them to the abbey will," Wat said.

"What if his grace has gone?" Gray asked.

Wat cast him a narrow look. "Then I'd have heard as much. You need not ride with us, you know. Mayhap, you should go back to the Hall and Aunt Rosalie."

"I believe I'll be more help if I stay with you, m'lord," Gray said quietly.

Wat shrugged. He didn't trust the man, but neither did he need to worry about one man among so many of his own lads.

The men wasted little time and were soon away. With the overcast sky, it was still dark, giving little hint of the time. Wat knew that with the nights as long as they were, they had hours yet before the eastern sky would grow lighter.

Nevertheless, his tension increased. He ordered torches lit.

Sym rode up alongside him after they crossed to the northwest bank of the Teviot near Denholm. Reining his mount close to Wat's, he said, "We didna leave anyone behind to see if they could find them tracks from last night, laird."

Wat said bluntly, "Do you think anyone else could find what Jed did not?"

"The light was bad," Sym reminded him. "By daylight—"

Wat shook his head. "I can't spare any more men, Sym. We have twice as many as Rutherford does, but I don't want to take unnecessary risk. Also, Tuedy's meeting place concerns me. Peat Law sits amidst a maze of cleuchs and hills, nearly all of which have water spilling down them, just as Black Law does."

"Sakes, laird, the Borders be rife wi' such places. Them hills yonder north of us be just as bad, and we'll be passing right betwixt 'em."

"Aye, but we'll meet the highroad to Melrose that way, Sym. As it is, we're unlikely to reach Peat Law by dawn. We need to increase our pace."

He gave the order, assuring himself that a faster pace would make it less likely that any of their prisoners could plan mischief. Even so, his tension grew. He almost wished that Sym would keep talking. It was harder than ever to keep his thoughts off Molly.

He was still struggling to avoid thinking about what Tuedy might be doing to her when armed riders descended from the hills around them, and battle erupted.

Wat barely drew his sword quickly enough from its scabbard on his back to block a sword slash from a rider right in front of him. The swordsman's horse plunged into his, but Wat's mount sidestepped it enough to let Wat draw his dirk and dispatch the other rider with an upward thrust into the other's ribs.

Wheeling his mount away, his gaze scanning all sides, he saw Sym and Jed battling two others, Len Gray a third nearby. With pandemonium reigning all around them, the torch nearest him went out.

When it did, and before his night vision recovered,

Wat felt a man-sized object crash into him. Sharp pain exploded in his upper left arm. His horse seemed to vanish from under him, and he hit the ground with a bone-shaking thud.

The night swallowed him into its darkness.

~

Molly felt an unexpected urge to burst into tears.

Having managed to loosen and remove four stones from the outer wall, she realized with despair that although she could get a firmer grip on those at the base of the wall, they were half-buried in the unyielding ground and would not move.

They were also uneven and larger than the ones she had removed. Only one of those was any size at all, and the hole she had made was not nearly large enough for her to crawl through.

Dashing tears from her cheeks, she muttered, "Stop thinking about failure, Molly Cockburn Scott. Think only of getting *out* of here!"

Though the nights were longer, they were not endless. When daylight came, at least she would see what she was doing. On the thought, she lit her candle again, held it near the opening, and saw that she would need at least three or four more stones out before she'd have a chance of squeezing through the opening.

Her tinderbox had little tinder remaining, so she left the candle lit.

~

Hearing a horse snort, Wat decided that either he was still alive or heaven did, as he had long ago thought it *must*, have horses to ride. Since God knew everything, He would surely know the value of having a good horse under Him.

"Laird, if ye're no dead yet, open your eyes."

Sym's voice sounded strange, but it *was* Sym's voice. Everything else seemed oddly silent.

Wat opened his eyes and saw a few scattered stars with Sym's head blocking most of his view. Then approaching torchlight revealed the older man's face close to his own. "What happened, Sym?"

"Rutherford's gone," Sym said bluntly. "They must ha' recognized his pony, laird, 'cause even wi' that sack over his head, they struck down the lad leading his horse and cut Rutherford hisself out as if he'd been a steer meant for butchering. Then them chaps made off wi' him, and most o' the others followed. I dinna ken how many there were, laird, but they dashed in and were gone again near as fast."

"What about our lads?" Wat asked.

"Jock Graham be dead, but there be only one other injury 'sides yourself, sir."

Wat winced. He knew all his men well, hated to lose any, and Jock had been Kip Graham's cousin. It was a pity, he mused, that Rutherford could hang just once.

"How is our injured man?" he asked.

"Better than ye look," Sym replied.

"I'll do," Wat said firmly, hoping he was right. "What about their lot?"

"A half dozen o' them fled wi' Rutherford and the rescuers that made away wi' him. The others willna trouble us further."

Trying to think and to assess how much damage his body had taken, Wat said, "Is someone following those who got away?"

"Aye, sure, my Jed and Ferg, along wi' half o' our men. I'm thinking Rutherford and them will no be able to hide their trail, leastwise not after dawn. Afore then, they could vanish, I expect. But Geordie and the men o' your tail be here, and we caught ourselves some'un that may be useful."

"Who?"

"Ned Cockburn," Sym said. "He's alive only 'cause Pete's Aggie recognized him, and Pete didna kill him lest his death upset Lady Molly. I didna say nowt about nowt to the man and told our lads to hold their wheesht, too."

"Good, I want to talk to Ned." Wat sat up, taking care to do so slowly. Someone had bandaged his left arm. It hurt like fury, but he could move it.

"We canna trade that villain for our lady Molly now," Sym said. "Even if we could catch them, we canna reach Peat Law by dawn."

"Someone organized this ambush, Sym. We need to know if Tuedy was involved. Our best hope is that he knows nowt of what happened here."

Sym grunted. "I dinna ken that, sir. If he knew we had Rutherford..."

He stopped there, but Wat easily followed his logic. "Then someone told him, and the number of men who knew we'd caught him is small."

"Gey small," Sym agreed. "I count just two. And, afore Tuedy said where to meet *him*, we'd ha' gone north through Denholm to reach Melrose, and avoided this cut. Knowing ye had to hie yourself, though..."

Wat nodded and wished he hadn't when pain shot through his head. "Send someone to Bellendean or go yourself, Sym. Tam has men out looking for Tuedy, and I want as many more searchers as we can get. But tell them to do it quietly."

"I'd send Kip Graham, laird. He'll need action to keep from thinking about Jock, and I be staying wi' ye. Herself did say I were no to take me keekers off ye."

"Begging your pardon, my lord," Len Gray said quietly from behind them.

"What?" Wat demanded, turning swiftly and thus causing himself another jolt of pain. "You walk like a damned cat, Gray."

Unfazed, Gray said, "If you're gathering searchers, may I suggest that we inform the Douglas, too. He can send people out from Hawick faster than Kip Graham can reach the men gathering at Bellendean."

"I'd liefer not spare anyone else," Wat said. Looking at Sym, he added, "You did say that our injured man fared better than I did, aye?"

"Aye, laird, and he'll do well enow. He willna be able to ride with us, but he says he can get hisself home again."

"Then, if you want to help, Gray, you can see our man safely home."

"I can, aye, *and* visit Hawick as we go. He can rest whilst I talk to Douglas."

"Ye seem mighty eager t' see the man," Sym said curtly.

"I am, and I hope he'll be as eager to talk to me."

"By God, you're a damned spy!" Wat exclaimed. "I suspected as much."

"Guilty, my lord," Gray said with a wry smile. "But not of spying for the Percies, if that's what you've also been thinking."

Chapter 19 ───────────

The tallow candle sputtered out at last. Plunged into pitch darkness again, Molly thought wistfully but briefly about how comforting its light had been. With a sigh, she felt her way back to her slowly widening hole.

"I hope Tuedy stays away all day," she muttered. The hole was big enough now to get her head through without scraping her ears off but would not yet allow passage of her shoulders.

She had stuck tight when she tried to put an arm through with her head and had been terrified for a time that Tuedy would find her like that.

Where had he gone? If he had gone raiding with Gil Rutherford, who else had gone with them, and how long would they be away? Were Will and Ned involved, as she had begun to suspect they were?

That Wat might yet prove to be right about them was vexing.

She dwelt on that thought as she applied the spurtle's handle end to the mortar. It occurred to her then that she'd never heard Wat gloat, about anything.

He was kind to his sisters and took full responsibility for them and for the rest of his household and clan. He was admirably even-tempered, albeit rather terrifying in his own way when he did get angry. She trusted his word.

Fervently, she hoped that he was searching for her and furious with Tuedy.

⁓

"What the devil are you trying to say to me?" Wat demanded of Len Gray.

"I served the fourth Earl of Douglas whilst I was in England," Gray said. "I spied on Harry Percy...that is, the current Earl of Northumberland, but only in hope of making friends with him. You must know that as Hotspur's son, and due to his father's and grandfather's enmity with the fourth King Henry of England, Harry Percy spent much of his minority exiled in Scotland."

"Aye, sure, we *kept* him in Scotland just as the English king kept Jamie in England, though not nearly as long. Even so, if the current Earl of Northumberland, likes us now, I've seen no evidence of it here in the Borders."

"Aye, but the fourth Douglas hoped to persuade him at least to support Scotland's right to its own territory. He sent me to keep an eye on him and judge when the time was right for a parley. But when the fourth Douglas died three years ago and his son inherited the earldom, I was reluctant to send messages to him, having no knowledge of him other than that his father deemed him a weakling."

"Fine words from *him*," Wat growled, knowing that the fourth Douglas had been much to blame for the disaster that had taken the life of his grandfather and thus robbed Lady Meg of her beloved husband.

"See you," Len went on, "Lady Rosalie's husband, Richard Percy, was a close cousin of Harry's and part of his entourage until the King summoned Harry to London. Harry sent Richard Percy to Wales to learn what remnants, if any, remained of the rebellion there. And, as you know, Richard died there. When he was dying, he asked me to look after Lady Rosalie, and I vowed that I would."

"'Twas good of you," Wat said, making his decision. "My people are raising Teviotdale, but I want them to do it quietly, without involving Douglas. My injured man will also find help easily enough getting home. So, Len Gray, unless you feel obliged to report to Douglas, I'd liefer keep you with me."

Len nodded. "I'd prefer that, too, my lord. I feared you might not trust me."

"I don't," Wat said. "But you're good with a sword, and that's enough for now. Where the devil is Ned Cockburn?" he demanded, letting Sym help him up.

"Here, laird," someone behind him said. "We didna like tae interrupt ye."

Turning, Wat saw one of his lads with Cockburn in tow. Someone had tied Ned's hands behind him and hobbled his ankles, so he could take only small steps. Shorter than his keeper or Wat, Ned was broad shouldered with a slim, wiry frame.

"I ha' nowt tae say to ye, Wat," he snapped.

"Well, I have something to say to you. Do you know where your sister is?"

"I do, aye. She's at Scott's Hall, where she has nae business to be!"

Wat wished he could see Ned more clearly. "You look and sound as if you believe that, Ned," he said. "Do you know where Ring Tuedy is?"

Ned shrugged elaborately. "I canna say I do."

"If I tell you that he abducted Molly from Rankilburn Kirk yestermorn and killed Father Eamon, our priest, will that aid your memory?"

Ned frowned but shook his head. "I still canna tell ye where he is, though I dinna hold wi' killing priests. But ye canna call aught that Ring may ha' done wi' me sister an abduction. The man be married tae her, after all."

"Not any longer," Wat said, adding a chill to his tone. "Molly declared that forced marriage unlawful because she was still a maiden afterward."

"Then she lied about that," Ned snapped.

"Nay, she did not. And take care of how you speak of her, for she is *my* wife now. I can swear, as will my grandmother, Lady Meg Scott, that Molly was chaste when she married me. The Abbot of Melrose agrees that her marriage to Tuedy was unlawful and that her marriage to me is a legal one, properly witnessed."

"Whether that be true or no, I canna tell ye where Tuedy keeps hisself."

"You were part and party to the attack on me and my men," Wat said coldly. "And Ring Tuedy has threatened to kill Molly if he does not get his way. If you cannot help me find her, I might as well just hang you from the nearest tree."

Even by torchlight, he saw Ned's face pale. Wat waited patiently.

At last, Ned said, "I canna tell ye what I dinna ken, Wat. I got clouted afore they took off, and nae one lingered tae tell me where they was a-going. I knew only that we were to rescue Gil."

"Your brother Will is with them, aye?"

"I canna deny that. Dunamany o' your own men must ha' seen him."

"I don't believe you when you claim not to know where they're going. So, before I hang you, tell me this much. Was Tuedy *with* the men who ambushed us?"

Ned hesitated for a long moment, making Wat fear that he would not answer.

Much as he wanted to shake the man, he forced himself to remain patient.

"Aye, then, he was," Ned said with a grimace and a sigh.

Wat nearly sighed, too. "I do believe that, at all events," he said. "Moreover, I'd liefer *not* hang my own good-brother, especially since, for some cause of which I am ignorant, and despite your foul treatment of her, Molly loves you *and* Will. She defends you both against all who speak ill of you."

Ned opened his mouth, doubtless to deny ever treating his sister badly. But a glance at Wat's face evidently changed his mind, for he shut his mouth again.

"Do *not* mistake my clemency for stupidity," Wat said with pure ice in his tone. "I will set you free but only if you promise to go home to St. Mary's Loch and tell your father that Tuedy has taken Molly and threatens to kill her. You will also tell him that he must either do all he can to help find her or suffer dire consequences if Tuedy harms her. If you cannot persuade him of that, I'll make you both sorry."

Waiting until he saw Ned's expression change from wariness to hope and something slyer and less identifiable, Wat said with gentle menace, "You should know before you go that my men are raising all of Teviotdale to find her. That means the Douglas will likely send his men out, too."

Ned nodded, but other than a nervous twitch of his lips, he revealed nothing.

"Since you will be alone," Wat added, icy again, "you should take the fastest route you know. No one will trouble a lone rider, riding urgently, so you can make all speed for Molly's sake. Just keep out of mischief on your way."

"Aye, sure, Wat," Ned said, nodding more fervently. "I...I dinna think Ring would really kill the lass, but I'll go straightaway, I promise."

"Untie him then, and find him a horse," Wat said in nearly the same frosty tone to the man who had brought Ned to him.

As they watched the two walk away, Sym murmured, "Ye dinna really think he'll go to Henderland or persuade Cockburn to aid her ladyship, *do* ye, laird?"

"I do not," Wat said grimly. "I think he'll head straight for wherever Tuedy, Will, and Rutherford are going and warn them that I'm raising Teviotdale, including the Douglas's men from Hawick, to search for them."

"That willna do us any good if they've left Teviotdale," Sym said.

"But I'll wager they haven't," Wat said. "Recall that Tuedy knew of Rutherford's capture when he sent his messengers to you at the Hall."

"Aye, and I said m'self that he must ha' known about that to suggest trading her ladyship for the reiver," Sym said, nodding. "Also, Tuedy likely learned about it from them two what escaped when ye captured the reivers."

"Which means that Tuedy's lair, the Hall, and Black Law must be close enough to each other for men to have ridden from one place to the other in the time available since we captured Rutherford," Wat said. "In fact, Tuedy's messenger had to ride to the Hall, and you had to ride here in time to meet me at Black Law."

"Aye, sure, laird. I do see how ye be thinking, but if we're a-going to make Peat Law anytime *near* dawn, we'd best ride."

"We're not going to Peat Law," Wat said flatly. "You will follow Ned Cockburn now, just as Jed and Ferg are following Rutherford's rescuers. Jed will be leaving our marks, so you will soon know if Ned is following Will and Rutherford. As you know, St. Mary's Loch lies due west of here, so if Ned takes the *fastest* route there, as he said he would, he'll cross the Hawick highroad and ride through Rankilburn Glen."

Sym nodded but frowned, too. "Methinks he'd be gey *un*likely to do that."

"Agreed," Wat said. "I think he'll head into some hills nearby, instead. For the two who got away at Black Law to have ridden to Tuedy's lair, and for Tuedy's lot to organize and ride here in time to ambush us, his lair must be nearby."

"Aye, but Herself did say—"

"Never mind Herself," Wat said curtly. "You are the best tracker I have."

"True," Sym said. "But Ned *could* just be taking another route to Henderland. If Tuedy wanted ye to meet him at Peat Law—"

"I think that was just a ruse to make us ride through these hills, so they could attack us. Tuedy does not want to exchange Molly for anyone, Sym, so she is likely closer than we thought. Now, take Aggie's Pete with you and get going. The rest of us will be close behind you. If I'm right, Ned will head into the rugged country west of the Hawick highroad, which is the *slowest* way to Henderland."

"What if ye're wrong?"

"Pray that I'm not," Wat said grimly.

How long, Molly wondered, had the others waited at the bridge before they looked for her? Surely, Wat must know by now that Tuedy and the false monks had taken her from the kirk, leaving poor Father Eamon and Emma dead on the floor.

But what if Len Gray was an English spy and had captured Lady Rosalie and Janet? What if Len, Tuedy, and the false monks were all in league together?

Her common sense recoiled from that notion. Lady Rosalie herself had said that Len Gray had been with her for the past two years, since her husband's death. Whether he was spying on Scots for Northumberland or the English king, or on Rosalie for the Percies, he would have had to keep secrets from Rosalie, who was Scottish. And she had said her husband *sent* Len to her. In any event, Len would have had to report to someone, somewhere. Yet he'd stuck like a burr to Rosalie.

Molly's thoughts returned to Wat until her imagination presented a picture of him lying at Tuedy's feet, stabbed by Tuedy's sword. At that point, declaring herself a ninny, she returned her attention to her primary objective.

A short time later, she realized that she could see the black outline of her hand clearly against the fading darkness. Dawn was breaking at last.

The next time she tried the hole for size, she could almost squeeze her shoulders through. But try as she did, she could not quite manage it. The sky was lighter but gray with overcast. She would at least be able to see where she was going if she could just get out. One more stone, she told herself, would do it.

A bird chirped as Molly straightened and reached for the spurtle. Animals were waking. Then she heard a less welcome sound, hoofbeats, fast approaching.

She dared not look again, to see if she could see them. She could only pray that, if it was Tuedy, he would not see the hole she had made in the wall.

Terrified, but aware that if he saw it from outside she could do nothing about it, she gathered her wits and snatched up the pallet he had given her. Rolling it, she shoved it under the shelf to hide the hole and the stones she'd removed to make it.

Wrapping her cloak around her, she waited, scarcely able to breathe. A minute later, muttering that she was worse than a fool, she dove back to the pallet and grabbed a stone—the only one she could grasp in one hand—from behind it.

Standing again, with her ears aprick for the slightest sound, she moved quietly the few steps to the corner farthest from the hole she had made and the door.

A thin beam of pale dawn light touched the top of the pallet and made a faint line across the floor, but Tuedy was at the door. Molly prayed he would not see it.

———

As Wat expected, Ned had crossed the highroad and headed into the rugged hills northwest of Hawick. They found Sym's mark, and soon found Jed's. Another set of marks that Wat and Geordie identified as Ferg's way of making the Scotts' cryptic sign indicated that Ferg had turned northward on the highroad.

"Might be another ambush in the making," Geordie said morosely, as they reined in their mounts to confer.

"We canna tell much from tracks on the highroad, laird. There be dunamany of 'em. There must ha' been at least a score o' riders."

Sym said, "Jed would ken fine, from them tracks we be a-following, that the rescuers ha' split up. I'd say mayhap a dozen besides Jed be a-going this way."

"Agreed," Wat said. "Others must have gone north, but I'd wager that Jed and Ferg *saw* them split up."

"Aye," Sym said. "And Jed would follow Ruther—" He frowned. "Nay then, he'd follow Tuedy. Jed kens the reiver be worth less to ye than her ladyship."

"He's likely following both," Wat said, although his heart ached at the mere hint that *anyone*, let alone the damned reiver, could be worth more than Molly.

Forcing himself to think aloud, if only to keep his thoughts on track, he said, "Rutherford will want to avoid Melrose and his grace's men. But his own lads can seek sanctuary on the Rutherford estates as long as Rutherford does not. Moreover, if Tuedy is keeping Molly near here, he won't want Rutherford's men crawling about. Sakes, he won't want Rutherford, but he may have no choice about him."

"If Tuedy has our lady Molly with him, she'll no be pleased to see her brothers," Sym said with a grimace. "D'ye still think Ned can lead us to her, laird?"

"That he is heading into these hills does encourage me," Wat said. "In any event, I don't want to take an army with me. Wherever Tuedy has hidden himself, he'll likely have watchers."

Sym stiffened, but if he was going to object, Geordie beat him to it, saying, "Ye willna go alone, laird, nor wi' fewer men than what this lot has wi' them."

"I did not plan to go alone," Wat said. "But neither do I want so many with me that every watcher will raise the alarm."

"With respect, my lord," Len Gray said, "I do have some experience with this sort of situation. Moreover, I am unknown to any of Tuedy's men. The two so-called monks who were with Father Eamon may have taken notice of me, but I think their attention was firmly on persuading your lady to go with them to the kirk. Had I, or any of us, objected to their doing so, they might have paid us greater heed. My point is that—"

"If you think I'll let you ride ahead to Tuedy's alone—"

"I know better than that, sir. But I have a keen eye, and I was thinking that we'll likely catch up with your Jed before we find Tuedy. He and I together might attend to watchers just as I'm told your men did when you approached Black Law."

"My lads did that in darkness," Wat reminded him.

Len continued to look at him, his lean body relaxed, his demeanor expectant.

Sym said, "The notion isna a daft one, laird. Jed kens these hills well."

"So do you and I," Wat said as another thought occurred to him. He met Sym's gaze. "What think you of that old sheepfold this side of Drinkstone Hill?"

"The one near the moss, aye," Sym said.

To Len, Wat said, "The place has been empty for years, because the moss turns into deep bog when it rains, and the daft sheep would walk into it and drown."

"Would Tuedy leave her ladyship in such a place?" Len asked.

"There's an old cottage there, or there was. I haven't

been there for years. Hills surround the sheepfold and there is no good track through them. Few folks want to climb up and down hills to reach such a place when there are other folds that require less exertion. So, if Tuedy sought an isolated place near the Hall that he could reach from the kirk without drawing attention, it would be a good choice."

"Someone might also ha' thought it would be a good place to keep stolen kine whilst he led searchers elsewhere," Sym said.

Geordie said, "Even so, laird, we dinna ken but that Tuedy may ha' left an army o' his own there to guard her ladyship."

"We'll continue following Ned Cockburn's tracks, Geordie," Wat said. "You and the other lads fall back, but I'll keep Sym with me. I ken fine that I can't dislodge him."

"And I, sir?" Len Gray said.

"Stay with us and keep your eyes skinned. If you see anyone above us on the hills, speak up. When we catch up with Jed, if we do, I'll decide then what to do with you."

⌒

The pantry door swung wide, and Tuedy filled the doorway.

Unable to read his expression with only the dusky interior light behind him, Molly took an involuntary step backward and bumped hard into a shelf there.

Something rattled, but she kept her gaze tensely fixed on Tuedy.

"What be ye doing there?" he asked.

"You are back earlier than I expected," she said.

"I feared ye'd miss me," he replied, his voice low, almost caressing.

It sent shivers up her spine.

Dampening lips that had unexpectedly dried, she tried to think of something to say without stirring his ire.

"Dinna be afeard o' me, lass," he said in that same strange tone. "We'll get on much better an ye treat me kindly."

"You have not treated me kindly at all," she replied tartly. Drawing a breath, aware that neither the statement nor her tone would soothe him, she swallowed hard.

He seemed almost conciliatory when he said, "If Wat Scott hadna persuaded ye to make mock o' our marriage, I'll wager I'd ha' made ye love me."

"I doubt that," Molly said. The man was daft. Naught that she could say to him would alter that.

"I'm thinking now that Wattie must ha' used the dark arts to make ye love him instead o' me."

"He did *not*. He wouldn't! He is a better man and a more honorable one than you could ever be, Ring Tuedy. He is kind and gentle. His people love him. I...I..." Realizing that she had nearly said that she loved him, too, she said instead, "He has many, many good qualities. You have none."

"There, ye see. Ye'd never ha' said that to me afore now. He's put some sort o' dark spell on ye. I wonder what the Kirk would think o' that."

"I...I don't know," she said, struggling to understand what he was doing but able to think only that she needed Wat and was uncomfortably aware of that hole in the outer wall. Had Tuedy seen it? Would he?

As disoriented as she had been when he'd brought

her inside, she knew only that the pantry stood near one end of the cottage. Also, although she had heard Tuedy's approach, she had not seen him ride in. Nor, now that she thought about it, had she seen the stockade or the barn-like outbuilding when she put her head outside.

She had seen only an overcast sky above and some lofty grass-and-shrubbery-clad hills so nearby that she had hoped to hide amid those shrubs.

That hope would die unless she could save herself now. Risking a glance past him, she tried to discern any sign of movement beyond him and listened hard for aught that she might hear outside. All was still.

Then a bird chirped, too nearby.

Tuedy looked toward the floor by the outer wall, his brow creased as if he wondered how a bird had got inside. Following his gaze, Molly saw with horror that the sliver of dawn light remained visible even with the pantry door open.

With a muttered curse, Tuedy bent to snatch the pallet away.

As soon as he did, Molly stepped forward, brought the stone from behind her back, and clouted his head as hard as she could. He collapsed to the floor.

Without a second thought, she whisked through the doorway and slammed the door shut. Flipping the hasp into place, she snatched up the iron bolt that hung by a slender chain from a nearby hook, and thrust it hard through the staple.

Having no illusion that Tuedy would be as unsuccessful as she had been at budging the door, she snatched up her skirts and ran to the only door she could see.

Opening it, she dashed outside, right into her brother Will's arms. They closed around her and held her tight.

The hills northwest of the river Teviot were just as much a maze as Wat remembered them being, but the tracks of the horses they followed were clear.

After crossing the highroad, and again when the tracks turned northward, the men they followed had tried to obliterate their tracks by dragging branches from trees or shrubbery across them for nearly half a mile. But the ruse had failed to fool Jed. He had left Wat's mark each time, showing them the way.

When at last Wat saw Drinkstone Hill rising above its companions ahead, he told all the men except Sym and Len Gray to fall back. "Keep far enough behind us," he told Geordie, "so that any watchers will see just three riders approaching that wee hidden glen."

Geordie objected to abandoning him, still suspicious of a trap, and of Len Gray.

When Wat's quiet "Do as I say" prevailed, he realized he had not worried for days about what his father or grandfather might think. Frowning, he wondered if he was giving his lads' acceptance of his authority more weight than it, or he, deserved.

"What's amiss, laird?" Sym asked. "Be your head still a-paining ye?"

"I deserve that it should, for letting myself get clouted as I did," Wat said ruefully. "But it aches only if I move it too suddenly. I was just thinking about my father and granddad, wondering what they'd have done in such a coil as this."

Sym shrugged. "They'd ha' done what needed doin', just as ye have," he said. "At your age, your da would have acted differently wi' the lady Molly, because he would already ha' been married and he already knew Cockburn. But if someone had snatched her, your da would ha' raised the dale, too."

"And Granddad?"

"I dinna ken what he'd a done had he met Herself in a forest, fleeing her family. Had she been abducted, though, he'd likely ha' acted a mite too hastily and wi' more flinging o' swords about. But he'd ha' found her, sure, and heads would ha' ended on pikes. Fact is, laird, men wha' lead other men ha' different methods o' leading. Some be good leaders, some fair, some bad. In me own opinion, a good man wha' kens his people and his own mind, as well, makes a gey good leader."

"But if a man is new to the position, how can he know if he's a good leader or a bad one?"

Sym grinned. "Easy as winking," he said. "He needs only to watch his men. Ye'd ken fine did your men no trust ye to lead them, me laddie."

"He's right about that, sir," Len Gray said from behind them.

Glancing back to see if Geordie and the others were still in sight and seeing only grassy, shrub-ridden hillsides, Wat realized that the words were not as comforting as Sym or Len might have intended them to be. Knowing that his men trusted him meant that he'd have to keep his wits about him more than ever and *not* let them down.

But he had greater cause than that to keep his wits about him now, if he was going to find Molly before Tuedy could do her irreparable harm. The fact that the brute might already have hurt her, or worse, did not bear contemplation.

When her beautiful face rose easily to his mind's eye, he felt certain that she was still alive, waiting for him to find her.

Glancing at Sym, he urged his horse to a faster pace. Whatever happened, he would *not* let Molly down.

*Chapter 20*_____

Will grabbed Molly by the shoulders and gave her a rough shake. "What be *ye* doing here? Were ye daft enough to run away from Wat Scott, too?"

"Let me *go*, Will," she cried, trying to pull away. "Was it not enough that you forced me to marry Tuedy? Are you set on letting him kill me now?"

"Dinna talk blethers, lass," he said, giving her another shake. "Tuedy wanted ye. He's no going to kill ye."

"He will now," she snapped. "I promise you."

"Then ye must ha' done summat to vex the man," Will said. "If ye didna like him, ye should ha' stayed at Scott's Hall."

"It was not *my* choice to leave," she retorted. "Tuedy sent men pretending to be monks, who told Father Eamon that the Abbot of Melrose was bringing Father to Rankilburn Kirk to talk with me. But when we reached the kirk, they killed Father Eamon. Then Tuedy brought me here. I don't even know where we are."

"It doesna matter where *we* are," Will said. "Where's Tuedy?"

"Cockburn, who *is* this woman?"

Her notice thus drawn to a stranger who eyed them

hostilely from a short distance away, Molly realized that he had also likely seen her run out of the cottage.

Straightening her shoulders and relieved when Will released her, she feared nonetheless that they would not let her get away in time.

Will said, "This is my sister, Molly, Gil."

Gil? Realizing that, despite being inches shorter than Will and pounds thinner, he was most likely Gil Rutherford, and that Wat had failed to capture him, Molly swallowed hard. Her stomach tightened.

"Tuedy married her a fortnight ago," Will added. "And now—"

Rutherford—if it *was* he—gave a shout of laughter. "Married? Tuedy?"

"I am *not* married to him," Molly declared more loudly than she had intended. "Tuedy abducted me from Rankilburn Kirk, and my husband is—"

Will grabbed her with one hand and clapped the other over her mouth. "Wheesht, will ye wheesht! The man doesna want to hear your daft ranting. Just answer me question, lass. Wha' had ye done wi' Tuedy? He brought us here, then left us to tend our horses and hied himself into the cottage."

A crash from inside answered his question before Molly could decide what to say. Hearing it, she stiffened, fighting the wave of fear that engulfed her.

Tuedy had broken free.

He burst through the cottage doorway and stopped short when he saw her.

"Good on ye, Will," he said, glowering at Molly. "Ye've caught the willsome wench. She wants a good thrashing, and I mean to see that she gets one."

"There, yonder," Sym said just as Wat saw Jed, waiting on his horse under an oak tree thirty yards ahead, at the base of the hill they had just skirted.

When they reached him, Wat said, "Ned didn't see you, did he?"

"Nay, laird," Jed assured him. "I tethered me pony out o' sight yonder and climbed up to ha' a look northward from the crest. I havena seen any watchers, but I saw Ned ride by a short time ago, heading—"

"—toward the old boggy sheepfold tucked away on the far side of that hill," Wat interjected impatiently. "How many other men could you see from up there?"

"Five or six riders well ahead o' Ned. Looked like Rutherford and a bigger one—mayhap Ring Tuedy—leading 'em, so I didna try to get closer lest they see me."

"Good lad," Wat said, hoping that the bigger man *was* Tuedy. "I want you to get back up there now and take Len Gray here with you. If he can creep about on a hillside the same way he creeps up on people, he'll be a good man to help you watch for trouble whilst the two of you see what lies ahead of us."

"Aye, sure, laird," Jed said with a nod to Len. "D'ye have a plan, then, sir?"

"Not yet," Wat admitted. "Keep an eye on us, though. We'll follow their tracks, and Geordie is close behind us with the others. So if you see aught that troubles either of you, especially where her ladyship is concerned, wave something."

"I'll wave me shirt or ha' Gray wave his," Jed said.

"What I'd *like* to do," Wat went on pensively, "is ride

into that glen, kill Rutherford for making such a nuisance of himself, and ride out with my lady unharmed. However, his grace wants to hang the reiver, and if Tuedy fears that he'll lose her ladyship, he may kill or gravely injure her. Therefore, we must do this in a way that keeps her safe."

"Likely, ye'll ken what ye should do when ye get there," Jed said confidently before he gave his pony a kick and rode back up the hill with Len following him.

Meeting Sym's twinkling gaze, Wat grimaced. "I'd rather have a plan now," he said. "But I don't."

"Well, dinna look to me," Sym said. "I ken only that altogether there be more of us than them. That willna win our lady from Tuedy, but it may give us that gallous reiver."

"I won't give a damn about Rutherford if anyone hurts Molly," Wat growled as he spurred his mount to its fastest pace.

~

"What are you on about, Tuedy?" Rutherford demanded. "If she's your lass, thrash her later. But lock her up now so we can decide what to do. I see nowt to suggest that there be food to eat here, and I'm famished. Can the woman cook?"

"I wasna expecting more visitors, Gil," Tuedy said. "'Twas just a stopping place for me and me lads till the fuss died down. But," he added hastily when Rutherford's eyebrows snapped together, "since Will said ye needed us—"

"Devil's curse on ye, Ring! D'ye mean to say ye've brung me here when someone may be searching for this woman o' yours?"

"I am *not* his woman," Molly blurted. "I am Wat Scott's *wife*!"

"What d'ye mean by that?" Rutherford demanded. "How can ye ha' two—?"

"Never mind her," Tuedy snapped. "I'm telling ye—"

"Will! Will!"

Molly recognized Ned's voice, and all of them turned to see Ned riding toward them. He wrenched his mount to a stop, and flung himself off.

"Hoots, what now!" Rutherford exclaimed.

Dropping his reins, Ned said urgently, "Will, ye should ken that—"

"Ye told me we'd be safe here!" Rutherford roared, turning his fury on Will. "'Tis more like a Cockburn gathering place!"

"We saved your hide, Gil," Will retorted. "Had we not known Tuedy would be here, ye'd still be riding wi' your own men. A bairn could follow *their* trail."

"Aye, perhaps," Rutherford snarled. "But ye said ye'd covered *our* trail, and yet here your brother is, so anyone might follow. Where do we go from here, eh?"

"Ned knows this glen as well as I do," Will said. "How d'ye think we found Ring and his men and arranged to ambush your captors? Had Ring not been here to aid us, as he'd promised to be, ye'd be standing before Jamie Stewart, awaiting his hangman. Show some gratitude for your freedom, man."

Molly sensed Tuedy moving closer to her. Standing, as she was, between him and Will, she felt sure that all chance of escape had died.

Ned said fretfully, "Will, I'm a-trying to tell ye! Wat Scott's raised all o' Teviotdale. He's even sent for the Douglas's men."

"That'll do him nae good," Rutherford said flatly. "Archie Douglas has nae desire to fratch wi' me or my men."

Molly eased away from Tuedy, closer to Will.

"Here now, what are ye doing?" Tuedy growled, reaching for her.

"Leave her alone, Ring," Ned snapped. Turning to his brother, he added, "She's the reason Wat's raising the dale, Will." To Rutherford, he said, "He'd like to catch you again, aye, Gil, but he told me himself that Molly's *his* wife now, legally."

Looking from one to the other, Rutherford's face reddened. "By the Rood," he muttered, scowling, "ye're all daft. And damned fools, as well!"

Argument erupted all around Molly, nearly deafening her.

She felt trapped, but as she tried to slip away, she caught sight, between Rutherford and Ned, of furtive movement on the hillside beyond them. Looking swiftly down, lest anyone else follow her gaze, she feared she had imagined it.

Glancing back up, she saw only bushes and trees on the grassy slope.

Tuedy grabbed her arm and jerked her toward him, startling a cry from her.

The other three men had stopped arguing, and she saw that Tuedy's men—four of the six louts she had seen before—were striding toward them, swords drawn, doubtless alarmed by the shouting.

She saw just one of the false monks with them and wondered where the other one was. Tuedy's grip tightened more, bruising her.

"You're hurting me," she said tartly as she tried to pull free.

Rutherford snapped, "Damn you, Tuedy, tell your men to put up their swords! Then take that woman inside so she can find us summat to eat."

"Dinna let Ring take Molly with him, Will," Ned muttered when Tuedy shouted at his men to sheathe their weapons. "Wat said Ring offered to trade her for Gil and threatened to kill her if Wat wouldna do it."

When Molly looked hopefully at Will, Tuedy's grip tightened until she gasped.

Will's jaw jutted forward. His whole body stiffened.

Into that pause, a more beloved voice with, for once, welcome ice in its grimly measured tones, said, "Take your filthy hands off my wife, Tuedy."

Rutherford whirled and ran toward the barnlike outbuilding, where he and his men had doubtless left their horses. But Molly's searching gaze had found Wat, astride his horse at the nearest corner of the cottage. He was looking right at her.

In a trice, Tuedy's dirk was at her throat, his strong left arm tight across her breasts, pinning her arms. He said, "Ye're a dead man, Wat Scott. Take 'im, lads!"

To Molly's shock, Wat smiled.

～

Wat fought to conceal his terror and keep smiling.

If Rutherford got away, so be it.

Without shifting his gaze, he could see that his unexpected smile had frozen Tuedy's men in place. But the sight of Tuedy's dirk at Molly's throat sent chills through him, and his hope of fixing Tuedy's attention on himself long enough to initiate a discussion died.

He and Sym had managed to draw close enough

behind Ned Cockburn to catch glimpses of him ahead as they rounded curves on the winding trail. Ned showed no suspicion that anyone was following him. But, as they rounded the last curve, leading into the glen, Jed appeared on the hillside above them, frantically waving his shirt.

Wat had been watching for him and waved but, at that point, still had no plausible plan other than to keep Ned in sight. Jed immediately vanished into the shrubbery.

Knowing that Jed's fervent waving meant danger to Molly, Wat had nearly spurred his mount on right then, but Sym's firm hand on his arm stopped him.

A fierce glare at the older man drew only a twinkle that on a younger one might have looked mischievous. "What?" Wat demanded. "They've got Molly!"

"Aye, and I see your granddad's devil has got ye," Sym retorted.

"If you mean that I'm angry—"

"Nay, laird. I'm thinking mayhap ye've forgot ye ha' men awaiting your commands—not only m'self but Geordie and the others."

Without hesitation, Wat said, "We dare not attack until I see what's what for myself, Sym. You wait for Geordie, whilst I go in and try to delay those villains until you and he can get the others into place. They cannot be but a minute or two behind us, so find a place where you can see me, and tell Geordie that no one is to ride in until I have Molly safe. Then I want you all to look and sound like an army."

When Sym nodded, Wat wheeled his mount and urged it on into the glen apace. Ned was just disappearing around the decrepit cottage, so he was able to approach from behind it. Only then did he realize that he had given Jed and Len Gray no further orders.

Now, however, facing the men in the cottage yard, he dared waste no time thinking about aught but Molly, and Tuedy's dirk.

Resting his knotted reins on the horse's neck, Wat shifted his own dirk from his right hand to his left and reached casually back to draw his sword.

Instead of charging him as he'd expected, Tuedy's men just watched, apparently mesmerized.

Gruffly, Will Cockburn said, "Ye heard the man, Tuedy. Let Molly go."

"I will *not*," Tuedy retorted. "I married the woman. She's mine."

"Nay, then, she's ours," Will replied, snatching his dirk from its sheath. "If ye draw one drop o' blood from me sister, I'll gut ye where ye stand."

Shoving Molly aside, Tuedy leaped toward Will, and the two men grappled.

Sword out, dirk in hand, Wat used his knees as he would in battle to urge his horse between the two men and Molly, backing her near the cottage wall as he did.

When one of Tuedy's men leaped forward and slashed a sword at him, Wat parried the stroke so deftly and hard that the other's weapon went flying. Without pause, Wat dispatched him and, with a sweeping gaze, sought the next attacker.

Horns blew, hoofbeats thundered toward them, and battle erupted.

Wat spied a would-be attacker darting toward him from the cottage and shifted position to meet him. But Len Gray stepped out of the building behind the chap and, in two long strides, grabbed him with one hand and slashed his throat with the other.

"Much obliged," Wat said to him as Len let the man fall and the sounds of battle rapidly diminished. "Did you see Rutherford?"

"Jed has him trussed up in that old barn by now, sir. We hied ourselves down the hill as soon as we knew you understood that her ladyship was in danger."

"Keep close to me, lass," Wat said quietly to Molly. "This is nearly over."

❧

Molly could not see Wat's face while his gaze shifted from the action in the yard to sweep over the nearest hills and back, so she could not imagine what he was thinking. Nor could she see what he was seeing, because his horse blocked her view. She had not considered before just *how* big the well-muscled bay was.

Wat still had his sword in hand, but he slipped his dirk into its sheath.

As his gaze swept again toward the hills, Molly heard a cry of rage that she recognized as Tuedy's. Astonishingly, the big bay's head ducked toward her just enough to let her see its bared teeth. Before she could react, its menacing head swung back swiftly and hard the other way as it reared, its front hooves lashing out.

She heard a grunt followed by the thud of a body hitting the ground.

The horse steadied, then tossed its head, whuffling, and stood quietly.

Darting forward far enough to see beyond the horse, Molly saw Tuedy lying in the dirt with Ned standing and Will kneeling by him, bloody dirks in hand.

Tuedy lay still.

"Is he dead?" Wat demanded as Ned wiped his dirk through the dry grass.

"He is now," Will said, straightening and slipping his own dirk into its sheath.

Hearing Molly gasp, Wat said, "You didn't have to kill him."

Will's gaze met his. "Aye, we did," he said. "Otherwise, he'd ha' stalked ye and plotted against ye until someone else killed him—or he killed you and our Molly."

"Sakes, man, *you* chose him for her husband."

Will shrugged. "I didna ken then that he were daft. She's better off wi' ye."

"I don't disagree with you," Wat said. "But, as keen on the rule of law as Jamie Stewart is, I expect he'll order a trial when he hears about this."

"Then dinna tell him."

"You know that I must. My father was an assistant march warden, Will. Until the King appoints someone new, as I hope he will, I'm obliged to act in his place."

"D'ye mean to arrest us then?"

Feeling Molly's anxious gaze on him, Wat said, "I do not, but I want your word as a Borderer that if Jamie does order a trial, you and Ned will present yourselves. If you do that," he added hastily, seeing refusal leap to Will's lips, "I *will* speak for you then."

When Will hesitated, Molly stepped close to him and said urgently, "Agree to that, Will. You know that Wat's word is good, and I know that yours is when you give it. And Ned will do whatever you say."

Wat kept quiet but watched Will closely. The man

looked at his own feet for a time and then looked straight at Molly. "I didna ken how mean Ring was, lass. I were thinking only o' what your marriage to him would mean to us by way o' keeping them contumacious Tuedys under control. But when ye snuggled up against me today in the midst of all the to-do, ye made me feel like a great gowkish fool for what I did. Do ye think ye'll ever forgive me?"

"You are my brother, Will. Of course, I forgive you."

"Good then," he said, turning to Wat. "I give ye me word as a Borderer that if his grace wants me, I'll go, and I'll take Ned wi' me. Will that suit ye?"

"It will, aye," Wat said. "It may take me a while to warm up to you, though, after what you put my lady through."

"Aye, but she's yours now, withal. Ye *should* be thanking me."

Shaking his head, Wat smiled and said, "Likely, you're right about that."

~

Molly had no time to speak privately with Wat, because Sym and Geordie approached them then, and Geordie said, "Do we bury Tuedy here, laird? Or d'ye want us to carry him home to his kinsmen?"

Will said, "Ned and I will see to the dead, Wat."

Molly saw then that some of Wat's men had prisoners, among which stood the false monk she had noticed earlier. "Walter, that man yonder killed Father Eamon and helped Tuedy abduct me. Tuedy k-killed poor Emma himself."

Wat dismounted then, opened his arms, and she walked into them.

"Ah, lassie," he murmured, tucking her head under his chin and stroking her hair. "Emma will be fine. She held her breath to make them think she was dead."

Molly's heart leaped, but she said, "Art sure, sir? There was so much blood!"

"Head wounds often bleed profusely," he said. "Emma even managed to follow your trail for a time before the others arrived to help her. As for that chap yonder, he and the others will go to Melrose and face the hangman for all they have done."

"Laird," Geordie said. "Jed has Rutherford ready to travel when we are."

"Then you and the lads can take him and these others to Melrose and present them to his grace with my compliments. I shall expect you to make our capture of the infamous reiver sound spectacular enough to win me a knighthood."

"Aye, sure, laird," Geordie said doubtfully. "Ye'll no be going with us?"

Holding Molly so closely that she could hear his heart thumping, Wat said firmly, "Tell his grace for me that I shall see him anon and will present my lady wife to him then. But since Rutherford interrupted my wedding night, you may also tell his grace that I must finish what I'd begun before the interruption. Since Jamie is also married to the woman he loves, I warrant he'll understand."

"Sakes, laird, I canna tell him any o' that," Geordie protested.

"Then take Sym with you," Wat said. "He'll tell Jamie all of it."

"I would, and I'd tell it well, too," Sym said. "But Herself—"

"*I'll* attend to Herself," Wat said. "You go with Geordie. Leave Jed and Len Gray to see us back to the Hall but collect our other lads, their prisoners, and any other louts you find along the way. And, Sym, see that Rutherford does not escape before you present him and our other prisoners to Jamie. When that is all done, you may come home again."

To Molly's astonishment, Sym said, "Aye, m'lord. It shall be as ye wish."

After seeing the others on their way, Wat helped Molly find her horse and mount it, and they set out for the Hall. Their two guardians followed them.

"You have scarcely said a word since we left that place," she said after a time. "Art vexed with me, sir?"

"Nay," Wat said, surprised. "How could I be? None of it was your fault."

"I know it wasn't my fault that the false monks fooled Father Eamon into believing my father would meet with me at the kirk or that those dreadful men killed him." She hesitated, biting her lower lip.

"Then, what is it, lass?" Wat asked quietly. "Something is troubling you."

"Only that when Lady Rosalie and Janet suggested that we ride outside the wall, I thought you might not like it. You *had* said I was not to go dashing out into the woods whilst you were away. And if we had *not* gone..."

"I see," Wat said when she paused. "If you had not gone, Father Eamon and our two grooms would still be alive. Is that what you were thinking?"

"Aye," she said, meeting his gaze. "Would they not?"

"Neither of us knows the answer to that, Molly. Likewise, neither of us killed them. Tuedy and the one you called a false monk did that, and they are dead, too. But we are alive, and when we get home, I'll show you *how* alive I feel right now."

Her beautiful eyes widened, and roses bloomed in her satin cheeks, but she did not comment.

"Do you recall what you said to me as I was leaving?" he asked softly.

She nodded, the roses in her cheeks darkening considerably.

He reached to lay a gentle hand on her knee. "Tell me," he said.

"I told you to come home to me."

"There was more to it than that, I think."

He loved seeing her blush. Sakes, he knew now that he loved everything about her. Recalling that he had often felt as if his father could hear his thoughts, Wat hoped that Robert could hear them now and would know that he had selected exactly the right wife for him. Surely, heaven allowed such things, especially to the newly deceased whose kin had been unable to say good-bye.

She was still blushing.

"Molly?"

"Of course I remember what I said. I said I wanted to learn more, and I meant it. I still want that."

"You said '*much* more,' as I recall."

"Recall it as you like, sir. I mean to have a bath when we get home."

"I love hearing you call the Hall 'home,' sweetheart."

"I love *you*," she murmured so quietly that he nearly failed to hear her.

"Say that again," he said. "Louder."

She looked at him speculatively.

He grinned. "Say it."

"Very well. I love you, Walter Scott. I missed you dreadfully and I wanted to feel your arms around me. But I still mean to have a bath when we get home."

"Aye, sure," he replied cheerfully. "I'll wash you myself."

Her mouth fell agape, and he chuckled.

Then his cock stirred and a craving unlike any he had felt before flamed through the rest of his body, making him wonder if she *would* get her bath.

Watching him, Molly wondered about that bath, too. Twice, they met men who had been searching for her, but no one delayed them for long. Wat simply told the curious that she was safe and to let other searchers know as much.

It was as well that naught detained them, Molly thought, because she was aching to get home and find out what he meant to do with her.

She had thought about him incessantly throughout her ordeal, and had often recalled the sense of safety he had given her. Just thinking of his quiet strength and soothing gentleness had calmed her then, making those traits seem most important. She had fled Henderland seeking shelter, after all, and Wat had provided it.

He had provided much more than that, too, in bed with her.

Now, riding safely beside him, she hungered for his touch and to feel his naked body against hers again. Even the brief pain he had caused her had promised something more. She could almost smell the spicy aroma of his skin and feel the hardness of his muscles and the possessive way he had held her. Just the thought of how easily he had stirred her senses made the heat flow through her again.

He said something then, diverting her thoughts, and they talked desultorily until they reached the Hall. She was astonished to discover how little time the journey took. She had thought that Tuedy had taken her miles and miles away.

At least one of the searchers must have raced ahead of them with the news, because the family was waiting when they entered the great hall. But, after hugs and greetings, Wat dealt summarily with them, too, and ushered her upstairs.

When Jed would have followed them, Wat told him to see to himself and continued up the stairway, only to meet another manservant at his door.

"Ye're to take the master's chambers now, laird," the man said. "Your lady mother arranged it all whilst ye were awa'. She said it were only rightful that ye and your lady should ha' the rooms. Also, Herself ordered bathwater for ye there as soon as we heard ye was coming. They've just took it up for ye, so it'll be hot."

"Bless them all," Molly murmured as they turned away from the man. "The way you've been looking, I feared you wouldn't give me time to get clean."

"I might not," he muttered back.

Stopping on the next step, she looked solemnly back at him. "Tuedy did me little harm," she said. "But just being near him, and in that horrid room, made me feel unclean. I *want* a bath, sir, and I think I'd like you to wash me."

"Then make haste up those stairs, sweetheart," he said, grinning. "I'll do my best to serve your every desire."

He made good on that promise, not only scrubbing her clean but making her laugh in the process. Then he helped her dry herself, wrapped her in a robe that some-one had left on the bed for her, and told her to get under the covers.

"But I want to wash you, too."

"Next time you may," he said. "But I can do it more quickly, and the water is rapidly chilling. Get warm now, so you can warm me up if I get cold."

"Make haste, sir," she said. "Your impatience is contagious."

~

Minutes later, almost dry, Wat climbed into bed and drew her into his arms. Although he was aching for her again by then, he was still a man who preferred the long view over the short. He took his time, kissing and caressing her all over, determined to show her many more of the treats that her body, and his skill, had in store for her. Then he took some time to show her how she could pleasure him, too.

To his delight, she proved as eager to please him as he was to please her, a treat that he had not enjoyed before.

When she began moaning and arcing to meet his teas-ing hands and fingers, he spread her legs and eased his way into her. If she felt any pain, she showed no sign of it. Still, he compelled himself to be as gentle as he could until his own body began torturing him in its eagerness to claim her.

Then, nature took its course.

Afterward, gathering her into his arms again, he lay

quietly for a time. She, too, was quiet until he said, "Art weary, sweetheart?"

"Nay, just savoring the taste and feel of you," she murmured. "I feel so contented here with you, in a...a cozy way that I never expected to feel."

"Ah, sweetheart, I love you, too," he said, kissing her again.

"Is there much more to learn?" she asked hopefully.

"Much, *much* more, but not tonight," he said, grinning but exhausted.

Dear Reader,

I hope you enjoyed *Moonlight Raider*. Readers who were not already acquainted with Lady Meg Scott before reading this book might like to read *Border Wedding*, the story of Meg and the first Sir Walter Scott of Buccleuch and Rankilburn. The book and its two sequels, *Border Lass* and *Border Moonlight*, are still in print as I write this and are also available in electronic form, in most formats, from www.Amazon.com and www.barnesandnoble.com, as well as other sources.

Lady Margaret Cockburn did marry Walter Scott, Lord of Rankilburn. He became the second *Sir* Walter Scott and the first Lord of Rankilburn to style himself primarily Lord of Buccleuch, taking the name from the family's first royal landgrant. The present Duke of Buccleuch and Queensbury is his descendant.

As I have mentioned before, there were many Walter Scotts. In fact, there was one in every other generation right down to my own grandfather, although our branch is not that of the famous author and poet. The Walter Scott of *Moonlight Raider* did capture the notorious reiver Gilbert Rutherford, and that feat did win him his knighthood (albeit not bestowed until the coronation of James II of Scotland).

During Walter Scott's long lifetime, he acquired much more land than his father had and accomplished many fine deeds. He remained loyal to James I until his grace's death, and eventually defeated the Douglases to become the most powerful lord of his time in the Scottish Borders. His efforts are often cited as the foundation for what is now Scotland's most powerful dukedom.

Margaret Cockburn's eldest brother, William, was an infamous reiver himself and had a son named Gilbert, although there is no evidence whatsoever that William was a cohort of the notorious Gilbert Rutherford. The author simply could not resist the coincidence of William's younger son's name. William also named one of his daughters Margaret, after his sister. William Cockburn and his brother Edward were arrested for and convicted of "the slaughter of Roger (not Ringan) Tuedy" of Drumelzier, but both men were (well after the events portrayed here) pardoned for that crime. No reason for Roger Tuedy's murder appears in the documentation, so creative license prevailed. I named my villain Ringan just to be fair to Roger.

My primary source for the Cockburns is *House of Cockburn* by Thomas H. Cockburn-Hood (Edinburgh, 1888).

Other sources include *The Scotts of Buccleuch* by William Fraser (Edinburgh, 1878), *Upper Teviotdale and the Scotts of Buccleuch* by J. Rutherford Oliver (Hawick, 1887), *Steel Bonnets* by George MacDonald Fraser (New York, 1972), *The Border Reivers* by Godfrey Watson (London, 1975), *Border Raids and Reivers* by Robert Borland (Dumfries, Thomas Fraser, date unknown), and others.

My primary source for Douglas history is *A History of the House of Douglas*, vol. I, by the Right Hon. Sir Herbert Maxwell (London, 1902). Another is *The Black Douglases* by Michael Brown (Scotland, 1998).

I extend a special thanks to Len Gray for the generous donation he made to the St. Andrews Society of Sacramento, which led me to create the character with his name in *Moonlight Raider*. I hope the result pleases Len and his wife, Nancy.

As always, I'd like to thank my long-suffering agents, Lucy Childs and Aaron Priest, my wonderful new editor Lauren Plude, master copyeditor Sean Devlin, Art Director Diane Luger and Elizabeth Turner (for *Moonlight Raider*'s terrific cover), Senior Managing Editor and stress-breaker Bob Castillo, Editorial Director Amy Pierpont, Vice President and Editor in Chief Beth de Guzman, and everyone else at Hachette Book Group's Grand Central Publishing/Forever who contributed to this book.

If you enjoyed *Moonlight Raider*, please look for *Devil's Moon* at your favorite bookstore and online March 31, 2015. Meantime, *Suas Alba!*

Amanda Scott

www.amandascottauthor.com
www.facebook.com/amandascottauthor
www.openroadmedia.com/amanda-scott

Amanda Scott's exciting Border
Nights series continues!
When lady Robina Gledstanes discovers
a stolen treasure, the English lass is beset
by scofflaw suitors seeking to add her
newfound fortune to their own. But only
one noble Scotsman sees that the true
prize is the fair Robina herself...

Please see the next page for a preview of

Devil's Moon.

South Teviotdale, the Scottish Borders, Spring 1428

Although the nearly full moon had slipped behind a cloud, ringing it with a silver halo and dimming the rugged landscape below, the five riders on the old drove road could see their way without difficulty. Their mounts were sure-footed and accustomed to moonlight raids.

Somewhat hampered by their booty—four gently lowing cows and a pair of nervous sheep—the small party traveled slowly downhill and northward through a cut that, due to its shape, men called "Leg-o'-Mutton." White Hill lay behind them, and they could make out the shadowy Witch Crags in the northeast distance.

Two other riders from their party acted as sentinels, the first riding the hill crests separating the cut from Slitrig Water, to the west, where the Slitrig flowed swiftly northward toward the town of Hawick. The second man rode near the timberline of the eastern hills, skirting their rockier heights.

The slope below those heights, on the riders' right, boasted patches of dense shrubbery and scattered trees near its base, then denser woodland above, with grass and rocky crags from the tree line to the peak. A narrow stream ran to their left.

The west slope of the cut was neither as high nor as steep as the eastern one, although on the Slitrig side, the western range sloped down more steeply. Woodland on both sides of the westward hills was less dense than the foliage to the east.

The riders knew every cranny and dip in those hills and would be home within the half-hour. The night was still except for the occasional nightjar's call and the soft bubbling of the stream that tumbled past them just to their left of the drove road.

The large man riding his sturdy roan next to the leader's black charger heaved a sigh. "Nowt to boast of in this lot o' beasts," he muttered in near disgust.

"We did not lift them to boast of it, Sandy," the leader muttered back. "We took them to feed our people."

"'Tis true, that, but chance beckoned us to take more, and had Rab—"

"With any luck, they won't miss a half-dozen beasts," the leader interjected curtly. "The last thing we want is to stir a feud with—"

A shout diverted their attention to the west slope, where the moon, emerging from its cloud, revealed a rider pelting down toward them.

"That be Shag's Hobby!" Sandy exclaimed.

Turning swiftly, the leader said clearly but without shouting, "Ratch! Shag! Hie those beasts into the woods. Keep them still and yourselves out of sight. Dand, get Hobby's attention and signal for him to follow us. We'll be riding apace by then, but be ready to slow before the next turning."

Sandy protested. "Sakes, me l—"

"Silence!" the leader snapped. "I told you, Sandy, call me nowt tonight save plain Bean. And if you're thinking we should ride all the way home like madmen, you're daft. You ken fine that Hobby's haste means riders are coming. We must make anyone who sees us now believe we're nowt save innocent travelers."

Sandy shook his shaggy head but obediently urged his mount to a faster pace, saying, "I doubt ye'll want to tell that tale if them riders catch up with us."

"Haud your wheesht! We're nobbut a mile from Coklaw, and we'll be only four riders with Hobby. If Shag and Ratch can keep the beasts hidden and quiet—"

"Aye, and if them wha' come didna already see us *wi'* the beasts—"

A shout came from Hobby, now more than halfway down the west slope: "A dozen riders coming up yon road through the pass, lads! Likely they're after *us*!"

Waving for him to follow, the three remaining riders did not wait but gave spur to their horses.

⁓

Twenty-four-year-old Sir David Ormiston, having ridden from Hermitage Castle in Liddesdale and forded Slitrig Water an hour before, on his way to Hawick and then home, crested the drove road pass above Leg o' Mutton and, in the increasing moonlight, saw three riders racing toward the cut's narrow end. A fourth rider, nearing the base of the slope below him and shouting as he rode, gave Sir David to understand that the other riders had set watchers to guard their passage.

The shouted warning amused him. They were a small group, and although he scanned the eastern slope for a second watcher, he saw none and had no interest in their activities. He acted for the Earl of Douglas and had business in Hawick.

Jock Cranston, the captain of his fighting tail, drew rein beside him. "D'ye think they be reivers, sir?"

"If they are, they seem to be unsuccessful ones. Do you see any beasts?"

"Nay, but they may be just heading out. Or mayhap they be English."

"Just four men, or five if they have another lookout yonder?" Sir David shook his head. "They were in an almighty hurry when I first saw them, but they've slowed, and—"

He broke off, stunned. The moon, abruptly free of the cloud that had dimmed it, beamed brightly down on the leader's big horse, turning its black hide glossy and revealing a big diamond-shaped white star between its eyes when it tossed its head.

"I know that horse!" Sir David exclaimed. "But who would dare—?"

Louder shouts from below interrupted him.

"They be taking flight," Jock muttered. "'Tis gey strange, if ye ask me."

"I'm going after them," Sir David said. "You and the others follow more slowly, Jock. I don't want *us* to look like raiders. If I'm right, that lot is heading for Coklaw, and I mean to learn who the bangster is that dares to ride Black Corby."

"Aye, it could be Rab Gledstanes's Corby," Jock agreed. "And we ken fine that Rab isna riding 'im. Whoever it be, the man rides like he kens the horse well."

"Corby is even better trained than my Auld Nick is," Sir David said curtly. "But if that chap runs him into a rabbit hole, or worse, he'll answer to me, by God."

"Ye could be wrong, sir."

"Just bring the lads, Jock. I'm away."

"Wi' the deevil in ye, too," Jock muttered loudly enough for him to hear. His only reaction was to smile grimly and spur his charger after the riders below.

The road he followed was safe enough, and Auld Nick was sure-footed. But he also knew that the speed he demanded from the big horse now was such that his crusty father, and likely others, would deem it reckless.

Nevertheless, he wanted to catch up with the riders ahead before they could vanish completely. A thought tickled his mind about who might be leading them, but he dismissed it half-formed and fixed his attention on the path ahead.

Glancing back as he forded the stream racing down the center of the cut, he saw that his men were following at a slower pace. The riders ahead had disappeared around the next curve before he had ridden a third of the way down the slope.

Auld Nick was willing, though, and the moderate pace that his master had set earlier from Liddesdale had not taxed him. The charger was eager to make speed.

Although the moon was bright whenever the scudding clouds let it be, the light it cast was too dim to read tracks from the saddle of a galloping horse, so Sir David did not try. Instinct and the black horse assured him that his quarry would race to Coklaw Castle, midway between the end of the cut and Hawick.

A quarter-hour later, the huge, square stone tower loomed ahead, pale white in the moonlight. There was no sign of the riders or their horses, but he knew Coklaw well. Its stables and yard lay hidden now beyond the tower.

Riding more sedately into the stableyard, he saw a lad

in breeks, boots, leather jack, and a knitted cap dashing across the yard from the stables.

Sir David shouted, "Here you, lad, come see to my horse!"

The lad failed to heed him, but another, no more than eleven or twelve years old, darted from the stable and shouted, "Aye, sir, I'll see to him for ye."

He did not recognize the youngster. "Do you know who I am?"

The boy's eyes flared like a nervous foal's. "Aye, sir. Ye be Dev—that is, Sir David Ormiston."

"Auld Nick will be hungry, lad. You're not afraid of him, I hope."

"Nay, sir. I'm no afeard o' any beast. I'll gi'e him oats and hay."

"Good then. I'm going inside."

The boy's eyes widened more. He glanced warily toward the stable and back at Sir David. "I can send some'un tae tell our steward ye be here, sir."

"Don't trouble yourself. If John Greenlaw's not snug in bed, he ought to be."

"Aye, but—"

"Never mind, I know the way," Sir David said, striding toward the tower's postern door, the one through which the other lad had apparently vanished.

⁓

Shutting the postern door, the person who had dashed across the yard ran up the stairs, muttering, "Lord, preserve me. There's no time. That was Dev, and he saw me. He thought I was just one of the lads, but he must *not* find me still up."

There was no time to lift the heavy bar into its brackets, let alone to bolt the iron yett to the wall, making that entryway impregnable. It wouldn't matter, anyway. Dev would go through the main entrance.

Just hurry then, get upstairs. Puffing now, startling at the sound of a crash downstairs—the door, the damned door, crashing back against the wall.

He's inside, not at the front!

Heavy, hasty footsteps pounded on the steps below.

The landing's just ahead. There's the door, push it open. Close it ... doucely, doucely! Throw the bolt. Hurry!

No time to change. Would the bolt hold? Footsteps on the landing!

He's here, Beany. You're in trouble now, and it serves you right.

The latch rattled. "Open this door!"

"I will not! It is the middle of the night. Go away! You've no business here."

The door crashed open. The big, dark-haired man filled the doorway. Even in the dim light of a moonbeam through the small window, anger blazed from his eyes.

⁓

Without hesitation, Sir David strode to the breeks-clad figure in the middle of the room and snatched off the knitted cap.

A cloud of tawny hair cascaded to her shoulders.

He'd been angry before; he was furious now. Grabbing her by the shoulders, he gave her a rough shake. "What demon possessed you to do such a stupid thing?"

"Faith, did you find our beasts and take them for yourself?"

His mouth gaped, but it was the last straw. Gripping one slender arm, he turned her toward her bed, sat on it, pulled her across his knees and gave her a smack on her leather-clad backside hard enough to make her screech. "That's one for Rab," he growled before smacking her harder. "That's for Black Corby." Then, with the hardest smack, he snapped, "And *that* one is for me."

~

Livid with anger, nineteen-year-old Robina Gledstanes struggled to free herself. "Damn your eyes, Dev Ormiston, let me go! May God curse you from here to your satanic home in Hell. Release me, damn you!"

"Such pretty language," he said sardonically. "Mind your tongue, Beany, or I'll smack you again."

"Don't call me that," she said grimly. "Only Rab..." Her twin's name caught in her throat, but she swallowed it and said, "Only he could call me that. And, come to that, I learned my pretty language from him—*and* from you."

Resting his big hand on her backside, he said evenly, "I doubt if Rab would accept that as an excuse for such curses flying from your lips any more than I do."

He's right about that, you wee vixen.

A shiver shot through her, and she sighed. "Just let me go, Dev, please."

He released her then, and she stood, resisting the urge to rub her backside. She would not give him the satisfaction of knowing how much it stung.

"Put on some proper clothing and meet me downstairs," he said grimly. "I have much more that I mean to say to you."

"I won't," she retorted. "I don't want to hear it, Dev. You have no *right* to call me to account."

"You'll do as I say, or by God, I'll strip you myself and take leather to you."

"You wouldn't dare!"

He sighed. "You know better than that, Robina."

You damn well should, so dinna be daft.

Angry, unexpected tears welled in her eyes at the sound of that persistent voice in her head. It was so clear that it was as if Rab were standing right behind her, watching them...and taking Dev's side against his own sister.

She stared down at the floor, fighting the tears, willing Dev to leave.

Instead, he added softly, "Besides, Robby-lass, who is here to stop me?"

"I am," said a small voice firmly from the doorway.

Startled, both of them whirled toward it and saw a tow-headed boy standing there with a raised dirk in his hand. The weapon was longer than his arm.

~

"Benjy!" Robina exclaimed, pushing roughly past Ormiston to confront her nine-year-old brother. "Whatever are you doing out of bed?"

"Sakes, who could sleep wi' such a din going on in here? What's Dev doing here anyway, Beany, and why were ye a-screeching like a banshee?"

"Hand me that dirk," she commanded. "And remember to offer it hilt first."

The little boy obeyed her, saying, "Ye ken fine I wouldna hurt ye."

"I ken fine that you belong in bed," she said.

"I'll take him," Ormiston said, moving past her and taking the dirk from her hand as he did. "You put some clothes on, Robina. I'll meet you in the hall."

"Where did ye come from, Dev?" the little boy asked, looking up at him.

"From Hermitage Castle in Liddesdale," he said. Then, putting a hand to the boy's shoulder, he added gently, "But you should address me as Sir David, you know, or 'sir,' not Dev."

"Hoots, nae one else here calls ye aught save Devil Ormiston. But Beany and me call ye Dev, though, just like our Rab did."

Benjy's voice faltered on the last three words.

Urging him gently across the landing to his bedchamber, Ormiston pulled Robina's door shut behind them, hoping it would stay put despite its broken latch, and said, "D'ye still miss him sorely, laddie?"

"Aye, sure, don't you?"

Ormiston paused to be sure his own voice would not betray him before he said evenly, "I do, aye, but it is our duty to go on with our lives, you know. I know it's hard, Benjy, but our Rab would want us to be strong."

"Even Beany?"

"Beany *is* strong," Ormiston said, wishing she were less *head*strong.

"But ye're sore vexed with her, aye? I heard ye."

Ormiston pulled back the covers on the boy's cot. "In you get now," he said.

"Dinna be mad at our Beany," Benjy said. "She gets sad, too, just like us."

~

Robina finished twisting her long hair into a plait and declared herself garbed well enough to avoid further censure. She had heard Benjy say that they always called him Dev and wondered what Dev would say to her about that.

Likely nowt, the voice in her head said. *He's far too*

wroth with you to let aught that wee Benjy says deter him
from scolding you. Mind your step when you go down,
and listen quietly to whatever he says. Do not challenge
or sauce him!

She grimaced, knowing that Dev was already waiting
for her, because she had heard him go downstairs. Before
that, she had heard the hum of his voice in Benjy's room
and of Benjy's answering him, but that was all.

Her backside still stung. Although she had known him
for nearly six years, she had never known him to be as
angry as he was right now. Sakes, what was she going to
tell John Greenlaw to explain her broken door?

She would think of something. Meantime, Rab's advice
was good, if only she could make herself follow it. Unfor-
tunately, Dev's very nature, and her own, almost compelled her to defend herself in every way against the man.

Not only was he the handsomest creature to stalk the
Borders, but he also seemed to think he was the smartest
one and the finest man ever to ride a horse, wield a sword,
or... sakes, to do anything!

Entering the hall, she saw that Dev had lit torches and
candles and was on one knee now, putting peat chunks on
the fire that he had stirred to life.

He straightened when he saw her, and she saw that he
looked tired.

He moved closer, eyeing her narrowly, and she mar-
veled yet again at how blue his eyes were, even by candle-
light. She could tell that he had been traveling, because
he had not shaved or had his man shave him. The dark
growth appeared to indicate such a lack for several days,
but it looked good on him.

He frowned. "What?"

The single word surprised her. She had expected him to begin ranting the moment he saw her.

"You said you had much to say to me. Are you still furious?"

"I am. Come and sit down."

"I'd rather stand, thank you."

His mouth quirked into a near smile. "You deserved every lick."

"I know that you think so." She nearly added that Rab did, too, but she did not want to have that conversation with him.

"I think you know that I'm right, too," he said. "What were you thinking?"

"That our people need food," she replied. "You know that the raids have begun again, and the Douglas does naught to stop them."

"I thought you were sending for your aunt and cousin to stay with you."

She shrugged and then wished she had not when his dark eyebrows snapped together again. To divert him, she said, "You know that you and your men cannot stay here tonight, Dev. Greenlaw would suffer an apoplexy. You'll have to ride on."

"I know. I'm expected at the Black Tower before dawn."

"You told Benjy you'd been at Hermitage," she said. "With Douglas?"

"Aye, but we are not going to talk about me, Robina. What became of your aunt and cousin?"

"I don't want them. This tower is impregnable. As you know very well, it survived the siege of 1403, and it will survive another one if necessary. Greenlaw saw to it then, and he will see to it again if he must."

He drew a deep breath, and when she saw his hands fisting, she took a hasty step back. He shook his head then—at himself, she knew—and his hands relaxed.

"You know I would never use my fists on you, Robby. But what do you think would have happened if, instead of my men and me, those chasing you tonight had been a raiding party? What if English raiders had followed you here?"

"We'd have barred the doors, of course. I told you!"

"Think, Robina. You ran across the yard and in through the postern door. You did not even bar it, nor would you have had the time, and Greenlaw is asleep. The risk you took if you went raiding, as I now believe, was unacceptable. I'm going to see that you don't endanger yourself so again. I promise you that."

"You can't promise any such thing. You don't have the right!"

"You said that before, lass. You'd do well to remember my reply."

Fall in Love with Forever Romance

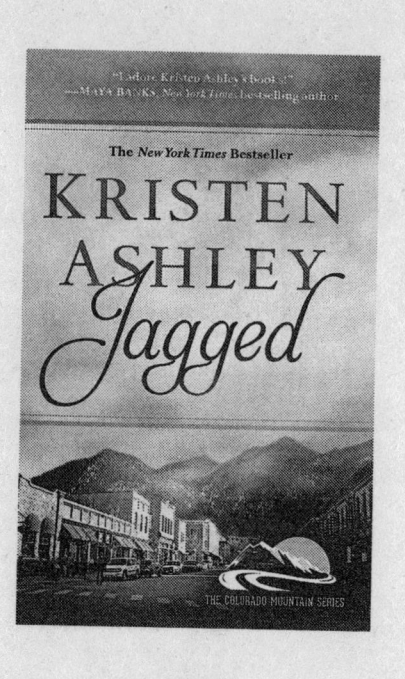

JAGGED

Zara is struggling to make ends meet when her old friend Ham comes back into her life. He wants to help, but a job and a place to live aren't the only things he's offering this time around...Fans of Julie Ann Walker, Lauren Dane, and Julie James will love the fifth book in Kristen Ashley's *New York Times* bestselling Colorado Mountain series, now in print for the first time!

Fall in Love with Forever Romance

ALL FIRED UP

It's a recipe for temptation: Mix a cool-as-a-cucumber event planner with a devastatingly handsome Irish pastry chef. Add sexual chemistry hot enough to start a fire. Let the sparks fly. Fans of Jill Shalvis will flip for the second book in Kate Meader's Hot in the Kitchen series.

Fall in Love with Forever Romance

MOONLIGHT RAIDER

USA Today bestselling author Amanda Scott brings to life the history, turmoil, and passion of the Scottish Border as only she can in the first book in her new Border Nights series. Fans of Diana Gabaldon's *Outlander* will be swept away by Scott's tale!

Fall in Love with Forever Romance

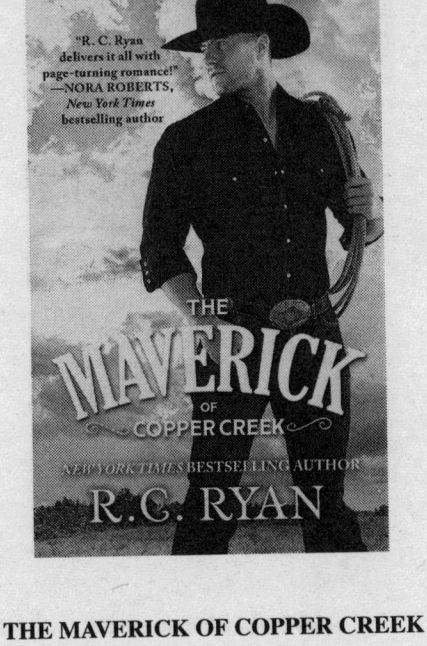

THE MAVERICK OF COPPER CREEK

Fans of Linda Lael Miller, Diana Palmer, and Joan Johnston will love *New York Times* bestselling author R. C. Ryan's THE MAVERICK OF COPPER CREEK, the charming, poignant, and unforgettable first book in her Copper Creek Cowboys series.

IT HAPPENED AT CHRISTMAS

Ethan and Skye may want a lot of things this holiday season, but what they get is something they didn't expect. Fans of feel-good romances by *New York Times* bestselling authors Brenda Novak, Robyn Carr, and Jill Shalvis will love the third book in Debbie Mason's series set in Christmas, Colorado—where love is the greatest gift of all.

Fall in Love with Forever Romance

MISTLETOE ON MAIN STREET

Fans of Jill Shalvis, Robyn Carr, and Susan Mallery will love this charming debut from best-selling author Olivia Miles about love, healing, and family at Christmastime.

Fall in Love with Forever Romance

RING IN THE HOLIDAYS

For Matthew McPherson, what happens in Vegas definitely doesn't stay there, and that may be a very good thing! Fans of Lori Wilde and Rachel Gibson will fall in love with this sexy series from bestselling author Katie Lane.